HEARING VOICES

AN
ISAAC BLAZE
THRILLER

AXEL CRUISE

Thanks to:

My editor, who is brilliant, name of Karin Cather;
My wife, who although I haven't met yet, I figure better safe
than sorry;
And my readers, who, provided they didn't steal it, are all aces
in my book.

For my parents,

my brother,

and The Penguin – who <u>always</u> gets his cut.

HEARING VOICES

ONE

I WAS ABOUT TO be tortured.

And not in a good way.

I was bound to a chair somewhere underground. Equipment had been brought in and neatly arranged on a table to my right. The room was dark and cold, and the blood on my forehead had dried to a thin film.

A man was standing in front of the table. He was smiling like a butcher's dog. And with good reason, too. He'd been waiting a long time for this. So long that he was making sure to savor the moment. I figured he was probably thinking *Everyone breaks*. But he wasn't going to break me. Not this guy. This guy was about to die.

And that's why I was smiling.

* * *

The SWAT team moved into position 6.3 miles south of Chicago's Loop. A place called North Kenwood. Right outside the old Kaizen boardinghouse.

It was a big gray-stone building. Think rich family, high ceilings, and original fireplaces, and you're pretty much there. The ground floor was a communal space; the first and second held bedrooms. All of the residents were still inside. I was inside, too.

I was sitting alone at a small table in the large ground floor lounge. I'd just finished a job in Cairo, Egypt. Now I was in Chicago. The activities room was big and white, with period cornices and a cream carpet. Daylight from the two huge windows in front of me made two yellow squares on the cream carpet. I glanced at the wall clock mounted high between them. Two thirty-nine in the afternoon. Tuesday.

Knight takes pawn, the male voice said.

I looked down at the chess set in front of me. It consisted of a folding piece of checked cardboard and thirty-two plastic pieces. A chess clock sat ticking beside the board.

Knight takes pawn. The male voice again.

It was a cool voice – English accent, spoke like it was grinning. It was also one of two that have always been in my head. Which is actually a pretty bad way of putting it, since they sound as if they're coming from right behind me. Like the proverbial angel and devil on my shoulders – except both are devils. One male, one female, each their own personality, and both giving me nothing but lip. Which isn't to say I'm crazy, just that there's a constant three-way conversation going on in my head, and that the situations I tend to find myself in aren't entirely my fault.

Hey. Quit stalling, Isaac.

I grumbled a bit and then moved the black knight as stated, taking my pawn off the board before hitting the clock. I leaned back in my chair. As things stood, black had expertly maneuvered its knight to a key center square and was poised for a king-side attack. Black's rook was also controlling the open file, and black was also up on material too. In other words: I was losing.

I considered the board for a second and then looked at the TV in the corner of the room. The news. The anchor was going through the headlines one by one while a guy with a keen eye for spotting cyborgs posing as humans was standing in front of the TV in his flannel bathrobe and telling the rest of us what was *really* going on in the world. Everyone else was scattered around the room. An odd bunch to be sure, but no more than you'd expect to find in a seedy boarding-house on the outskirts of town. Most were older, a couple had definitely done time. One woman was just zombieing around. She was holding a juice box with a straw sticking out. She had been for the past couple of hours. There were two janitors in the room, as well. They were dressed in faded overalls and doing everything but cleaning. They were just standing there together, expressions lazy, mumbling to each other. I glanced at the wall clock again. Watched 2:39 change to 2:40. That was the exact moment I heard footsteps.

They were loud and they got louder. They had a distinct and even rhythm that was out of sync with the chess clock and doubling the pace. They were solid and purposeful and enough for me to deduce three things: she was female, she was Armed Forces, and she was here for me.

I listened to her approach. She was walking fast and her momentum stayed constant. She hadn't used the main entrance. She'd used the side entrance. Her eighteen-second journey should have taken thirty. This was urgent.

I heard her march straight past the reception desk and into the lounge. Her footsteps turned silent as she hit the carpet, but there was no change to her momentum. No hesitation at all. There were nine of us to choose from, but she made a beeline straight for her target. I had nowhere to go.

She stopped right beside the chessboard. I saw her boots

plant down just two feet to my left. My eyes flicked up at her. She was young and good-looking. Twenty-seven give or take, so about my age. She had a long black ponytail, astonishing blue eyes, and she was wearing a lightweight tactical vest over a thin black sweater. Not much of a uniform. But enough. She was alone and didn't say a word and neither did I. The guy in the flannel bathrobe was looking. His eyes were wide and his jaw was hanging. But, apart from the two bewildered janitors and the gawking receptionist, he was the only other person who seemed to be aware of what was going on.

I figured I had three seconds.

The chess clock ticked *one*.

My eyes locked onto the girl's hip holster and equipment belt. Then they shifted back to the chess set, and then to the girl's feet, and then to one of the tall windows in front of me. A quick zigzag motion. Her weapons, my weapons, her position, my exit.

Really? the male voice said. *You're thinking Cuckoo's Nest?*

The clock ticked *two*.

My eyes went to the zombieing woman, who had drifted nearby—to her juice box, then to the girl's shoulder radio, then to the small table in front of me, and then back to the equipment belt.

Yeah…

But? I replied—speaking internally and not out loud. Which, as I've learned, is the proper social etiquette when speaking to a voice in your head. You just get weird looks otherwise.

The male voice said, *Take another look at the girl.*

My eyes flicked up again. The girl hadn't let her gaze slip from me since the second she'd walked into the room. Her eyes were electric blue. There was absolute confidence behind

12

them. Which was also fitting now that I knew who this girl really was.

The clock ticked *three*.

I did nothing.

The girl kept looking straight at me. I was looking up, she was looking down. My left hand had moved toward a bishop but was now frozen just an inch away from it. Her hands were loose by her sides, never having moved once.

Two more SWAT guys crept into the room.

They had submachine guns in hand. They stood together, blocking the only doorway, eyes scanning side to side, assessing everything. The guy in the flannel bathrobe took one look at them and started inching backward toward one of the big windows. The two janitors backed up against the wall on the other side of the room. Everyone else went about their business.

The girl said, "You need to come with us. Now."

She was wrong. I didn't *need* to do anything. This wasn't an arrest. Not technically. And certainly not yet anyway. So I stayed calm and didn't move.

The girl stayed calm, too. Her eyes simply swept toward the windows and then came back to me. I got the message. *More backup outside*. Not that this girl needed backup. She didn't. Not by a long shot.

Hmmm. Now why would she be here? asked the male voice.

You sure it's her? I asked.

Definitely.

Then I've got no idea.

So what do we do?

What else? I said. *We find out.*

The girl was watching me closely. She must have been able

to see the internal debate going on behind my eyes because, after a beat, she said, "Ready now?"

I replied by giving her a wry smile, like maybe I might try something, but she just shrugged back at me as if to say: *Up to you. But I wouldn't advise it.* Which was solid advice.

So again, I did nothing.

The girl unclipped her handcuffs from the back of her belt and dropped them on the table, right beside the chessboard. They made a heavy *thud.* I looked down at the silver bracelets and sighed.

The male voice said, *All right, so maybe Cuckoo's Nest wasn't such a bad idea.*

I stopped the chess clock and then picked up the cuffs and clicked them on my wrists, making sure to hold them up and show the girl that they were tight. Then I pushed my chair back and stood up.

The girl nodded back at the doorway and turned sideways to let me pass. As I walked past her, we exchanged glances and then she fell in step behind me. I looked over at the guy in the flannel bathrobe. He was pressed up hard against a window, shaking his head at me as if to say: *Don't do it!* I acknowledged the warning, giving him a nod back that said: *Stay frosty.*

I focused on the two SWAT guys ahead of me. They both turned sideways to let me pass, and then each of them took hold of one of my elbows and started walking with me. Once we were clear of the activities room, I heard the guy in the flannel bathrobe shout, "*See?* I told you!"

They led me back toward the side entrance. As we passed the reception desk, the receptionist tentatively handed two DVDs to the girl.

There go the surveillance tapes. Like we were never here.

Outside, it was cool and there was slight breeze. I saw a van blocking the north gate in front of us. It was black and unmarked and had heavy tints on the windows. Two SWAT guys had taken aim. Both had rifles, one was closing in. The one coming toward me was the biggest of the four guys I'd seen so far. A real bruiser. Half a foot taller than me, bald, and mean. But not even half as dangerous as the girl. He slung his rifle over his shoulder as he walked toward me. The other guy stayed behind the van, his rifle still trained on my center mass. The big guy gave me a quick pat down, finding nothing but a fold of cash in my front pocket. He eyed the bills very carefully and then held them up for the girl to see. He did a quick count.

"Seventeen-hundred and change," he said.

"Seventeen-hundred-*thirty-two*," I said.

I put a lot of emphasis on the *thirty-two*. Like I was going to be sure to count it all when I got it back, and if any was missing, I'd know whose pocket to look in. The big guy didn't appreciate it. His face went red and angry, and he opened his mouth to say something, but the girl waved him down.

Lucky for him, said the male voice.

A moment later, a couple more SWAT guys hurried round from the main entrance. They saw me, saw the cuffs, and then looked to the girl. She gave them a nod, and then they jogged back round the building, presumably to a secondary vehicle. The signal to move out was then issued to the rest of the team, but a ringing phone made them all tense up—except the girl. She did not tense up. She just casually swiped the phone and held it to her ear. I listened carefully. A muffled voice came through. It was male and it was shouting. A gravelly voice, approximately forty-five years old, and very angry. The boss.

"Yes, sir," the girl said, rolling her eyes. "On our way now."

More muffled shouting ensued, and then the boss hung up. The girl put the phone away, smiling and shaking her head. She gave a nod to the big guy, and then the team sprang back into action.

They ushered me hastily into the back of the van, where there were two bench-like seats running parallel to the sides. Six sets of chains were bolted to the floor, three to each bench. I was put in the middle of the right bench and the big guy hooked me up to the corresponding chains.

Now I had two sets of cuffs on.

The girl sat directly opposite me, and the big guy and one of the elbow-grabbers squeezed in on either side of her. The other two guys slammed the back doors shut and then I heard them walk round and take the passenger and driver's seats.

I assessed my surroundings. The back doors had no windows, the floor was riveted steel, the roof had a few dim lights. A solid steel wall served as a partition between the front and back of the van. I was in a metal box. Nobody could see in. Nobody could see out.

A still moment passed, and then the girl checked her watch and banged on the partition twice, and then the van started up and pulled away.

A lot of people died in the next four hours.

TWO

THE BACK OF the van was both noisy and quiet. The metallic wash of the slack chains against the steel floor was loud and constant but nobody spoke. All four of us were rocking and bouncing around. The van wasn't moving particularly quickly, but the ride was bad. Probably because of all the steel. It was weighing down the suspension. The van was feeling every imperfection in the road. It juddered and jarred and sent vibrations through all of us. It was like being in an old subway car. Uncomfortable, not that any of us were showing it. The three of them just sat across from me and stared straight at me. I stared back.

Three against one.

Or three against three.

Depending on how you looked at it.

The girl's name was Isabel. She didn't know it, but our paths had actually crossed a while back. And suffice to say: she'd made an impression. Both figuratively on me, and in a much more literal way on the poor bastard she'd been after. Seriously, whatever the guy had done, it couldn't have been worth it. Because I can still see his head even now. It looked like a lump of red Playdough.

She was leaning back against her side of the van. Her electric blues were set firmly upon me. There was still total confidence in them. She had a languid smile on her face, like she knew something I didn't. Which, of course, she did. She knew what game she was playing. All I knew was that game wasn't going to end well for someone. I kept my gaze fixed with hers, but let my focus drift out to the guys either side of her.

The big guy was sitting to her left. He was leaning forward with his elbows on his knees. His rifle was standing up between his legs and he kept jostling the muzzle between his hands. He was staring at me with a slight smile but an altogether ugly expression. Then again, maybe that's just how he looked. The guy on Isabel's right had been watching my hands very carefully, but now he was looking down at the rivets on the steel floor. Alert, but with no real interest in me, anymore.

So far these guys had proven themselves to be competent. This had been a good operation. They hadn't stormed the building because there had been no need to. I had been sitting alone at a table. I hadn't barricaded myself inside, wasn't using the residents as hostages. There was no emergency situation. And no need to cause one. Which is why Isabel had just walked in. She hadn't made a big deal about it, just got close to her target and made it clear that I was surrounded and had nowhere to go. They hadn't used helicopters or dogs or sirens or anything else that might have tipped me off. They had been quiet and efficient and confident. And they had got the job done.

The male voice said, *All right, so what have we got here?*
Run it through, I said, my gaze still fixed on Isabel.
OK. Unmarked clothes.
Unmarked van, I said.
Side entrance.

Surveillance tapes, I said.

Few witnesses.

Right, I said. *And even fewer mistakes*

Well, the male voice said, *I didn't see a badge.*

What happens when you don't have jurisdiction

Technically kidnapping, the male voice said.

Yeah, but only technically. Then I thought about that. *OK, more than technically.*

So we agree, the male voice said.

Yup.

They're Them.

Have to be, I agreed.

Huh. They don't give up, do they?

I said, *Wouldn't be any fun if they did.*

Still doesn't explain Isabel, though.

The van headed north for the better part of thirty minutes. The ride stayed bad, the pace stayed steady and inconspicuous. Then we lurched to a temporary stop and idied in position and the noise of the chains died down and I began to hear city noises outside—cars beeping, people hustling, workers shouting, a jackhammer going nuts in the distance. Downtown Chicago at three o'clock. The beginning of rush hour. A red light. The van's engine was still rumbling and making the whole vehicle buzz. I arched my back off the side of the van and adjusted my position. Isabel didn't move. The guy to her right shot his eyes up from the floor and checked my hands and chains. The big guy just snorted at me. Then he grinned and snorted again.

Yeah keep snorting, asshole, the male voice said. *Because it's going to be real hard to do that with a broken nose.*

You know, we could just ask her, I said.

You know, you two really are hopeless, the female voice said.

Well look who decided to join the party, the male voice said. *I thought it was quiet in here.*

Yeah, well, I needed a break, she said.

I wasn't complaining.

Whatever. She's got this great southern accent. Raspy and playful and full of mischief.

So what's shakin', babe? the male voice said.

What's shakin' is I leave you two alone for what, an hour? Next thing I know we're double cuffed in the back of a van.

Uhhh… it was his fault?

Thanks a lot, I said.

The female voice sighed. *Well, she is pretty. I'll give you boys that.*

I smiled across the van and Isabel's eyes narrowed back at me.

Care to weigh in on our situation here? I asked.

The female voice yawned. *All right, way I see it, Bright Eyes here can wait. Real question is how?*

How what? the male voice said.

How they found us, I said. Which was a damn good question.

The female voice said, *They didn't track us from Cairo.*

The male voice said, *I don't know, that was a pretty big mess back there. Not to mention our exit strategy went straight to hell.*

No, Cairo is out. If they had us there they'd have moved in there, the female voice insisted.

What's the big deal either way? Not like we couldn't get out of here right now if we wanted.

True, but as usual you're missing the point, she said.

Oh do tell.

Think about it. We've been in Chicago for what, all of four hours?

Give or take.

And our last run in with these guys was when? Back in Rome?

Yeah, so?

So, she said patiently, *we've left these guys chasing shadows for going on six months now—Amsterdam, Moscow, Vegas, Tokyo—but as soon as we hit <u>Chicago</u> they're all over us?*

Hmmm, I see your point. So what's the answer?

Well, I don't know. But something's got these guys watching the Windy City, and we just got picked up because of it.

Isaac?

Beats me, I said. *I'm just trying to figure out where we're going.*

The van drove on and made an easy right turn. Then it made three more. It was the ninth block we'd circled so far. Clearly the importance of countersurveillance had not been lost on these guys. They were snaking around town, making sure we hadn't picked up a tail. It was making it difficult for me to keep track of where we were, and Isabel seemed to be picking up on this. Our eyes were still locked onto each other but her lips had now curled up into a sly grin that seemed to say: *Don't tell me we lost you?*

Truth is, they had.

The driver must have taken every possible twist and turn from the boardinghouse and, within five minutes, I had lost our position. But then we had hit downtown and I had gotten lucky.

I had gotten lucky because three hours ago I had been on a downtown bus, watching the elderly couple in front of me get shocked awake by the jackhammer going nuts outside a

British-style pub, in the heart of Chicago's financial district, in the southwest part of the Loop, right on the corner of West Adams and South Clark Street. Hearing it again had given me a second chance. I had used it to estimate our position, and had been tracking our progress ever since. We were currently four blocks north and one block west of it.

The van hit a pothole a few minutes later and bounced the four of us up and down. The guy on Isabel's right was sitting next to the wheel arch and got a good smack. The big guy just absorbed the impact and hardly moved. But both of them immediately looked at my hands and checked my cuffs.

A competent team.

I tuned back in to the conversation that was still going on in my head.

That could work, the female voice was saying.

The male voice said, *I know, that's why I brought it up.*

So tell him.

Tell me what? I said.

The male voice said, *I think FB was right.*

FB?

Flannel Bathrobe.

Oh, I said. *Right about what?*

Remember the headlines?

Bits and pieces. But go ahead, give me the 411.

Started with Atlanta, the male voice said. *The World Congress Center.*

Yeah, some big deal about a business conference, right?

Tag-line is Big Business Tackling Big Problems. *They've been building it up for a while now. Everyone's real excited.*

Something about China next, wasn't it?

The cyberattack, the female voice said.

What got hacked?

According to their government? Nothing.

There's a surprise. All right what was after that?

A couple of things, the male voice said. *Both local, and both of which might have something to do with all this.*

Edge of my seat here, I said.

OK, first up is Chicago's FRB. They had a proble—'

Whoa, whoa, whoa. Seriously? Again with the initials?

What?

What the hell's FRB?

FRB. Federal Reserve Bank,

Well, why didn't you just say that?

I'm trying to save time.

Think it's working? the female voice said.

You feel like taking another break?

Guys… I said.

As I was saying, the male voice said, *three days ago Chicago's Federal Reserve Bank reported a, quote, "minor system glitch."*

Let me guess, it wasn't so minor?

Well, he said, *they got everything up and running again. And within twelve minutes, too—which they claim is impressive. Problem is, it seems twelve minutes was more than enough time for some of their funds to go missing.*

You don't say. So how much they lose?

Undisclosed.

Any link to the China cyberattack?

Some new punk trying to prove himself? Could be.

What was the second thing?

Research facility over on the west side. Apparently one of their lab techs made a big mistake.

How big?

Big enough to make it go boom.

Hmmm… All right it's interesting stuff, but I still don't see how either gets these guys involved. FBI, Homeland, or NSA would take lead. Unless of course—

There's more to one of those stories than meets the eye…?

It was food for thought but I didn't have much time to chew. The van slowed and swung a tentative left turn, then stopped short. We were perpendicular to the road. I could hear traffic stream behind us. Then I heard a metallic clang and rattle in front. It sounded like metal shutter being rolled up. The van moved forward again. We turned a long curve, spiraling down, before coming to an abrupt halt. Then the engine was cut and the chains stopped rustling and the van shut down.

We had arrived.

Obviously, this was not a maximum security detention facility. That would come later. First they wanted to talk to me. They had questions and they wanted answers. So right now we were somewhere they could interrogate me. And since these guys had no jurisdiction, the only place they could do that was in the covert facility they had been illegally operating out of this whole time.

I heard the two guys up front get out. They slammed their doors and walked round to the rear of the van. I heard another set of doors open when they got there. Then everything went quiet. The three guys opposite me stayed still. Isabel still cool. The guy on her right still indifferent. The big guy still ugly.

Two seconds later, the van exploded open and two red dots hit the inside partition. I saw the secondary vehicle. It was a black unmarked sedan. It had pulled up right behind us. Its front doors were wide open, and two SWAT guys were semicrouching behind them, using them like shields and aiming their rifles into the van. The two red dots quickly found me. One to my left shoulder. The other to my stomach. Then the SWAT guys outside shouted something I guessed was some kind of operational code, because the SWAT guys inside seemed to react to it and stood up. Isabel, however, didn't move. So neither did I. We hadn't broken eye contact since leaving the hospital, and our staring match was continuing quite unchecked. The big guy seemed to clock this and decided to take the initiative. He started at me but Isabel was quick to stop him.

"Wait," she said, while also silencing the others with a simple hand gesture.

They all waited.

Then her eyes narrowed slowly, like she had gleaned some critical piece of information about me. She paused a moment, smiled, and then said, "OK, take him."

The big guy quickly unhooked my chains and then hauled me out of the van and into the middle of a basement parking garage. It was the lowest level of three, ash gray, and packed with vehicles. There was a row of reserved spaces against the far wall. Three were empty, and one was full of trash. There were no other free spaces. A couple of dumpsters sat against another wall, and graffiti and general dirt covered everything. A typical parking lot, but dirtier than you'd expect for this part of town.

Isabel started walking. The big guy and the indifferent guy grabbed my elbows and hustled me along behind her. The other two guys from the van followed behind us, and the two from the secondary vehicle stayed with the van and sedan. We walked past the dumpsters and over to a corner where there were two elevators on offer: standard or service. All six of us crammed into the latter. A flash of Peter Sellers brought a smile to my face. The elevator's button panel had been replaced by a rectangular piece of opaque glass with a blue tint. Isabel swiped a card over it causing a small green light to flick on. The cage held still for a few seconds and then the gears initiated and the shutter came down and the box jolted and we began to move.

Going down.

THREE

THE ELEVATOR CAGE opened onto a square platform of metal grating with a short staircase on either side. In front of me was a large rectangular room. Two cube-shaped offices had been built out of the left corners and a huge monitor was mounted on the wall between them. The central workfloor encompassed several small work stations, with three computers to every desk. All of the screens were black. A cursory once-over revealed no identifying markers of branch or affiliation, which in itself confirmed who I was dealing with. Colorwise, everything was either black, white, or gray. There were about a dozen people in all, plenty of good tech, and lots of situation boards. Stacks of papers cluttered the work floor. Various pipes and cables snaked along the ceiling and down the walls. *Scruffy*.

I was led down the right-hand staircase, its metal mesh clanging under our footsteps. The SWAT guys kept a solid box formation around me as we moved along the right-hand edge of the work floor. The people on the work floor stared, but only for a moment. They were definitely uncomfortable with the proceedings.

Isabel peeled off quickly and headed toward one of the

office cubes. The box turned right and onto a short corridor, where a wiry, agitated man blocked our path. His sleeves were rolled up and his chest was concave. He had chewed finger-nails, a tired shirt half-untucked, and worn-out matte shoes. He looked like he really needed a cigarette. I didn't think much of him, and the feeling seemed to be mutual. He gave me a once-over followed by a dirty look and then, in a grav-elly voice, asked the big SWAT guy for my possessions. The big guy handed over my cash.

"Seventeen-hundred and change," he said.

"Seventeen-hundred thirty-two," I said.

The big guy snarled and shot me a look. Gravel Voice looked at each of us in turn and then down at the fold of cash resting in his flat palm. He seemed to have mixed feelings about it. He gave the big guy a look, and the big guy replied with a very slight shake of his head. *No, he didn't have any-thing else on him.* Gravel Voice turned and gave me another dirty look. Then he contemplated something for a second. Then he nodded at the big guy and jabbed his thumb behind himself. He said, "You know where to put him."

It was a typical interrogation room: White walls, lino-leum flooring, a silver-gray door. One table, two chairs. There was a one-way window and a single camera in a top corner.

The big guy sat me down. Hard. Facing the door. My cuffs were swiftly exchanged for the ones bolted to the desk. My third set of the day. The SWAT guys made a quick exit, but there was no locking of the door. The room went quiet.

Well, that was rude, the female voice said.

Things will pick up yet, I said.

And in the meantime?

We wait.

Great…

Interrogation tactics are all about discomfort. More discomfort equals better results. Physically speaking, the basic premise is to mismatch body state and environment. Begin with panic and speed, then slow everything down. Spike adrenaline, keep it elevated, and then let it sit. Wear out the suspects. Then break them. Psychologically, it can be as simple as an unlocked door with no way to reach it.

I looked down at my hands. They had almost no freedom of movement. There was a thick, semicircular steel loop growing out of the table, about one foot in from the edge of my side. The chain connecting my cuffs together was looped through it. The table was also made of steel and it was bolted to the floor. All I could do was shuffle my chair up close and rest my forearms on top of the table's cool surface.

I looked at the empty chair across from me. It had arms, mine didn't. Another psychological ploy. I turned my head and looked at my reflection in the one-way window on my left. I figured there was probably someone standing behind it looking back at me. I took a guess that they were standing just off-center and shot my eyes to that spot and smirked like I could see them. Then I looked away from the window, hoping someone was freaking out.

Seriously, the female voice said, *Has that ever worked for us?*

I gave the room another once-over. Walls, door, table, chairs, camera, one-way glass.

A typical interrogation room.

Typical, except for one thing.

It was spotless.

See, normally these rooms are all scuffed up and feel

worn-out. They look sad and tired, just like you'd expect. But this one didn't. Every surface was gleaming. The table was sharp and there were no scratch marks around the metal ring. The one-way window was crystal clean and super shiny. This room was definitely not scruffy.

In any case five minutes went by and nothing happened. I just sat there in silence. I couldn't hear a thing coming from outside the room.

The male voice said, *I think it was your move.*

* * *

The male voice and I were well into the endgame of our chess match when I saw the red light blink on the corner camera. The door opened about a minute later, and I watched a small metal trolley get wheeled in. Behind it was a short man followed by two suits I'd seen on the work floor before. The trolley had two shelves. On the top shelf was a laptop, a mess of wires, some gadgets, and a roll of paper. The bottom shelf was more of a basket and was filled with more wires and other assorted junk. A folding chair was also brought in.

The two suits hooked me up pretty quickly to a pressure gauge over my left bicep and a sensor clipped to my forefinger that would monitor whether I was getting enough oxygen, and my pulse. No eye scanner meant it wasn't one of the better polygraphs I'd ever come across—not that I couldn't have beaten one those if I had needed to.

The suits left the room. The short man stayed. He was younger than me. Early twenties, probably fresh out of university. He had thin, short blond hair, he was skinny, and he was wearing glasses. His laminate ID called him "Peter." He sat on the folding chair behind the trolley to my left, with the laptop in front of him and the window behind him. He was four feet away from me and completely harmless. I glanced at his watch and noted the time: 4:28. An hour waiting.

The door to the room was still open. It was very thick, which explained why I hadn't been able to hear much before. If not for the one-way window, the room would've probably been totally soundproof.

Gravel Voice hustled past the door, right to left, toward the other side of the glass.

Another minute passed. And then, finally, an elegant man sauntered into view. He was black, slim, and had neat hair. He was wearing a pristine dark suit and brogue shoes—an ensemble courtesy of London's Savile Row. He had a gold lapel pin in the shape of a bird, and he was clutching a rectangular brown folder under his arm.

I hadn't seen this man on my way in. He would have stuck out, too. He was, like the interrogation room, the exact opposite of scruffy. He stood just outside the doorway, looking back thoughtfully at something in the main, central work area. I wondered what might be on the big screen. The guy stayed standing like that for maybe twenty seconds until I cleared my throat and his eyes shifted into the room. He looked directly at me, and took a long solemn breath, and then stepped inside.

He glanced up at the corner camera, nodded once, and then glided to the seat opposite me. The door closed behind him. The guy must have been sixty-five years old but his body hadn't aged past fifty.

He sat down gently. His posture was perfect, tall and proper. He pulled his seat up close to the table, and then his long, manicured fingers opened the folder beautifully. He reached into his jacket and took out a fountain pen and placed it neatly beside the folder. Then he clasped his hands together on top of the folder and focused his attention on me.

He said, "My name is Adrian Hays."

Which was really no good for anyone.

FOUR

ADRIAN HAYS DIDN'T say anything else for the next sixty seconds. His posture remained perfect and his hands remained clasped on top of the folder. His breathing was silent and patient.

Then he said, "I believe a man should have two things firmly ingrained into his being. A sense of dignity," he paused, "And a sense of respect."

The guy dressed English, spoke American. And his voice was something else. Deep and velvety, like a radio presenter or voice-over specialist.

"I believe in treating people the same way I wish to be treated," he said. "To that end, I will not lie to you, and, in doing so, I believe that *you* will not lie to *me*."

I glanced at the polygraph and then back at Hays.

"I also believe in verification," he said.

"You believe in a lot," I said.

"A man is his beliefs. At the end of the day they are all he has."

"Beliefs can change."

"So can a man."

"Beliefs can be influenced."

Hays nodded once. "Perhaps."

"Then a man is nothing more than his circumstance," I said.

Hays cracked a smile. "And what of *your* circumstance, Mr. Blaze?" He unclasped his hands and addressed the folder. It was a nice reversal. He didn't miss a beat. He said, "You are a man who, and I quote, possesses a *genius*-level intellect.'" He said it like a question, and then looked up at me as if over a pair of glasses. I knew what he was doing. He needed to draw out this part of the interrogation so the polygraph could get an accurate baseline. And while I could have just said nothing, the overriding fact of the matter was that the guy had just called me out. So I said, "Go for it."

"OK," Hays said. "Let's try some multiplication." He nodded at Peter who brought out a calculator, and then he reclined in his chair and crossed his legs and pondered at the ceiling and searched for numbers.

"Nine-hundred-eighty-two," Hays said. "That is, 982 by 326 by 64. . . " he paused, looked at me, smirked, "multiplied by pi."

I watched Peter begin to input the numbers on the calculator, and then I turned back to Hays.

The male voice said, *Why always maths?*

Beats me, I said. *But you got the answer, right?*

Of course.

Be interesting if it was the amount stolen from the Fed Bank, the female voice said.

Peter finished inputting the numbers and hit the *equals* button. Hays was staring patiently at me, awaiting my answer.

I said, "It's 85366346."

Hays glanced at Peter and Peter shook his head.

Hays said, "Looks like you're wrong, Mr. Blaze."

I said, "Yeah, but am I, really?"

Hays glanced at Peter again. Peter looked back at the calculator's readout, not understanding at first, and then getting it. He looked up at me, amazed. "He said the answer backward."

Hays just grunted. "And I suppose if I were to ask you to divide that by say…" he glanced down at his lapel pin and brushed it with his thumb, "oh,… 9,346?"

"I'd tell you the answer was 6,887," I said.

Peter hurried to check my answer but Hays just raised a hand and gave him a *don't bother* head shake. I still couldn't see any connections between the numbers, or anything else.

"Impressive," Hays said.

"I thought so."

Hays gave me an odd look.

"*I?*" he said. "Or *we?*"

I gave him a look back: *touché.*

Hays turned over a page in the file. He searched a finger over it and then tapped on a word.

"Tell me about voice-hearing," he said.

I shrugged. "Means I hear voices."

He nodded slowly and thoughtfully. "And how many voices do you hear?"

"Two."

"Two?"

"One male, one female."

"And what's that like?"

My eyes drifted sideways.

All I'm saying is there are other questions besides maths, the male voice was saying.

The female voice said, *So you expect him to what, ask a geography question?*

Do you know what the capital of Svalbard is?

Do you think anyone gives a crap?

My eyes went back to Hays.

"Crowded," I said.

"Yes, I imagine so," Hays said. "Must be hard to think, sometimes."

"But at least I don't get lonely."

"Nor do you ever get to be alone."

I glanced at his left hand. No ring. "You like being alone?" I asked.

"Solitude stimulates the creative mind," he said.

"Einstein also said it was monotonous."

"One of the voices tell you that?"

"They're not just good with numbers."

"Your conversations must be sparkling."

"Sure beat the hell out of this one."

Hays exhaled slowly and seemed to size something up in his mind. "So… " he said. "You're mad?"

"I prefer to think of it as *sane adjacent.*"

Hays smirked and shook his head. He looked up at the ceiling and brought something to memory. "Voice hearing," he said. "A condition quite separate and distinct from schizophrenia and other mental disorders in that *no* debilitating neurological effects are present. Voices associated with voice hearing may be viewed as a direct link to the unconscious mind, which, if unsuppressed, may grant a voice hearer free and unfettered access to the deepest resources of their mind."

"You've done your homework," I said.

"Yes," he said. "And I'm afraid it means insanity pleas are off the table."

"Right," I said. "Because I'd get a trial."

Now it was Hays' turn to give me the *touché* look.

Hays tapped on the open folder with a flat hand and said, "You know what I see when I look at this?"

"Paper?"

"Discrepancies."

"I'm not surprised," I said. I nodded at the window. "Your man back there doesn't exactly scream *attention to detail* now, does he? Guy can't even keep his shirt tucked in." I turned to the window and called, "No use doing it now." I turned back to Hays and shook my head. "Seriously, I'd get rid of that one."

Hays exhaled slowly again. A patient man.

He said, "Finished now?"

I gestured for him to continue.

He said, "I look at this file and see a man with perhaps unlimited potential. Mr. Blaze, you are by all accounts intelligent, resourceful, capable, even charismatic."

"Not to mention good-looking."

"My point, Mr. Blaze, is that you are a man who should be out in the world—a man following in the footsteps of Einstein, Tesla, and Da Vinci. A man who should be revered and respected. And yet, here you sit. A man who is *not*. Not *ever*." He leaned forward and went back to the folder. "A man whose file implicates him in over three hundred felonies. And a man whose file concludes *is unpredictable, unreasonable, and without any clear set of principles, intentions, motivations, beliefs, moralities, or allegiances, which, in combination with his high intellect and proclivity toward provocation, means he must not be engaged lightly and must be considered dangerous at all times*."

Hays looked up from the file and reclined again. He

watched my reaction carefully. I thought about the profile and recalled somewhat fondly a two-month period during which I'd been in and out of four psychiatric hospital. Four separate psychiatrists had evaluated me and reached similar assessments. All four of them now had files of their own as a result.

Hays said, "So tell me, Mr. Blaze. What circumstances change a man's destiny in such a way as yours has been?"

I tutted at him.

"You're engaging," I said.

Hays looked down at my handcuffs.

"Yes," he said. "But not lightly."

We shared a grin. Hays really seemed to be enjoying himself now, and, quite honestly, I was starting to like the guy.

"You know, our circumstances aren't that different, Hays."

"How so?" he said.

"Well for one, they've both brought us to this table."

"And you believe that puts us on equal footing?"

"I never said we were equal."

Hays nodded. "So this table has two sides."

"But you're at the wrong one."

Contempt pulled up one side of his lips. "Said the man cuffed to it."

I shrugged. "And yet for the moment neither of us can leave."

Hays gave me a look. "Believe me, Mr. Blaze, I'm exactly where I wish to be."

At which point we were interrupted by a noise from behind the one-way window. It sounded like a knock, like maybe it was a signal from Gravel Voice.

Peter turned his head toward it and then turned back to his laptop. Hays's eyes slid quickly to the side and he leaned forward. He contemplated the noise carefully and then exhaled slowly and shifted his eyes back to me. Clearly, he was not pleased by the interruption. He looked frustrated and irritated and he stared at me hard. He was about to say something when a second, much louder noise came from behind the door. Hays twisted in his chair to see what was going on and Peter and I glanced over, too.

The door opened slowly. It was Gravel Voice. His face was pale, his hair was even more disheveled, and his clothes were battered. His nose was busted and bleeding badly. He was teetering over the threshold like a drunk. We all stared at him. He coughed and spluttered and then let out a sharp, pathetic cry as his right knee collapsed—the result of a hard kick from behind. He dropped vertically and his knees crashed down onto the floor. His torso began to fold over, but a hand caught the back of his collar and held him up in a kneeling position. The room fell silent as three sets of eyes traced the hand back to its source. Hays found two electric blue eyes waiting for him.

Isabel stood in the Doorway. She was looking straight at Hays. Her right hand was holding Gravel Voice's head in front of her, level with her stomach.

"I was told to make this hurt," she said to Hays.

Her left hand came up and a nickel-plated Colt M1911 came with it..45 ACP ammo and an additional suppressor. It nuzzled itself squarely against Gravel Voice's left temple.

A single pull followed.

There was no hesitation. Just a loud bang followed by a wet slapping sound. The side of Gravel Voice's head exploded open and a stream of red ejected into the air like ketchup from a squeeze-bottle. It squirted right across the room, chasing the bullet all the way to the wall. The stream had enough hang time for us to see it glisten before it splattered onto the ground.

Isabel didn't even blink.

Her right hand simply released its grip and the corpse thudded onto the floor. It put Hays in a trance. His mouth dropped opened but nothing came out.

"Item eighty-six," Isabel said. "Where is it?"

Hays didn't say or do anything. His brain had been presented with a confirmed threat to which it had only three responses: fight, flight, or freeze. Hays's had picked freeze.

But Peter's hadn't. He was rising out of his chair. His limbic brain had picked flight and his legs had just gotten the message: *Go, go, go*! But Peter didn't get far.

Isabel's left hand came up again.

A single pull followed.

There was a momentary sense of something flying behind Hays' back and then there was another death. The bullet smashed through the left lens of Peter's glasses and a quarter of his face exploded. The one-way glass was sprayed with red and accompanied by another a wet slapping sound, like someone throwing out a bucket of bathwater. Peter had been halfway to standing when the bullet hit. He dropped onto the carpet, knocking the trolley over and taking the laptop with it. My left arm jerked as the wires connecting me to the laptop were ripped out.

"You're going to die," Isabel said to Hays. "Sorry darlin' but that's just the way it's got to be. Deal is you give me a straight answer and I make this painless and quick. OK? Good. Now, where is it?"

Hays managed to gather himself enough to shoot me a look. His eyes were wide and said what his voice couldn't.

But they didn't find what they were looking for. I just kind of shrugged at him. What did he expect me to do?

Hays's face twitched awkwardly. His eyes darted down to my cuffed hands, his face washed with confusion and panic and about a million other emotions until he finally realized it was over. A gasp of air steadied him. I watched him accept the situation. It was almost dignified. Almost.

He closed his eyes and swallowed hard and turned back square to the table and resumed his proper posture with his back to Isabel. I understood that completely. He couldn't face those eyes a second time. He didn't want to see it coming, either. He paused a moment, probably saying a silent prayer, and then opened his eyes slowly and looked right at me and said, "Shanghai."

Isabel smiled behind him.

"Thanks, Sugar."

The left hand rose again.

Hays screwed his eyes shut. There was a still moment, and then I watched as dignity was overpowered by fear. There was a sharp screech of chair legs and then another loud bang.

Hays dropped.

The blue eyes shifted to me.

FIVE

ISABEL STOOD SQUARELY in the doorway, her icy cool eyes beaming into the room, the Colt hanging loose by her side. She'd lost the tactical vest. The thin black sweater was hugging her figure nicely. A good portion of it was soaked with Gravel Juice. She closed her eyes and stretched her neck to each side and then took a deep breath and sighed. She brought her right hand to face and used her thumb to wipe a couple of red dots off her cheek. She looked down at her hand and smiled at some inner amusement as she rubbed her thumb against her other fingers.

Then she stepped in through the doorway and immediately—and without looking—put a bullet in the corner camera. It was an elegant move, her left hand just casually swung across her body and back again.

Very cool.

She stretched her neck one more time and then rocked her chin up and flicked her eyes over to me.

"All right, so what's the trick, Slick?"

I felt a giddy smile break out across my face.

Isabel raised an eyebrow and then nodded at Hays's fallen chair. "Mind if I sit?"

I gestured with my hand to approve. "Please."

She walked forward and kicked the leg of Hays's fallen chair. It popped straight back up into position.

Very cool.

She sat down and placed the Colt on the table. Directly in front of her, barrel facing me. She eased back and down in her chair. Put her right elbow on the chair arm and rested her head on her hand and began gently biting and sucking at the end of her little finger with the side of her mouth.

I stayed where I was. My hands cuffed to the table, my arms resting on top. We proceeded to watch each other for a little while, just like we did in the van. Then a smile started playing at her lips.

"Question," she said. She nodded toward the bloody strip one-way window. "What kind of person doesn't flinch at seeing that?"

"Same kind that doesn't flinch at doing it, I guess."

"But not the kind that gets caught."

"At least not unintentionally."

Isabel narrowed her eyes at me.

"OK, I'll bite," she said. "Why would you want to get caught?"

"Better question is why haven't you shot me, yet?"

Isabel smiled and then glanced down at Hays.

"You know Savile Row here was a pretty big deal," she said.

"Yeah? How big?"

"As it turns out, one of SAD's head honchos."

"That's big."

"You bet."

"Congratulations."

"Right back at you."

"Me?"

She leaned forward in her chair.

"See, Savile Row here didn't go after just any poor bastard the CIA deemed worthy—no, no, no. In fact in the two decades he's been in charge, Savile Row here has only ever been concerned with the absolute highest priority cases. I'm talking real Nostradamus stuff. Bond villains."

"Example?"

"Well, you remember that Korean guy a few years back, worked out of Nepal, big time loan shark but with a twist?"

I nodded. "Guy gives you a loan, takes your kidneys as collateral. Then the recession hits and he gets all entrepreneurial. Starts selling kidneys to every poor bastard at the bottom of a transplant list. Fifteen thousand per, twenty-five for a pair. Ends up with one of the biggest organ trafficking networks in history."

"That's the guy," she said. "And Savile Row's the one who caught him."

I shot my eyebrows. "No kidding."

Isabel nodded. "Yup. And up until three days ago he was working on something even bigger."

"Which was?"

"Apparently not big enough," she said. "Because next thing anyone knows, he's put the whole thing on pause and is taking these guys in a completely different direction."

"Sounds intriguing."

"It should," she said. "Because, as of four hours ago, that direction was you."

"That why you let Hays talk to me first? Find out why?"

"And what a waste of time that was. This table has two sides? Who talks like that?"

I laughed.

"Still though, it does raise an interesting point," she said. "If Savile Row here thought you were worth something…"

"Someone else might, too?"

She leaned back in her chair, satisfied. "Pretty perspicacious, huh?"

"What?"

She smiled. "One of the words Savile Row used to describe you. Means you notice and understand things that aren't obvious. We all had to look it up."

"And here I thought these guys didn't like me. I guess Hays really did believe in a sense of respect."

"Yup. And besides, Gravel Voice had enough choice words for you to pick up the slack."

I glanced up at the ceiling. "Speaking of noticing things," I said. "You ever wonder how nobody ever finds these places?"

Isabel thought for a moment. "It is a pretty snazzy set-up isn't it?"

"And right here on South Franklin Street."

She gave me a look. "So you did figure it out."

I smiled. "Among other things."

She laughed. "*Oh, really?*" she said. "And just when did you figure me out?"

"About three seconds after I met you."

She shook her head.

I shrugged. "You're probably right," I said. "I mean the odds would be astronomical."

"Odds?"

"That I'd run into one of Harriet Granger's girls."

Isabel went quiet and serious.

Then her left hand went for her Colt.

SIX

ISABEL STOPPED HER hand almost before it moved. She had tried not to react, but her left hand had betrayed her. The result was a twitch so imperceptible it basically hadn't happened. Except it had happened. She knew it, I knew it, and she knew that I knew it. She looked down at her hand and smiled. *Well played.*

"Well now," she said. "That *is* impressive." Her eyes flicked up at me and she leaned forward again. "And what would you know about that?"

I smiled. "So you're Isabel?" I said.

She went quiet again. Her eyes narrowed, and I could see her thinking hard.

"Tell me what you know," she said.

"Tell me why Hays was a target."

"Why is anyone? Someone wanted him dead."

"What's item eighty-six?"

"What's it to you?"

"Harriet still got that pen?"

"Who are you?"

I took a breath like I was about to speak and then didn't.

We fell silent. Isabel kept thinking hard. She stayed quiet for a while and then leaned back and smiled a mischievous smile.

"You know, I could just *make* you tell me," she said.

"You could try."

"Maybe I will." She tilted her head to the side and a playful expression came to her face. Then I felt her left leg stretch out under the table and begin moving up the inside of my right leg. My eyebrow twitched. I heard the male voice tell me to be cool. I was glad the laptop had smashed because the polygraph would have been going haywire. I still couldn't get over the way her eyes seemed to glow. There was something so feline about her, so alluring and yet so dangerous. She watched my reaction. Saw her effect. I was melting and she knew it. She kept her leg there, teasing me for a whole minute. Then she retractcd it. "Relax handsome. You're not my type."

"Perspicacious?"

"Male."

At which point I heard the male voice have a heart attack.

Isabel kept watching me, the playful look still on her face, but something else now forming behind her eyes.

"So where do we go from here?" I asked.

"Well what would you do in my position?"

"You could read my file. Maybe you'll find some answers in there."

"Or I could just shoot you."

I nodded. "There's that."

"Besides, what makes you think you're worth reading about, anyway?"

"Guess I'll return those Tony Robbins CDs then."

Her eyes slid to the open folder—which was now hanging halfway over the edge of the table. She thought for a moment and then checked her watch and shrugged. "What the hell, I've got time."

She grabbed the folder and leaned back into chair and started leafing through the file.

"Hmmm," she said. "Isaac Blaze, male, twenty-eight years old, blah-blah-blah… highly intelligent, hears voices, possibly unstable… blah-blah-blah…"

She stopped reading and held up the top few pages of the file and looked at me. "You know what the problem with psych profiles is?"

"Makes you realize there are people getting paid to do guesswork?"

"In other words, they're useless," she said, and then tossed the pages with a flick of her wrist. They were stapled together and landed awkwardly on the floor in a kind of paper tepee. They landed right next to the hole in Hays chest and immediately started wilting and turning red as they soaked up the spilled blood.

Isabel said, "Better we stick to the facts. So let's take a look at your background."

Good luck with that, I thought.

Isabel read through the next few pages making all kinds of interested and surprised sounds as she did so. While she did that, the male voice began narrating in a deep mysterious tone, *Not much is known about the origins of Isaac Blaze. He is a man shrouded in mystery and secret. Traversing the terrasphere for reasons unknown. Appearing suddenly, only to vanish just as quickly. Some say—*

"1998," Isabel said.

"Year of the Tiger," I said.

"And the year Isaac Blaze bursts onto the scene."

"That's what it says?"

"Best these guys can figure, anyway."

"And before then?"

"You don't exist. No birth certificate, no medical history, no school records, no nothing."

"They don't speculate?"

"Not particularly."

"Nothing about an ancient prophecy being fulfilled, alignment of the planets…"

Isabel gave me a look.

I said, "It mention how they found me in '98?"

"Hotel manager gave you up," she said.

I shook my head.

The female voice said, *I knew that guy was a rat.*

Isabel flipped through some more pages and got deep into the file. She mumbled some of the dates she was reading about. "Berlin, 2001, Moscow, 2005, Rome the same year." A couple of entries seemed to make her smile. I listened to the list and exchanged some fond memories with the voices. But then Isabel read of a couple of dates that meant absolutely nothing to me. And that got me curious.

I asked, "Anything in there about Israel in '08?"

Isabel didn't answer. She seemed to have reached something interesting. She had been speed reading through all of the previous information, but now she was reading very carefully. She looked a little confused.

"Something wrong?" I asked.

"February '09," she said.

I recalled the date.

"What about it?" I said.

"You were in Panama?"

"I might have been."

She looked up from the file.

"February 2009. Panama. Yes or no?"

I said nothing. There was something in her eyes.

"Answer the question," she said.

"What's your interest?" I said.

"Answer the question," she said again. Her voice had risen.

The female voice said, *She's not messing around here, Isaac*.

She really wasn't. Not one bit. Her eyes had gone cold and she was staring at me hard. Her jaw was clenched tight and I could feel her struggling not to stick the Colt in my face. Clearly Panama '09 was important to her. And the question of my being there was important, too. But what had happened? I didn't know. I said nothing.

The next few moments were tense to say the least. I had no idea what was running through Isabel's mind. If she had lifted the Colt, I may well have been killed. But she didn't lift the Colt. Instead she seemed to let the matter drop completely. And instantly. One second I was on trial, the next I was a free man. A favorable judgment. The playful smile came back to her face. Her eyes went back to the file and she perused the rest of it quickly. There were photographs at the back which she briefly studied, and then she closed the folder and tossed it onto the table again.

"You've done some bad things," she said.

"Allegedly," I said.

"You deny it?"

"I lead a full life."

"As a fugitive?"

"Outlaw."

She rolled her eyes.

I said, "Ask me. You can't beat a good game of cat and mouse."

"From what I've read it's more like the Coyote and the Road Runner."

"Except Wile E. Coyote never caught the Road Runner."

"And these guys never caught you. Not before now, anyway."

"Oh they've caught me before," I said.

"They have?"

"A few times, in fact."

"Not according to this."

"If you let a fugitive escape your custody would you put it in a file?"

"I thought you didn't get caught unintentionally."

"I don't."

"So what happened?"

"They got lucky."

"But they didn't get lucky this time."

I shook my head. "Nope."

"Which brings us back to…"

"Why get caught?"

She nodded.

"Easiest way in," I said.

"To this place? It's *one* way. I don't know about easiest though. And it's definitely not the most stylish."

"But it did put me in the same room as Hays."

"So you were after Savile Row, too?"

"Actually, no."

She nodded. "But you could have been, yeah, I get it."

"How did you do it?" I asked.

"Get in here?" she said. She leaned to her right and reached around to the back of her belt with her left hand. She held up a laminate ID. The same one she'd used in the elevator. "SSO Elizabeth Taylor," she said. "Pleased to meet you."

"You're joking," I said. "Elizabeth Taylor?"

"Doesn't say much for these guys, huh? But then, that's the problem with these black book operations. Half the time even they don't know who their assets are. Everyone's a ghost."

"And with snazzy places like this…"

She nodded. "You turn up, you must be one of them."

You got to hand it to her, she does make it sound easy, the female voice said.

She makes it sound a whole lot of things, the male voice replied.

"OK," Isabel said. She leaned to her right again and clipped the ID back on her belt. "So if Savile Row wasn't on the menu, you got taken for what, just to see what I was up to?"

"What can I say, I'm a curious guy," I said.

Isabel thought about that for a moment then shrugged.

"All right," she said. "But now let's say you hadn't wanted to get caught."

"How would I have escaped your capable hands?"

She nodded.

I said, "Way I see it you made two mistakes."

"Now this I've got to hear," she said. She pulled her chair up close and folded her arms and leaned across the table, right over the Colt.

I said, "First mistake, you stood too close to me."

"Did I?" she said.

"Second mistake was your gun."

"What about it?"

"It was holstered."

"Believe me, I'm a quick draw," she said.

"I do believe you."

"But?"

"You didn't have position."

"Because I was standing too close?"

I nodded. "Any kind of draw would have put that gun straight in my face. Literally."

"Which would make for an easy disarm," she said. "Assuming you have the necessary skill, of course."

"Of course."

She shrugged. "Big deal. So I take a step back when I draw. Call it half a second to make my move."

"Plenty of time," I said.

"It might have been. Depends what you had in mind."

"Remember the table I was at?" I said.

"Small, wooden, and square," she said.

"And light and solid and most importantly not bolted to the ground like this one."

"So I make my move…"

"And I flip the table."

"I get a blocked view, you get maybe another second."

I shook my head. "I get options," I said.

"Options, huh? All right. Option one?"

"I make a break for the window."

"*Cuckoo's Nest?* Please."

"Not the greatest plan I'll admit, but you didn't have them covered."

"We didn't think you were an idiot."

"Thin glass, superficial cuts, I'd have been fine. In any case, that was option one."

She pulled a face. "What else you got?"

"Option two: I flip the table and you get a hostage situation."

"The woman with juice box?"

I nodded.

Isabel said, "And I take it this is where the bishop comes into play?"

"So you saw that?"

"I see everything."

"And what eyes you do that with."

She smiled. "Not my type, remember?"

"That's twice you've said that."

She rolled her eyes. "The bishop," she said.

"It's what I had."

"That thing was sharp."

"I know, right? They really need to pay more attention at the factory."

Isabel said, "So option two is you flip the table, grab Juice Box, and then it's what, 'Throw your weapon or this one gets a bishop in her jugular?'"

"Pretty much."

"And what happens when my guys come in?"

"Nothing. They'd look to you and you'd tell them to throw their weapons too. And after that you get on your shoulder radio and tell your boys outside to stand down as well."

"And then what? You walk out with Juice Box, get into a car and drive off beyond the horizon?"

"I don't know, I didn't think that far ahead. But something like that, yeah."

"You really think we'd just surrender?"

"What other choice did you have? CIA on American soil? Any kind of problem would have been a disaster. And a *hostage* situation? You'd have brought down the entire agency. Hays would've been swapping Savile for Death."

"Except you wouldn't have really hurt that woman, would you?"

"Yeah, but that's irrelevant. Point is, it would be a situation. I'd have gotten away clean."

Isabel thought about it for a moment.

"You know, you're probably right," she said. "There's just one problem."

"Which is?"

"Who says I would've needed my gun?"

"Yeah, those CDs are definitely going back."

"Think about it," she said. "Suppose I had just walked in and started smacking you around instead. What then?"

"I might have enjoyed it."

She laughed. "OK, but how about this. Forget SWAT, forget Savile Row, forget all of this crap. What if it had been *me*—the *real* me—who had come for you?"

"Well…" I said. "I'm sure I would have thought of something."

"Think it would've worked?"

"I guess we'll never know."

"I guess not."

Her wristwatch started beeping: three quick beeps and then a pause and then three quick beeps again. Isabel checked her watch and hit a button. The beeping stopped. Then she glanced down at the Colt. She picked it up. She looked it over and contemplated for a moment. Then her eyes flicked up at me.

"Looks like our time's up, handsome," she said.

"So what have you concluded?" I asked.

"That you, Isaac Blaze, are an unknown."

"And?"

"And I don't mess with the unknown."

"Harriet's Golden Rule," I said.

Isabel smirked and then stood up and holstered the Colt.

"Call this a *favor*," she said.

"No bullet, then?"

She tutted. "Never kill a man who owes you a favor."

I nodded. "Rule Five."

Isabel turned toward the door and then turned back.

"Oh and by the way," she said. "Wile E. Coyote did catch Road Runner."

"He did?"

"Just once," she said. "In a Looney Tunes TV special back in nineteen-eighty. Chuck Jones put it together. The special was called *Bugs Bunny's Bustin' Out All Over* and there was a Road Runner short called *Soup or Sonic*. Wile E. catches him in it."

"Aired on May 21st," I said. "How did you know?"

"I like cartoons," she said. And with that she turned away and walked to the door.

"How about a hand with these?" I called.

Isabel paused in the doorway and looked back over her shoulder, grinning. "Well, Isaac Blaze, if you're as good as you *think* you are, I doubt you'll have a problem with those."

And then she was gone.

Hot damn! the male voice said.

Worth the trip, right? I said.

So what are we waiting for? Let's go after her.

Aren't you forgetting something? the female voice said.

I looked down at my cuffed hands.

SEVEN

ANDCUFFS COME IN a wide variety of specifications. Long chain, short chain, hinged, rigid—the list goes on. And each type of spec offers a different level of restriction. But no matter how strong or thick or constricting the metal bracelets are, they are only ever as good as their lock. And when it comes to handcuffs, locks and keys do not tend to vary much at all. In fact they are usually the same.

The reasons for this are numerous—the most intuitive being that you don't want to have to keep uncuffing and recuffing a prisoner every time you trade officers. What this means for the savvy criminal is that it pays to carry a concealed key. And while I know a lot of savvy criminals who do, I don't. That would be cheating.

I was currently affixed to a pair of Smith and Wesson 103P handcuffs. They were stainless steel and had double locks. Each cuff had one keyhole. The keyholes were facing away from me. Technically, that was Isabel's third mistake. She had dropped the cuffs on the table and allowed me to put them on myself. I had tightened them well enough but I had also made sure that the keyholes were facing outward. Which made them easier to get to. If the keyholes are facing toward you then you have to twist and turn your hands before your fingers can get to them.

The keyholes themselves looked like small magnifying glasses. Next to each keyhole was a horizontal oblong-shaped hole that indicated whether the double lock was engaged or not. If the hole has a thin vertical bar running through it, the double lock is not engaged. Neither cuff had a bar showing.

I started looking around the room. Picking locks is easy enough, but finding something to do it with is another matter, entirely. You need a strong yet malleable metal. Bobby pins are ideal, and I remembered seeing two females wearing them on my way in. Normally, I carry a bobby pin on my person. They have so many uses that, quite frankly, it's common sense. Of course, as luck would have it, today was an exception. So I had to improvise.

The male voice said, *What about Hays's fountain pen? The nib would work.*

You see Hays's fountain pen? the female voice said.

The male voice said nothing. The pen had long since rolled onto the floor.

What about the folder? the male voice said.

I looked at the folder, but the female voice was ahead of me.

Strike two, she said. *Not even a single paper clip*.

The male voice said, *I hope _you_ have an answer.*

Oh I have an answer… . I glanced to my left. My reflection was smudged in the one-way glass. Brain matter and blood were sprayed all over. I followed the snail trails and raspberry-colored chunks down the one-way glass and down the wall and onto the floor and past a leg of the overturned folding chair until I reached what was left of Peter's head. It was resting in a pool of blood, looking straight at me.

The male voice sighed. *Looks like our shoes are going to get wet.*

I stood up and stretched my left leg out, leaning on the table for balance, and reached for Peter's broken eyeglasses with my foot. The right temple was lying under his head and was still wrapped around his right ear. The left temple was sticking up in the air. It had nothing to grip onto. I pushed the left temple to the floor with my foot and dragged the frames toward me. They slipped and slid easily due to the copious amount of lubrication there was. Once I had reeled them in, I sat down again and used my right foot to maneuver the frames onto my left foot, which I cautiously lifted up and used to toss the frames onto the table. They landed next to my left hand. I picked them up and wiped off the blood and the glop against my right forearm.

The glasses were perfect. They had titanium frames— thin, wiry, and strong. They were also long, which was very useful. I pulled off the rubber ear-grips and bent a temple tip into shape by leaning over and using my teeth.

Yuck, said the female voice.

Yuck is right, said the male voice. *I mean, who knows whether Peter washed behind his ears?*

Ignoring those comments, I pushed the tip into the right cuff's lock and jimmied it counterclockwise first, which released the double lock and brought a vertical bar into the center of the oblong hole, and then I jimmied clockwise to release the cuff completely.

The trick is not to be aggressive. You need a delicate touch. You want to exert just the right amount of pressure with the pick and no more. Too much and the pick can break and jam the lock.

Too little and it'll be your patience that breaks. The length of the pick I was using definitely helped in this regard, but, after years of practice, I had a developed fairly deft touch, anyway. Once my right hand was free, I repeated the entire procedure with the left cuff. The whole enchilada took about ten minutes.

I stood up, ripped off the polygraph equipment, shook out my arms, and stretched my shoulders and back. I looked down at the three bodies. Peter was lying next to me. Chest-down, arms by his sides. There was a mess of equipment all around him. The folding chair was overturned behind him, and the laptop was near his head, lying facedown like an open book. His head lay in and beside large pool of blood. There were swipe marks where I had dragged the eyeglasses. The pool had expanded all the way down to his waist and had spread out half a meter from both sides of his body. I could see a murky reflection in it.

I looked over at Hays. He had been shot in the chest. He had managed to stand up and turn around before Isabel had shot him. He was sprawled in a kind of Superman-flying pose. He was lying on his right side with his right arm out-stretched above his head. His hand was almost touching the wall with the one-way glass. His head was about level with Peter's feet. The small trolley they had wheeled in was stand-ing in that angle. Two of its wheels standing in Peter's blood, the other two in Hays's. And right in the middle of Hays's pool was the paper tepee.

It was the first part of my file—the first thing anyone would have read about me. The pages were exactly where Isabel had tossed them, still stapled together, still in a tepee shape, but now totally saturated in Hays's blood. I bent down and picked them up by the corner staple, which was the tepee's point. I laid the pages on the table, peeling each page carefully off the next as I tried to read them. From what I could make out, they consisted of a single statistics page, followed by a twelve-page psychological profile. I figured it had been written by some hot-shot profiler who had largely based their opinions on an amalgamation of previous works from better sources, some of whom might have actually had first-hand contact with me. As Isabel said: useless.

I picked up the brown folder and started going through it very carefully. It began with my background information. Or rather it attempted to begin with it. Like Isabel told me, these guys had almost nothing. There was nothing from before 1998. No medical records, no financials, no nothing.

But they did have my DNA on file. They had collected blood from an early crime scene and I had been in their system ever since. Later forensic collections had enabled cross referencing which had allowed them to confirm my presence at various other times of interest.

I carried on through the file and came to the part about my alleged previous exploits. There was a big table of data that stretched over twenty-nine pages. The table was split into three columns. The first gave a date, the second gave a location, and the third gave a bullet-point summary of any relevant details. Each row corresponded to a different case. There were 321 cases in total. Some had plenty of details, others had almost none. All of them were asterisked to indicate further information was available. I started scrolling down the table. Forensic evidence tied me to about 70 percent of the cases. It was circumstantial at best but more than enough for these guys. And it's not like they were wrong, anyway. The remaining 30 percent of cases had been attributed to me via a mix of eyewitness testimony, educated speculation, and pure rumor. The thirty-fourth entry brought a smile to my face. It was about three-quarters of the way down the eighth page. It was dated April 2011. The location was the Rue de Paradis, in Paris, France. The details amounted to a single bullet point: *Isaac Blaze shot nine times in the chest.*

The male voice said, *Now that was a fun contract.*

That poor medical examiner, the female voice said. *He just about hit the roof.*

We all laughed at the memory and then I continued scrolling down the table until I found the entry about Panama 2009. I read over the details and recalled the events.

Doesn't make sense, the female voice said. *Panama was nothing.*

Maybe not to us, I said. *But you got to figure there are some people who are still seriously pissed off about what happened.*

Forget figure, the male voice said. *We know there are.*

Maybe… the female voice said. *But I mean, come on, we didn't even kill anybody.*

Maybe that was the problem, said the male voice.

Or maybe there was another party going on at the same time, I said.

Whatever, the female voice said. *Point is, that girl was about ready to kill us over it and for some reason she didn't.*

Mentioning Harriet must have rattled her pretty good, the male voice said.

I don't know, she looked more angry than rattled. A little desperate even. Almost like it was personal, said the female voice.

Thoughts, Isaac?

We can ask her about it later, I said.

I finished scanning the table and the next thing in the file was a forty-page special report. Three expert data analysts had been brought in and asked to put it together. What they had produced was something akin to a scientific research paper. The report began by compiling every piece of data they had about me. Everything from my movement patterns to my restaurant choices. They had even included "facts" from the psych report. Charts and graphs had been produced and then compared and contrasted. The analysts had commented on their findings, come up with a series of parameters, and then finally extrapolated the data to predict my possible future targets.

The male voice said, *That's a long list.*

What did you expect? the female voice said.

Not the Tate at number three, that's for sure. A 67 percent probability we'll hit in the next two months? What's that about?

You rely on psych reports, you get corrupted data. Might as well use astrology.

Well it does state Egypt as being a current target, I said.

Yeah, along with China and Turkey and Texas.

After the report, there was an annexed list of file references. Each reference would link to a separate file that expounded on every case summarized in the table. Following that was pages of what I assumed were Hays's personal notes. But I couldn't read them. Not even a little. The handwriting was so bad I actually started laughing. It was just a spidery mess of lines. Like someone had tried to sketch a piece of wire-wool, from an abstract perspective, with their off-hand, while sky-diving. I looked down at Hays and shook my head and tutted.

The last thing in the folder was a dossier of photographs. Naturally, the subject was me. Different years, different places. But none of the pictures captured anything important. They were just random surveillance shots.

I closed the file and stretched my shoulders and back again. I looked over at Gravel Voice. He was sprawled on the ground, stretching away from the doorway toward the left corner of the room. His body was slumped like Peter's: chest down, arms straight by his sides. He was also missing about 25 percent of his head. There was a neat hole on the left side of his head and a bloody mess on the other. The neat hole was about the diameter of an index finger. There was a black ring around it. The Colt's muzzle had been pressed tight to his temple and when the gun had fired a blast of superheated air had seared the imprint into his skin. You could have fit a grapefruit in the other hole.

A long spew of red and pink stretched from the top of Gravel Voice's head to the wall with the one-way glass. The bullet had lodged itself about a third of the way up the wall, a few inches out from the corner, directly below the corner camera. There was a small red stain around it.

I bent down and searched Hays's clothes. He wasn't carrying much. Which wasn't surprising since that would have completely destroyed the way his suit draped. Anything excess would be in a desk drawer somewhere. I found no wallet on him.

Naturally, his cell phone was in his right inside jacket pocket, meaning it had been lying in a pool of blood for a good long while. It didn't even power on. Not great. As for the left side of his jacket, it held just two items: a logo-less car key and a small rectangular widget. The widget had a small piece of red-tinted glass and emitted some sort of short-range signal. No way to tell what for, but at least it was moderately interesting. The gold lapel pin had caught my eye in the interview, so I took it as well. I had to roll Gravel Voice over in order to search him properly. It was wasted effort though. He didn't have my money anymore. I stared down at Hays one last time and then ventured out into the rest of the facility.

EIGHT

I WALKED OUT OF the interrogation room to the end of the short corridor. There was a single door either side. The door on my left was standing open. There was a trail of scuff marks and tiny red smudges leading from it to the interrogation room. I stepped inside. It was a small rectangular room. Same length as the interrogation room but only a third of the width. A long low countertop had been built out of the right wall. There were a couple of computer monitors and some recording equipment on top of it. One monitor was linked to the corner camera and showed nothing but static. The other monitor was just a standard computer.

The left wall held the other side of the one-way glass. There was a scuff mark in its center, and the floor directly below had a fair bit of blood on it.

The male voice said, *OK, so there Gravel Voice is, he's watching us, he's watching Hays, he's agitated, he's impatient, he needs a cigarette—*

And then the door opens, the female voice said.

He turns to look…

Isabel cracks him on his nose.

His head flies back against the glass…

Our interrogation gets interrupted.

Isabel proceeds to pound on him for a bit…

And then she drags him away and we saw what happened next, I said.

Poor bastard.

I went back into the corridor and opened the door opposite. There was nothing much in it. It was lined with shelves and stocked full of cardboard boxes. They were all filled with various kinds of paperwork that, for whatever reason, hadn't been digitized.

I walked back up the corridor, past the interrogation room, and into the only other door there was. It was a toilet. I took the opportunity to wash my hands. I had three peoples' blood on them: Hays's from touching the tepee, Peter's from wiping his glasses, and Gravel Voice's from rolling him over. I used the facilities and then washed my hands again.

There was a small mirror above the sink. I looked at my reflection and then leaned in closer. The left side of my face was covered in tiny red sprinkles. There was probably good amount in my hair too, but I couldn't see it. Red doesn't show on black.

I pumped some more soap from the dispenser, lathered my face, and washed it all off. I repeated the procedure a couple of times. Then I stepped out into the main work area.

Everybody was down. Eighteen bodies. The twelve people I'd seen on my way in, plus the six SWAT guys. A single shot to each with clinical precision. We hadn't heard any of it because of the almost soundproof interrogation room.

Damn she's good, the female voice said.

She is one of Harriet's, I said.

The male voice said, *Now, that's just mean!*

I looked up at the big monitor on the wall between the

two office cubes. I remembered how Hays had been staring at it so intently before he walked into the interrogation room. Whatever had been up there before hadn't pleased him, and I myself had mixed feelings about its current display. On screen now was a simple message. Three capital letters followed by four numbers: *IOU 1732.*

I sighed and shook my head.

I was smiling, though.

I walked between the desks and the bodies and checked out both of the office cubes. They were identical. Desk, chair, computer, phone. Each office had a bunch of paperwork on its desk and both had a single filing cabinet filled with more. No pictures, no personal effects. They were plain, simple, efficient, and anonymous.

And that was it.

The entire facility.

Brutal.

But brutal is what these guys were all about. The Special Activities Division is the CIA's pièce de résistance. The guys who get shit done. They recruit from the elite and then train them to be better. SAD is pure special ops. A totally deniable asset. They operate covertly and all around the world. The problem, of course, is that with all their operatives out there getting shit done, there's usually nobody sitting around at home to defend it.

So these guys had been really unlucky. Because this time there had been people at home. Hays had been running an OP on American soil and scrambled together a seven-strong team specifically for it. Unfortunately for him though, one of those seven turned out to be Isabel, and she was an army all by herself. The six SWAT guys didn't stand a chance.

And everybody else here was an analyst. They didn't even have weapons because that wasn't their function. They were here to provide tactical support to the boots on the ground. It was a command center. Nothing more.

I came back to the work area and sat down at a desk. I nudged a mouse and woke up a computer. I didn't need a password because it was already logged on. Nobody had had a chance to log off. I clicked around for a couple of minutes and acquainted myself with their system. Then I did a search for their most recent files and threw everything up on the big screen.

The first thing I saw was my own wanted poster. It was part of a system alert that had been triggered six hours ago. The poster was a digital copy of the paper version I'd seen many times before. All the agencies had their own version, and, for the most part, they looked about the same.

SAD's version used a couple of surveillance photos for my headshots. They were side by side in the middle of the poster. One showed a more or less straight-on capture of my face, and the other showed a three-quarter profile. My name was written above them in block capital letters. At the top of the poster was a blue banner that read: *Most Wanted Fugitive*, followed by a long list of reasons why. Underneath the headshots was a short description of me that laid out my height, weight, eye color, and other statistics. It said my last known location was Europe. Then came a caution that I was to be considered extremely dangerous, and finally there was a reward note stating that information leading to my arrest was worth $250,000.

The male voice said, *That's their problem, right there. Who's going to call these guys when Russia's offering a cool mill?*

Not to mention what the other side of the law is offering, the female voice said.

I brought up the information from three days ago. That was when Hays had started all this. Prior to that, he'd been working on something else. Something big, Isabel had said.

And Isabel was right.

Hays had been running point on a HUMINT operation for the past nineteen days. He had a team deployed to Tehran, Iran. Four days ago, their efforts had yielded a piece of information that had instantly changed their mission parameters. Human Intelligence had suddenly become Direct Action. It was a huge and unexpected shift. But these guys were the best for a reason. The team had adapted quickly, worked up a solution, and, less than sixteen hours later, they had moved into a preliminary position, ready to engage.

But then they had been ordered to hold.

And they'd been holding for the past three days.

The male voice said, *No wonder he needed a cigarette*.

I remembered the dirty look Gravel Voice had greeted me with. He must have been thinking: *Iran's on hold for this guy?*

And, ego aside, he had a point.

Why had Hays come after me? I mean, sure, SAD wanted me pretty bad. But bad enough to pause a live mission in Iran?

Flattering.

But unlikely.

And yet taking control of Chicago's eyes was the first thing Hays had done. The facility was currently tapped into every surveillance camera the city had to offer. From the moment Hays had walked in on Saturday morning, all traffic in and out of Chicago had been thoroughly scrutinized.

Advanced facial recognition software had been running 24/7, with a specific focus on high value targets.

The male voice said, *Damn thing tracked us all the way from O'Hare*.

The female voice said, *Doesn't make sense*.

Facial Rec's come a long way. Plus we have been a bit devil-may-care recently.

No, I mean look at what he's been working on. It doesn't make any sense.

The female voice had a point. Once Hays had finished going all Big Brother on Chicago, he had immediately started looking into the laboratory explosion that had been in the news.

Looks like I was right, the male voice said.

We're all surprised, the female voice said.

The details of the case were fairly simple. Thursday night, at 1902 hours, an explosion had occurred at the HBL laboratory in the west side of Chicago. The research team had been developing a new kind of jet fuel for the Air Force. Eight people were killed. They were identified as a team of researchers who had been working late. A couple of security guards had been injured.

The explosion was believed to be the result of a faulty combustion chamber. It had gone boom like it was supposed to but the chamber hadn't withstood the blast. There was some minor speculation suggesting human error rather than technical was to blame, and that either someone hadn't sealed the chamber properly, or someone hadn't run a proper diagnostics check beforehand. But all opinions ruled it accidental.

The female voice said, *Hmmm*.

And *hmmm* was right.

SAD didn't investigate accidents.

The male voice said, *So either these guys had nothing better to do—*

Which we know they did, the female voice said.

Or Hays thought that something about this explosion needed his immediate attention, I said.

Which was all well and good in theory, but, from what I could see, Hays had exactly no evidence to support such a claim. None at all. Not, of course, that he needed any, mind you. As one of SAD's head honchos, Hays had simply walked in on Saturday morning, told everyone how it was, and taken over.

What about this other stuff? the male voice said.

I went through it. This other stuff indicated that, while Hays may have had his suspicions about the HBL explosion, according to the system files it was far from being the only thing on his agenda. Hays had actually been looking into a number of incidents. The HBL explosion was merely the first. The other cases varied in their nature and included a shooting spree in Tangiers, an embassy bombing in Madrid, and a prison riot in Texas. All had occurred within the past seven days. All had resulted in mass casualties.

But none appeared to be connected—at least not obviously.

Either of you see a connection? the female voice said.

Not me, the male voice said. *You, Isaac?*

Uh-uh, I said. *Locations are spread, victim profiles are random. Definitely nothing to do with us, anyway.*

And yet, the female voice said, *there's something here that compelled Hays to drop everything else for.*

And then come after us, I said.

So what did he see that we aren't?

And how did it get him killed?

NINE

WHOEVER WANTED HAYS dead *really* wanted Hays dead. Case in point, they'd hired one of Harriet Granger's girls. And they were the best. Which naturally also made them the most pricey. Which implied big players and high stakes. Or in other words: exactly the kind of thing I like to stick my nose into.

I went through all the cases again. This time in detail. Or at least in as much detail as was available. Which wasn't much.

A curious point in itself.

The six cases in front of me had all occurred within the past few days. Nineteen hurt, thirty-five dead. I studied the data, compared the findings, and analyzed the results. And I reached the same conclusion as before: No connection.

The male voice said, *Maybe we're going about this all wrong.*

How so? I said.

Well, we all agree that there must be some kind of connection between these six cases, right?

Right.

And we also agree that whatever this connection is it's about as easy to see as the reason any man would intentionally wear skinny jeans, don't we?

Yeah, I hate those things.

What's your point? the female voice said.

The male voice said, *Point is, maybe the question isn't <u>what</u> Hays saw, it's <u>how</u>. As in how did he come to see this super-thin-yet-ultra-crucial connection in the first place?*

You think he had a source?

Last time I checked, HUMINT is what these guys are all about. You know, when they're not doing all that other shit, that is, the male voice said.

OK, say you're right. Say Hays did have a source. How come the informant's not in the system?

Obvious answer, because Hays didn't share the intel.

Why not? Makes no sense.

Yeah but Hays did a lot of things that don't make sense. Not least of which was bringing us here, he said.

That's important?

Sure it's important. After all, this place is far from equipped to handle prisoners.

It's got an interrogation room, she said.

No, it's got a spotless interrogation room. Or at least it did before things got messy.

Yeah, and?

And that implies it was hardly ever used. In fact I'm betting we were the first to have the pleasure.

I still don't see the big deal, she said.

The big deal is that this place was built for only one purpose: operational interaction from a <u>distance</u>. It's all about the tech and the analysts. It was never meant for anything more. Least of all handling bad guys. Then he said, *It doesn't even have a holding cell.*

Then why have an interrogation room, at all?

Exactly, the male voice said. *They shouldn't. In fact that whole corridor is in reality completely superfluous. This facility should be nothing more than the main work area. The big screen, the computers, the analysts. That's all it needs.*

So what happened?

Good question, said the male voice. *Maybe when they actually started building this place, they found they had more room to work with than they thought, and with nothing on the plans, someone had to make a snap decision. And while this place could have never been turned into a full-fledged secret prison, a discrete and highly accessible interview facility could be useful, nonetheless. For emergencies, sure, and maybe they'd never use it, but what the hell, it couldn't hurt, and they had nothing better to do with the space, anyway.*

I can think of a dozen better ways to use it, she said.

A dozen? Whatever. The point isn't that they built an emergency interrogation room, the point is Hays used it.

Which is why everybody was staring at us on the way in, I said.

Right, the male voice said. *They were staring at us because even they knew something was off.*

Hmmm, the female voice said. *So let me get this straight. Hays turns up on Saturday morning, pauses the Iran mission, opens a new investigation on American soil that he doesn't have any evidence for and won't share any intel about, and won't loop anyone else in on, and then, once he does have a lead, which apparently is us, he brings us here, to an emergency contingency interrogation room, just so he can what, interrogate us, himself?*

Like I said, a lot of things that don't make sense, said the male voice.

Plus the fact that whatever intel Hays did have, it not only got him killed—

It also made him ultraparanoid too.

All right, you might be on to something.

Thank you.

Except it only confirms what we already know, I said. *That the intel in question is highly valuable. But it doesn't get us any closer to finding out what it actually is because whatever Hays knew died with him.*

Which means we're still on square one, the female voice said.

Square one? Not necessarily, the male voice said.

Meaning?

Meaning that there are only two possible reasons this intel gets Hays so paranoid. Either he couldn't trust his own people any more, or whatever this is about was personal.

So?

So just because we found nothing here, it doesn't mean Hays didn't have intel somewhere else.

Like where? the female voice asked.

Where? I don't know.

Not real helpful then is it?

And just what do you suggest? asked the male voice.

We go after the source.

Go after the source? You do realize I came up with that theory, right?

Please. Anyone could have come up with that.

We could also come at this from the other angle, I said.

Which is? asked the female voice.

We find out who wanted him dead.

OK, so we have options, the male voice said. *Where do we start?*

Where else? I said. *With Hays, himself.*

TEN

I WORKED THE COMPUTER. The facility might have been remote and top secret, but it was still a CIA installation, and as such it had all the privileges of an office at Langley. So I made use of them. I accessed their database—an effortless task given that they were all top-level analysts working off a shared system that I was already logged into—and ran a name check on Adrian Hays. Obviously, I knew that Langley wasn't going to have any record of one Adrian Hays working for them. The CIA had to remain perfectly clean, and SAD was anything but.

But.

The CIA did have access to basically every identity database the US had to offer. Everything from every state's DMV records to insurance company records, Medicare/Medicaid, inmate databases, and Social Security. So while Adrian Hays high-level-CIA-operative wouldn't exist, Adrian Hays nothing-to-see-here-I'm-an-American-taxpayer would.

And did.

The database listed fifty-three people named Adrian Hays in the US. Refining that list was a matter of common sense. First and foremost: get rid of the white guys. And that parameter alone cut the list to just sixteen. Age profiling, educational considerations, and the fact that most people live where they work, took care of the rest.

Adrian Hays, I said to the voices. *Sixty-five years old, graduated top of his class from MIT. Majored in mathematics with a minor in philosophy.*

Explains a lot, the female voice said. *Probably got recruited straight out of college.*

Says he works at Mizuho Bank, the male voice said. Which was more or less what I was expecting. Like Isabel said, everybody here was a ghost. But there are two types of ghost. The first is the kind you see in movies, with no name, and very particular sets of skills, and bank account numbers in their hip. The type of guys that go to Iran. Not the type that wear Savile Row suits and have perfect manicures. Those well-kept hands of his weren't the result of a lifetime in the field, and, judging from his reaction to Isabel, wet work was definitely out of the question. So Hays was type two.

Assets like Hays get embedded into companies and corporations that have access to high-quality information streams. Banks, law firms, and corporate accountants are the normal choices for placement. As employees, they can operate unnoticed and do whatever it is the CIA needs doing, which, in most cases, is sticking its nose where it doesn't belong.

The Mizuho Financial Group was as good a place as any. It was one of the Japanese megabanks, with assets of around $1.6 trillion and offices all over the world, including—surprise, surprise—one that was located in the heart of Chicago's financial district, in the southwest part of the Loop. I leaned back in my chair and stared up at all the pipes and cables snaking across the ceiling. Hays's office was thirty floors above me.

The male voice said, *It's possible Hays kept something in his office. Or maybe in a safety deposit box.*

Maybe, I said. *But that would limit his own access. Which would be counterproductive to an active investigation and counterintuitive if this really was somehow personal to him.*

Plus it's not like altitude would have helped his paranoia, the female voice said. *If he wasn't comfortable bringing intel down here, there's no reason he'd feel different about storing it up there.*

And that's assuming he had any physical intel at all. Or even a source for that matter. If this was personal, he might not have had either.

The male voice said, *No source? Well something has to have happened fairly recently, otherwise there's no reason for any of this to be happening in the first place.*

Agreed, I said. *Something definitely got Hays going, and the best way to find out what is to see what he's been up to recently.*

Which was fairly easy to do given that I was currently in a CIA facility and Hays was the second type of ghost.

I pulled up his credit card info on the big screen. I looked at every transaction from the past six months. Rather unsurprisingly, it told me that Hays was creature of habit. His daily and weekly routines were crystal clear and very rigid. He paid the same amounts on the same days of the week for the same assortment of groceries. He pumped the same amount of gas at the same Texaco station on the same three-day schedule. He got manicure treatments every two weeks. All his patterns were right there and easy to see. Variations even more so. My initial instinct was to look for any recent one-off transactions. Something like a small coffee shop or diner. Somewhere Hays would never normally go, and therefore a possible meeting place for a source. What I found instead was a recurring charge of $178.75 at around 10:30 pm every Tuesday and Friday.

That's *some* *dinner,* the female voice said.

Sure is! And would you look at that, the male voice said. *The last charge was seventy-six dollars more expensive than usual.*

And just eight hours before Hays started all this, I said.

I followed the money to a place called *Antelope*. I brought up the website. It was a gentleman's club. And not the sleazy kind. It was a meeting place for society's high and mighty. Very exclusive. Very Hays.

We're going to need a suit, I said.

I closed down all the stuff onscreen and brought up the Iran operation again. It didn't feel right to leave those guys stranded out there. They were totally in the dark about their situation. And they were in the worst situation possible. They had been made. The enemy was moving on their flank and they didn't even know it. Gravel Voice had a satellite over their position, so I had a real-time feed up on the monitor. I could see everything that was, and everything that would need to be. And for them to engage, they were going to need all sorts of tactical assistance, and there was nobody left here to provide it. But they couldn't just pull back. From what I had read, there was a lot on the line there, and these guys weren't the type to let that go, even if they were outflanked. They also needed to know that their exfiltration was going to be a lot harder now.

I looked at their circumstances, considered the support facilities Gravel Voice had in place, and thought about their options. I brought up their communication log. They had a satellite-phone on the ground and used it to check in every six hours. Their last communication had been five hours ago. It requested an update from Command, to which Gravel Voice had, for the fourteenth time, replied with: *Hold*. The team had then confirmed with a *Copy*, and there was nothing further. They had no idea that, as of four hours ago, they had become sitting ducks.

I sent them a message.

I started searching the rest of the system. There was plenty of interesting stuff to peruse. Atlanta's newly appointed senator, for example, was leading a considerably more experimental lifestyle than even I would have guessed. There was also a big oil deal over in Ukraine that was being monitored very closely and for very good reasons. I didn't have time to read everything, but I wasn't going to let it go to waste.

Marcel? the male voice asked.

Marcel, I agreed.

I opened a browser and started typing. In this day and age, digital warfare is the most crippling. So knowing a few guys with perpetual pizza stains on their shirt can give you a powerful resource. The best and scariest of these guys hang around on what's called the *Darknet*, which itself is part of the Deep Web, which is part of the Internet that can't be accessed by search engines, and, therefore, a place for the technologically savvy to share certain information. To access a site in the Deep Web, you need to already know its name and any passwords you may need. As for the Darknet, you need specific software before you can even get started. Which, of course, wasn't a problem: I was using an SAD computer.

Marcel—one name, like *Madonna*—was an old

acquaintance of mine and one of the best hackers in cyberspace. He and I had a standing agreement: I would send him interesting information as soon as I found it and he would provide his services as and when I needed them. It was an arrangement that had been more than lucrative for him and more than lifesaving for me.

Marcel had a number of Darknet sites setup for various purposes, and the one I accessed was essentially a drop point where I could upload any kind of digital information, such as the entire file system the SAD facility had. The site had a secondary function, too. Once an upload was complete, a powerful virus was sent back to the donor system, and destroyed any and all data on the server. I set the upload in motion and then sat back from the computer and spun round in my chair, thinking.

I figured my next move was to go to Hays's home, which, according to the DMV, was about an hour's drive in a place called Barrington. If Hays did have intel stored somewhere, his home would be a good place to look, especially if this was personal. I couldn't just waltz into the Antelope club, either. Not in jeans, anyway. I'd need to look the part, and a closet of Savile Row was going to be very handy.

The facility's surveillance footage had already been wiped by Isabel, but the camera feeds were still operational. They showed no movement in the parking lot, and I didn't see anything suspicious on the perimeter, either. I stood up and walked over to one of the women on the floor. I knelt down and removed two bobby pins from her hair and put them in my pocket. Then I went back to the interrogation room, grabbed the brown folder, and left.

ELEVEN

THE SERVICE ELEVATOR lifted me back up to the parking lot. It clunked into position. Then the cage shutter came up and let me out. The parking lot was still full, but the black van and follow car were nowhere to be seen. The row of reserved spaces was still the only place with vacancies. Except now there were only two, not three. The one that was full of litter was still available, and sitting in one of the others was Hays's car.

I knew it was Hays's car because only Hays would have driven what it was. *Ostentatious* was the operative word. In the elevator, I had bet on either a Jaguar or a Bentley, and, sure enough, it was a pristine Jaguar XK 120 Coupe. It was all black and highly polished. It had a long nose and thick wheels, and the interior was all custom—right down to the gearshift.

I walked over and unlocked it with Hays's key. I sat down in the plush seat and the male voice said, *Ooh, rich Corinthian leather*.

The car was as spotless inside as out. In the glove box, I found Hays's wallet and a bottle of antiseptic hand gel. There was also a very expensive hand moisturizer and a pair of leather driving gloves. I put a splodge of the moisturizer on the back of my hand and massaged it around. It was good stuff. My hands felt great afterwards. Smelled like peaches.

I started the engine and the Jaguar growled to life. It made a huge noise in the underground chamber. I backed out of the space, spiraled up the ramp, and came to a closed metal shutter. It was dull gray and corrugated and had a maximum clearance warning across the top. There was a ticket machine standing in front of it. I rolled down my window and inserted a ticket I found in the side door. The machine sucked in the ticket and then there was a clang and a rattle as the metal shutter started rolling up. The machine didn't give me a ticket back, so I just drove out.

I had to stop immediately, because I was right on the edge of the road, perpendicular to the traffic flow, which was in full rush hour hustle. After driving around the block perforce, I came to the building's southwest corner, where there was an outdoor public parking lot that was packed with various vehicles, including the black van that had brought me here and the follow car that had followed. They were sitting quite unassumingly at the edge of the lot. I stared a little too long and got beeped from behind. I drove past the main entrance.

The male voice said, *Damn, that's a big building.*

The female voice said, *And how many times must we have passed it before?*

I know, right? Makes you think what else we might be missing.

Which was what I thought about all the way to Hays's house.

The drive up to Barrington took around an hour and a half.

Barrington was a suburb in northwest Chicago. I found myself in a nice upper-middle-class eighbourhood with clean streets, neat lawns, and perfectly trimmed hedges. The houses were all fairly similar. All of them set back slightly, behind short driveways, and in the shade of leafy trees. A quiet seclusion. Very Hays.

I made sure to drive easily like Hays would have, reveling in the exquisiteness of the classic automobile, and owning the road. I fished the garage clicker out of the side door and pressed when I was two houses away. I pulled into Hays driveway and rolled straight into the open garage. It was all about timing and precision. I didn't want to draw any attention to myself. Hays had simply come home from the bank. I engaged the handbrake and then waited for the garage to close before I got out of the car.

The garage door moved on a motorized track that was fitted to the ceiling. The track had a light on it which had automatically come on when the door opened. The garage was plain and square, with ample room for the Jag, and everything else squared away on purpose-built shelves and cabinets. There was an adjoining door to the house on the wall in front of me. There was an alarm panel beside it. A standard plastic box, consisting of a keypad, and a rectangular screen above. On the side of the box were two small light bulbs. One was unlit, the other was shining red. The system was armed.

Disabling any kind of security can be tricky. It all depends on what you're dealing with. Small keypads like this were usually beaten by cracking open the case and playing with the wires inside, much the way one would hotwire a car. I looked around and saw a toolbox on one of the shelves. I could have taken a screwdriver and got to work, but then I took a closer look at the keypad, and the male voice said, *Well, that helps.*

The combination of Hays's hand cream and the silicon buttons had resulted in the numbers *1*, *2*, and *8*, all becoming slightly faded.

I said, *Standard code would be four digits.*

So one number repeats, the male voice said.

Which yields twelve possibilities.

Which is better than twenty-four.

But still more than the standard three attempts.

Right. Except there's only one code it can be.

Yes: 8-1-2-8, the female voice said.

Obviously, I said.

How about you type it in, first. Then you can have an attitude.

I entered the code. The small red light flicked off and the other light flicked on green.

You were saying? said the female voice.

All right. Someone care to explain why? I said.

It's simple really, the male voice said. *8-1-2-8. It's the fourth perfect number and it is four digits long. Beautiful mathematics. Classic Hays.*

The door opened into a small laundry room, which led into the kitchen, which looked brand new. The countertops were made from slabs of granite, and they were all gleaming. The refrigerator, cooking stations, and all of the appliances were shiny stainless steel. The pantry was empty. And I didn't find much in the fridge, either—just a couple of water bottles and a case of chilled beers. The beers were some kind of imported brand I didn't recognize. I lifted one out and broke off the cap and took a long pull. Not bad, at all.

The rest of the house was just as immaculate. Wooden floors, antique furniture, and not a speck of dust. A faint trace of lavender was hanging in the air. I traced the source to an air freshener that was plugged into one of the wall sockets in the hallway. The house had a large study/library, which is where I figured Hays spent most of his time. The color scheme was chocolate brown, dark green, and deep red. The lighting was dim, and the walls were lined with floor-to-ceiling book-shelves. There was a large antique desk in the corner, a cozy fireplace, a framed surrealist painting on a wall, and a free-standing globe. There was also a grandfather clock, because, of course, there would be.

I walked over to the antique desk and sat down in the chair behind it. The chair was a hefty item, handcrafted from thick wood, and finely upholstered in dark green leather. It had arms and a high back and was impossibly comfortable. There was nothing on top of the desk. No computer, no sta-tionary. Just a Newton's Cradle on the far edge, with all five balls hanging perfectly still.

In the top drawer of the desk, I found a selection of plas-tic cards. They were all about the same size as a standard credit card. One of them was completely black and engraved with a gold antelope-head insignia. There was nothing else of note in the desk.

I reached over to the Newton's Cradle, pulled a ball out to the side, and let it go. It smacked into the other four and then a single ball swung up on the opposite side and the pro-cess repeated. It was pleasing, soothing, and almost hypnotiz-ing. I stared at it for a while and felt myself sink deeper into the chair.

The male voice said, *Ten bucks says there's a wall safe behind that painting.*

I glanced away from the Cradle and across the room. The surrealist painting hung in the center of the wall, in the gap between two bookcases. I didn't know much about surrealism, but, according to the female voice, it was a copy of Salvador Dali's *Swans reflecting Elephants*. I liked it a lot. Below the painting was a shelf that contained a crystal decanter set. The six tumblers were sharp and gleaming, and the decanter was half full of an auburn liquid I assumed was only the finest whiskey.

I walked over and took a closer look. The painting had a very thick and ornate frame that was overlaid in gold leaf. I gripped it on each side and lifted it off the wall. It was much lighter than I expected, which made sense, since Hays would have had to be able move it. I leaned it gently against a bookcase. There was in fact a wall safe behind it.

Except it wasn't a wall safe. It was just a steel panel. Square, shiny, and solid. It had no keypad, no discernible lock, and therefore seemingly no way in. I searched my fingers over it, pushing, and prodding, and knocking, and banging. Nothing happened.

Ideas? I said.

Err… try the widget, the male voice said.

I knew that.

I took the small rectangular thing with the red glass out of my pocket and held it up against the steel panel and moved it across the surface slowly. I heard something click and then the panel flipped back automatically, like a garage door.

The safe turned out to be a half-meter cube. Inside it was a black and white photograph, a money clip holding a thousand dollars, and an A5 writing pad.

There was also a stack of brown folders.

TWELVE

I TOOK EVERYTHING BACK to the desk and sat down in the upholstered chair again. I took another pull of the imported beer and then I picked up the photograph.

It was a surveillance shot taken high up from across the street. It showed two people—a man and a woman—standing outside what looked like a hotel entrance. There were two big double doors behind them and a small rise of stairs before them. There was heavy rainfall and large puddles on the pavement. The man had his back to the camera. I couldn't make him out at all. Not even his age. But he seemed to be handing something to his female companion, who was facing the camera, and looked to be about sixty years old, with shoulder length light hair. In the bottom right corner of the photo there was a time stamp that read: *23–09–2015, 11:42:06*.

The day before the HBL bombing.

On the back of the photo the letters "CT" had been scribbled, followed by *confirmed*.

Initials? the female voice said.

Likely, I said.

I put the photograph down and started browsing through

the stack of brown folders. There were six of them. They were just like mine. Each folder began with a vital statistics page, followed by a full psychological profile. Naturally though, these psych profiles took up much less paper than mine, and where my folder had been padded out with my alleged activities, these were thick with background information. Birth certificates, medical histories, resumes, it was all there. These people had been scrutinized to the finest detail, and in most cases the folders were fully comprehensive.

The question was why?

Clearly they were persons of interest. Three were male, four had served. But there were no real links between them. And certainly no links to me. There was no one with the initials *CT* either.

I picked up the A5 writing pad. It only had about a third of its sheets left, but it was full of handwritten notes. Unfortunately that handwriting belonged to Hays, and thus I was looking at another collection of wire-wool portraits. I spent the next fifteen minutes trying to decipher it and only managed to make out a few words. And not even useful words either. I only recognized them because they referred to the HBL explosion and five other cases that Hays had been working on. At the bottom of the first page, Hays had scribbled something that he had then circled furiously. It was perhaps the most important thing of all I had no chance of reading it. Whatever insights the pad held would remain a secret.

The female voice said, *Not exactly the nugget we were hoping for, is it?*

Yeah, but when is it ever that easy? I said.

I sighed and threw the pad back on top of the desk and leaned back in the chair. I took a long pull on the imported beer and just stared at the pile of folders in front of me. The

Newton's Cradle was still going at the edge of the desk, one ball swinging out on one side, and then colliding back in to the other four, transferring its momentum, and causing another ball to swing out on the opposite side. Each collision made a tiny metallic tap, thus setting a metronomic beat.

I just couldn't understand it. What could possibly have been so important that Hays was not only willing to pause a live operation—in Iran, no less—but to actually endanger the lives of his operatives by leaving them out in the cold? I drained the last of my beer and tried to think it out, but was ultimately left frustrated.

I got up and examined the rest of the study. The bookcases were packed. Volumes of theology and philosophy were balanced with hard science and mathematics. One book in particular caught my attention. It was on a low shelf, almost hidden. The spine was well creased and the edges were tatty. It was entitled: *The Mind; Strangeness of Genius*. It was a scholarly text dealing with the interplay between various neurological abnormalities and genius. The premise was that one did not exist without the other. I flipped lightly through it. The introduction was filled with examples of historical figures, such as Leonardo Da Vinci and Nicola Tesla. Each chapter thereafter focused on one neurological condition at a time, and explored its effects on mental acuity, creativity, and information processing.

Near the end of the book was a small chapter that focused on voice-hearing. Hays had paraphrased it quite succinctly. The chapter immediately and explicitly sectioned off voice-hearing—as distinct from schizophrenia and other forms of psychosis—before giving a thorough breakdown of the condition. It talked about the necessity of engaging and not suppressing the voices, and how the earliest documented case was of a young boy who lived in an Italian monastery.

The boy was an orphan and the monks who had taken him in quickly came to realize he possessed a gift that they subsequently claimed was the ability to hear the voice of G-d. They cited examples of the boy's inherent ability to analyze and expound on ancient and complex scriptures just minutes after being presented with them. Eventually word spread and the scholars of the time came to test the boy. Their approach was simple. They asked the boy a variety of questions, both scientific and otherwise, that they believed no nine year old could be expected to understand, let alone answer. To their astonishment, the boy would audibly repeat the question to himself, and then he would go very quiet, as if concentrating very hard, and then, suddenly, he would begin to answer the question in a manner far beyond his own conceivable understanding, and, in most cases, the understanding of the scholars, themselves.

When the boy was asked how he arrived at his answers, he said he was merely repeating what the voice told him—which on some level seemed to be true. The scholars were quick to note that the boy clearly had no understanding of the answers he was giving. He even struggled to pronounce some of the words he was using to explain his ideas. But while the scholars of the time did not accept the "voice of G-d" conclusion, they did admit that the phenomenon was inexplicable. It wasn't until many years later, with the advent of modern psychology, that a theory could be put forward. And, although it was still to be proved, the current theory suggested that the voices were in fact a manifestation of the unconscious mind, thereby giving some voice-hearers the ability to tap into this largely mysterious, though potentially limitless, part of the mind.

I turned the book over and looked at the author's picture. The guy looked about how you'd expect: a hard Eastern

European face, wild hair reined in with a comb, and a coarse beard. My eyes lingered on the picture, and a moment later my mind reached back seven years and served up a memory. I was twenty-one, in Russia, in a bar, and about to get into a lot of trouble. Moments before, a man had come in from the cold and sat down on the stool next to me. He was wearing a long black coat and a big fluffy Cossack hat. It was so cold that his breath clouded when he spoke. He ordered vodka, naturally, and then turned to me and told me his name was Ruben Fields.

The same name that was under the photograph on the back of the book.

The male voice said, *Huh, so he actually did write it?*
Apparently.

I put the book back on the shelf and continued around the study. I pulled out a couple of other books that had catchy titles or seemed like they might be interesting and briefly read some excerpts. Eventually, I came back to the desk and the heap of papers on top. I thought about sitting down again, but the voices told me I hadn't worked anything out yet so I left it alone.

The grandfather clock showed 7:30. Two and half hours until Antelope opened. Since I couldn't do anything else until then, I reasoned it was as good a time as any for a quick nap. I took the liberty of using Hays's facilities and then drained another beer from the fridge and went upstairs.

The master bedroom was simple: bed, trouser press, more antique furniture. It was uncluttered, neat, and very calming. The mattress was hard—to toughen-up the vertebrae—and the pillow was shallow to ensure the spine stayed aligned. I lay down on the bed and set the alarm clock on the nightstand for nine.

* * *

Sleep is easy for me. It always has been. I can fall asleep almost instantaneously and on demand. And I always wake up in the same way, too—instantly, with no grogginess and no need to stretch or guzzle coffee or do any other morning ritual in order to get going. I'm just up and wide awake. I'm like a machine, off and on. But sleep is also something that for me is an altogether superfluous endeavor. I'm never *tired*. My body gets fatigued, yes, but never my mind. And so while I do need some sleep, two hours per day is my self-imposed limit. Any further dedication to the practice would be folly. I just don't seem to need it.

In any case, the alarm didn't wake me. I was already up and working out. Staying strong is absolutely vital in my line of work. I went through a simple bodyweight routine, not the push-ups and sit-ups crap the average weakling considers strenuous, but proper gymnastics stuff like planches, v-sits, and handstand presses.

Then I used Hays's shower and came back to the bedroom and opened the wardrobe and found fifteen hangers and fourteen suits: a two-week rotation with one spare. I was looking at easily $10,000 worth of exquisite material. Each suit was a fine piece of craftsmanship, but it was the dark blue that caught my eye. It was a three-piece affair, and I matched it with a white shirt, a bronze tie, and a bronze pocket square. Hays was a little taller than me, and the tailoring was quite precise, but it sat well considering. A little tight in the shoulders, maybe, but hardly noticeable. I had to try on four pairs of shoes before I found a snug fit. Hays wore size thirteen, whereas I was a comfortable twelve. The voices told me all about *barleycorns* as I put them on. Then I stood up, put the gold lapel pin in its place, and checked the final look in the mirror.

Looking sharp, the male voice said.

Yeah, very dapper, the female voice said.

I adjusted my tie. *Not bad, right?*

A getup like this was going to allow me to blend in seamlessly at the club.

I went downstairs and collected all of the brown folders and put them in the Jag's trunk, along with the photo and the notepad. I took a trash bag from a roll in the kitchen and put my old clothes and shoes inside and then threw it in the trunk too. I put the membership card and money clip in my jacket pocket, and then I closed the empty safe and replaced the painting on the wall.

THIRTEEN

I T WAS DARK outside and a few degrees colder. Which made it cold enough to force a gentleman to offer his jacket, but not *cold*. The moon was out and alone in a black sky. And underneath it the Jag was prowling over the roads and racing me back toward town. It handled exceptionally well. Until you're doing 100 mph or more a car like this is barely half awake.

Uptown Chicago on the other hand was wide awake. People were out, lights were on, and the night was young. I had no problem finding the club. Antelope was a big place. Almost half a city block, in fact. It was surrounded by a stone wall, and further hidden from view by a line of trees just inside its perimeter. The surrounding wall had only one way through, which was the main entrance. It consisted of a thick black gate sitting between two tall stone pillars. The gate was standing open and ahead of it was a strip of tire spikes and a security hut. I drove around the place a couple of times to check things out and then parked the Jag on the opposite side of the street to the gate and waited.

A few minutes later, I saw a new-model Ferrari pull into the club. A security guard came out of the hut and greeted it at the gate. He was holding a clipboard and what looked like a barcode scanner. The Ferrari's driver-side window came down and an arm poked through holding a small black card. The security guard scanned it and then scribbled something on his clipboard and then went back to the hut and lowered the tire spikes before ushering the driver ahead. I watched the same procedure unfold again when another supercar pulled in just moments later. It all seemed simple enough, so I waited a few more minutes and then drove over.

I pulled the Jag in slowly, being careful about its long nose and the strip of tire spikes. I followed procedure. The guard came out of his hut, I rolled down my window and poked my arm through with the card I'd found in Hays's desk. But the security guard didn't take it. Instead his eyes narrowed, and looked past the card in order to get a better look at me. He stared at me and I stared back. He had a black eye and a bad expression. His eyes began shifting around the inside of the Jag.

Then he glanced at the trunk.

I didn't see any good coming from that. And driving around with a body in the trunk would ruin the way the Jag handled. So I cleared my throat and waved the card up and down in as arrogant a way as I could. It worked. His eyes snapped back to me and he took the card and scanned it and muttered an evening greeting. I replied in kind. His scanner beeped a couple of times and then he gave me back the card and asked for my name. I said, "Hays."

The guy considered my answer for a second. He was definitely skeptical, but eventually he turned to his clipboard and scribbled something down. He did, however, make a point of saying that he'd never seen me before, to which I responded by facing forward and raising my driver's window. He gave the Jag a once-over again and then begrudgingly stepped back to the security hut and hit a button inside the door and waved me through.

I rolled over the retracted tire spikes and down a short driveway and came upon the club. It looked like an embassy building or something. Which I suppose, in some ways, it was. The Republic of Rich Bastards.

I pulled up at the front steps and a valet ran over to open my door. It was a Hispanic guy in a red blazer and we quickly switched places. I greased his palm with a medium bill in the process, which seemed to utterly flabbergast him. He looked at the bill and then stared up at me from the driver's seat. His face was all confused. I figured I must have either tipped way too much, or not nearly enough. Either way he quickly closed the door and drove the car away. I watched him go and then took a deep breath of the cool night-time air and stared up at the building's magnificent gothic architecture and noted the copious amount of security cameras.

This might be trickier than we thought, the female voice said.

I glanced back at the security hut by the gate.

Yup.

The reception hall was tall and grand. Red carpets on polished floors and rich mahogany stained darker than dark. A magnificent split staircase grew up the far wall and a giant crystal chandelier glowed proudly above, picking out golden highlights all around. There was a concierge desk on the right with a young guy stood behind it. He was trying his best to conceal his stare, looking hard at his computer screen but not directly at it. I clocked his name tag as I walked over. Like Isabel and SAD, blending into these sorts of places is all about confidence. Act like you belong and you do.

"Anything I should know tonight, James?" I asked.

It caught him off guard. A first name usually does. His shoulders tightened and his arms pinned themselves to his sides. He cleared his throat to buy some time and then clicked around on the computer. He said, "Um… Senator Kane is sponsoring tonight, sir. There's one seat available in the eleven-thirty, the one o'clock is full, and the two-fifteen is now double."

He looked up at me, hopeful he'd done some kind of satisfactory job.

I said nothing and just adopted an all-knowing and unimpressed stare.

His eyes went back to the computer. "Also…" he said, but now speaking in a whisper. "The *cleaners* are passing through tonight. Oh and Ms. Celina is taking orders, as well."

"Good to know," I said, and then walked away without saying anything else.

As I made my way deeper into the opulence, I started to get a feel for the place. First thing I noticed: no security cameras inside.

I turned left at the stairs and stepped into a large lounge, with low lights, and high back chairs, and small tables, and fireplaces, and newspapers, and a haze of cigar smoke. It reminded me of Hays's study. Exactly what I imagined the place would look like. It was a proper gentlemen's club. Which, in some ways, was sad, because clubs like this were on the way out. Gone were the days of old men, smoking jackets, and low conversations in wood-paneled rooms. According to a recent magazine article I'd read, now it was all about rooftop parties and fancy-colored drinks. This must have been true, because the lounge was totally deserted. In fact, the only signs of life on the ground floor were coming from the dining room on the other side of the staircase.

Upstairs was where the main action was. It was also where the secrets were. Every so often, I came upon a couple of guys standing outside a closed door. They were a generic bunch on the whole, but with enough differences between them to imply they were personal bodyguards rather than in-house security. But the goings on in those closed rooms weren't all that hard to imagine. All you had to do was look at what the open doors offered. I saw gambling, drinking, smoking, sniffing, a Madame called Celina—there was no attempt to hide it. But then, that was the point of the club. It handled the happenings within, and the *cleaners*, as they called them, handled everything without.

I came back downstairs and walked into the dining room. It was a formal setting with sturdy wooden chairs, black-and-gold tablecloths, and polished silverware. The majority of tables were two-seaters and there were five men sitting down in total. Two together and three singletons. They were all between thirty-five and fifty, and they were all wearing suits of equal value to my own. The three singletons were eating quietly and didn't give me much more than a passing glance. The duo had empty dishes between them and were talking in hushed tones, but they took the time to stop what they were doing and shoot me a look that echoed the guard's sentiments: *Never seen you before.* It made me tense up slightly but

I kept cool and responded with a look of my own: *Never seen you before either… assholes.*

The male voice said, *That'll be where Hays sat.*

I looked away from the duo and across the room where I saw a surrealist painting hanging on the far wall, toward the far right corner. The female voice told me it was a reproduction of Dali's *Apparition of Face and Fruit Dish on a Beach*, which I thought was a good name, since the painting was exactly that.

If you like that, the female voice said, *then Lobster Telephone is going to be right up your alley.*

I went and sat at the table in front of the painting. In the corner ahead of me was a set of double doors. They had double hinges and porthole windows, and led to the kitchen. Above them was a wall clock that showed 10:36 pm. And coming through them was the person who would tell me who Hays's source was.

FOURTEEN

M AIDS, PROSTITUTES, WAITERS. If they ever got together, we'd be looking at the most-well informed intelligence agency in the world. There isn't one person in the history of those professions who hasn't seen, heard, or stolen something they shouldn't. And they don't even have to try. We make it so easy. Anybody in their right mind would demand a warrant before giving law enforcement the same kind of access we freely grant to *the help*: our homes, our cars, our food, our innermost desires and fetishes.

Our private clubs.

We let them in and we pay them for their trouble. So while these rich bastards had gone to such lengths to hide their extracurriculars—building Antelope, vetting the membership, and using "cleaners"—it was all for nothing. Because, from day one, they had brought in outsiders. They had invited exposure, and I was going to capitalize on that.

It was 10:36 pm, which meant I was dining at the same time, at the same place, and on one of the same nights that Hays always had. And that meant the waiting staff—who worked in shifts—were going to be an excellent source of information—especially whichever one of them had been working on Friday.

I watched the waiter come out of the kitchen and putter around one of the singleton tables. I saw him clock me the moment he came through the double doors but he didn't react. He just cleared the singleton's table and then headed back through the double doors.

My stomach started growling.

In the center of my table was a menu. It was a single card, a little bigger than A5, black, and embossed with a gold antelope-head insignia at the top. It was standing upright in a little wooden holder. I pulled it out and perused the options. The damn thing should've have come with a health warning: *Do not read if you have a pre-existing heart condition,* because $178.75 was only just enough to get one person reasonably full. Two people would leave hungry. And while these guys clearly had no care for money, the third item really was taking the piss. A so-called *Gourmet Salad*. Ingredients included delicacies such as fresh lobster, caviar, truffles, and aged balsamic. The price? Seventy-six dollars.

Eye-watering.

And all the more reason Hays needed a cover life at the bank. Between his antique-laden house, the prestigious Jag, the Savile Row suits, and the presumably outrageous membership fee to Antelope, Hays would've had a lot to explain. Now I wasn't sure exactly what an SAD pay check amounted to, but it definitely didn't say SAD on it. So Hays needed a plausible source of income, and Mizuho Bank certainly fit the bill. Having said that, it was my firm belief that a $76 salad should always be severed with an extensive audit on the side. But having said *that*, the taxman was probably a member here too.

I put the menu back in the holder and, a short while later, the double doors swung open again, and the waiter came back out of the kitchen. Again he noticed me but didn't come over. He went back to the singleton and muttered a few words. The singleton shook his head. He was only half listening, grinning at something on his phone. The waiter slipped a hand into his pocket and came out with a membership card. The singleton took the card and then slid his chair back and stood up. Forty-five, gray hair, richly relaxed, and in all probability another asshole. He put the card into his inside jacket pocket, glanced at the other four patrons, quickly and in turn, then glanced over at me, for a little longer, and then walked straight out of the room. The waiter then reset that table, still ignoring me.

The male voice said, *Try putting Hays' card on the table.*

Hhn?

I think that's the signal.

I took out Hays's card and placed it on the table.

Four seconds later the waiter was standing next to me.

"Good evening, sir. How are you?" He had black hair slicked back, a nice dark suit, and a shiny bow tie. He stood ramrod straight, as if at extreme attention. I looked up at him. His accent was French, his nameplate said *Nicolas*. He asked, "Are you ready to order?"

"I'll have the rib eye," I said. "Medium rare. Sides as they come."

"Excellent, sir. And to drink?"

"Anything you'd recommend, Nicolas?"

"The house red is particularly good this month."

I thought about Hays' imported beer. "How about dark ales?" I said. "Or maybe something exotic?"

He puckered his lips and glanced sideways and then leaned a little closer, like a secret.

"Nothing I wouldn't hesitate to recommend," he said.

Nursing? the male voice said.

The female voice started laughing and I fought a smile as best I could.

"I'll defer to your expertise," I said to Nicolas.

"Certainly, sir. Thank you, sir." He picked up Hays's card, slid it into his pocket, and then he took my menu and the small wooden holder and swiftly collected an empty plate from another singleton before ducking into the kitchen again.

The female voice said, *You know what, I think he's actually Belgian.*

Belgian? What makes you say that? the male voice said.

His vowels are off.

And you think if we charm him enough, he'll talk?

Actually, I was thinking it might stop him spitting on our food. But yeah, that too.

So thirty seconds later, when Nicolas came back and presented the wine, I laid it on thick. And in French.

"Nicolas, vous êtes Belge?"

"Très bien, monsieur. Comment saviez-vous?"

"Mes grands-parents sont aussi."

"Ah bon?"

"Oui, bien sûr."

And so on and so on.

And, before long, I had his entire life story. He told me he had moved to America seven years ago. He'd been headhunted for his expertise in fine wines—first by a prestigious restaurant on the West Coast, and then by Antelope, who paid him double for only half the work. He now waited three nights on, one night off. Which, in other words, meant he had to have been working on Friday night. Which was perfect.

Nicolas continued to regale me for about ten minutes,

but then had to get back to work. Another one of the singletons was ready to leave, and I watched the same process unfolded as before. Waiter and diner muttered a few words, then Nicolas gave him back his membership card, then the guy stood up and glanced at each of the other diners in turn, and then glanced at me for a little longer, and then walked out. I watched him all the way and then reclined in my seat and shifted my thoughts to something James had said. To an Antelope member that was particularly noteworthy. Especially after what I'd found on the SAD system.

So Senator Kane is a member here, I said.

He's a member here. And "hosting," the male voice said. *Whatever that means. Guy's not even here.*

Well, Atlanta is a little out of the way. Maybe he's coming later.

Or maybe he is here and we just didn't see him, the female voice said.

You think he's behind one of those closed doors? the male voice said.

Could be. And maybe he's doing what he was in that photo.

*Well, there goes my appeti*te, I said.

Yeah, but think of the possibilities.

He's a senator. I get it.

And a billionaire.

A billionaire with a temper, the male voice said.

You guys have got this all figured out, don't you?

Oh, we're definitely going to have some fun with that one, the female voice said.

Nicolas returned with my steak and then went to see off the

last singleton. Same process, again. Muttered words, membership card, glances, departure. Which left me and the whispering duo alone in the dining room. And when Nicolas headed back into the kitchen, the duo glanced over at me again. I was getting pretty tired of it. But they were on the opposite side of the room, in the diagonally opposite corner, which meant I would have to raise my voice to say something, which I didn't feel like doing. So instead I looked them dead in the eye and held my gaze while I picked up my steak knife *just so*. I held in the air long enough to suggest all I needed to and then sunk it straight into my steak.

The duo turned away.

The rib eye was good. Not $112 good, but good. And I wasn't exactly about to complain, since it was Hays's treat. The male voice, on the other hand, had plenty to say. A whole routine, in fact, about fine dining and how the whole experience starts out with such promise only to end up with a confused diner, a big white empty plate with a tiny smudge in the middle, and a waiter with an expression that says, "Would Sir like a microscope?"

Once that rant was over, the three of us began discussing the Iran situation. The SAD team had received my information just over four hours ago, and, if they were moving on it there was a fifty-fifty chance they were now out of the hot spot—which, although didn't mean they were home free, did give them a fighting chance.

I finished the steak and polished off the sides and then ordered ice cream for dessert. I spent the rest of the meal thinking about Isabel. I couldn't wait to see her again.

I finished the ice cream, dropped the spoon onto the dish, and sat back from the table, almost satisfied. Nicolas was standing by a maître d' stand, bolt upright, and looking nowhere in particular. The wall clock showed 11:22, which is when the whispering duo stopped whispering. One of them raised a hand and snapped his fingers at an already well-aware Nicolas, who was walking over to see them off.

But this time, the standard routine changed.

The usual brief muttering went on for considerably longer, and about halfway through it, Nicolas glanced back over his shoulder at me. His eyes were like slits, full of suspicion. Then he turned back to the duo and the muttering continued. Except now, Nicolas was doing most of the talking. The duo was just listening and nodding.

The male voice said, *I wonder what they're talking about.*

I said, *Yeah, but what could he possibly say? He gave us his life story, not the other way around.*

I sat quietly, brought my wine glass to my lips, and watched the three of them as I drained it. Eventually, the muttering stopped and the duo stood up. Nicolas produced two membership cards and then one of the guys circled his index finger around, like he was saying *between us*, and then he nodded at Nicolas, who glanced at me again, and then nodded back. After that the duo turned toward the door, but not before giving me their dirtiest look, yet. I smiled and raised my empty wine glass at them and nodded a toast: *Assholes.* One of the guys stepped toward me and was about to say something, but the other guy stopped him and hustled him out of the room. Nicolas stood still for a moment and then cleared their table and reset it. He went in and out of the double doors and a minute later came over to check on me.

"Was everything satisfactory?" he asked.

"My compliments to the chef."

"Thank you, sir."

I nodded to where the duo had been sitting. "Everything OK over there?"

"Of course, sir," he said. And then he said, "Will Monsieur Hays be gracing us tonight?"

"He didn't make it out of the office."

"Ah, oui. A lawyer is always busy, *n'est-ce pas?*"

"You mean banker," I said.

His hand shot up to his mouth. "That's right, sir. *Banker.* My apologies. It's easy to forget those details."

My eyes narrowed.

Was that a test? the female voice said.

I scanned the empty dining room. What had those guys said to him? And what might happen if I wait to find out? Surely nothing I couldn't handle, but equally nothing I particularly had any interest in engaging in either. The dining room was suspiciously empty though. I looked at Nicolas and circled my index finger around and said, "It always this busy?"

"Things tend to pick up around midnight," he said.

"Midnight?"

"Generally, our members like to work up an appetite, first."

Closed doors.

An appetite.

Maybe Kane was here.

"And you serve them all?" I asked. "By yourself?"

"We provide canapés to all our players. My underlings are currently serving."

I nodded. I had seen all that. Maybe I was just getting paranoid about all this. In any case I decided it was best to move things along. Get what I came for and get out.

"So what did you think of our new recruit?" I said.

"Sir?"

"Friday," I said. "Mr. Hays brought her here for dinner. You met her."

"Did I, sir?" he said knowingly.

I nodded. Assuming salad equals female had been a risk, but I was pretty sure I'd just hit a bullseye.

Nicolas said, "I'm afraid I couldn't possibly remember, sir."

So much for charm, the female voice said. But it wasn't all that surprising, really. This guy may have been recruited for his wine knowledge, but he was also a sly one. Equipped with just the right amount of cautiousness for his station.

I said to Nicolas, "I only ask because Mr. Hays has been pretty secretive about the whole thing. Which normally wouldn't bother me one bit. But see—and this is just between you and me—there's been a lot of restructuring going on recently. 'Tempestuous times,' to quote Mr. Hays."

Nicolas said nothing.

"Now the way I see it—and again, I'm quoting Mr. Hays, here—'Tempestuous times call for perspicacious measures.'"

Nicolas said nothing.

"So, while I'm sure this new recruit is going to do wonders for us, I'd really like to be perfectly certain. For all our sakes."

Nicolas said nothing.

"You didn't happen to catch her name, did you?"

"As I said, sir, I couldn't possibly remember."

I smiled and looked down at the table and thought about jamming my ice-cream spoon into his eye. I figured it would jog his memory, and the female voice seemed to agree, but the male voice said, *Might I suggest a more practical approach?*

I looked back up at Nicolas.

"You know, Nicolas, my aunt was a waitress," I said.

"Really, sir?"

I nodded. "Almost fifty years," I said. "Some out of the way place up in New York. Nothing as refined as this establishment, though. Bad food, worse customers. Real pains in the ass. You know the kind, I'm sure."

He couldn't help his eyes shift over to where the duo had been sitting. He snapped them back quickly though.

"Now anybody else would have quit," I continued. "Gotten fed up and left. But not my aunt. She thrived. Made more in tips than the average working woman's salary. And you know what her secret was?"

He raised an eyebrow.

"Flat shoes, impeccable manners, and total discretion," I said. "Especially that last one."

He squeezed his eyes approvingly. "Privacy is very valuable, sir."

Told you, the male voice said.

I reached into my jacket and took out Hays's money clip. I released a couple of Benjamins and noted the subsequent bulging effect on Nicolas's eyes. I then continued to release bills, such that for every one I released, Nicolas's eyes bulged a fraction wider. By the time I stopped, there was over a thousand dollars on the table, and Nicolas looked like that Howling Wolf cartoon. His memory did seem to improve, though.

I tapped on Ben Franklin's face and furrowed my brow. "I'm trying to remember, Nicolas. Benjamin Franklin… bifocals, never president, and married that girl… what's her name?"

Nicolas leaned down a touch, his eyes glued to the green. "Sophia, I believe."

And just like that, I had everything I needed.

"That's right," I said. "Yes, it *is* easy to forget those details."

Nicolas conveyed his understanding with a long blink, and then he took out Hays's card and I put it back into my jacket along with the money clip. I stood up and started at the exit and then stopped and turned around.

"Oh, and by the way, Nicolas," I said, looking back at the table and seeing no trace of Benjamin Franklin anywhere. "The gentleman who ordered the steak tonight…"

Nicolas glanced at the ceiling, scoffing. 'I couldn't possibly remember, sir."

"*Merci*, Nicolas."

"*Il n'y a pas de quoi,* Monsieur."

I walked back to the entrance hall. By now, the upstairs rooms had gotten loud—clearly much busier now. There was loud cheering and choice words. I glanced at the reception desk on my way out and saw James trying to hide his stare again. He had a long way to go. I stepped outside and saw nothing but a Hispanic blur, as the valet sprinted off to get the Jag.

Guess that clears that up, the male voice said.

We're not tipping him again, Isaac, the female voice said.

I smiled and waited by the entrance steps. I took another deep breath of cool nighttime air, looked up at the black sky, and refocused.

Sophia was Sophia Brooks.

And Sophia Brooks was a brown folder.

FIFTEEN

SOPHIA BROOKS'S CURRENT whereabouts had not been in her file. That was Problem One. I drove a few blocks away from Antelope and parked the Jag on a curb, under a streetlight. I got out, retrieved the A5 notepad from the trunk, and started going through it again. If Hays had physically met with Sophia then there was a good chance she was still in Chicago. And since Hays had the entire city under surveillance there was a good chance he had known exactly where she was—and an equally good chance he would have written that down.

Possibly even circled it furiously.

I held the pad right up to my face and tried to decipher the mess inside the circle at the bottom of the first page. I had found Hays's handwriting funny at first, even charming. Now it was just pissing me off. I stood there under the streetlight trying to pick out single letters by comparing each squiggle with squiggles from the few words I had previously managed to decipher elsewhere in the pad. And after ten minutes I was pretty sure the first letter was an S.

Or an F.

Or a W.

At which point I threw the pad at the base of the lamp-post and started venting. *How the hell does someone like Hays produce this crap?* I said. *I've seen clearer forms of communication etched into caves. I mean, you can't even call it writing. It's an atrocity. A crime against the written word.*

I went on like this for a little while until a married couple walked by and gave me some very odd looks. I realized that I must have spoken some of that out loud.

Then the male voice said, *Hold on, I've got a brilliant idea.*

I doubt it, the female voice said.

I said, *What is it?*

The male voice said, *What's the one group of people who are notorious for having the worst handwriting?*

Doctors.

Bingo.

Bingo what? the female voice said.

Well, if doctors have the worst handwriting who then by default must have the best deciphering skills?

The female voice and I said nothing.

The male voice said, *Really? Silence? Come on guys, we watched that episode of Curb together.*

At which point I started smiling.

I got back in the car and drove around uptown until I found a twenty-four-hour pharmacy. Naturally, being America, I was going to hit either a Walgreens or a CVS pretty quickly. It turned out to be a CVS. It was a pretty big one, too, though understandably empty at that time of night.

There was a tall guy behind the prescription counter. He was wearing a white lab coat and looked altogether bored out of his mind. I walked up and asked him if he could do me a solid, explaining how my fiancée had the worst handwriting and that tomorrow I had to be at this address in order to meet the mother-in-law. He then offered me some Prozac and we both shared a laugh. He was of course more than happy to oblige and took one look at the pad and instantly recited the address. It was an impressive feat. So I tried to capitalize. I asked the guy to read on and see if any special instructions had been left for me. Pick up a bottle of wine or something. Again the guy obliged but admitted that his previous triumph had been somewhat of a fluke. He said it really was some of the worst handwriting he'd ever seen, and that the only reason he got the address so easily was because he used to live near the area and recognized the street name. He didn't think he could decipher the rest, but I asked him to give it his best shot anyway, which he did. He started going through the pad and quickly seemed to pick up on the HBL references which made him pretty suspicious for a moment until I explained that my wife-to-be was a journalist and assured him that nothing he was reading was sensitive. The guy carried on, but after a couple of minutes and a whole lot of squinting, he gave up. He said the chicken scratch had beaten him and that apart from continuous reference to a test of some sort he couldn't make out a thing. He wished me luck and wrote down the address for me, and I bought a bottle of water and thanked him and left.

The male voice said, *A test?*

We'll ask Sophia, I said.

The female voice said, *I can't believe that worked.*

The male voice said, *Larry David: Genius.*

*

The address led me to a very run down area on the South Side. A bad neighborhood.. Windows were boarded up, corners were being run. Sophia Brooks was holed up on the the fourth floor of an old apartment building. I drove past and parked a hundred yards down the street—this time not under a streetlight.

I got out and retrieved Sophia's folder from the trunk and then got back in the driver seat. I took off my jacket and tie, and then switched on the dome light and read through her file, again.

Sophia Brooks was twenty-nine years old, highly intelligent, and extremely well trained. She was the same breed as the guys in Iran. Formerly special ops, now ex-SAD, and living off the grid. And, seeing as how she started all this, presumably on high alert, too. In other words, not your average target. Which was problem two.

I looked out of the car and surveyed the scene.

The male voice said, *Old buildings.*

The female voice said, *Old security.*

I scanned all of the surrounding windows. They were all dark.

Whatever we do needs to be quiet, I said.

Fire escape?

Uh-uh. She'll have that covered.

Too loud, anyway, the female voice said.

Well, we can't just knock on her door, the male voice said.

Funny, that's exactly what I think we should do.

You're kidding, right? At this time of night? In this neighborhood? Heck, I'd be unloading a shotgun before I answered the damn door.

We better hope she doesn't have a shotgun, then.

But she will have a gun. That much is guaranteed. And

firing will be her first instinct, too. I mean, she ain't gonna be looking through no peephole now, is she?

So we'll have to draw her out, I said.

I got out of the car and filled both of Hays's driving gloves with soil from a patch of foliage outside one of the buildings. I put the gloves in my pants' pocket and then walked over to the apartment building. The front door was in the bottom left corner of the building as you looked at it. It was old and battered and its lock was easy to pick. I used one of the bobby pins I had taken from the lady at the SAD facility and had the door open in under a minute.

The building had no lobby to speak of, just a misplaced table and a row of post-office boxes against a wall. "Drab" would be an understatement. There was a two-tone color scheme: beige and off-beige. The walls were split horizontally by it. The apartment doors were unevenly spaced and a murky brown color. Numbers were painted on and peeling off. The hallways were long and poorly lit. One hallway continued straight ahead and ended with a stairwell. The other hallway extended right and ended with an elevator. Wet-dog smell and human urine viciously assaulted my nostrils.

The stairwell was bare and seemed to be the origin of the building's smell. The potency was much stronger there. I climbed the four flights rapidly and came out onto another depressing hallway. There was a cracked street-side window at the far end. The only ceiling light was flickering lazily. I walked slowly toward the window and then the hallway made a left turn. Rooms *49*, *51*, and *53* were on the right-hand side. Light shone out from under the middle door.

Sophia Brooks was awake.

I took two steps forward and the floor creaked loudly under my weight. I froze. My eyes shot to the bottom of Sophia's door. I stared at the strip of light and held my breath. No shadow passed by. I quickly scanned the other doors too. No lights came on. I took a breath. Adjusted my position. I put my back against the wall. Floorboards are sturdier at the edges. I took out Hays's driving gloves and began sidestepping down the hallway, throwing soil on to the floor as I went. I passed over room *49* and edged up to *51*, where I dumped the remainder of the soil. Both gloves were now empty and the hallway was covered in soil. I paused and listened through the wall. I could hear Sophia in there.

I stayed still for a full minute and then came away from the wall and knocked hard on *51* four times. Then I walked straight down the center of the hallway, making tracks through the soil and lots of loud creaks. I turned the corner and then flopped to the ground, left leg outstretched, right leg crossed underneath, arms splayed, and torso slumped against the wall. I made sure my left shoulder peaked out around the corner just enough.

Then I waited.

I heard a door open a few seconds later. The hallway fell silent. I imagined Sophia. Her gun would be drawn, a double-hand grasp, with arms straight and feet planted. She'd have jumped back a few feet into her room, staying well away from the doorway, and aiming her gun straight through it. Nothing happened for a moment, and then I heard a faint shuffling sound. Sophia would now be positioned to the side of her doorway, looking straight down one side of hallway, and checking things out. I heard another faint shuffle shortly after, meaning she had now semi circled around her doorway and was checking the other side of the hallway.

I heard her step out.

I imagined her seeing the tracks in the mud, every instinct telling her not to follow it, but, in the same way a ringing phone must be answered, a curious trail must be followed.

I waited.

Thirty seconds later, the hallway creaked.

She took two more quick steps and suddenly she was standing right next to me. I imagined her looking down at me, her gun still drawn, her eyes still darting around the scene. I could hear her breathing. She was calm. Well trained. I didn't move.

Then she kicked me.

She kicked me straight in my outstretched leg. Not quite a soccer kick but with enough force to see what was what. I gave no reaction. So she kicked me again. Harder this time. I made a mental note of that, but still gave no reaction. Thankfully, she didn't kick me again. She just stood there for the next minute, perfectly still, and in total silence. I heard her clothes rustle as she twisted and checked the street-side window and then, finally, I heard her holster her weapon and take a long breath and crouch down in front of me for the inevitable pulse check.

Gotcha, the male voice said.

I felt two fingers touch the left side of my neck and I exploded. I had her in a carotid choke so fast she didn't even have time to gasp—let alone escape. She had undoubtedly been taught ground techniques, but she was rusty and I was not. She stopped struggling very quickly. Her body went limp and I released my grip. Her neck smelled like coconut. I carried her back to *51*.

* * *

The room was a dull mucus-green. The carpet was dark and thin and worn and crusty. A cloudy light bulb hung from the ceiling by a dirty white electrical cord. The bed had a ripped duvet and took up most of the space. The bathroom door hit the toilet and could only be opened halfway. The sink and shower looked like hell.

I put Sophia in the only chair there was and then patted her down. She had nothing in her pockets, but I found a small, serrated hunting knife tucked into the waistband of her jeans.

I had felt it before when she had fallen into my lap. It was exactly the kind of thing special forces use and it looked brutal: a six-inch fixed blade, solid steel, and sharp. It was perfectly counterbalanced by the handle, and coated with a matte black finish. It was a custom design, fit for a number of things, including gutting fish and dressing deer. Or people. I used the knife to tear some strips from the bedding. A bit of water from the sink strengthened the would-be restraints. I tied her hands together behind her and each foot to a chair leg. Then I turned the chair so that the back was facing the wall mirror and I could keep an eye on every part of her. Once I'd done all that, I stood back and looked her over.

This is her? the female voice said.

I know, right? I said.

What I was seeing was far from what I expected. Sophia had moved like a Marine in the hallway—stealthy, controlled, and fully Aware. But everything about her appearance pointed to the contrary. She looked more like a junkie. She looked messy and exhausted. Insomnia was streaked across her eyes, and her blonde hair was straggly and untamed. Her fingernails were chewed and dirty. But her clothes were new. Her jeans were still rigid and dark blue and totally unfaded from never having seen a washing machine. Her bulky blue sweater was likewise unstressed. It was still soft, and hung loose over her wiry figure.

Something was very wrong with this picture.

I started searching around the rest of the room. Possessionwise, there was less than I had hoped for. There was a burner phone with no call history, a couple of half-full take-out containers, and a newspaper with a half done crossword. That was it.

Opposite the door was a dirty brown rag which served as a curtain. I nudged it back, peeked out of the filthy window, and checked the street. Everything was quiet. There was nobody out there and the Jag hadn't been defaced or stolen. Yet. The window led out onto the fire escape, but only if you could open it, which I doubted could be done without a brick. I nudged the curtain back into place and then went and sat at the foot of the bed. On the wall in front of me a group of concentric circles had been drawn in black marker. It looked like an archery board. And it was full of gashes.

I looked at Sophia.

Well? I said.

Well we know one thing for sure, the male voice said. *Right?*

Right, the female voice said.

Definitely, I said. *The HBL explosion was no accident.*

SIXTEEN

NORMALLY, WHEN A person regains consciousness and finds themselves tied to a chair, they either struggle vigorously against the restraints, they start shouting, or both. Sophia Brooks did nothing. She didn't even open her eyes. She was not a normal person. She was expertly utilizing her combat training. She knew that any information she managed to gather now could be invaluable later. It was all about picking up resources and trying to reclaim some advantage. Then, when the time was right, she'd make her move.

The only problem was, she wasn't fooling me. I was sitting on the end of the bed, playing a game on the burner phone. I wasn't watching Sophia, but I had been listening to her very carefully. A slight change in her breathing pattern had signaled the shift in consciousness. I maxed the phone's volume and it beeped and buzzed as I completed a couple of levels while Sophia sat there pretending to be asleep. I let this go on for a while and then I put the phone down and said, "So, this is where seventy-six dollar salads leaves you?"

Sophia didn't bother wasting time. She took her cue and gave up the act. Her torso straightened and her head rolled up into position and her eyes opened and darted to me. I saw frustration and anger in them. There was something else in them too. And it definitely wasn't fear.

"Hi."

"Where's Hays?" she said.

"He's dead."

And with that the something disappeared from her eyes.

"How?" she asked.

"His heart stopped beating."

Sophia smirked. "I suppose that means you're here to kill me then?"

The male voice said, *It does?*

I said nothing and just shrugged at Sophia.

She smiled and shook her head. "No," she said. "You're not."

I raised an eyebrow.

Sophia's eyes swept the room with a single glance and then come straight back to me.

"It's obvious," she said. "Just look at the situation. You took me out with ease. Impressive, yes, but the point is, I'm sat here talking about it. You didn't finish the job. So you're not one of them."

The male voice said, *One of them?*

The female voice said, *How should I know?*

I said nothing and let Sophia keep talking.

"You knew where to find me," she said. "Only one other person knew that and you're saying he's dead. And I believe you. But it wasn't you who killed him, was it? You wouldn't have needed to look through my stuff otherwise. Because that implies you're looking for something. And if you're looking for answers then you don't know what's going on. And that means you didn't work for Hays. And if you didn't kill him, you're not here to kill me. So the only question left is: Who the hell are you?"

The male voice began, *Not much is known about the origins of Isaac Blaze. He is a man shrou–*

"Homeland? FBI? What?" Sophia said.

The female voice said, *Now she thinks we're government?*

"Might as well tell me," Sophia said. "I'll be dead soon, anyway."

I said nothing.

She said, "You won't get anything out of me. You know that, right?"

"No, you'll talk."

"Will I?"

"I can be very persuasive."

A nervous smile crept onto her face.

"Everyone breaks," she said. "Right?"

A silence ensued.

I said, "I'm not going to hurt you."

"No you're just going to tie me up."

"Well you did kick me. Twice."

Sophia said, "Let's just get this over with, shall we?"

"I'm not going to hurt you," I said again.

"Then why would I tell you anything?"

"I thought you were going to be dead soon?"

"I will."

"So what do you care if I know what you know?"

She said nothing.

"You've got nothing to lose," I said. "And who knows, maybe I can help you."

Sophia gave me a once-over and snorted. "Help me?" she said. "You don't know the first thing about me."

I glanced at the newspaper crossword.

"As a mule," I said. "Eight letters."

She gave me a look and came back with, "Phallic appendage attached to the cranium. Also eight letters."

I pondered at the ceiling. "Hard one."

She couldn't help smiling, but then I picked up the knife from the bed and she went very quiet. I looked down at the knife and held its tip between my thumb and forefinger. I bobbed my hand up and down, feeling the blade's weight, and then I flicked my wrist and tossed it into the air. It flipped a full three-sixty and I caught it by the tip again.

Sophia said, "Nice trick."

"I've got some skills."

"You got a name, too?"

"I do, actually."

Sophia kept her eyes on the knife.

"This what you used in Taipei?" I asked.

"You've read my file?"

I flipped the knife again and immediately upon catching it threw it straight at the wall in front of me. It hit dead center of the concentric circles, right in the bullseye. Sophia glanced at the wall and then her eyes slid back to me.

I said, "Sophia Brooks, twenty-nine, Aquarius. There was some other stuff, too."

"Who are you?"

"Someone who knows you bombed the HBL lab."

Sophia said nothing. Confusion kept mounting on her face and I could see her running countless calculations in her head.

"Nothing to lose," I said.

"You can't help me."

"Unless of course I can."

"But why would you?"

"Why wouldn't I?"

"You won't believe me."

"And if I do?"

"It probably gets you killed."

"Guess we'll see."

"Yes we will."

I smiled. "So you are going to talk."

SEVENTEEN

SOPHIA BROOKS WAS not going to make this easy. Stubborn, yes, but then I had knocked her out.

She was looking at me hard, still running calculations. Still very dangerous. I could see her hands in the mirror behind her. They were completely still.

I said, "Tell me about Hays."

"What about him?" she said.

"You were working for him?"

She rolled her eyes like it was the stupidest question in the world and then said a very flat, "No."

"But you used to," I said.

"Yeah. *Used* to. Past tense."

"When did you meet?"

"Friday."

"Where?"

"Some private club. Real sophisticated."

"Antelope."

She nodded.

I said, "Why'd you bomb HBL?"

Sophia said, "I…" and then trailed off and looked away from me. She started shaking her head. Gave a weak shrug.

"You're saying you don't know?"

Sophia said nothing.

"So you just woke up one day and decided to build a bomb and kill a bunch of people?"

"I didn't *decide* to do anything," she said.

"Then explain yourself. Why?"

"I don't know why."

"How can you not know why?"

"Because I don't remember doing it."

"Then how do you know you did?"

"Because Hays told me I did."

Silence.

The male voice said,… *What?*

Don't look at me, the female voice said.

Sophia saw my bewilderment. She snorted and shook her head again. Then her eyes watered up and shined over, and she shifted her gaze down to the depressing carpet, and stared at a stain a few feet in front of her. She said, "You ever had reason to wonder if you're crazy?"

I said nothing.

The voices started chirping like crickets in my head.

"TV," Sophia said. "I was watching it on TV. A news report. They were talking about the casualties and there was a red bulletin message streaming across the bottom of the screen that said: *Disaster at Research Facility*. I remember watching it so intently and then I remember looking away from the TV and realizing I was standing on a sidewalk outside an electronics store with no idea where I was or how I'd got there, and then—" she stopped and looked at me, "You know that button on a DVD remote that lets you skip ahead, not like fast forward, but like a skip-stop kind of thing?"

I nodded.

"Right, well it was like that," she said. "I was outside the electronics store and then I was suddenly standing over three bodies."

"What bodies?"

"SAD bodies."

"You killed three assets?"

"They shouldn't have come after me."

"Why wouldn't they? After what you did?"

"But that's my point. I hadn't done anything."

"Hmmm."

"I was out," she said. "Finished with SAD. Finished with all of it. They were supposed to leave me alone. Hays gave me his word."

"And you thought that was a license to just blow shit up?"

"I hadn't done anything."

"Then why'd they come after you?"

"That's what I went to ask Hays."

I thought about this for a moment.

"Go on," I said.

"Guy was a robot," she said. "Did everything just so. Had to. OCD or something. Mega annoying."

"But useful if you wanted to track him down."

She nodded. "Friday night? Where else would he be?"

"So you just rocked up to the club? How'd you get in?"

"Please."

I remembered the guard with the black eye. Nodded.

"I found Hays in the dining room," she said. "Had his nose in a glass of wine. Sucking up the bouquet like it was cocaine."

"And he looked up, saw you, and what, just invited you to dine with him?"

She snorted. "What else was he going to do? Etiquette demanded it."

"I don't buy it."

She shrugged. "Hays was that guy. Always played it calm."

"What about the other patrons?"

"What about them?" she said. "I mean, sure, those assholes weren't happy about it—a woman in the dining room? I don't think so—but it's not like they could do anything, could they? All that stuff going on upstairs, the last thing they wanted was any kind of commotion. Besides, at that point I was Hays's guest, so they had to let it go."

A woman in the dining room? Guess that explains all the hostility, the male voice said. *Hays had already pissed them off once. Us showing up must've looked like he was doing it again.*

I asked Sophia, "What did Hays say?"

"He said I should turn myself in. That there was no better option."

"You probably should have."

"Except I hadn't done anything. Which is what I told him. But then he…"

She went quiet. Looked away.

"Then he what?" I said.

She turned back.

"But then he said I bombed HBL."

"Yeah… so?"

"So he was *right*," she said. "I *had* done it. I *had* bombed HBL. I'd killed *eight* people."

"Eleven people."

Sophia stared at the floor. "I couldn't believe it," she said. "But it was true. I suddenly got this flashback of me standing outside the lab and looking down and seeing the bomb in my backpack." She looked away again. "I just started freaking out after that," she said. "Seriously, Hays had to get me out of there."

"You let him take you in?"

"No, of course not. But Hays didn't try to either. He should have, but he didn't. He brought me here instead."

"Why?"

"Because I'm being set up."

I nodded. "As long as by 'being set up' you mean 'guilty.'"

"I told you you wouldn't believe me."

"Can you blame me?"

"Hays believed me."

"Hays believed a lot of things."

"He's also dead now."

Which was a good point.

I said, "All right, what else did Hays say?"

"He said there was a much bigger game being played. Something about a test."

"What test?"

"I don't know. He just said I was being used and in serious danger."

"In danger from whom?"

"Whoever set me up."

"Hays never told you who they were?"

"Only that if they found me they'd kill me."

"And he stuck you *here*? SAD must have a dozen safe houses in Chicago. Why not use one of those?"

"Haven't you been listening? SAD is after me."

"I thought you said Hays believed you?"

"He did. But he was the only one. He said no one else would. Said he didn't trust them. He said he needed to cover it all up. That it was the only way to protect me. So he brought me here and told me to stay put until he sent someone."

"Who was he sending?"

"I don't know. They never came."

"So you've just been waiting here since Friday?"

She nodded.

"No wonder you look like hell."

Sophia shot me look.

I turned my palms to the ceiling, "Well… you *do*."

"I can't sleep," she said.

"You do a pretty good impression though."

Sophia growled.

I said, "What about the other cases?"

"What other cases?"

I took out the photo from Hays's safe. "Who's CT?"

"What are you talking about?"

I sighed and turned away from her. I looked at the knife sticking out of the wall in front of me.

The female voice said, *Quite a story.*

The male voice said, *It's quite a load of something.*

You don't believe her? I said.

Believe her? Man this story's got more holes in it than Denzel at the end of Training Day, the male voice said.

Yeah. But it is compelling. And fits with what we know.

Which just means she's a damn good liar, the female voice said. *Don't forget, Isaac, according her file, this disheveled blonde was rated Master of Deception. By SAD. And I think we can all agree that what she did in 2011 means we need to be seriously careful here.*

So you both think she's lying?

Lying… the male voice said. *Or she's just batshit crazy.*

But why would she lie? What's her angle?

Long term? Unsure. Right now? To get out of that chair.

I checked the mirror behind Sophia again. Her hands were still relaxed. She was sitting quietly, watching me think.

The problem is her eyes, I said. *Fabricating a story is one thing, but those red streaks across her face are damned real. And if the insomnia is real…*

Or maybe she just pepper-sprayed herself, the male voice said.

Pepper spray?

Like I said, batshit.

I don't buy it.

I'm telling you, Isaac. You take off those restraints and that knife won't be in the wall for very long.

I deliberated on that a while longer. Sophia said nothing. She was watching me carefully. All things considered, I had to keep in mind that I was dealing with someone extremely smart and extremely dangerous. An accurate reading was going to require breaking her. And that was something I wasn't entirely sure I could do.

Eventually I said, "Let's go back a bit. You said you were out. Finished with SAD."

"I was."

"But why?"

"You mean why'd I leave?"

"Yeah."

"That's irrelevant."

"No, it's intriguing."

"Are you going to untie me or not?"

"Tell me what happened."

Sophia said nothing. She just exhaled through her nose and then turned away from me and stared at the floor.

"You were one of their best," I said. "Going places for sure. Maybe to Hays's job. Or maybe even past it. Then two months ago you just up and leave. Why?'

Sophia said nothing.

"Must be something juicy," I said.

Sophia said nothing.

"Something to do with a mission?"

Sophia said nothing.

"A mission that went wrong?"

She looked up at me.

"That bad, huh?"

Sophia smiled. She did it slowly and deeply, and I don't know whether it was the light, or the slight downward angle of her head, but that smile was evil. It put me right on edge. I checked the mirror. Her hands were still.

And then they weren't.

Sophia's hands snapped into fists, and for a split second I thought she was about to make a move. I felt a pulse of adrenaline hit my stomach, and my hand reached for the gun beside me. But then her head snapped back, like something had pulled down on her hair, and her chin shot up to the ceiling, and her neck stretched to its limit, and then her whole body pulsed wildly, like she'd been hit by lightning. Her head jarred first, and then a wild shiver raced down her body and through her extremities, causing every muscle to momentarily contract at peak force.

Sophia was winded.

Her chin collapsed onto her chest.

"You OK?" I asked.

A stupid question. Obviously she wasn't OK.

But before I could ask another one her chin shot up again.

And her head jarred again.

And her body pulsed again.

And much stronger this time.

"Stop it," she said.

"Stop what?"

Sophia's eyes screwed shut. "I said stop it."

But I wasn't doing anything.

Sophia breathed in and out. Her chest was heaving.

Then the next zap came and her whole body started shaking.

She started screaming. "I don't remember. I don't want to remember. *Stop it!*"

She was really freaking out now. Some kind of seizure. I just stared at her from the bed. I didn't know what to do. Nothing in her file had mentioned anything that could explain what was happening. No medical conditions, no psychological issues. So all I could do was watch. The episode lasted about thirty seconds and then her head fell down and her chin collapsed onto her chest for the third time.

I was totally lost with it.

Sophia's face was full of pain. She was panting hard.

I got up and walked around her. Sophia winced and cowered in the chair.

Guys? I said.

Well it's definitely not an act, the female voice said.

What is it?

Looked like she remembered something, the male voice said. *Right before she smiled. Something flickered in her eyes.*

You think a memory did this?

I think it triggered it, yeah.

But what kind of memory could do this?

Best guess, some kind of majorly traumatic incident. Something her mind couldn't properly process at the time and instead locked it away.

Like bombing the HBL lab?

Or maybe something worse, the female voice said. *What did she say? Everybody breaks? Maybe that's what happened. Maybe she was captured and tortured. A mission gone bad.*

The male voice said, *Well, whatever happened she definitely hasn't been rehabilitated. That's for damn sure.*

I sat on the bed again. Lay back and stared at the ceiling. Waiting, and thinking. Ten minutes later I heard Sophia say, "You going tell me who you are now?"

I sat up and looked at her. She was sitting in the chair, perfectly calm, even-tempered. Her hands were loose behind her. She was relaxed and in total control.

As if nothing had happened.

I got up and walked around her again. I bent down and put my hands on her knees and leaned in close so we were face to face. Sophia looked me dead in the eye. She was rock steady in the chair.

"What now?" she asked, smiling.

What now, indeed.

The male voice said, *You know we <u>are</u> in Chicago.*

I kept staring at Sophia, an inch from her face, half trying to smell for pepper, half wondering whether I should apologize or not. Three minutes went by. She didn't flinch once.

I said, "Fine."

"Fine what?" she said.

I stepped around her and started untying the restraints.

"You're letting me go?"

"Don't kick me."

She looked back over her shoulder.

"So you believe me?"

I said nothing.

"Who are you?"

EIGHTEEN

IT WAS JUST after 1:00 a.m., and the streets were anything but empty. Chicago at its quietest. A black sky, deserted sidewalks, and about a million cars still on the road. Which was a damn shame. I really wanted to see what the Jag could do.

Sophia was sitting next to me, staring out of the passenger-side window. She had a faraway look in her eyes and hadn't said a word since we left the motel. She'd taken five minutes to wipe down the room and eliminate all trace of herself, and then she had begun to collect the few belongings she had, stopping when she came to the gun on the bed. I had nodded at her, *Go ahead*, which had puzzled her for a moment, until I qualified it by pulling the knife out of the wall, and nodding again, *But I'm keeping this*.

Then, both armed, we had walked out of the motel, and down the street to the Jag, and driven off. I started to say something, but then I thought better of it. Sophia was lost in thought. She was mute and despondent, and her body was continually juddering as the road's character developed. Something was eating away at her, and I wondered if it was the same thing that was eating away at me. The seizures. I just couldn't get my head around it. Nor could I get the image of that evil smile out of my mind. And then there was how she had come around with no recollection of anything.

I reached behind to the back seat and retrieved Sophia's file. I threw it into her lap. Sophia's attention snapped back to the present and she broke away from her stare and looked down at the brown folder and then over at me.

"It's a good read," I said.

Sophia said nothing. She just looked down at the brown folder again, and after a couple of seconds opened it up. I turned back to the road and put my foot down again.

I didn't take a direct route. Mainly because there's no such thing in Chicago. But also because the couple of back seat drivers in my head had me try and cut a corner to beat the traffic, which naturally put us in a worse lane than when we started. Sophia was uninterested in the traffic, looking up only a couple of times from her file when I exchanged *pleasantries* with some of the other drivers. Eventually though, the traffic eased up a little, and soon the Jag was prowling through River North, following the Chicago Brown above, until North Franklin met West Chicago.

I pulled up exactly on the boundary of the Near North Side. I parked in a small parking lot and cut the power and the engine stopped growling and the Jag settled down. I looked over at Sophia. She was still reading through her file, and, for the first time, she looked peaceful. Maybe I was still feeling guilty about before, but I didn't want to take that from her. So I took a breath and sat back in my plush seat and closed my eyes and started to tell her about my morning. I told her about the SAD facility, how Hays had died, how I'd tracked his movements, and how I'd found the brown folders in his house.

"Really?" Sophia said. "Behind a painting?"

"*Swans Reflecting Elephants*," I said.

"And there were eight of them?"

"The rest are in the trunk."

She glanced behind us. "They all serve, too?"

"About fifty-fifty."

"And you thought one of us was a source?"

"It was a theory."

"Why me?"

"You're the one who met with Hays."

"What did you do, bribe a waiter?"

I said nothing.

"It was the French guy, wasn't it?"

"He's Belgian, actually."

"Whatever."

'Yeah, he talked."

"I should go back and kick his ass."

"It's a moot point. Your trail was always going to be easy to pick up. After all, a woman in a gentleman's club does tend to stick out."

"Unless, of course, they're a hooker."

I gave her a look.

She smiled. "Hey, the zombie look is in right now."

I said nothing.

Sophia said, "Still doesn't explain how you actually found me, though."

"Ah, well I had some help there."

"Help?"

"Hays had an address."

"He did? Then why not just go to the address in the first place?"

"Two reasons," I said. "First, I wanted to know who I was dealing with."

"And second?"

I nodded to the glove box.

Sophia opened it and took out the A5 pad. She flipped through and just said, "Wow."

"I know, right?"

"Unbelievable," she said. "This is *Hays's*? Guy wrote like an imbecile."

"Pretty much."

"And you managed to read this?" She kept trying to shift perspectives, holding the pad close to her face, and then far away, squinting hard, and then looking at it sideways, and making all sorts of faces in the process. She said, "I don't see an address."

"See that big furious circle at the bottom of the first page?"

She flipped back and squinted hard and then shook her head. Again she just said, "Wow."

Sophia put the pad back in the glove box and threw her folder up on the dash. Then she raised her left hand and rubbed her eyes and pinched her nose.

I said, "You know that pad also mentions a test."

Sophia opened her eyes and looked at me. "A test?"

I nodded. "The answers are probably all right there."

Sophia said nothing.

I said, "You said Hays knew who was setting you up?"

"Yes."

"But he wouldn't tell you."

"No."

"But he needed to cover it up."

"Which you're telling me he did. Official story is that HBL was an accident, right?"

"It is."

"So there you go."

I shook my head. "Doesn't make sense."

"None of this makes sense."

"No, I mean if Hays was willing to not only believe you, but to help you too, *and* go to such lengths to do so, why wouldn't he tell you what was going on?"

Sophia didn't have an answer.

I said, "You shouldn't have trusted him."

"Oh and what exactly would you have done?"

"Me? I'd have flooded social media. Facebook, Twitter, Instagram, the lot. I'd have told whoever wanted some to come and get it. And then obliterated them when they showed up."

"And suppose I'm not that cocky."

I shrugged. "Then you should have run. From SAD and whoever else. You've got the skills."

She snorted. "Run from the people that taught me how. Yeah, great plan."

"As opposed to the genius of staying isolated in *that* hell hole? Yes, I think so."

Sophia turned away from me, pinching her nose again. She took a long deep breath. Exhaled slowly. She nodded to herself.

And then her left hand dropped down from her face and her right hand flew up into view, holding her gun.

The hammer cracked into the cocked position.

NINETEEN

SOPHIA HELD THE gun rock steady and pointed straight at my head. She had moved seriously quickly. She had kicked off the center console and her back was nestled against her door, putting her square to her target. Her arms were out straight and the barrel was less than a foot from my right ear. Both of her hands were wrapped around the butt. I turned my head to the right and stared straight down the barrel. Then I refocused behind it and onto Sophia. I raised an eyebrow. "Feeling brave, are we?"

"Last time you took me by surprise," she said. "Now *I'm* in control."

She had a wild look on her face. Her eyes were twitching and she was slightly panting.

I said, "You sure?"

Her right hand squeezed tighter. I saw her knuckles blanch. There was no slack left in the trigger.

The male voice said, *Is every girl we meet going to stick a gun in our face?*

Sophia smiled. "What's the matter? I mean, this *is* what you said I should do, isn't it? Obliterate them when they show up?"

The female voice said, *Yes, kudos on that one, Isaac.*

Sophia said, "Time to start talking. Who are you?"

I said nothing.

"Who are you working for? Which agency?"

"Does it matter?"

"Yes."

I smirked and looked away. "You wouldn't believe me."

"Tell me."

"I don't work for anyone."

"You're lying."

I shrugged. "I told you you wouldn't believe me."

"Yeah, because you have to work for an agency. You couldn't have known HBL was a bombing, otherwise. Let alone that I did it."

"Couldn't I?"

She shook her head. "Impossible. Same goes for having access to my file."

"I already explained that."

"Yes. *A wall safe. Behind a painting*. What, you think I'm stupid?"

"Well you did forget to switch the safety off."

She shook her head. Didn't flinch.

I sighed. "Maybe you're right," I said. "In fact, maybe I really am one of the people Hays warned you about. Maybe I did kill him. Maybe I took your information by force."

"No," she said. "You didn't kill Hays. You're not one of *them*. You'd have killed me, already. So the only way for you to get my information would be through government channels."

Now I had to pinch my nose.

"OK, say you're right," I said. "Say I do work for an agency. That would explain how I got your file and possibly even how I linked you to the bombing as well. But it still wouldn't explain how I knew where to find you, would it?"

Sophia said nothing.

"You said it yourself, Hays didn't tell anyone what he was doing. He said they wouldn't believe you and that he didn't trust anyone. And if Hays was the only person who knew where you were, and I didn't beat it out of him, nor find all this stuff in a wall safe, how did I find you?"

"Easy," she said. "You took over the surveillance cameras. All of Chicago, probably. Facial recognition would've picked me up in seconds."

"Doesn't say much for your skills, then."

"So I'm right."

"Except for the fact it's been four days."

"Interagency communication for you."

"And you think after all that they'd send in just one guy?"

"Wet work is usually solo."

"You really think an agency would put a hit on you?"

"I was SAD. I know how things are done."

I said nothing.

Sophia said, "Let me guess, I was supposed to be found in that motel room, right? Slit wrists in the bathtub, suicide note on the bed, *sorry, can't go on*, the usual crap?"

"You're still alive aren't you?"

"I'm well trained."

"All the more reason an agency would've sent more than just me."

"Doesn't say much for *your* skills then."

"Only that they're better than yours."

"I'm the one holding the gun."

"You're also the one who got tied to a chair." ،

Her eyes shifted to the window and back. "Where are we? Headquarters?"

"This look like a federal agency to you?"

"Isn't that the point?"

"By that logic wouldn't you be surrounded?"

"Yes."

"Meaning your plan is to kill me and go out in a blaze of glory?"

Sophia said nothing.

The gun didn't move.

I said, "I don't work for anyone."

She said, "Then how did you know about HBL?"

"Put the gun down and I'll tell you."

"Tell me and I'll put down the gun."

"And if it goes off in the meantime?"

She smiled. "I won't lose any sleep."

I said nothing.

She kept smiling.

"Oh, I get it," I assured her. "Because you *can't* sleep."

Her smile turned into a punch-drunk giggle. She nodded.

I said, "Can you shower?"

"What?"

"Shower."

Sophia said nothing. I could see the huge amounts of calculations going on behind her eyes. But I could also see they were running increasingly slower. Again she said, "What?"

"It's what gave you away," I said.

Sophia blinked hard. Said nothing.

"You have explosives training, right?"

She glanced at her file on the dashboard. "You know I do."

"And *you know* that building a bomb is a messy practice."

"So?"

"So evidence doesn't just get left at the crime scene."

She shook her head. "I didn't build that bomb at the motel. Hell I don't even know if I built it, at all."

"But you did carry it."

Sophia said nothing.

"A backpack, wasn't it?"

She still wasn't with me.

"The kind of thing one wears over one's shoulder…"

Sophia eyes widened and her left hand came off the gun and slapped the side of her neck. "Shit."

I nodded. "Simple contact transfer. Explosives to backpack, backpack to shoulder, residue to neck. I smelled it back in the hallway. You know, when I took you down, and all."

Sophia started rubbing her neck.

"C11," I said. "Kind of a milky-coconut aroma. Not bad on you, actually."

Sophia kept the gun in position and a stern look on her face, but I could see all of those calculations beginning to yield the same answer now: *Maybe he isn't lying.* And even more important was their inevitable conclusion: *Maybe I do need him.*

The gun came down.

I said, "Ready now?"

She said, "Tell me why you believe me."

I shook my head. "I never said I did. That's why we're here."

Sophia eyes shot out the window and a sudden fear flashed across her face. She rushed her gun back into position but I'd had enough. I thrust up my hands and flipped the gun around and aimed it right back at her.

"If I wanted you dead…"

Sophia recoiled against her door. She stared down the barrel and then up at me. Her eyes were wide and twitching harder. She was holding her breath. Her jaw started shaking. I waited for her to settle down, then lowered the gun, stripped it bare, and threw the pieces on the back seat.

"OK," I said. "Ready *now*?"

Sophia said, "What the hell is this place?"

"You'll see."

"At least tell me your name."

I shrugged.

"I'm Isaac Blaze."

TWENTY

WE GOT OUT. The first thing to hit me was the smell. There was a doughnut shop upwind. It was a twenty-four-hour place. A fresh batch must have just been taken out of the oven. It flushed the air with that tantalizing bakery bouquet.

No matter what city you're in, there's always some kind of *action* to get a piece of. You just have to know where to look. And River North is as good a place as you'll find in Chicago. There are plenty of clubs and eateries peppered around, and along with Wicker Park, River North is hipster territory. But there's no shortage of shady characters, wise guys, and players of the long-con this side of the river either. And the corner property we were standing outside of was a well-established watering hole for some of the most infamous of them.

It was a jazz and blues club. Had one of those neon saxophones above its entrance. It was lit up all purple and blue. The club was still open and seemed to be in full swing. Hipsters listening to cool riffs. I could hear the minor thirds and dominant sevenths flowing out of the club and riding the breeze outside, hanging around for a moment, and then floating away down each path of the momentarily silent intersection.

Behind the club was a big abandoned building. A gated alleyway ran between the two. The gate wasn't locked. I led Sophia through it. About halfway down the alley, we found a basement-access staircase with an old door at the bottom. It was black, solid, and visibly reinforced. There were three cameras positioned around it, and another five set up at various points in the alleyway. All were in operation. All were undetectable too, unless, of course, you already knew where they were. The old door had one of those sliding spyholes. It shot to the right as we came off the stairs. Angry eyes looked out. We heard a sinister voice coming from behind the door. It said, "If half of five is three, what is one-third of ten?"

An old-fashioned system, but it was reliable.

Sophia gave me a look: *Seriously?*

I shrugged: *If you don't know the answer, just say so,* to which she replied with a two-word look, and a one word answer.

"Four," she said.

The sinister voice came back with question two.

"A man gave one son ten cents and to his other son he gave fifteen cents. What time is it?"

The male voice said, *Hmmm, good one.*

Sophia folded her arms and stared at the ground and thought for a long moment. Then she smiled.

"One-forty-five," she said.

Which made her two for two. Ten cents plus fifteen cents make twenty five cents. Or a "quarter." So a quarter to two sons. *A quarter to two.*

Question three was fired immediately.

"The universe is vast, eternal in nature. My name is Olbers, my question, your answer."

This time Sophia bit her lip.

The female voice said, *No way she gets this.*

I said, *Yeah, but do we know it?*
Please.

I smiled and folded my arms and leaned on the wall and watched Sophia struggle with the fact that she didn't know the answer and what that meant she would have to do. I began to whistle. Sophia held out as long as she could and then, finally, she gave it up. She closed her eyes and exhaled slowly. Turned to face me with eyelids low and another two-word expression., to which I responded with a throat clear and the right answer. I said, "Why is the night sky dark?"

Sophia turned back to the door. Nothing happened for a moment and then the spyhole shot to the left and a set of heavy sounding bolts was released. The door opened slowly.

I said, "After you."

Sophia chuckled and stepped back. "As if," she said.

So after me it was. I stepped through the doorway and Sophia followed cautiously one step behind.

The door closed behind us.

Mr. Sinister was nowhere to be seen.

Sophia said, "What the hell kind of question was that?"

"A physics one."

"You know about physics?"

"Apparently."

"Where are we?"

We were stood in a small square foyer with blacked-out walls and a single umbrella stand in a corner. On the wall to our right were a couple of framed posters that advertised theater performances from the late 1800s. Directly ahead of us was a door-sized dark purple curtain. It was hanging down, perfectly still. I pulled it back and we walked through.

It was an old speakeasy. Low lighting, with a haze of smoke, and Oscar Peterson creating the atmosphere. The room was rectangular with an old, dark hardwood floor. The curtain opened into the center of one of the long sides. There was a line of booths along each of the short sides. Each one was gloomy and had its own framed poster hanging over it. One of them advertised a Houdini act and pictured young man hanging upside down in a tank full of water with a strait-jacket binding his body and a thousand-dollar reward for any-one who could prove he was cheating. There were three pay-phones and then a door that led to the toilets and coatroom. On the other side was a long bar, complete with bartender and classic barstools. And directly in front of us, on the oppo-site side of the room, in the middle of the other long side, was a dark stage.

There were fifteen circular wooden tables arranged in front of the stage. Two cocktail waitresses were sitting at one of them. I knew them both. One was called *Jess* and the other was her twin sister *Lucy*. They sat easily and provocatively, glancing over at us in tandem with their long lashes and lan-guid smiles. I'd go into detail, but seriously, you have no idea.

And in any case their charms had no effect on Sophia. She had tensed up beside me and was looking back through the curtain to the alleyway door. She was still running calcula-tions in her head—each of them adjusted to cope with a new factor: She had no weapons, now. She stared at the exit and reached a conclusion. She turned back to the room. Her eyes scanned everything, narrowing at the stage and pausing on Jess and Lucy before finally coming back to me. I just nodded at one of the tables. Sophia looked at it but didn't move for a while longer. Eventually though she did walk forward and take a seat. But she remained on edge.

I sighed and shook my head and then went over to the bar.

As soon as I sat down, a man appeared center stage.

He had emerald eyes and jet black hair. He was wearing an open-necked black shirt behind a silver-gray suit. He stood in the center of the old wooden stage, completely still, surrounded by shadows, looking nowhere and everywhere at the same time.

The male voice said, *Here we go*.

I looked at Sophia.

She had already been drawn in.

The man waited just the right amount of time before grinning and taking a single step backward and disappearing into the shadows.

Sophia stared on intently. The stage was now empty. The room was silent. Then Jess and Lucy suddenly giggled and Sophia's eyes shot over to them and the instant they landed Sophia felt a hand on her shoulder. She jumped in her seat, stunned to see the man standing behind her and staring back. I smiled, having seen things play out from a different perspective, nodding at Jess and Lucy who both smiled back and gave me a wink.

Sophia stared up at the man and the man stared down at Sophia. His hand kept still on her shoulder and it remained there until Sophia realized something: She couldn't move.

The man walked around the table. Sophia tracked his movements with her eyes. Nothing else would move. The man sat down opposite her. He crossed his legs, reclined in his chair, and proceeded to say exactly nothing, which only made Sophia grow more and more worried. She tensed and strained and her eyes darted around. And then, at the moment her fear peaked, the man closed his eyes and reached into his inside jacket pocket and made things even worse.

TWENTY-ONE

THE MAN BROUGHT his hand out slowly. His fingers were slightly pinched and he placed what they held gently on the table.

Sophia began panting hard.

Her head was still stuck looking up and behind her. Her eyes were wide and glued to the table.

I was watching everything from the bar. Sophia's whole body strained to move, but she was paralyzed. She was fighting panic. She was even struggling to breathe.

The man had tried to do the same thing to me the first time we'd met, but for some reason—probably the voices—he couldn't. Which, considering the state Sophia and countless others before her had been left in, I was thankful for. For some reason his mere presence alerts the lizard part of your brain and immediately puts you on edge. He made you feel like gravity had suddenly doubled. It was suffocating. And it was suffocating Sophia right then.

Her eyes were fixed on the table, stretching ever wider, and beginning to tear up. Her entire body was still straining hard. The pulse in her neck was visible. It was pounding. She was terrified. She needed to get away. Because no one is ever prepared to deal with what the man takes out of his jacket. It's just too much.

Which, as an outside observer, told you both everything and nothing about the man's power.

Because, of course, there was nothing on the table at all.

The female voice said, *I hate watching this.*

The male voice said, *I wonder how long she'll last?*

As it turned out, the answer was six minutes. Sophia fought the entire time, but couldn't endure the strain any longer. After five minutes, she began hyperventilating. A minute after that, she had simply shut down. Her body went limp, her chin dropped to her chest. The man remained impassive.

I heard a dull thud behind me. Glass hitting wood. The bartender had filled a lowball glass. He was a big meaty guy— thick forearms, full head of hair, young face. He was wearing an open white shirt over a white tank-top undershirt. The bottle he was pouring from had no label, but I recognized the drink instantly. It was something called *201*. It was red-gold and always served neat. And it was a hell of a drink. The bartender poured a single finger and then casually swiped his hand sideways, sending the lowball sliding down the bar. I caught it, stared at it for a moment, then looked across at the bartender, who gave a wry smile.

I drank it in one gulp, keeping a straight face as I slid the lowball back to the bartender. Then I swivelled back around, leaned back against the bar, and kept playing it cool, even though I was pretty sure my throat was bleeding.

The female voice said, *Idiot.*

I heard the bartender snort way off my left and then I

heard a news report. There was a small TV mounted in the top left corner behind the bar. A breaking news bulletin had just hit the screen. I turned my head toward it. It stated that there had been some kind of commotion at O'Hare Airport earlier in the day. Information was as yet vague but details were to follow. There was nothing about a massacre at a secret CIA facility, though.

I looked over at Sophia again. The man was still sitting opposite her. He seemed to be thinking about something. He was drumming his fingers slowly on the table. I watched him. He kept thinking for a few minutes more and then he turned his head at looked right at me. I nodded. The man paused a moment and then pushed his chair back from the table and walked toward me.

The man was in his late forties. He had grown up all over the Middle East, immigrating to America in his late teens. He was scary smart, a master of mental manipulation, and one of the most well-informed people I knew. His name was Armand.

I said, "You ever going to teach me that trick?"

He smirked and flicked something at me. I caught it with my right hand.

A bobby pin.

I just pocketed it and rubbed the red marks on my wrists that the three sets of handcuffs had left.

Armand came and stood beside me. He didn't sit on a stool, choosing instead to lean on the bar and face the opposite direction to me, which is how we continued our conversation. "So," he said, "Cairo?"

"Not half as much fun as I hear Tokyo was."

Armand said nothing.

I said, "What happened to retirement?"

He smiled. "Didn't take."

"You don't say."

Armand looked up at the TV and chuckled to himself. The bartender slid another 201 down the bar. It went right behind my back and straight into Armand's cupped hand. It was a double.

Armand said, "I'm not the only one."

"Harriet?"

"So you know."

I nodded.

"Met one of hers today," I said. "Lovely girl."

Armand smirked and held the lowball up to his lips. "I'm not sure Mr. Hays would agree."

I turned my head and Armand gave me a sly sideways look before slinging back the two fingers of 201.

The female voice said, *How the hell does he know these things?*

"I remember when they built it," Armand said. "Was supposed to have an underground passage to Union Station."

"Oh yeah?"

"You know it's 293 meters tall?"

"Not 294?"

"The seventh tallest building in Chicago," he said. "And twenty-first in the United States."

I said nothing.

"Sixty-five stories high, with cylinders that light up on its roof." He shook his head. "Couldn't stand out more if it tried."

"All right, I get it. I should have known. Lesson learned."

"Ah, but is it?"

"It is."

"So you know what's hiding in the sixth tallest building then?"

I didn't take the bait.

I said, "You heard from Rachael?"

Armand smiled. He placed the lowball back on the bar and slid it back across to the bartender. "Fighting again are we?"

"You know how it is."

He shook his head again. "She checked in a couple of weeks ago," he said.

"Anything interesting?"

"Il suo italiano sta migliorando."

"Daverro?"

"*Si*. But that's *all* I know."

"Ah, but is it?"

He said nothing.

"Don't tell me it's that case, again?"

"Rachael can take care of herself."

The lowball came back down the bar again. Another double. Armand caught it, shooting me a look as he did. I shook my head, *far be it from me*, and he slung it back quickly. I turned back to the stage and we went quiet for a while.

Then Armand got back on topic and said, "You realize, of course, you're too late."

I grinned. "Why, because Hays is dead?"

Armand sighed. "See now this is exactly what I'm talking about, Isaac. Sooner or later you're going to piss off the wrong person."

"Meaning up until now I've only been pissing off the right ones?"

Armand said nothing.

I nodded at Sophia. "So what do you think?"

"Strong girl," he said. "Almost lasted as long as the twins. Not bad for CIA."

"Former CIA."

"But SAD."

"Yeah."

"How long has she been out?"

"Couple of months."

"Doing?"

"No idea."

"And she resurfaces here?"

"With a bang."

He nodded. "Indeed."

I said, "I thought C11 was supposed to be hard to get?"

"Not if you make it yourself."

"You think?"

"How else would she get it all over her?"

I said nothing.

Armand said, "How did you find her?"

"I didn't. Hays did."

Armand looked at me. "She got caught?"

"And quickly."

"Why'd she do it?"

I took a breath and turned to face him. "You might want another drink…"

I repeated Sophia's story word for word. I also told him about what I'd found at Hays's house and what Hays had been working on at the SAD facility. Armand had already worked out the HBL connection, but by the end of the story, he was pretty intrigued.

"Seizures?" he said.

I nodded. "Like she got hit by lightning."

Armand turned around and rested his back against the bar and we both looked over at Sophia.

"And she can't remember anything?" he said.

"Or so she claims."

Armand went quiet. Then he said, "OK. So we start with Friday?"

I smiled. "What happened to pissing off the wrong person?"

"Don't push it, Isaac."

"All right, all right, yeah, start with Friday."

Armand nodded and started at Sophia, but then the voices reminded me of something and I called after Armand, "Actually, no. Start with Wednesday. September 23."

TWENTY-TWO

ARMAND WALKED BACK to the table and I got a beer from the bartender before following. My throat really felt like it had caught fire.

I took Armand's chair and Armand stood behind Sophia. She looked calm and very peaceful. I took a swig of beer and then put the bottle on the table and sat back and watched Armand go to work. He rested his hand on Sophia's shoulder, paused, and then, slowly, he began.

"Sophia, can you hear me?" His voice was calm and even and appropriately hypnotic. Sophia reacted to it instantly. Her body picked up like a marionette and she sat there with perfect posture, just like Hays had during my interview.

She nodded.

Armand said, "Good, Sophia. That's very good. Now I want you to continue being in that relaxed and deeply pleasurable state, still listening to my voice as you continue to drift there, but slowly I want you to become aware of what's running straight ahead in front of you. You can see something can't you?"

Sophia nodded.

"Do you know what it is?"

Sophia tilted her head to one side. She seemed unsure.

Armand waited a moment and then tapped her twice on her shoulder and said, "It's a road, isn't it?"

Sophia nodded.

"Yes, that's right, it's a road. And it stretches far off into the distance, doesn't it? Far beyond the horizon."

Sophia nodded.

"And it's a very *safe* road too. Quiet, familiar, yes, that's right, you know this road. In fact you walk it every day, don't you? You're even walking on it now, one step at a time, slowly, safely—*safer* with each step."

Sophia nodded. Her breathing rate began to drop.

"But the best thing about this road is the scenery. It's so peaceful and calm. Just like you are sitting here now. In fact that's exactly what it is, isn't it? You can see what's going on right now all around you."

Sophia nodded.

"And that's why everything up ahead is so blurry until you get there. Because that's the future."

Sophia nodded.

"Good, Sophia. And now, as you keep walking ahead, at the same steady speed that you always do, still listening to my voice, still relaxing with each step, you begin to realize that you can slow down. You can stop and rest if you want. Why don't you try that now Sophia, it's OK, go ahead and stop."

Sophia didn't nod this time. She was sitting completely still. Her breathing rate had dropped to maybe four breaths per minute.

Armand said, "It feels good to take a break doesn't it Sophia? To just stand there and take in the scenery and be able to perfectly relive any moment of your day?"

At that point, I wasn't even sure Sophia was actually

breathing, anymore. Her chest didn't seem to be moving at all. She was like a statue. She was smiling, though. Which, I thought, as long as it wasn't that evil one, had to be good thing.

Armand said, "OK, Sophia, now I want you to turn around and look back down the road. Back the way you came. You can see the whole day, yes? It's all stretched out in front of you, all the way to the horizon, every hour, every second, right back to this morning. You can see it can't you?"

Sophia nodded.

"And you are walking toward it now, too."

Sophia nodded.

"Good, Sophia. Excellent. Now let's walk a little further. Let's go over the horizon. Let's go into yesterday, OK?"

Armand paused and Sophia kept smiling.

"It's fun isn't it, Sophia?"

Sophia nodded.

"And easy, too."

Sophia nodded.

"Yes, of course it is. In fact why don't you stop and take a take a look around. Go ahead, tell me, Sophia, what day is it now?"

"Monday."

"Of course. Monday. Yes. And what time is it now, Sophia?"

"Ten o'clock."

"In the morning?"

"Yes."

"And you're doing?"

"A crossword."

"And the clue is?"

She told him.

"And the answer is?"

She told him.

"This is fun, isn't it?"

Sophia nodded. She smiled.

"So let's keep walking," Armand said. "Yes, that's it, and a little quicker now too, over the horizon again, and straight through Sunday… and then again through Saturday… and not stopping for Friday… or Thursday… but slowing down now for Wednesday, because this is where we want to be, isn't it?"

Sophia nodded.

"Yes, that's a good idea, Sophia. We *should* stop here. How about at midday? Yes, that sounds good, doesn't it? With all the day surrounding us, so we can see it all?"

Sophia nodded.

After that Armand paused for about a minute. Then he said, "Are you there now, Sophia?"

Sophia nodded.

"What's the date today?"

"September 23," she said.

"Excellent, Sophia. *Very good*. Now tell me, what do you see? What's happening?"

Sophia stayed perfectly still and quiet, barely breathing for about three minutes. Then she said, "It's raining."

Armand said nothing.

"But I'm not wet," Sophia said. "I'm inside."

"Inside where, Sophia? Where are you?"

Her head turned to the left. "A hospital."

I leaned forward.

The male voice said, *She was in hospital the day before the bombing?*

Armand said, "Tell me what's inside. What do you see, Sophia?"

Her head moved again. Side to side, like she was looking around. Her eyes stayed closed but I could see them moving around under her lids, scanning her environment. She said, "People. I see people."

Armand said nothing and let her continue at her own pace.

"They are like me," Sophia said. "But *they're* all lying down and I'm not. I'm—"

She reeled back in her chair.

"The man is here."

"What man?" Armand said.

"The man in the white coat. *He's* the one who hurts me."

"Don't worry, Sophia. Nothing can hurt you now. Remember, I'm right here with you." He tapped on her shoulder again. "You are safe, OK?"

Sophia nodded and straightened up again.

"Good," Armand said. "Now, try describing the people for me."

So Sophia did.

And it was amazing.

Sophia began describing each person she saw in incredible detail. Hair color, eye color, build, gait, distinguishing features, everything. She was hesitant to look at the guy in the white coat, and Armand didn't push her for more than the vaguest description—dark-skinned with bushy hair—but the other people came through crystal clear. And five minutes later, after hearing only the first two descriptions, my mind was racing. Because I knew those people.

They were the other brown folders.

TWENTY THREE

I STOOD UP FROM the table and went back out to the Jag. I collected all of the folders from the trunk, as well as everything else I'd picked up along the way—the notepad, the photo, Sophia's belongings from the motel—and then went back inside and sat down opposite Sophia again. She was still describing all the people she could see lying down in the hospital.

I put the folders on the table, opening them one at a time and showing Armand the profile picture that Sophia was currently describing to a tee. By the time she had finished, Sophia had put all five of the other brown folders at the same location as her, at the same time, on Wednesday, the day before the bombing.

Armand said, "OK, Sophia. That's very good. But let's move on now. You said it was raining?"

"Yes," she said. "I can see out of the window."

"Tell me what you see."

"Traffic."

"A main road?"

"Yes."

"Do you know which one?"

Sophia pulled a face. Her eyes started scanning around beneath her eyelids again. I saw them stop on something. Sophia squinted at it but then she shook her head.

"No."

Armand said, "OK, Sophia. That's fine. What else can you—"

"Oh wait," she said excitedly. "I see a taxi."

"A taxi?"

"It's stuck in the traffic," she said. "But it's black." Her eyebrows shot up and she smiled. "I think I'm in London."

Armand said nothing and let her continue on her own again.

Sophia turned her head down and to the right. She said, "I also see a man. And a woman too. They are together, talking."

"An old woman?" I asked.

Sophia said nothing.

Armand gave me a sharp look. I held my hands up apologetically. Interrupting a person in as deep a trance as Sophia's could cause bad reactions. It disorients them, and can snap them straight back to reality with no idea where they are or what's going on, which naturally makes them hostile, which is pretty much the last kind of state you want an unstable ex-SAD operative to be left in. I picked up the black-and-white photo and pointed.

Armand said, "OK, Sophia. Tell me about the couple. Start with the man. Can you see his face?"

Sophia pulled another face.

"No, they're too far away."

"Then look closer, Sophia. Concentrate."

Sophia squinted hard.

She concentrated.

And then she suddenly reeled back in her chair again.

"The woman," she said. "She scares me."

Armand said, "It's OK, Sophia. Don't worry. She can't hurt you. Nobody can. I'm right here, remember?" He tapped her on the shoulder again but Sophia was much more reluctant to straighten up this time.

Armand said, "Focus on the man, Sophia. Look past the woman and try and see his face."

Sophia tried to comply but she kept turning her head to the side and looking away. She said, "I…"

"You can do it," Armand said. "Just *look*, Sophia."

"I…"

She reeled back in her chair again.

"No," she said. "The woman knows I'm here."

"It's OK, Sophia. Nobody can hurt you."

He tapped her shoulder again. It did nothing. Sophia wasn't convinced. She started squirming around in her chair, breathing hard and twisting and turning.

"No, I don't want to," she said. "Please don't make me."

She sounded like a child. Very scared and pleading with her parents to make it go away.

Armand said, "OK, Sophia. OK." He rested his hand on her shoulder and this time he kept it there. Sophia began to calm down. Her muscles relaxed and she stopped squirming and the room's brief distress subsided.

Armand said, "Go back to the road, Sophia."

Armand said nothing for a couple of minutes, allowing Sophia a short break and a chance to catch her breath. But during which time he seemed to contemplate something very seriously. I didn't say anything. I didn't want to screw anything up. The couple of minutes went by in silence, and then, once Sophia seemed steady again, Armand said, "Let's start walking again, Sophia. But forward now, OK? Into Thursday. Toward the evening."

Sophia nodded.

"What do you see now, Sophia?"

Sophia didn't reply.

Armand said, "Sophia?"

She opened her mouth to speak but then closed it again. Her face washed over with confusion. She stayed quiet.

"Sophia?"

"Nothing," she said. "There's nothing here. I can't see anything at all."

Armand tapped her shoulder again. He said, "You have to *look*, Sophia. You can do it. Now tell me what you see. Look around and *tell me*."

Sophia squinted hard, turning her head and looking around all over. But in the end she just shrugged and shook her head, hopelessly.

"There's nothing," she said again. "It's just… *black*. I can't see *anything*."

I looked up at Armand. He was looking down at Sophia. His face had turned stern and he seemed to resume contemplating whatever he had been before. He said, "Sophia I want you to listen very carefully, now. I want you to keep walking forward until you can see again. And then I want you to stop and tell me exactly what you see when you get there. Do that now, OK?"

Sophia nodded and the room fell into an apprehensive silence. One minute went by, and then another. And then another.

Then Sophia said, "There's been an explosion. It's on the TV."

I looked up at Armand. He nodded back. We knew this part of the story already. The sidewalk outside the electronics store—after the explosion, before Hays.

Armand said, "OK, Sophia. Good. Now go backward again. Go back to Wednesday. To the hospital."

Sophia nodded.

Armand said, "Are you there, Sophia?"

Sophia didn't reply.

"Sophia?"

Again she didn't reply.

Armand said, "Sophia, can you hear me? Are you back at the hospital?"

Sophia remained silent.

"Sophia?"

"It's gone," she said. "It's all gone. I can't see it anymore."

TWENTY-FOUR

WHAT HAPPENED NEXT will stay with me forever.

Armand walked around Sophia and searched through the stack of folders on the table in front of me. He pulled Sophia's folder out from the pile and then started pacing back and forth behind Sophia as he read it. Whatever he had been contemplating before was now consuming him. He was clearly very uneasy. He had a serious look on his face and he seemed to be lost in his own thoughts.

And that began to have major consequences.

Because he left Sophia in the dark.

Literally.

I watched Sophia closely from across the table. She was turning her head side to side again, her eyes moving around behind her lids, looking all over. She was scared. That much was obvious. Her body was tense. She was breathing harder. Her lower lip was quivering and a subtle tremor was beginning to ripple through her body as well. She looked cold. Like she was sitting in a freezer. And as time went on she got worse.

But Armand took no notice. In fact he didn't seem to care at all. No shoulder taps, no reassuring words, no guidance.

He wasn't saying anything. He just kept pacing around behind her, searching through her file, completely lost in his thoughts.

I kept watching Sophia.

She kept getting worse.

Ten minutes went by and her breathing became labored. She began twisting and turning in her seat again, too. Every so often her head would snap to one side as if a loud noise had gone off behind her. I didn't know what was going on inside her head, but wherever she was, trapped in the dark or not, she definitely didn't want to be there.

The male voice said, *We need to do something, Isaac.*

The female voice said, *Yeah, this isn't right.*

I looked up at Armand again. He was still pacing around.

I took a swig of beer, replacing the bottle on the table a lot harder than I needed to. The glass hit the wood and made a loud thud.

Armand kept pacing.

Another minute went by.

The male voice said, *Seriously, Isaac, do something.*

I looked at Sophia. She was in a bad way now. She was shivering and sweating and her breathing had become ragged. Her head kept shifting from side to side, like she was sensing a threat all around her but was unable to see it. Her chair started rocking with her movements. Her arms were squeezing her sides and her hands were gripping her seat like vices. The chair legs began scrapping around on the wooden floor.

I said, "Hey, *Armand*."

Armand stopped pacing. He looked up from the file and turned to me. There was something in his eyes. They stared at me for a moment and then they fell down to Sophia.

But by that point it was too late.

Sophia's eyes burst wide open and she shrieked. I recoiled in my seat and Sophia snapped her leg out under the table, kicking my chair hard and sending me all the way over. The same momentum also sent her flying backward and crashing into Armand who was frozen right behind her. I saw them collide a split second before I smacked down onto the ground. The back of my chair punched straight into my spine. There was a loud crack, and I wasn't sure whether it was my spine or the chair, but I was bouncing back off the impact immediately afterwards, my legs coming over quickly and my head snapping forward and curling under my weight, which was piling onto my shoulders and neck as I flipped right over.

I ended up sprawled on my stomach, at an odd angle to the chair.

Sophia was on her feet. She grabbed my beer bottle before I could stop her.

She had a weapon.

The voices started screaming at me to get up. I was fast. Sophia was faster. She had broken the beer bottle on the table.

Now she had a sharp weapon.

The voices started screaming again.

I listened and moved.

I lunged at the table.

And then everything slowed right down.

Time froze and I saw everything in crystal-clear ultra-high-definition. Sophia stood behind the table while Armand tried to scramble to his feet below her. Sheets of paper fell everywhere. Shards of brown glass flowed across the table top and rained to the floor. I was aware of Jess and Lucy and the bartender, how they were moving and their precise locations way off to my right. I could see the entire room at once. I could see every part of Sophia. Every burst vessel in her eyes, every bead of sweat on her forehead. Every detail was magnified and being assessed. I could see the determination in her face and how her chin was beginning to stretch up toward the ceiling. All of this information was right there in front of me.

But it was her right hand that I was truly focused on.

Because her right hand is what had made my brain shift into super high gear and cause everything to slow down in the first place. Because although she did now have a weapon—her fingers firmly wrapped around the bottle's neck, the jagged edges of the bottle's broken body glinting in the light, razor sharp, and pointing straight at me—the real problem was how she intended to use it. Because after all the variables had been taken into account—speed, trajectory, comparative density, logic—an answer had emerged that was impossible. Because at that speed, and at that trajectory, and with all those other variables as they were, the bottle was going to end up somewhere it couldn't.

Because Sophia's hand was now swinging *in*.

And *up*.

And there was nothing I could do to stop it.

Time restarted and I watched the bottle slam into Sophia's neck. Everything came together in an instant. Her chin reached the height of its movement, stretching her neck to its extreme, and her right hand flew up from her side and buried the jagged glass into her own throat. Blood sprayed everywhere.

And then Sophia was folding at the waist.

My hands finally smacked into the near edge of the table, punching the other side straight into her hips. It smacked her left and then bumped off to the right toward Armand. I kept stumbling forward but managed to stay on my feet. The table hit Armand and pitched over sideways and I carried on past it and fell straight on top of Sophia. She had gone down awkwardly, with the bottle in her neck and her hand still wrapped around it.

At which point she yanked the bottle out of her neck.

A jet of blood blasted all over me.

A fountain of red sprayed up into the air, erupting like a volcano and flooding Sophia's chest. I threw my hands over her neck, but I knew it was pointless. Within seconds, she had lost more blood than her body could bear. Her neck just kept gushing. I had been blinded by the blood but I could feel her arteries squirting away under my palms, each one less powerful than the last, until finally her heart gave out and there was nothing left to pump.

I rolled off her.

I lay there next to the body for a full minute, my shirt drenched, and my face and arms stained red. I wiped my eyes with the crux of my elbow and when I eventually opened them I saw Jess and Lucy kneeling beside me, the bartender next to Sophia, and Armand standing above us with an expression I'd never seen before.

TWENTY-FIVE

I LAY THERE NEXT to Sophia until Jess and Lucy helped me up. We all just stood around Sophia, saying nothing. Armand kept the same expression on his face the whole time—the one I didn't recognize.

He knew something.

And he didn't like what it was.

After a few minutes, the lake of blood surrounding Sophia stopped expanding. But we all just kept standing there in silence.

Then Armand knelt down and pulled up each of Sophia's sleeves.

Jess and Lucy both gasped.

The male voice said, *What the hell?*

The cruxes of Sophia's elbows were black. Her veins were fat and lumpy and looked hard under her skin. They bulged upwards, spreading out like tree roots. They grew up and down her arms, changing from black to deep purple and then to light pink and green. The lower branches covered her inner arms and almost reached her wrists. The upper branches wrapped around her biceps before disappearing back under her skin at her armpits. In the center of her inner elbow was a ragged puncture hole. Huge and swollen and crusted over. It was like a fat worm had bitten in, bored under her skin, and then started growing. I had no doubt that Sophia would have been in immense and constant pain. And all of it had been covered up by her baggy sweater.

Armand breathed out. He gave a solemn nod and then stood back up, but when I went to speak, he just held up his hand, and shook his head, and nodded at my clothes. I looked down at myself. I was soaked. The shirt was made of a high-quality cotton thread and had soaked up the blood to the point of total saturation. It had been light and airy before but was now heavy and plastered to my back. The navy-blue suit-pants were in a similar state. My arms were tanned red. I could taste blood.

I looked up at Armand again and he nodded at the stage. I reached into my pocket and pulled out the Jag's keys and tossed them to the bartender. Then I walked away from the body. I got up on stage and walked through a concealed door at the back. There was a secret passageway behind it. It was about twenty meters long and led to the basement of the building behind the jazz club. Back in the days when raids were common this was how the clientele got out in a hurry. From the outside the building behind the club had looked totally abandoned. But that was far from the case. Armand had bought it for a very specific purpose.

I came out into a dark and dingy basement. It was a big area, but it had been utterly gutted. The brick work was fully exposed and the support columns were all rusty. And apart from a string of makeshift lighting and couple of steel folding chairs there was nothing in it.

Except a hose.

It was rolled up on a cylindrical wall dispenser in one of

the corners of the room. It was the exact same spec as a regulation firefighter instrument. It was very long, off-white in color, and had a giant chrome nozzle. I peeled off Hays suit and threw it onto one of the folding chairs. My skin was slick with Sophia's blood, but I could feel it beginning to clot.

A couple of minutes later the bartender emerged from the passageway. He was carrying my old clothes from the Jag's trunk. He dragged over another one of the folding chairs and put the clothes on it. Then he walked over to the hose and I went and stood against a wall, directly over one of the many gutters in the floor. The bartender picked up the giant nozzle and unhooked the hose from the wall and spooled off some length. He turned the faucet underneath the dispenser and then walked out and stood about ten feet in front of me. I saw the hose swell up like a balloon animal. The bartender took a wide and staggered stance, using both hands to aim the giant chrome nozzle squarely at me. I remember being more intimidated then than when Sophia had pointed her gun at me in the car. The bartender gripped the nozzle's retracting lever, his big meaty forearms rippling and tensing, and then, just before he pulled it, I saw him smile slightly, and remembered to cover my crotch.

The water was so cold it took my breath away. Or at least it would have if it hadn't also smacked me back into the wall and winded me first. It was super powerful. Like a bloody jet-washer. And the bartender didn't let up either. I stayed pinned against the wall for the better part of ten minutes, during which time the male voice reminded me of a story I'd heard many years before, from a very reliable source, about his first day in a Russian prison. Like all prisons, a preliminary induction had to be conducted. This began with the fresh meat first getting searched—a horror story in itself—and then they got lined up for their mandatory shower. Naturally this was done in the middle of the prison yard, with the other inmates watching, and a similar hose to the one being used on me. Except theirs was connected to the septic tank.

Moral of the story: You *do not* get caught in Russia.

Once I was clean again, I went to put on my old clothes. The jeans were fine but my old shirt wasn't. It still had a mix of Hays's and Peter's blood on it. I looked at the bartender. He just shrugged. He rewound the hose and then we walked back through passageway.

I came out onto the stage and saw Jess and Lucy on hands and knees with huge sponges to the floor and buckets of soapy water standing by.

Sophia's body was gone.

All that was left was a big red stain.

Armand was standing a few feet back, just in front of the purple curtain. His arms were folded and he was staring down at the floor. The same expression was still on his face. He looked up at me standing shirtless on the stage and then walked across the room, past the three payphones, and into the door in the far corner. He came out a few seconds later with a dark shirt and a dark deck jacket draped over his arm. I jumped down off the stage and put them on.

Then Armand said, "MK-ULTRA."

TWENTY-SIX

MY FOOT PUNCHED the pedal flat to the floor. The engine howled and I got pressed right back into my seat. I flew out of the parking lot, looping around the block before hitting the shift and redlining the Jag and hurtling back down North Franklin. Armand's words kept streaming through my mind.

The male voice said, *I knew it.*

The female voice said, *Here we go…*

What do you mean "here we go"? Armand just confirmed it.

No, Armand just confirmed he drinks too much, said the female voice.

Drinks too much? You're really going to keep playing skeptic? Why shouldn't I?

How much more proof do you need?

More proof? she asked.

Memory loss, insomnia, the marks on her arms, they're all documented side-effects of the program, he said.

And blowing up HBL? Was that another side effect?

Side effect? Don't you see? She was a puppet. They made her do it.

And why exactly would they do that? asked the female voice. *What could the CIA possibly have against HBL?*

How should I know? Maybe nothing. <u>Probably</u> nothing. Remember, this is all part of a test, said the male voice.

You think they'd kill eight people just for a test?

Not like they haven't done worse. And it's fifty-four people. The other five cases are part of this, too. The brown folders are the subjects.

The female voice said nothing.

Just think about it. It explains everything. They've been at it for sixty years and now they've finally got the program to work.

And they're using it on their own people? she asked.

Sophia was out, remember? Ex-SAD.

You really think you've got it, don't you?

Like I said, it explains everything.

Oh yeah… Except of course for Hays, the safe-house, and the entire SAD investigation.

The male voice went quiet.

I kept flying down Franklin, zooming under the Brown line.

The male voice said, *All right, all right, how about this. We know Sophia went off the grid two months ago, right? Left SAD, and for absolutely no reason.*

The female voice said, *So?*

So maybe there was a reason.

Like what?

Like maybe she didn't "leave" so much as she "went dark."

For what purpose?

Well, let's say some faction within the agency really is keeping the program alive. Maybe Sophia stumbled onto something she shouldn't have, said the male voice.

And you think she'd try and investigate all by herself?

She was one of their best.

What about Hays? asked the female voice.

Hays was big player, for sure. But maybe not big enough. Something like this would go far higher up than him. But maybe he had suspicions of his own, and when he heard Sophia's story— when he saw the marks on her arms—it confirmed them.

The female voice said nothing.

Think about it, would you? said the male voice. *She goes under, she makes some progress, but then she gets caught and ends up as one of the test subjects. Next thing she knows, she's blown up a building.*

Which explains why the SAD would be after her, and why Hays was helping her, said the female voice.

Exactly. If Hays had been investigating his own agency then everything he did starts to make sense. Why he played it so close, why this all took priority over Iran.

Because he wouldn't have known who to trust.

So you agree.

No, she said, *you're an idiot. If Hays was investigating, why on earth would he cover up those six cases? That's his evidence.*

Then maybe he was in on it.

In which case he wouldn't have helped Sophia.

You got a better explanation? he asked.

Than MK-ULTRA? Yeah, I've got a few.

So let's hear one.

It's simple really, said the female voice. *She was a junkie.*

A junkie?

Explains everything. The memory loss, the insomnia, the marks on her arms. She was in withdrawal.

Withdrawal? Seriously? And what about blowing up HBL? Was that part of the withdrawal too? asked the male voice.

She needed cash, she took a job.

And Hays? What was that all that about?

How should I know? Maybe he was just looking out for his own.

The male voice said nothing.

The female voice said, *See? It <u>does</u> explain everything.*

Oh yeah… Except of course for the brown folders, the memories, and <u>everything that just happened</u>.

The female voice said nothing.

The male voice said, *Ah ha!*

Look, whatever. The point is it's not MK-ULTRA.

Hey, Isaac, you want to help me out here?

Does it matter? I said. *Fact is someone did something so horrific to her that she went and did <u>that</u>.*

The voices went quiet and I kept flying down Franklin.

The truth was I didn't care *what* had been done. MK-ULTRA or not, it was irrelevant. It was the *where* and the *who* that was really causing my blood to boil. Sophia had described a hospital. Combine that with her PTSD-like symptoms and it began to look like the hospital was actually a mental-health facility. And if someone thought they could mess with the patients, the kind of people who couldn't even defend themselves, they were dead wrong. Because, while I may not be helpless anymore, I had been once. And so, while I'd initially gotten involved in this whole thing for a thrill, now it was personal.

Now someone was going to pay.

The male voice said, *We should start with the woman.*

Agreed, the female voice said, *Judging by Sophia's reaction she's whose behind this whole thing.*

It's irrelevant, I said. *The woman, the mystery guy, the white coat—we're taking them all.*

181

I was about a mile south of Armand's place and still had my foot down. With the 'L' above me and tall buildings either side, I quite literally had tunnel vision. I was coming up fast on West Ontario. I needed to turn right to join the Kennedy. O'Hare was about twenty minutes away and I wanted to get there as quickly as possible.

I had left all of the brown folders and such with Armand. Between me and the voices, I had that stuff well memorized. I had kept the photograph though, which, along with Hays's remaining money and a full British passport, was in my pocket. The passport came from a stack that I kept with Armand. He was a trusted acquaintance and my main point of contact in Chicago and as such he offered me a place to store many such utilities.

I came to a stop at the intersection and brushed my hand over my face. I saw Sophia standing in front of me again— behind the table, out of reach, with the shattered bottle in her hand, and her hand sweeping in and up. I saw her eyes. Wide open. Bloodshot. Determined. In total control of what she was doing. I saw the bottle smack straight into her neck.

One of the voices started to say something, but sudden noise shut them down. Noise, and then total silence. I felt a shockwave smack straight into my back, sending my chest forward and my neck whipping back. My eyes opened slowly. I saw my left hand drifting away from my face. There was a burst of light. I watched it spray out across the car. Felt it raining against my cheek as it passed straight in front of my face. And then I got hit by another shockwave. My seatbelt kept getting tighter and tighter. But just as I began to understand what was happening, my head finally hit the headrest behind me and everything speeded up again—ultra-fast-forward, deafening noise. I saw flashes of road and then sky and then road again.

And then everything went black.

TWENTY-SEVEN

THE FIRST THING I felt were my feet dragging. There was some kind of thick sludge on the ground. My jacket was missing and I could feel a meaty hand clutching each of my wrists. My arms were out to my sides, each one resting across a set of thick shoulders, while my body slumped down in between. I was still way out of it but I was slowly coming to. I began to hear the voices.

. . . You guys need to wake up to reality, the male voice was saying. *The CIA has been experimenting with mind control since the fifties.*

They're poisoning our crops too, the female voice said.

They are *poisoning our crops. That thing in Nebraska proved it.*

Yeah, and let's not forget about the Pigmen.

All right, look, I'm not saying it's all true, but you can't deny that the CIA has done some shady shit.

I'm not denying it. I'm just saying you're an idiot.

Yeah, well twenty-thousand documents say I'm not.

Oh come on, <u>mind control</u>? You can't be serious.

It's a fact. They never shut the program down. And let me tell you something else—

What the hell happened? I said.

Well look who decided to wake up. By the way great road awareness back there, Isaac.

We got hit?

By a bloody truck.

How bad is it?

Left shoulder's going to be sore for a while, but we should be fine.

What about the face?

You know we did try to warn you, the female voice said. *Next time pay attention.*

I stayed completely lifeless, slumped between whoever was carrying me, with my head hanging down, and my feet continuing to drag. I did a complete system check. I began contracting each muscle group to see if anything was damaged. I started with my calves and worked up to my upper traps. I found my left shoulder to be throbbing, as was my head, but nothing was broken. Like the male voice said, I was sore but I'd be fine.

I said, *How long was I out?*

The female voice said, *Best we can figure, about an hour.*

So they drugged us too?

Must have, the male voice said. *Probably straight after we got hit.*

My senses were slowly starting to come back online again. The more they did, the worse the smell got. The air was warm and thick and dank and putrid. I could hear plenty now, too. The guys who were carrying me had heavy footsteps and they were pounding along in standard 4/4 time. There was a constant rattling noise coming from their backs and way off in the distance I could hear a rush of water. There was also a high pitched dripping sound that echoed all around us. But it was the cacophony of squealing rats that confirmed where we were.

I said, *The sewers?*

The female voice said, *Well it'd help if you opened your eyes, already.*

I slowly lifted my eyes and tried to see ahead, but my hair was hanging down and obscured my view. It was wet and gloopy, and that meant a head wound.

Dammit, I said. *My face.*

The female voice said, *Will you stop worrying about our face for once. Every time it's: How's my face? Please, not the face!*

Hey, I don't do radio.

Do you do useful?

Wow, you're in a bad mood.

Well one of us should be. We're in a damn sewer. Now pipe down and check these guys out.

I let my head continue to hang. Let it keep swaying with our movements so that my eyes could catch as much as possible. But my entire body remained lifeless. To my left I saw a couple of boots pounding along. They were completely soiled with mud, each one slapping down onto the muck. I saw a second pair of boots pounding along on my right.

I couldn't quite make out the faces of my two escorts. With my head hanging, the top of my sight ended at their sternums, meaning I was limited to about a three-quarter picture. But I wasn't concerned about that. Between their boots and their sternums lay all the information I needed to fully understand the situation.

For a start, they were both wearing dark combat trousers,

all black, and dirty, and similar to worker's pants. The guy to my left had a side-piece slung in a battered leather holster that was hanging off his right hip, and the guy to my right was sash-strapped with some kind of semi-automatic rifle. Both guys were unfit to say the least. Duck-walking more than marching, their pot-bellies leading the way. The pig-like wheezing coming out of each of them was continuous. Clearly they were heavy smokers. Judging by the pungency, they were each sucking down three packs a day, minimum. They were huffing and puffing and kept grunting to each other in Russian between breaths. Needless to say, they didn't sound very intelligent.

As I was carried further, the thick sludge underneath us got progressively looser, and soon small splashes of water were being kicked up every time those heavy boots smacked down. We eventually stopped 144 steps after I had regained consciousness, having taken only one right turn after step seventy-six. The two guys were really wheezing badly now, coughing and spluttering and having a very tough go of it. We stood still for a moment and then the guy to my left let go of my wrist and my body dropped down and flopped heavily against the guy to my right.

"*Bweestra*," he wheezed painfully.

I squinted an eye open and saw the other guy crowding a door in front of us. The tunnel we were in had curved walls, and was essentially a giant tube, but a section of it had been cut away for the door.

"*Bweestra,*" the guy holding me said again.

Yeah, _bweestra_, the male voice said. *Your comrade here smells.*

But the guy in front was hurrying. He was patting himself down, frantically ferreting into his multitude of pockets. When he finally did pull out what he was looking for, the male voice started laughing. *You've got to be _kidding_.*

The guy had pulled out a key ring with maybe thirty different keys on it. And, for the next two minutes, he proceeded to agitate and fumble around with them, desperately trying over half the possibilities in the door's lock. His chubby fingers were of no use to him. Each key he tried would frantically scratch around the lock before finally slipping into the hole. It was like he was in that classic nightmare scenario where you're trying to get into your house before the chasing psychopath gets you.

"*Bweestra*," the guy holding me said for the third time. He was trembling under my weight and it seemed his muscles were on the brink of giving out. Luckily though, his partner did get the door open.

A victory.

Or maybe not.

Because as the door swung open, both guys seemed to shuffle backwards. The guy in front was definitely hesitating. He took a long moment to put his keys away, glancing back at his partner before finally taking a step forward. He peeked through the doorway. The room beyond was pitch black. I couldn't see anything. Only that the guy was making sure to lean no more of himself inside than was necessary for a look. His head swept left, then right. Then he reached inside and banged his fist three times on the inside wall, sending echoes through the chamber. The guy froze over the threshold, listening carefully until the echo died out. Only after that did he take a breath and step inside. The guy holding me rushed in after him, stepping quickly over some kind of sludge guard in the doorway that my feet tried unsuccessfully to go straight through. It was solid metal and would have really hurt if not for my rugged footwear.

Five paces into the room, I was thrown hard into a chair. I continued to play dead, but made sure to exaggerate my whiplash in order to get the blood-soaked hair out of my face. The chair didn't budge at all. It was made of metal and bolted to the floor. One of the guys grabbed my hands behind me and pulled them down. The other one handcuffed my wrists to my ankles.

It was a punishing way to be tied up. The handcuff chains weren't very long and pulled hard on my wrists and ankles. There was therefore continuous strain on my knees, quads, and hip extensors, elbows, shoulders, and neck. The back of the chair was digging into my trapezoids and the lip of the seat was digging into my hamstrings. My butt was trying to take my weight, but, because of the way I'd been stretched, it wasn't directly under my center of gravity, and therefore couldn't quite do that—which added to the tension on my joints. Everything was being stretched and pulled underneath the chair.

This kind of bind forces you to stay completely still. You move your leg an inch and you could dislocate your shoulder. Prolonged exposure to the position results in chronic joint and muscle pain, which persist and build, and keep building, until eventually your muscles just give out, and something tears. Having said all that, I had been tied up in worse positions.

But major props to the two idiots for even knowing it.

And, judging by the grunting that followed, they both seemed pretty happy with the job they'd done, too. But they didn't around. They just tied me up, checked I was secure, and then hustled straight back out of the chamber. The door was slammed shut. It was locked, then unlocked, and then locked again.

I glanced around the darkness. The room was much colder than it should have been. Drier, too. I could hear a noise coming from somewhere behind and above me. Some kind of mechanical whirring. My hair was wet and cold and I could feel the blood on my forehead drying quickly. There was just a faint haze of ambient light seeping through small cracks in the walls. Shadows hung like heavy drapes around the room. My eyes were working hard to adjust.

The female voice sighed. *Really, Isaac? Twice in one day?*

On the bright side, these shoes are really proving their worth, I said.

Yeah, that guy back in Cairo wasn't kidding, the male voice said. *The Timberlands of the Sudan.*

You know I'm still pissed about that pyramid tour.

I don't blame you.

Two thousand bucks straight down the drain, I said.

And don't forget about the girl who was leading it.

How could I?

The female voice said, *You guys are just doing this to annoy me now, aren't you?*

Why are you in such in a mood, anyway? the male voice asked.

I'm not in a mood. I just want to find out who the hell knocked us off the road. And then I want to kill them.

The male voice said, *You know on some level you have to admire her bloodlust.*

Admire? I said. *Or fear?*

The female voice said, *Isaac!*

All right, all right. Jeez. Give me a minute would you? I did just get knocked off the road.

Then another voice said, "Great, this is all I need."

TWENTY-EIGHT

MY GAZE SHOT to the corner of the room. I squinted and stared and hoped to hell that there was something there. Three voices in my head was more than enough. Four would've put me over the edge.

The new voice said, "I mean, sorry to interrupt and all, but if you're going to lose your mind could you at least do it quietly?"

The male voice said, *Oh yeah, by the way, you've been mumbling out loud to us since you woke up.*

I kept staring at the corner. At first I couldn't see anything, but then my lips stretched up into a smile.

I said, "I thought you were going to Shanghai?"

"There was a problem at customs."

I saw her eyes flick open. They were amazing. They beamed through the darkness, glowing electric blue, throwing light onto her body. Her outline took shape immediately. Her silhouette slowly began to gain features, and soon the dangerous and alluring Isabel was right there in front of me. She was still wearing her SWAT gear. Dark combat trousers, thin black jumper, heavy boots. She was sitting against the wall with long chains affixed to her wrists. They clanged as she adjusted her posture.

"So," she said. "Intentional, or did these guys just get lucky, too?"

"Neither. It was an accident."

"Of course it was."

"How's Harriet?"

Isabel said nothing.

"Let me guess, she said '*Don't get involved with Isaac Blaze*?'"

"Among other things."

I smiled. "She didn't tell you who I was did she?"

"You make it sound like I care."

"Yeah, well, don't take it personally. She has her reasons."

"Please. I've hardly given you a second thought."

"But you have given me the first one," I said.

She said nothing.

"Been here long?" I asked.

"Few hours."

"Care to elaborate?"

"Not particularly."

The sound of water moving through pipes filled the room.

Isabel said, "And just for the record, I didn't *need* Harriet to tell me anything."

I said nothing.

"Hey, I'll admit you've got a pretty interesting file, but come on, if only half of it was true, you'd be on every major watchlist in the world."

"And I'm not."

"Kinda gives you away doesn't it?" she said.

"I don't know. Does it?"

"Well it certainly limits you," she said. "But once you

factor in what you've done, the necessary training it would take, your complexion, and a name like *Isaac*, yeah, it's pretty obvious."

"So what's the answer?"

"You're Mossad. Ex now to be sure but once upon a time I'm guessing you were in whatever their version of SAD is."

"*Shayatet*-13."

"So, I'm right?"

"No, not at all. Not either of them. But I am flattered, though."

Isabel grumbled. "You know what your problem is?"

"I attract the wrong kind of women."

An unwanted smile crept onto her face and forced her to take a breath. "Forget it," she said.

I grinned. "Look if you really want to know, I'll tell you. But I'm pretty sure you'd rather have the *other* answer."

Isabel didn't reply on principle.

"You want to know how I knew you were one of Harriet's girls, right?"

Isabel shook her head. "You think you're *so* cool."

"So you don't want to know?"

A long silence followed.

Then, "Just tell me."

"All right," I said. "It's everything."

She gave me look from the shadows.

"I mean it," I said. "It's everything about you. How you walk, how you talk, even how you breathe. It all speaks volumes. It's like how Marines can always spot one of their own."

"You think we're the same?"

"I think you've been trained very well."

"Just not as well as you."

"Few are."

"No argument there. Takes something real special to get caught twice in one day."

I said nothing.

She snorted. "*Everything about me.* Do me a favor."

"OK, you're right about that. It wasn't *everything.*"

"Obviously."

"But it was something. And it really did let you down."

Isabel said nothing.

"Actually it's been letting people down a lot today."

"Just tell me already."

"It's your scent."

"My *scent?*"

I laughed.

"Relax," I said. "I'm not saying you smell, or anything. I'm just saying there's only one way to pick up that particular redolence of gunpowder, bourbon, and sawdust."

Isabel's eyes narrowed. She went quiet for a while and then it dawned on her. "Wait, you've been to Harriet's place?"

"Mm-hmm."

"But you're…"

"I know."

"But that means…"

"Yup."

Isabel went quiet for a long time after that.

The female voice said, *Well that ought to change things.*

Guess we'll see, I said. *You guys figure out who took us yet?*

Depends.

On what?

Whether we are where we think we are, the female voice said.

Suppose we are.

Then yeah, we've got a list.

I listened to it and figured it could have been worse.

Then Isabel said, "You got a way out of here?"

"Does seem like one of us should, doesn't it?" I said.

"So go ahead, impress me."

I shook my head.

"And you wonder why I doubt your ability," she said.

"Hey I'm just following Rule Eight."

Isabel said nothing.

Rule Eight was more or less a repetition of Rule One. But it had its own subtleties and it was there for a reason. Rule Eight was: *Don't do anything until you know who you're dealing with.* And usually it means you're going to have to be patient. But we found out quickly enough because the next thing I heard was the sound of a key frantically scratching around a lock.

TWENTY-NINE

THE GRUESOME TWOSOME burst into the room. They were clutching their rifles with both hands and kept moving their heads back and forth between Isabel and me. We just stared at them. Eventually their brains finished processing the zero situation and they shuffled around my chair and took up position behind me, one over my left shoulder the other over my right. They were still breathing hard.

The door was directly opposite me. It was standing open and a trapezoid of light beamed onto the floor. It was a dim sewer-green color and a long shadow was cast on top of it by the figure standing in the doorway. It was a man. He was wearing a full-length black coat and heavy boots. He was carrying a mid-sized briefcase in his right hand. He was older than his henchmen by a couple of decades but was in much better physical shape. He was strong and lean, and clearly the brains of this operation. He stood silently in the doorway, staring into the room. The eerie light from the tunnel lit him up from behind and his shadow covered me completely. He crossed the threshold and then we were five.

He turned the light on. I glanced up at the ceiling. There

was a fluorescent tube mounted right above me. It was old and dirty and emitted a dull white glow. But that was more than enough to illuminate the chamber, which was completely gray. We were in nothing more than a subterranean concrete box. I saw Isabel in full color. The chains on her arms were thick and bolted into the wall behind her. Seven more sets of chains were likewise bolted all the way down the same wall to my left. Isabel was sitting calmly against it. Her eyes swept across the room. She wasn't worried.

Tweedledum and Tweedledee were still behind me. They were about three feet back from me, still breathing hard, still totally incompetent.

The door slammed shut. I looked across at the man in the black coat. He took a couple of paces toward me and then stopped. He stared down at me for about a minute. Then turned away and put his briefcase on top of a long wooden table pushed up against the wall. He flicked the locks open, lifted the lid, and looked over the contents. Then he glanced back at me and smiled.

See? I said. *Now there's a face for radio.*

The male voice said, *I can't believe he actually caught up to us.*

The man's skin was the color of jaundice. It was all leathery and creased like an old catcher's mitt. He was completely bald and his head was covered in scar tissue. A particularly deep scar cut diagonally across his lips, distorting his smile like a Picasso.

I had met this man, Vlad, five years ago. It was a brief acquaintance to be sure less—than five seconds in fact, and one in which no more than four words had ever been exchanged between us. But despite all that, the interaction had in no doubt ruined him.

He turned back to the briefcase. His hand began dipping in and out of it, moving back and forth across the table as he set it. He proceeded to do this in silence, every now and then stopping to glance back and grin at me.

The male voice said, *Oh yeah, he's really enjoying this.*

The female voice said, *Can you blame him?*

Isabel was watching Vlad intently. He continued to dispense the briefcase's contents until finally thirty metallic implements of various shapes and sizes rested atop the old piece of wood. They were all surgical in nature. And they were all pristinely sharp. Perfectly arranged in three rows of ten, each one ranked specifically according to cutting depth.

Vlad was, among other things, a fully licensed surgeon and a first class forensic anthropologist. And although originally from Ukraine, he had once been one of Russia's finest interrogators. But Vlad was a modest man, too. He didn't care for fine clothes or any of the flash, brash, and crass that Hays had adored. Vlad had simple interests. His work was his passion. He loved it. And that wasn't a good thing if you were sat where I was.

Vlad took two final things out of the briefcase: a hammer and a stack of old cloth. He laid the hammer to the left of the three rows, perfectly straight and vertically flush with them. He put the cloth in one of the corners. Then he closed the briefcase and put down it on floor, under the table, out of the way. Then, keeping his back to me, and his gaze on the equipment he had laid out, he took a deep breath, and wiped his hands slowly over his head. His fingertips pushed backward from his forehead, spreading out slightly as though running through hair, reaching all the way to the back of his skull, which was covered in scar tissue. His fingers lingered on the ridged skin. I figured he was remembering exactly why he needed to relish this moment.

He said, "*Ne bylo by schast'ya, da neschast'ye pomoglo.*"

He was still looking down at the table. His voice was calm, but his fingers were pressing hard into his head.

Nobody said anything.

The handcuffs were digging into my skin. My joints were beginning to burn.

Vlad turned to face me. A jagged half-smile crinkled up on his face.

"*Ne bylo by schast'ya, da neschast'ye pomoglo,*" he said again.

His accent was thick and heavy. Roughly translated he was saying: *I'd have no luck, if not for misfortune.* It was an idiom similar to what Lightnin' Slim, Albert King, and Ray Charles had cried out about in years past, but Vlad meant it to convey his realization of a blessing in disguise.

"For example," Vlad said, switching to English in order to accommodate Isabel, but keeping his focus squarely on me. "It would seem like such an unfortunatality that Dima was killed today. And yet, just hours later, the universe restores balance by giving me you in return."

I stared back unimpressed. "You know that *unfortunality* isn't a word, right?"

Vlad didn't reply. His hands just crushed into fists at his sides.

The female voice said, *Yeah, sure, make him _more_ mad. That's just what we need.*

Vlad turned back to the table and took off his coat. He folded it up and then draped it neatly over his suitcase. Then he walked back to me, cracking his neck side-to-side, and rolling up his shirt sleeves. More scars revealed themselves along his inner forearms. They were long and thick and gnarly and reminded me of Sophia's veins.

Vlad said, "Isaac Blaze."

I gave him a bashful look. "Name dropper."

He punched his right fist into his left palm and started cracking his knuckles.

"This will be an immense pleasure for me," he said.

"That's great. But any chance we can speed this up? I've got a plane to catch."

Vlad switched hands and kept cracking knuckles. He was standing just a few feet to my right. His eyes were blazing and I could see him doing everything in his power to hold back his furious anger. He had to restrain himself. If he gave in now he'd never get out what he had to say. He said, "Who… is… this… man?"

I said nothing.

Vlad grinned again and then rushed at me, leaning down and shoving his head right in my face and sniffing me like a rabid dog. "It is a question that has plagued me ever since that day," he said.

I leaned away to my left, squinting my right eye closed as his saliva hit my cheek. Vlad lingered in my face. Growling. Fighting the urge. He had to restrain himself. He stood back up and stepped away again. "But I have come to realize I was wrong," he said. "The question should not be *who?* It should be *what?*"

I blew out my cheeks.

The male voice said, *Oh boy. Here comes the monologue.*

"It is an odd thing to be a torturer," Vlad said. "Because you start as the devil and you finish as the priest."

I exchanged a look with Isabel.

Vlad began to pace around my chair.

"I learned my trade quickly," he said. "And for over thirty years I have practiced and honed it. But even before my first year was up, I had begun to develop a sharp sense for discerning truth. For knowing *exactly* when a person has nothing left to give."

I sighed. "I'm not going to have time to get one of those giant Toblerones, am I?"

Vlad stopped behind me and slapped his right hand onto my left shoulder. He squeezed hard. I felt his fingernails dig into my skin through my shirt. "It seemed I had a talent," he said. "Yes, I was quite gifted, in fact. And the better I became the more I learned."

He let go of my shoulder and walked around in front of me again. He looked up at the ceiling, closed his eyes, and brought something to memory. He said, "Hope is in reality the worst of all evils because it prolongs the torments of man."

I exchanged another look with Isabel.

Vlad looked back down at me.

"You know this quote?" he asked. "It's Nietzsche. And he was right. Hope, courage, love, faith, they are nothing. They just prolong the pain. This is a truth I see for myself many times before. Those who believe, they suffer the most."

He looked at the table and gestured with his hand.

"I have thirty tools of confession. The 'Three Rows,' I call them. And do you know where most people achieve absolution?" "Is it number one?"

"Number four," he said. "In thirty years that has been all it takes. Only a rare few have needed number five, and only one man has ever surpassed that. He was very special. Truly exceptional. But even he only made it to number eight. In thirty years never has anybody gone past the first row. *Never.*"

He paused and his gritted his teeth and looked at me.

"And then thirty-six of them did."

THIRTY

VLAD REACHED INTO his trouser pocket and pulled out a folded piece of card. He opened it up and then shoved it into my face. It was a photograph. Black and white, and just like Hays's.

Except I was in it.

The photograph had been taken by a street camera, which judging from its downward angle had been mounted on a tall pole. The image was slightly blurred and had been taken in the middle of a bazaar in Istanbul, Turkey. I had been caught in a three-quarters profile, in the midst of a large crowd, looking back over my shoulder.

Vlad said, "Five years I show this picture. I show it to my friends, my colleagues—I even show it to my sheep."

The male voice said, *Sheep?*

The female voice said, *His victims.*

Oh.

Vlad took the photo out of my face and stared down at it. He said, "Five years I ask *who is this man?* And five years I get the same answer. One-hundred-fifty-three sheep and nobody know you."

I shrugged. "I don't have Facebook."

Vlad kept staring at the photo. "But then we catch people from Istanbul. We catch all of them three months ago. And they *do* know you." He gritted his teeth again and crushed the photograph in his fist and then he spun one-hundred-and-eighty degrees and threw the photograph at the table like a baseball-pitcher. He gave it everything he had and screamed after it. Then he started stomping around in front of me, two steps one way, two steps the other. He kept his eyes glued to me. His face was all red and aggravated. He said, "Thirty-six sheep. Man, woman, child, whatever. They all say *nothing*. Not one. They endure *everything* I can give. All the rows. All of them. Nobody gives you to me. And you know why?"

I said nothing.

He jabbed his finger at me and stepped in and screamed in my face. "Because they fear *you* more than they fear *me*!"

I leaned away again. I saw Isabel looking at me with questions in her eyes. I began to say something but Vlad thrust a hand into my face, cutting me off.

"But *today*," he said, "today I will finally get my answer. Today, Isaac Blaze, I will finally learn *what* you are." His grip tightened. He shook my head around and then threw it back. Then used the same hand to gesture at Isabel. He said, "I must thank greatly the lady for helping in this regard."

I recentered my head and spit out the taste of Vlad's hand. I raised an eyebrow. "Yeah, and why's that?"

Vlad grinned. "She give us way to track you. Show us where you are within five feet."

I looked at Isabel. "You put a tracker on Hays's car?"

She shrugged. "I was curious where you'd go."

"How'd you know I'd take the Jag?"

"Please."

Vlad put his hands on his knees and leaned down and looked between us both.

"This one I like," he said.

"You're not her type," I said.

"He's not anyone's type," Isabel said. "Ugly is universally declined."

"Hey, come on. That's not his fault, is it Vlad? Just one of those *unfortunalities.*"

Vlad stood there taking fire from two directions. He was taken aback for a moment by our whole attitude, but then he rolled his neck again and leered lasciviously at Isabel.

"We have girls like you in Ukraine," he said. "They unwilling too at first. The young ones the most. But over time they learn to be willing. And you too will be made willing."

Isabel said nothing. She didn't need to. Her pupils had turned to sharp pin-points, magnifying her glowing ghostly blue irises. I saw Vlad dying a thousand deaths in them. So did Vlad. He went very quiet. Eventually he said, "OK, I will do you courtesy of punishing sins in order. *Herashor?*"

Isabel said nothing.

Vlad said, "In meantime, please enjoy entertainment." He nodded at the table. "Is acquired taste, but I think you like number nine."

Isabel looked at the table.

Vlad smiled and turned to me.

"Because that's when we cut out his tongue."

The male voice said, *The hell it is.*

The female voice said, *Need a plan here, Isaac.*

I looked at Isabel. Putting aside the fact that she actually seemed to be liking the idea of me getting my tongue hacked out, the way I saw it, it was me and her against Vlad. And while we were tied up, he had Quasimodo and his twin

206

brother weighing him down. I looked down at my left shirt sleeve. It was rolled up to my elbow. It was also one of the best places to conceal something. Like a bobby pin. I could feel the one I'd put there before leaving Armand's. I just needed to get to it.

Vlad said, "Number nine. After that there will be no more talking."

I contemplated that for a second.

Then I turned to Isabel.

"You know I haven't forgotten about that seventeen-hundred bucks."

"Seventeen-hundred-*thirty-two,*" she said.

I smiled and turned back to Vlad.

Vlad snorted. "Yes, always with the jokes."

"Ileana seemed to like them."

The swing came fast and hard. A violent blow. Savage and powerful and well deserved. Vlad's fist smashed into my left cheek and sent my head reeling to the right. He used so much power that he ended up stumbling off balance and a few feet from where he began. I coughed and spat out a stream of blood. I looked up to face him. He was seething at me like a bloodhound.

"You don't speak her name!" he yelled.

I said nothing. Just sniffed up and spat out some more blood, and then smirked at him. Which of course made him more mad, which is what I wanted, but then he realized that, and quickly collected himself. He snorted again.

"Time for jokes has passed," he said.

He walked to the table and made a show of picking up one of the instruments. He moved his hand slowly over the top row, counting from right to left, until he reached the last but one. The ninth instrument. His hand stopped right above it and then daintily picked it up. It was a short-headed scalpel. Vlad held it up above his face and watched the light glisten off the blade's edge. That thing was going to have no problem slicing through my tongue. He looked back at me and smiled.

The male voice said, *Only one way out of this one.*

Easy for you to say, I said.

Vlad replaced the scalpel and then drew his hand back along the top row, right to left, until he reached the beginning, and the first item.

I felt a pulse of adrenaline hit my stomach. I glanced at Isabel. She understood.

Vlad picked up the first instrument. It was the exact same instrument as number eleven and twenty-one, the first instruments in the second and third rows respectively. It was a ten-inch long metal spike. Which made it fairly easy to see where this was going. Vlad was going to drive that thing about nine inches into me, probably through a joint, and definitely through a pressure point, or bundle of nerve fibers. The spike would then stay there, constantly radiating pain waves, while Vlad worked his way through the next nine instruments, whereupon we'd then reach row two, and the next spike would be driven in, doubling the underlying pain, which although would be physically unbearable, would be nothing in comparison to the psychological torture of knowing that even if you made it through this row as well, there was still another row left. I figured the first spike would go through a knee cap. The shoulder was also a good option, or maybe under the armpit.

The male voice said, *Not something we need to find out, Isaac.*

The female voice said, *Yeah, do it, already.*

I pinched my shoulder blades and brought my hands together behind me.

Vlad picked up the hammer. He turned around. He licked his lips and hit the end of the spike three times with the hammer.

Tink, tink, tink.

I gripped my right hand with my left and started squeezing hard. My quads tensed up and my feet kicked out and the handcuffs pulled tight against my wrists.

Vlad stepped toward me.

I looked away from him and stared at the door, hoping to hell he'd choose the kneecap.

Vlad walked up to my chair. But then he went behind me. He hammered on the spike again.

Tink, tink, tink.

I gritted my teeth. Kept squeezing my hand.

Isabel was watching us closely. Sitting still, not moving a muscle.

Vlad stayed standing behind me.

I kept staring at the door.

Then Vlad came and stood in front of me. Three feet away, with the spike and hammer in front of his chest. He hit them together for the fourth time.

Tink, tink—CRACK.

My right thumb broke.

It popped straight out of place, crunching inwards, and allowing my whole hand to fold into itself, at which point I released my grip, and the bracelet flew straight off my wrist, and all of the stored tension unwound, and I kicked Vlad in the testicles as hard as I could. His legs were wide open and my foot flew up between them and smacked any chance of procreation right out of him.

The hammer and spike fell to the ground.

Vlad doubled right over and I kicked him in the face. And then Vlad was on his hands and knees, vomiting wildly, and Isabel, who was already standing up, wrapped one of those long chains around his neck.

It all happened in a flash. Less than eight seconds from *pop* to headlock.

The two goons didn't know what to do. They were slow to react and clumsy when they did. It took them a full three seconds just to get their rifles pointed at Isabel. Which of course was useless since she had Vlad in a headlock and was using him as a human shield. His face was a bloody mess.

Isabel said, "Put them down."

Russia replied with random noise.

I was making noise, too. I was sprawled in the chair in a crazy awkward position. The left side of my body was still tied up and being pulled under the chair, and the right side of me was loose but sporting a broken thumb and over-stretched groin.

Vlad began to shout something, but Isabel tightened the chain around his neck and strangled him into silence. Tweedledum then stuck his rifle into my neck and told her he'd kill me, to which Isabel just smiled and told him to go ahead. That led to a brief standoff, but then, after about a minute and half, Tweedledee got his own idea, and shouted the plan to his comrade. He spoke fast and with a lisp and I couldn't really understand him very well. But then again, I didn't need to. After that earlier display with the keys, I had no doubt it was a terrible idea. In any case, the rifle did come out of my neck.

The two goons started walking forward. They retrained their rifles on Isabel, and edged toward her slowly, each one coming around one side of my chair, and then moving closer together as they passed me.

Isabel backed into the corner.

The female voice said, *Get on with it, Isaac.*

I turned in my seat and thrust my right hand into my left elbow. It was shooting with pain but I pushed past it and rummaged through the shirt fold, using my index and third fingers to locate the bobby pin. Then I reached back around the chair and jammed the bobby pin against the handcuff, and although it did scratch around for a moment, it fell into the keyhole pretty quickly. Had Tweedledum been in my position, he would have been screwed. Not that he would have had a bobby pin. Or for that matter the flexibility to reach back around the chair. In any case, in the time it took me to do all that, the goons had no time to get to Isabel.

The handcuff came loose.

I lunged at the guy on the right. Broke his neck, and in one motion had the other guy in a guillotine choke. He ended up bent over with his head against my chest and my arms linked beneath his neck. I pulled. Hard. Waited for the *click* and then let go. He flopped down on top of his comrade.

"Guess the bell-tower's going to be quiet tonight," I said.

Isabel watched the whole thing from the corner. I took a bow in her direction and said, "You're welcome."

"Whatever," she said.

She was still pulling on the chains and draining the last bit of life out of Vlad. His head was a beetroot and his lips had turned a dark blue. The last thing he saw was me tipping an imaginary hat to him. Then the chains crushed tighter and Isabel finished him with a violent jerk. Vlad collapsed onto the ground.

Isabel said, "Now help me out of these."

I shrugged. "Well, if you're as good as you think you are—"

"Just get them off."

THIRTY-ONE

Y THUMB WAS in a pretty bad way. Technically, nothing was broken. I had just dislocated it. But that didn't mean the pain wasn't terrible. The small adrenaline-burst from before had worn off and the pain was getting steadily worse. Having said that, it was a familiar pain. After all, that wasn't the first time I'd intentionally dislocated my thumb to escape from handcuffs. Not by a long way. And, by this point in my life I'm basically an expert on resetting joints. So I knew what I had to do. I curled my left hand's fingers very loosely around my right thumb, and then I took a breath, and gritted my teeth, and tightened my grip, and yanked my thumb up, stretching it out and realigning the bones, and then I snapped them back into place. I tried to bury the accompanying scream but it came growling out of me and echoed around the giant sewer pipe we were walking through.

Isabel snorted at me.

I blew out my cheeks and looked at her.

"Pain threshold that low, we'd have never made it to number nine."

I said, "You're welcome."

"And what am I thankful for?"

"Saving your ass, for one."

She shook her head. "You owed me a favor, remember?"

I shook out my hand and wiggled my thumb about. It still hurt like hell but it was working.

Isabel said, "Be honest though, you *were* scared."

"Of *Vlad*? Uh-uh."

"You sure about that?"

I nodded. "Torture's all about theatrics. You want to really scare someone, you've got to go all out."

"And an underground chamber where no one will hear you scream isn't good enough?"

"It's a start, but see, *The Three Rows*, that's just not a scary name."

"I don't know, some of those tools were pretty sharp."

"Yeah but laying them all out on the table, that's about as mundane as it gets."

"So what would you do?"

"I'd use something else. Something bold. Way I see it, a torture device needs to make a statement. You bring it out, and that's it. Nuff said."

"Example?"

"Well I'll tell you this, if he'd have brought out a small guillotine, I'd have been pretty damn scared."

"Yeah? How small?"

We kept on walking, side by side, retracing my route in. Sixty-eight steps from the chamber, we made a left turn and then stayed on that bearing. Underfoot, the murky water started getting thicker.

Isabel said, "So what's your deal, anyway?"

"My deal?"

"You really hear voices?"

"Be hard to smell them."

"You always talk with them out loud?"

"I thought I was alone."

"One male, one female?"

"Yup."

"They got names?"

"What? No, that would just be weird."

Isabel paused for a few steps and then said, "There's more to the Hays thing, isn't there?"

"Like you wouldn't believe."

"Care to elaborate?"

"Not particularly."

"Whatever."

We walked on.

"You got the time?" I asked.

Isabel checked her watch. "3:42," she said. "About seventy-five from O'Hare."

"And about an hour from the Near North Side," I said.

"Rules out the West then. And anything North would put us nowhere. The southeast landfill is most likely. Easy access for a van too."

The female voice said, *Girl knows her stuff. Looks like Harriett did a good job with this one.*

Isabel said, "So you and Vlad…"

I shrugged. "I assume you did your homework?"

"Vladimir Kurshenkov. Used to work for a group in the Ukraine. Standard trafficking operation. Small scale but high-value cargo. Did plenty of work over the Trans-Siberian area.

Big market for drugs and weapons. Even bigger one for girls. Then he spent the past two years working private security."

"Right. But before any of that, Vlad was Ukraine Intelligence."

"He was a good guy?"

"I guess. So long as you consider SZRU to be *good,* that is."

Isabel said nothing.

"Guy had two major talents," I said. "Interrogation and logistics."

"And you knew him from way back then?"

"*Knew* would be a bit of a stretch. We met briefly about five years ago. Tverskaya Street, Moscow."

"Oh really? And just what exactly did you do in such a short space of time that caused a man to chase after you for five years?"

I turned to her and leaned in secretively. "All right," I said. "As long as it stays between us girls."

Isabel scowled back.

"I stole a note from his wallet," I said.

"*Sure,*" she said. "That guy chases you all this time just for stealing some cash."

"Ah but it was important cash. *Special.*"

Isabel gave me look. She was unconvinced.

I sighed. "Well… I might have slept with his wife, too."

"Might have?"

We passed the point I had regained consciousness and started plodding through the thick gunge underfoot. Fifty yards later, we heard the sound of the freeway.

Isabel said, "That'll be the Edens Expressway."

"Which means we're almost out of here," I said.

We proceeded cautiously. We were both wearing solid

boots, but the gunge stank and had almost no purchase, so neither of us could afford to lose our footing. Pride was of paramount importance. As a result, the last fifty meters of tunnel turned into a ten minute slip-and-slide race.

Isabel said, "What was with all the scars?"

"Let's just say the Odessa Mafia doesn't take failure well. Especially when they find out you're working for SZRU."

Isabel looked at me.

"Wait, you outed an undercover agent?"

"Not intentionally. But yeah."

"And *they* gave him all those scars?"

"It was pound-of-flesh sort of thing. They owned him after that."

"Wow," she said. "You ever lose a wink of sleep over that?"

"Just the next night. With his wife."

Isabel rolled her eyes.

"What?" I said. "She was lonely. And she was married to Vlad."

The end of the pipe was jail-barred. A broken door lock was sticking out of the sludge below. We pushed through the door and emptied into the south-east dumpsite that Isabel had predicted.

Putting aside the smell and gunk and the fact that we were literally standing in shit, the place had a certain charm. A silky fog was hanging in the air and moonlight silvered the haze. Mountains of waste towered around us, and I saw Isabel taken aback by the same thing all first time landfill visitors are disturbed by. It's not the heaps of waste that's the issue. You never see any horrified gasps or emotional outbursts or sudden realizations of environmental responsibility. What affects people most are the thousands of children's toys.

Isabel looked back down the sewer pipe.

"What the hell was that place?" she said.

"Just another part of Chicago's fascinating sewer history," I said.

"Fascinating? *Really?*"

"Well the city *was* built on a swamp. See, way back in the early nineteenth century, Chicago didn't have streets so much as it had impassable slop-filled troughs. It was a consequence of being only a few feet above the water level of Lake Michigan."

Isabel's eyelids dropped halfway over her eyes. She was looking at me like a teenager in a high school geology glass.

I said, "The cost of digging down was deemed too expensive so Chicago had to be raised up instead. Some buildings were jacked up, others were literally rolled to new locations. New foundations were laid and sewer pipes were installed, and then everything was built over with roads. But even a relatively small amount of rainfall could cause sewage overflows into the Chicago River and other waterways. And before long, sewage started pouring into Lake Michigan, thus polluting the city's only source of drinking water. But even the so-called *greatest engineering feet in modern times*—the reversal of the Chicago River in 1900—wasn't enough to plug the problem. So–"

"So the Deep Tunnel Project. Yeah, I know. In 1975, and it won't be done for ten or fifteen years."

I was a little thrown by that. As was the male voice who had been narrating to me the whole time. I said, "OK, but what you're forgetting is how bad the 70s were for the mob."

"The Chicago Outfit?"

"You bet. Law enforcement was penetrating them from all angles, and before long they were hemorrhaging cash."

"And they thought moving product through the tunnels would stop that?"

"That was the idea, yeah. They used their pull at the city planner's office to quite literally make a drug pipeline. Moving operations underground meant just that. There are storerooms all over the Deep Tunnels."

Isabel said, "But that didn't work."

"Not as well as they'd hoped, anyway. They reduced the bleeding, but they couldn't stop it."

"So what did they do?"

"What do you think? They sold off some assets."

Isabel looked out at the landfill. "You think the mob owned this place?"

I nodded. "What, you never watched *The Sopranos*? It's classic waste management disposal."

Isabel said nothing.

"The Odessa Mafia was making all sorts of purchases back then. The 70s were conversely a good time for them and they were looking to branch out."

"I thought they set up in New York and LA?"

"Yeah, that's where they are *now*, but they were here for a short time, too. In any case, it took them about twenty years to really get going here in the States."

"By which time a certain baldy at Ukrainian intelligence had been assigned some undercover work."

I shrugged. "I don't know if he was *always* bald, but yeah, he'd have been well aware of all these facilities."

Isabel said, "Well use this place or not, they really shouldn't have left it with those two laggards."

"Way I see it this is exactly where they belong."

Isabel shot her eyebrows. "Huh. You know what, that was pretty interesting."

"Told you."

We turned our backs to the tunnel and looked out at the landfill, again. In front of us were two tracks of deep footprints that disappeared off to the right and behind a garbage heap. The prints were slowly puffing back out and between them was a continuous double line. It was a trail that, of course, had to be followed, and Isabel and I found a transit van waiting at the finish. Its fender and entire right side were bashed in. It was originally maroon but was now also sporting some silver stripes courtesy of the Jag. The tires were worse for wear, a side mirror was missing, and the windshield was cracked. There was a logo on the side belonging to the landfill company.

Isabel said. "Well, it's not much, but it should be enough to get us out of here."

She started walking toward it.

"*Us?*" I called after her.

"So you're staying here, then?"

Nothing to say to that.

Isabel slid open the side door and rummaged around for a moment. She came out with a battered leather jacket, which she put on, and then she threw me my deck jacket. I checked the pockets. Hays's photo was still there. As was his money and my passport. But I had lost Sophia's knife.

I opened the driver's side door and scraped off my boots using the door frame. I got in and found the van's seats to be less than accommodating. My ass had been spoiled having driven Hays's car all day. I checked the fuel gauge. Barely an eighth of a tank left. I shook my head.

The male voice said, *Truly useless.*

I started the van. Mercifully, it turned over on the second try. The pedals were covered in crap and were stinking up the cab. It wasn't going to be a great ride.

Isabel slammed the side door shut and trudged around to the passenger door. She scraped sludge off her boots like I had and then climbed in beside me. She took out a baseball cap from her jacket and nestled it on her head. Then she settled down in her seat and turned to me and said, "Step on it, would you?"

I shot her a look. *Excuse me?*

She shot me one back. *You're excused. Now drive. *Finger snap.**

THIRTY-TWO

THE RADIO WAS tuned to local news and blaring out continuous updates on the recent events at O'Hare. The report confirmed that there had been seven casualties. Details of the attack had not been made public yet, only that it had taken place in the arrivals lounge. Speculations that Ukrainian ambassador, Dima Kolochev, had been the target were unconfirmed, and his condition was as yet undisclosed. All flights were either cancelled or severely delayed. Details were to follow. I turned the volume down and looked over at Isabel.

She shrugged. "Like I said, there was a problem at Customs."

"Busy day," I said.

She smiled and waved it away.

"So what did he do?"

"Enough to get me involved," Isabel replied.

"Who put the hit out?"

"Does it matter?"

"Might."

"How so?"

"Well you did get caught."

Her smile vanished. "I didn't get caught."

"OK."

A long silence followed. I just stared out of the window and drove on. Isabel stared out of her window too, but about fifteen seconds after I started whistling, I heard her grit her teeth.

"I know what you're doing," she said.

I rolled my eyes toward her and whistled a couple of notes at an innocently higher pitch: *Me?*

Isabel scowled and turned away and looked back out of her window.

She lasted less than a minute.

"All right, look," she said. "That guy was out. Seven bodyguards and still he went down. Eight, ten seconds tops. Then it was game over. Your friend Vlad didn't know what the hell was going on."

"So what happened?"

Isabel didn't answer. Just shook her head for a while. But then she told me.

"You're joking," I said. I started laughing.

Isabel said, "It's not funny."

"It's a little funny."

"It's unbelievable is, what it is. I mean seriously, what are the odds?"

"So then what happened?"

"What do you think happened? Next thing I know I've got all seven bodyguards to deal with."

I thought back to how cautiously Tweedledum had opened up that storeroom.

The male voice said, *No wonder they were scared.*

Isabel said, "Unbelievable. Pure bad luck. Nothing more."

"Yeah," I said. "Until Vlad took out that picture and…"

Isabel grinned. "I was talking before he even asked the question."

I shook my head.

Isabel said, "And by the way, what was all that Istanbul stuff about? Thirty-six people? All the rows? I'd have given you up in a heartbeat."

"*You* did."

The van's engine strained as I picked up the speed. We passed a sign for a gas station. Five miles until we got there. Isabel turned and rested her elbow on the door, looking out into the distance and biting at the end of her thumb to conceal a smile.

Five miles later, we stopped for gas at a small station. It was pretty much deserted, but it had fuel pumps and a convenience store, which was all we needed. I got out and filled up the van. Isabel chose to stay in the car.

Inside the station I loaded up three bags of food along with a few bottles of water, a pack of tissues, and a roll of duct tape. I was wearing Isabel's cap to cover the blood on my head, and, although the clerk's eyes were following me around the store, he wasn't really paying much attention. The red counter he was stood behind had an old TV on top and that was where his focus really lay. The TV was blurting out the same report as the radio. The O'Hare situation was making big news. I looked out of the store's big front window. Isabel was still sitting in the van and for the first time she didn't seem *on*. She looked relaxed.

The male voice said, *Six SWAT guys, twelve SAD analysts,*

Gravel Voice, Hays, a Ukrainian ambassador, his seven body-guards, <u>and</u> Vlad.

Hell of a girl, I said.

I walked up to the counter and asked Hi-I'm-Greg—the red-eyed night-station supervisor—if there was a phone I could use. Hi-I'm-Greg kept his eyes on the TV and pointed to a lone phone booth outside.

I said, "It work?"

He shrugged.

"Thanks a lot."

I paid him for the goods and walked out. I opened the driver's door and chucked the bags onto the middle seat. Isabel looked down at my selection of junk foods. She was unimpressed.

"They were all out of quinoa," I said.

I took the duct tape and got to work on strapping up my thumb.

Isabel yawned. "So what's the plan Stan?"

"Plan is I need to get to London."

"The Hays stuff?"

"The Hays stuff."

"Any chance that transport goes on to Shanghai?"

"Could."

I tore off the strip of duct tape with my teeth and then chucked the roll back on the seat. I tested out my thumb by trying to scrunch up one of the paper bags using just my right hand. Not great. But it seemed to be functional enough.

Isabel said, "Well?"

"Well, what?"

"Shanghai."

"What about it?"

"You gonna help a girl out, or not?"

"What's in it for me?"

"I'll owe you a favor."

I tilted my head to one side and scrunched my face little.

Isabel said, "All right then what do you want?"

My mind wandered a bit with that one but then I said. "OK, I'll take the favor."

"Great. So how are we getting out?"

"I need to make a phone call."

THIRTY-THREE

I WALKED OVER TO the lone phone booth. It was not in good condition.

The female voice said, *Dali should've just painted one of these. Phonebooth Toilet.*

The male voice said, *Who are we calling, anyway?*

Our new best friend, I said.

I thought we were your only friends?

True dat, the female voice said.

Hold on you don't mean…

That's exactly who I mean, I said.

I thought we were going to save that nugget for something bigger?

Who says we can only use it once?

Isaac, you sly son of bitch.

I picked up the receiver, put some of the change in the slot, and punched in a number on what felt like the biggest keypad in the world. The ringtone shifted away from the norm after the fifth ring. It went to a slightly higher pitch against a background of light crackling—the result of a line-tap and location-trace. Ten rings total and then an animated male voice came through at rapid pace.

"What it is, *what it is?* My man. Isaac Blaze. Figured you'd be getting in touch, soon."

I said, "I need a number."

"You look like hell."

I looked around. My eyes settled on one of the gas station's outside CCTV cameras. It was pointing right at me. It moved up and down, giving me *the nod*.

"Show-off," I said. I turned back to the phone booth but the line appeared to go dead for a moment. "Marcel?"

The line stayed quiet and then a wolf-whistle erupted out of the receiver. "*Damn*," Marcel said. "Mega babe at your seven."

I turned around again and saw Isabel leaning against the front end of the van. The CCTV camera was pointed straight at her. So was Greg's nose. Isabel's hair was floating on a gust of wind and a she was taking a long pull on a bottle of water. Her neck was stretched up and long.

The male voice said, *Luckiest van in the world.*

Isabel finished her drink and caught me staring. She threw a gesture that, among other things, said *Hurry up.*

I gestured back: *Going as fast as I can.*

Marcel said, "Aw, man. Don't tell me. She's with *you*?"

I shrugged happily at the camera.

"Man, you must have been kissed by a wizard or something. Seriously, how the hell do you keep lucking into these women?"

I turned back to the phone booth again. "What are you complaining about? You've got Laquonda."

"That shit's been over for time, man. And that's some top-shelf stuff right there."

I said nothing.

"Hey, man, you know I only got your best interests in mind, right?" said Marcel.

"Yeah, I know."

"Good. Now, you got a name for me, or what?"

"George Kane."

"Yeeeaaaah, now we're talking. Bout time for this motherfucker, too. Dude sells drugs and gets a billion dollars cause he calls it *pharmaceuticals*. My cousin does the same thing and gets twenty-five to life."

I had nothing to say to that.

Marcel said, "All right, I got you. How you wanna play it?"

"You remember Venice?"

"Oh-nine or '12?"

"Oh-nine."

"Cool." He started laughing. "Damn, this fool ain't gonna know what hit him."

"He's just lucky I need a favor. You saw what I sent you, right?"

Marcel whistled. "Dude has problems for sure. I mean, *a Dalmatian*? That's just messed up. And who was the other guy, anyway?"

"His Royal Highness Sheikh Zayed Hussein bin Ali al-Hamad."

Marcel whistled and tsked. He said, "So tell me, man, what's the world's luckiest bastard up to now?"

"As a matter of fact, London's calling."

I heard a loud beep on Marcel's end of the line. He went quiet for a moment and then said, "Yo, Isaac, that guy Hays? Says here the Po-Po just brought in his car."

"Let me guess, it was totalled?"

"To say the damn least."

"Word to the wise, never take your eyes off the road."

"Hold the phone, you saying *you* was driving?"

"Still think I'm lucky?"

"Hey man, I don't see no bandages. Just a fine-ass girl."

I laughed.

Marcel said, "Aight, patching you through to Kane, now."

THIRTY-FOUR

ATLANTA SENATOR GEORGE Kane was two years into his term. He was one of the rarer breeds of politician in that laypeople outside of his home state had actually heard of him. And even stranger—they actually liked him.

What happened was that, in 1995, a small start-up called Silverton Pharmaceuticals began making waves in the pharmaceutical and biotechnological industry. Its twenty-three-year-old director was somewhat of a prodigy and his innovations quickly led to the company's becoming one of the largest and most profitable in the sector. But Kane didn't stop there. He kept building on that success and began branching out into other industries. Silverton Pharmaceuticals became just one subsidiary of the Silverton Group. The group's holdings rapidly increased and diversified through a series of mergers and acquisitions such that it now dealt in everything from children's toys to weapons manufacture. When the group went public in 2006, Kane made a reported $28 billion. And that $28 billion was the reason that Kane was so beloved.

Upon making his fortune, Kane began a spending spree that attracted worldwide attention. "*What will he buy next?*"

and *"Look what he's bought now!"* became the strap lines for many TV and radio shorts that thrust Kane into the public eye. From a private island paradise to massive weekend trips to Vegas, the thirty-three-year-old was living large.

But Kane made sure to spread it around, too.

He routinely provided steak dinners at soup kitchens and would make huge donations to charities. When the financial crises hit in '08, he bought out over one hundred collapsed mortgages, allowing all of those people to not only keep their homes but to own them, outright. One time he walked into a hospital and took care of every single patient's bill. And, while Kane did vanish from the spotlight for a while, when he came back, he came back big—with political ambitions and a clear vision for the future. And with the public's goodwill in his hands, he secured his place in the US senate at the very next election.

And I had the power to change all of that.

Atlanta was an hour ahead of Chicago, meaning dawn was already well underway there. The phone rang five times and then the senator came on the line.

"Kane," he said. He sounded alert.

I said nothing.

Kane said, "Hello?"

"This is the part where your lizard brain tells you everything you need to know, and why, when I tell you that you have ten seconds to clear the room, you'll do just that," I said.

"What? Who is this?"

"Seven seconds."

"Who is this? How did you get this number?"

"Five seconds."

"*I'm alone, dammit!* Now who are you?"

"Put me on speaker."

"Why?"

"So you can see your phone screen."

I heard the acoustics of the line change.

"You done it?" I asked.

"You're on speaker."

"You watching the screen?"

"Yes."

"Good. Keep watching."

Kane went quiet. Then, "MOTHERFU—"

I pulled the receiver away from my ear. Kane was yelling at the top of his lungs and the expletives kept flying for a whole minute. It was actually quite impressive. Funny, too. Eventually though a sentence did manage to make it through all the cussing and Kane said, "Listen here you son of a bitch! You're not going to get away with this. You hear me? Who the hell do you think you are?"

"Does it matter?"

"You're damn right it matters. If I'm going to be fucked, I want to know who's standing behind me."

I laughed. "You know, it never ceases to amaze me," I said.

"*What?*" He was still yelling.

"How brave a man can get when there's a phone between him and his adversary."

"Listen here, asshole—"

"No, *you* listen, George. This isn't one of your TV debates. You can't just talk tough and then not back it up. This is the real world. You piss me off and I'll kill you. Then I'll call CNN just for the hell of it."

Kane quieted down, but I could hear him seething down the phone.

"Look," he said. "I know how this works. Just tell me what you want."

The male voice said, *Well that was easy*.

The female voice said, *Like he has a choice*.

Kane said, "Hello? Hello?"

I said, "It's simple, George. I need a plane and you've got one."

"You want my *jet*?" He was back to yelling at the top of his lungs and fired off another round of f-bombs.

I held the phone away again and started laughing.

The female voice said, *This guy is something else*.

Kane shouted down the line, "There's no way I'm giving you my jet!"

"You mean '*One* of my jets'," I said. "And yes, you will. In fact you're going to lend me the one at Wright-Patterson."

"But I can't just—"

"One pilot, two passengers, no questions. Shanghai via London. You've got five hours."

I hung up.

THIRTY-FIVE

I WALKED BACK TO the van and grabbed a water bottle from the cab.

Isabel was still leaning on the front of the van. I perched next to her.

"Well?" she said.

"We've got transport."

"Shanghai?"

"Via London."

"We're flying?"

"In style."

"You do realize O'Hare's going to have every other airport on alert, right?"

"I wouldn't worry about it."

Isabel raised an eyebrow.

I said, "How well do you know your senators?"

"Give me a state."

"How about Georgia?"

"Kane? Yeah I just read an article about him. Biotech, right? Forbes has his net worth estimated at around twenty-four billion dollars."

"So you've heard of him."

She shrugged. "He'd make a good target," she said. "Or client, I guess."

"Or resource," I said.

"You have something on him?"

"Thanks to Hays."

"What is it?"

"Let's just say Cruella de Vil ain't got nothing on George Kane."

"He's into… *dogs*?"

"Dalmatians."

Isabel shook her head, disgusted. "Typical," she said.

I drained my water bottle and tossed it into a trash can by the fuel pump.

I said, "You know there is still one thing I don't get."

Isabel finished her water and threw it into the trash after mine.

"Shoot," she said.

"Why did you go on the mission?"

"What, you mean with the SWAT team?"

I nodded. "See, I get the whole SAD infiltration thing. That's what got you to Hays. But going on the mission makes no sense."

Isabel smiled. "No choice," she said.

"Hhn?"

"Remember that big monitor they had?" she asked.

"What about it?"

"First thing I see when I step off the elevator? Your face in twenty-foot HD."

"That's a whole lot of handsome."

"The SWAT guys, the analysts, Gravel Voice, they're all standing in the middle of the work floor, looking up at it, and

Hays is standing below it, halfway through a briefing. I come off the elevator and twenty heads spin round to look at me."

"That had to be unnerving."

"To say the least," she said. "Those SWAT guys were locked and loaded."

"Good job you had ID then."

"Yup. But then again that had its own consequences. They had a class-five-agency priority target and I was a senior field officer."

"Meaning you couldn't just hang back and wait for the SWAT guys to leave."

She nodded. "Next thing I know I'm taking point on the OP."

"Huh."

Isabel said, "All right, now I've got a question."

"The big deal about Hays?"

She nodded. "What did you find out?"

"Well, for one, there's no better coding system than bad handwriting."

Isabel raised her eyebrow again.

I pushed off the front of the van and walked around it, kicking each of the tires as I went in order to check their pressure.

Isabel said, "Well, at least tell me where we're going."

"Wright-Patt," I called back. I finished checking the tires and opened the driver's door. I took off Isabel's cap and chucked it into the cab.

Isabel was still leaning against the front of the van, staring back at me with her mouth slightly open. "You're kidding, right?"

"I figure five hours," I said. "Traffic should be light."

"I'm not going to Wright-Patt."

I smiled. "So you're staying here, then?"

I got in the cab and closed my door. I put my seatbelt on and started the engine.

The male voice said, *You know if Kane double-crosses us we're going to have a big problem.*

The female voice said, *Yeah, but he doesn't have the balls.*

Isabel got in beside me. She did not look happy. She grabbed her cap and pulled it down over her eyes. Then she pushed her seat back and put her feet up on the dash and folded her arms.

I said, "You know we're switching at the halfway point."

"Yeah," she said. "Keep telling yourself that."

* * *

Three and a half hours later, I was still driving. About two hours into the journey, we'd pulled into a big service station. We couldn't very well have kept driving the beat-up van, so we got some more food and then stole the plainest sedan we could find. We had both been pretty quiet up until that point, but we started talking afterwards. Mostly we exchanged stories about hits gone wrong. I asked her about Panama '09 and got exactly nothing back. Same went for Shanghai and Item 86.

In fact, for all the questions I asked, I somehow ended up telling her all about Cairo, instead. "…so now the woman is staring at this wire cage and, you know, she doesn't know *what* to do. And the guy, he's just standing there like everything's normal, right?"

Isabel was laughing.

"Anyway," I said. "Eventually this guy turns around and sees the rest of us watching in disbelief, at which point the light bulb goes off, and he holds up his hand and starts nodding like *Ah, yeah, I see the problem*."

"And that's when he pulls out the passport?"

"Slaps it straight on the counter, right next to the cage."

"So what did the woman do?"

"She opened it up," I said.

"And?"

"What do you mean *and*? And inside there's a 40mm head shot of the chicken."

Isabel was in stitches.

I said, "Turns out the guy was trying to move the number-three-ranked cockfighter in the whole of Egypt. He was part of some big circuit. Cairo police had been after them for years. Whole thing blew up my exit strategy."

I'd estimated pretty well. Just over five hours after leaving the gas station, we finally came up on Wright-Patterson Air Force Base. We were about five or ten klicks east of Dayton, Ohio, and the base loomed.

The first gate we came to was a big black thing that was covered with warning signs. It was a general access point and only open between 0530 and 1830. There was a security hut just inside and, although one of the officers gave us a full checking-out, Kane's name got us past without undue hassle.

Kane had strong ties to the Air Force and especially with this particular installation. Wright-Patterson houses a major USAF Medical Center and is also home to the Air Force Institute of Technology. Kane's Silverton Group designed and equipped them with the most cutting-edge advances, something that earned him plenty of clout with the US armed forces.

We drove in cautiously. The place was huge. In addition to the Medical Center and Institute of Technology, Wright-Patterson had two thousand families stationed on base as well as a myriad of historic spectacles. It was where the Wright Brothers had unlocked the final secrets of applied aerodynamics and developed the 1905 Flyer. We passed the museum, the hospital, and the Materiel Command Headquarters.

It was the second gate that gave us trouble.

It was huge, solid steel, and doubly guarded with two security outposts. Behind it was a vast field with a lot of things happening way off in the distance. One set of fatigues came out from each box, leaving their respective partners behind. They were both heavily armed. Rifles slung over shoulders. One of them held a clipboard. He came round to my side of the van. The other guy went to Isabel's. I rolled down the window. The guy put one hand on the roof and leaned down to check us out. His name tag said *Phillson*.

He said, "Help you folks?"

He had a harsh voice and no accent. He knew we didn't belong and I could see him judging the situation and making threat assessments in rapid time.

I said, "You're expecting us."

He shook his head. "You're not on the list."

I looked down at his clipboard. He hadn't checked it once.

He said, "Nothing scheduled for 1100 hours."

I said, "Senator Kane's orders. You've got a fixed-wing waiting for its payload."

Kane's name meant nothing to him.

The other guy completed his circuit of the car and came and stood next to Phillson. They both stood back from the window and whispered. The other guy was taller and built like a fortress. He was holding his rifle diagonally across his body, his right forearm rippling over it. Phillson's rifle was hanging loose in front of him. He was holding up the clipboard with one hand and making a sweeping motion over it with his other. These guys were the exact opposite of the Gruesome Twosome from the landfill. Smart for one. Competant for another. Showered was another word. But most importantly: Trained. They knew how to handle themselves. They knew how to handle their weapons. They both kept looking back at me. Then Phillson said something with a lot of emphasis, after which they both shook their heads at each other.

The big guy leaned down and said, "Nothing on the list. Time for you two to head on out."

I shook my head. "Sounds outdated," I said. I nodded toward one of the booths. "Ring it in."

The guy grunted. His eyes flicked between me and Isabel, who was making threat assessments of her own. He stood back up and made a phone gesture to the guy in the left outpost. Phillson then began his own circuit of the car.

I saw Isabel's left hand conceal a knife. Sophia's knife. She had taken it out of my jacket before giving it back to me. The girl was good.

"Easy… " I whispered.

She shot me a look: *You take it easy.*

I looked ahead at the guy in the hut. He was on the phone.

The male voice said, *You sure Kane doesn't have the balls?*

The female voice said nothing.

Thirty seconds went by. I started calculating escape strategies. I figured the best way out was in a set of fatigues. I had a preliminary response all worked out when the guy in the hut got off the phone.

But then he shouted, "Fixed-wing. Deuce."

Isabel and I both took a breath. *Safe.*

The guy by my window acknowledged the response and leaned down to my window again.

"Quarter mile," he said. "Go straight and then make a right. Follow that down to the blacktop. Hanger six."

Phillson had made two complete circuits of the sedan. He was in front of the car, walking backward toward the gate. He did that finger-circle thing and then the gate split open. The big guy stepped back from my window and waved us through with a couple of fingers.

I drove us to the runway. It stretched far off into the distance and had a line of hangars on each side. Most of the hangars were open and had mechanics and such working away inside. There were a few planes out on the runway, many of which were super-fighters. Kane's was ready for flight, idling on the tarmac outside of Hangar Six.

Kane's jet was the lady out there. It was compact and sleek, but it still dwarfed our measly sedan. I pulled up alongside it and got out with Isabel. The plane had a huge Silverton Group logo on its side. Its stairs were down. Standing at the bottom was a pilot. He was wearing a full getup—cap and all.

"Wheels up in five," I called over.

He nodded and started up the staircase. Isabel surveyed the jet and then gave me a look which seemed to say I'd done an adequate job. Then she walked ahead and I watched her climb up the stairs. The sun gleamed off the jet and the breeze blew Isabel's hair. I took a deep breath and smiled.

One mile up and nobody around.
Whatever would we do to pass the time…?

THIRTY-SIX

L ONDON.
Four thousand miles east.
Seven hours and twenty-three minutes later.

Kane's jet was refuelling for the second leg of its journey to Shanghai, now one passenger lighter, and I was standing in front of a wastepaper basket, in Heathrow's Terminal Five arrivals area, trying to look casual.

In this day and age, it's all but impossible to get a weapon through Customs. Yes, it *can* be done, but, frankly, it requires more hassle than it's worth. What that means for today's man-on-the-move is that supply stashes are an absolute necessity. And with this demand came opportunity. Pay a certain guy a certain annual fee and you can entitle yourself to a certain ad hoc service whereby, depending on your indicated needs, a suitable welcome pack will be made available to you at any international airport.

I had called ahead from Kane's jet and, normally, I would have been given a locker number along with instructions as to where the corresponding key could be found. But because the UK is so security-anal, there are no luggage lockers—at Heathrow or anywhere else—and so I was instead told to go to the left baggage concierge desk and hand in the ticket, which I would find taped to the inside lip of the nearby wastebasket.

I retrieved the ticket and handed it over to the guy behind the desk. He looked at it and then at me. He nodded. Then he went into the storage room and came back with a black backpack. I slung it over my shoulder and walked easily through the terminal and out of the airport.

Already there was a problem.

The backpack was lighter than it should have been.

I picked up speed when I got outside, hustling my way to the end of the taxi line, where I got into a black cab and told the guy to head north. I kept an eye on the traffic around us until I was sure I hadn't picked up a tail. The sky was black and the roads were as clear as you find them in a capital city at 10:45 on a Wednesday evening. A tail would've been easy to spot. Nobody was following.

I told the cabbie to head for Oxford Circus and we cut out westward a few miles later.

I looked down at the backpack and unzipped it. Inside, I should have found cash, a fresh burner cell, and the weapon system I'd asked for. Instead I found a small roll of English pounds, a few thousand rubles, a half-used medical kit, a tangle of bloodstained bandages, and a plastic bag full of what I assumed was cocaine.

And a Colt Python.

The male voice said, *Whoa*.

Whoa indeed.

The Colt Python is a bastard. A six-inch, six-round, double-action .357 bastard. And make sure you get the royal-blue finish, too. The Python, despite being long-since discontinued, is, in my estimation, the best revolver ever made. And, believe me, you won't find anybody carrying one of these around who isn't also packing at least a seven-inch python of a different kind.

So it was a bag of mixed fortunes.

I took out the Colt and held it low in the footwell. I flicked open the cylinder. Five bullets left.

The male voice said, *Definitely a story there*.

The female voice said, *Disgusting*.

I looked down at the bandages. The ad hoc service could be used in reverse too. As a *drop-off* as well as a *pickup*.

To be fair, I said, *we've left worse things with that service*.

And for the fee we pay. We damned well can, the female voice said. *But this is unacceptable. We're getting screwed*.

The male voice said, *At least we got a Colt*.

A gun with five bullets and a risk of hepatitis is what we got. And thanks to Isabel's taking Sophia's knife—it's <u>all</u> we got.

We'll deal with Customer Service, later, I said. *Right now, we've got other priorities*.

The cab dropped me at Oxford Circus forty minutes after leaving Heathrow. The cabbie demanded £100 English pounds, which I—as a guy who hears voices—paid him.

I watched the guy drive off and then went in search of a trash can. I found one and dumped the backpack. I only kept the cash and the Colt.

I took out Hays's photo.

I was no Londoner, but I'd been there enough times to have picked up a vague notion of what was where. The acclaimed medical district, for example, was just north of Oxford Circus, and, I figured, as good a place as any to start looking.

I started walking north. It was pretty damn cold out. I turned west on Margaret Street and then north again onto Harley Street. Fifty yards later, I saw a massive street sweeper rolling slowly westward.

I stopped walking.

THIRTY-SEVEN

I WAS STANDING IN the photo.
Same street.
Same sidewalk.
One massive difference.
The building was gone.

It was crumbled like a stock cube and lying in a heap—an eight-story building reduced to three and change. Gray-colored stone was stained black with flash burn. Reams of yellow tape cordoned off the nucleus of the site and crowd-control barriers set a police perimeter further out. Inside the perimeter were numerous first responders. Ambulances were backed up to the rubble, medics rushed around like worker ants. Two fire engines sat drained in the center. Three ladders extended to where the building's fourth floor used to be and three firemen performing leg-lock maneuvers at the top were looking down onto the blackened bricks and relaying information to the guys at the bottom. I saw a couple more firemen winding up long hoses and more than a few gulping down water and wiping their brows. They all looked exhausted.

A giant crane was looming over everything, powered down right then, but obviously having worked hard.

But what exactly had happened?

I moved up to the back of the crowd. They were all gathered one block west of Harley Street, in the middle of the intersection with Wimpole Street. The police barrier closed an entire city block. What was left of the building took up the southwest block of the intersection, Wigmore Hall took the northwest block, a coffee shop had the northeast corner, and the Royal Society of Medicine occupied most of the southeast quadrant.

Four news vans had been abandoned behind the crowd. All four news teams were set up at various points along the edge of the police barrier. Three of the news teams were currently rolling; one was waiting to come on air. A reporter was in a frenzy, trying to balance on one leg as she stuffed her other foot into a high heel and get powdered up at the same time—all the while barking at her cameraman to ready his equipment faster. I made my way through the crowd and up to the edge of the barrier just as she started speaking.

It had happened four days ago. In the early hours of Sunday morning. An explosion at the Lyndale Institute on Wigmore Street. The rescue operation was now in its final stages, with the last of the bodies having been pulled earlier in the day. The final casualty count was still unknown at this time, but estimated to be in the high sixties. As for the cause of the explosion, that was an unknown, too.

It had taken sixteen hours to put out the fire. And another forty-eight just to remove the surface rubble and stabilize the building. Luckily, its top three floors had collapsed more or less vertically, thereby containing the mess somewhat, but a good portion had rained on to the street—hence the massive sweeper. It had been a huge effort, but now, finally, things were starting to move forward.

Counterterrorism officers had only been granted access in the past few hours, and, along with the London Fire Brigade, were in the initial stages of their investigation. Arson, accident, or attack? That was the question.

The reporter then began an on-site analysis, speculating about causes and consequences, and talking about the mood of the scene, all three subjects of which were devoid of fact. She did however mention that the prime minister, mayor, and police chief would all be giving a statement at some point in the next twelve hours. After that, she went into a loop, repeating everything for anyone who was just joining them. The other three news teams had nothing different to offer.

As I stood there watching the scene unfold, and, even though I was blended into a decent-sized crowd, I began to feel very uneasy. Exposed, somehow. Like I was being watched.

I looked up and around at the surrounding buildings. I scanned the windows and the rooftops. I couldn't see anything. I slid back through the crowd and walked over to the coffee shop.

Nothing suspicious.

But I did see something familiar.

The diagonal point of view matched Hays's photo exactly. The Institute's front doors were approximately three-hundred feet away from me. It was where the man and woman had been standing. The coffee shop's front doors had a small dome camera mounted above them. Hays must have gotten the image off of it.

I ducked into a small alleyway beside the coffee shop, concealing myself in the shadows. I felt better there. More secure.

So what do we think? I said.

The male voice said, *Err… you're paranoid.*

Besides that.

Sixth floor, the female voice said. *That was origin of the blast. Took out the two floors above and the two below.*

I glanced around and saw remnants of those five floors lying all over the sidewalks. The big chunks had been hauled away over the past two days but there was still plenty left. Smaller pieces of debris had been flung well clear of the blast and were scattered beyond the police perimeter, all up and down Wigmore. Some bits had even made it into the alley I was standing in, and I figured there must have been more collecting on nearby rooftops as well. There was still a lot of cleanup to do—not least of which was the concert hall—which had taken a major beating.

I refocused my attention on the Institute. I watched the investigators through the gaping holes in the building facade. Assessing the scene, accumulating evidence, drawing conclusions.

The female voice said, *Someone's covering their tracks.*

The male voice said, *Yeah, and we all know who.*

And we're back…

I'm telling you the CIA has got secret labs all over the world. They never stopped experimenting. Why would they?

Hey, Isaac, do me a favor and roll our eyes at this fool.

Guys… I said.

All right, point is we need to get inside that building.

Not going to be easy, the male voice said. *We'd have to*

bypass that congregation of camera crews, spectators, and various responders.

Then how about giving me some suggestions? I said.

The female voice said, *Best bet is to lure a policeman into this alley. Spin him a tall tale about something he should see, and follow it with a quick takedown. One swift clothes change later and we'll have the all-access pass we need.*

The male voice said, *Hey guys, imagine Isabel in a police uniform.*

That's not helping, said the female voice.

It's not hurting.

You're a pig.

Don't act like you weren't thinking about it, too.

The female voice said nothing.

I kept scanning the scene. Windows, rooftops, passing cars, everything.

The male voice said, *Isaac?*

I kept scanning. I still felt like I was being watched.

Isaac?

No, I said. *Too risky. We've got to wait for everything to die down. The last of the bodies was pulled out this morning so the investigators will have the scene for a good while, yet. We'll go in tomorrow night.*

Then what do we do all day?

Coffee shop.

Coffee shop?

Good place for recon. Lots of people, lots of facilities.

Nobody's watching us.

We wait until tomorrow.

I leaned against the coffee shop. It was going to be a busy day. Cleanup crews would be out in force and the various press conferences would be taking place too. I continued to watch the scene unfold until a sudden noise from behind had me turning quickly and reaching for the Colt.

THIRTY-EIGHT

THE COLT NEVER made it out of my waistband. It was a false alarm. Just some homeless guy moving about under a cardboard blanket behind the alleyway's dumpster. He had been watching me and I saw his head duck away as I turned around.

I walked down the alley and found him huddled in a ball. His hands were wrapped tight around his shins and his head was down on his knees. He was covered in rags. Two gray woolly hats were stretched over his head, each one covering the holes in the other. His sneakers were worn through. His jacket had fit him once but now hung loose. He was sitting on a pile of cardboard, rocking back and forth, shivering from the cold, and shaking with fear. He whimpered as I loomed over him. Then, slowly, he gathered his courage, and looked up at me.

He looked about forty-five years old, which meant he was probably thirty. He'd clearly been living like this for a long time. His stubble was turning white and his face was covered in dirt.

I looked hard into the guy's face, searching his thoughts, reading his story. He was sickly thin and very jittery. I detected no alcohol or cigarettes on his breath, nor did I see any signs of drug use. Just a decent guy who had been dealt a bad hand.

I said, "Hi."

He didn't speak. Just whimpered and nodded.

I motioned my head at the Institute. "Know anything?"

Again he said nothing. All I got was another whimper and a vigorous shake of his head. He was scared of me, and that wasn't helping. But I gave him a sterner look all the same, which seemed to do the trick. His eyes widened and then clamped shut. He said, "There was a guy."

His voice was raspy and weak. Like he hadn't used it in a while.

I said, "What guy?"

He kept rocking back and forth. Didn't answer. I grumbled a little and saw him wince at the possible consequences.

He said, "He was hanging around after it happened."

He was talking so quietly I could barely hear him. He remained huddled in a ball, with his eyes closed, and his head down.

I said, "I'm not going to hurt you."

He kept rocking.

"All right, I will hurt you if you don't stop rocking."

He stopped rocking.

I said, "Good. Now look at me."

He looked at me. He was very scared.

"The guy," I said, "What did he look like?"

"Just a guy."

"A white guy?"

"No. Black."

"What was he wearing?"

He shook his head. "Black. All black."

The male voice said, *Great, so we're looking for a shadow.*

254

The homeless guy watched me think.

I said, "You think this guy had something to with the explosion?"

"I don't know. He was just hanging around."

"Yeah, but something about him was off, right?"

The homeless guy nodded. "Yeah. *Off*."

"Off how?"

"Guy just seemed too interested," he said. "Like way more than anyone else. But with the coffee shop, too."

"The coffee shop?"

He nodded. "I saw him talking with Chloe."

"Who's Chloe?"

"She works in there. Gives me the leftovers each day. It's why I hang around here."

"What were they talking about?"

"I couldn't hear. But the guy kept pointing at the doors."

"The doors? Wait, you mean the camera?"

"Yeah, yeah, the camera. He was real interested in it."

"Has he been back since?"

"No. I haven't seen him."

"What else did you see?"

He shook his head. "Nothing."

I took the photo from Hays's safe out of my pocket.

"What about these two?" I said. "Were they around?"

He took the photo in his hand. He looked closely. He tried hard. He shook his head again.

I put the photo back in my pocket.

The homeless guy adjusted his position causing the cardboard underneath him to shift about. I saw a photograph. I reached down and took it.

"This your family?" I asked.

His face dropped down.

"Was," he said.

We went quiet. I had nothing more to ask him and he clearly had nothing more to tell me. He had clamped his eyes shut again and started back up with the rocking and whimpering. His hands were clasped together in front of his face and he seemed to be praying into them.

The voices and I had a quick discussion.

Then I reached into my pocket. The homeless guy held his breath.

I heard him release it a couple of minutes later. He must have opened his eyes and quickly realized two things: first, that I wasn't there anymore; and second, that there was five-hundred pounds between his hands. I was back at the end of the alleyway, looking out at the scene again. I heard a shifting of cardboard and then a brushing of feet as he exited the other end of the alley.

I stayed in the alley until six in the morning. The work effort had continued all night and was still in full swing. The crowd had thinned around 2:00 a.m. but was now beginning to pick up again. The people were drawn to it. They migrated slowly, morning-groggy and with stiff joints. At 6:15 a.m., the coffee shop's *Sorry we're closed* sign flipped over. I was fourth through the door.

I hate coffee and so insulted the establishment by buying a bottle of water with my two Danish pastries. I sat down by the large front window and watched as the morning patrons came to fuel their socially-accepted—though ultimately undeniable—addiction. Three gold coins exchanged for a Styrofoam cup, portioned with a magical brown elixir, one sip of which turned the walking dead into the agitated living.

The day progressed as expected. The crowd went strong until about 8:45 a.m., but eventually the need to go to work thinned it out to almost nothing. The police investigators remained in control until around 10:00 a.m., after which the city planners, surveyors, and structural engineers had taken over.

The mayor and Metropolitan Police chief held a joint press conference at 11:00 a.m. The prime minister had issued a televised statement two hours earlier due to him being on an official visit to France, but all three figures made roughly the same speech. They began by expressing their sadness and heartfelt condolences to the victims and their families. Then came the assurances of situational control, followed finally by promises of increased vigilance and security. The police chief got the brunt of the press questions. He had one answer for all: He couldn't comment on an active investigation.

The cleanup crews began their fifth day of work. The crane came to life and the huge skips were continuously hauled away and replaced with new ones. They worked incredibly quickly and must have shifted fifty tons of rubble by noon. And with the site now clear of bodies, that pace should have been easy to keep up. But investigators were hesitant to let them tear down the building just yet. Not until they had a definitive cause.

After lunch, I made a quick trip to a nearby electric store and bought a flashlight. I also converted the dollars and rubles I had into sterling at a post office. When I got back to the coffee shop, I made use of one their computers and researched everything I could about Lyndale Institute.

It was a billed as a private mental health research institute. Top doctors, premium facilities. Their research covered many areas but their primary focus was PTSD, along with other trauma-related illnesses. They were proud of their work with the Armed Forces, and were credited with the development of a leading therapeutic model.

In addition to their research facilities, the Lyndale Institute also treated psychiatric inpatients.

I went through all the pictures on their website—the doctors, the board of directors, their associated partners. I found nobody resembling the woman in Hays's photo. Nor did I find any clues as to what "CT" might be. As for MK-ULTRA, that was obviously dead end, too.

I tried searching for videos of the explosion and found a selection of footage. Problem was, it had all been shot on mobile phones. So obviously it wasn't great. The footage was shaky at best. Taken at night, and in a panic. The Institute couldn't really be seen in any of it. Apart from the odd flash of orange flame, the building was entirely masked by a thick layer of black smoke. Even the best of the footage consisted of little more than a black screen and the sound of distressed sirens blaring in the background.

Useless.

The final thing I did was check the international news. Dmitry Kolachev had now officially been confirmed dead, as had all seven of his bodyguards. Chicago police were naturally unable to comment on an active investigation. As for the news coming out of the other side of the world, Shanghai was altogether quiet. At least for then, anyway.

By seven in the evening the Lyndale Institute was silent. No police, no press, no cleanup crews. They were all gone. As were the spectators. The panic was over, nothing to see. The police barriers were still in place, and that section of Wigmore was still closed off, but a traffic diversion had been set up very early on, and pedestrians were now giving the wreck no more than a curious glance in passing. London, as ever, was moving on quickly. Nothing can ever keep it down.

Sixteen hours after opening, the baristas had rags to tables. It was dark outside and I was the last patron left.

At no point in the day had I seen a black guy dressed all in black.

THIRTY-NINE

I WALKED OUT OF the coffee shop and ducked into the alleyway again. The homeless guy wasn't there. I looked across the intersection and gave everything a final once-over. It was all quiet. This area of London was full of specialist medical practitioners, meaning it basically shut down after 6:30 p.m. The Marylebone High Street was further north and audibly busier. There was some slow migration passing through Wigmore and moving in that general direction, but, overall, the sidewalks were empty and so was the road.

I strolled across the intersection, casually ducked under the yellow tape, and walked into the Lyndale Institute.

Structurally—and only in that sense—the first floor had held up pretty well. Most of damage was superficial and had actually been caused by the Fire Brigade. They had smashed in through the large double-door entrance and knocked out all of the windows.

I powered up the flashlight and played it around.

The first thing I saw was a head.

It was completely white and had been severed at the neck.

It was lying in the middle of the reception hall, right at the foot of the big Greek statue it belonged to.

I said, *Aphrodite?*

The female voice said, *Athena.*

You know, as signs go, that's probably not a good one

Good thing we're not superstitious, then.

The statue stood directly in front of a grand staircase that had now completely fallen through. The reception hall had been decorated elegantly with marble flooring and a corniced ceiling. Now it was covered in dirt and ash and piles of broken stone. Anything that had once been white was now at least a dark gray.

I walked around the first floor, following the snaking path the firefighters had plowed through the rubble. Numerous corridors led off to various offices, all of which were cluttered with paperwork. No light bulb was left unshattered. The furniture was all totally ruined. I passed a set of elevators that were jammed open. Each one had a pile of black brick and shattered glass inside.

The male voice said, *Probably best to take the stairs.*

I found a fire-escape plan at the bottom of a stairwell on the west side of the building. According to the plan, the first floor had been totally administrative. The second floor had a bunch of treatment rooms, plus a communal area for those visiting the inpatients. Third and fourth floors had been fitted out as specialized inpatient wards, with plenty of beds, more treatment rooms, and even a couple of isolation rooms, too. The fifth, sixth, and seventh floor contained the research departments. Neurology, psychiatry—pretty much what you'd expect. The eighth floor wasn't clearly defined, but I figured it had probably been offices.

I played the flashlight over the fire stairs. Each step had a pile of debris at either end, but they were made of concrete, so looked sturdy enough. I made my way up to the second floor and came out in the communal area. It was a huge room and it hadn't held up well, at all. The ceiling was bulging in the middle, like a boil about to burst. Huge cracks crept down the walls. The dainty cornices were crumbled all around. Dust was still sprinkling down, covering the carpeted floor.

The male voice said, *This is just sad.*

It really was. Around the room I saw abandoned board games, a litter of playing cards, an overturned easel, vacant wheelchairs, and some empty food trays. It looked like a nursery. It basically was too, only this one took adults and was much more depressing. Having said that, anyone on this floor would have survived.

On the northern wall, there were two tall arched windows. They faced the street, and were separated by a wall of arts and crafts. Sixty sheets of various-sized paper were tacked to the wall in a kind of collage. Some had fallen down, others were peeling off. All were either torn or covered in blast residue. They were the products of the art therapy sessions. Most were in crayon, but a few had been painted. They were preschool-level masterpieces of stick men with giant heads and turned-out feet, all of whom were wearing—I supposed appropriately—crazy smiles. There were plenty of yellow balls with lines coming out of them in many a top corner. And there were thick signatures in many a bottom. These pictures made up the majority. But in and among them were other works. More surreal works. More disturbing works. The kind that had somehow managed to achieve an Edvard Munchian level of despair by simply removing the smiles from their stick men.

The male voice said, *Yeeesh.*

The two windows had been smashed. I imagined the Institute blowing outwards, its bricks hurtling across the street and raining against the concert hall. The damage was extensive. I stood under the window arch and looked up and down the street. The lights went out in the coffee shop. A barista left a few seconds later. Then I looked down and to the right to the Institute's main entrance.

Down and to the right.

Sophia's exact head movement while under hypnosis.

The male voice said, *Close, but she sounded like she was higher up. Plus…*

I turned back to the room.

No beds, I said.

The female voice said, *Let's try the next floor*.

I kicked around through the mess, doing a quick circuit of the entire second floor, checking out the facilities, looking out for any kind of clue, but turning up nothing but dust.

Back in the stairwell, the next flight up had much more debris on it. Its handrail had also collapsed. I cautiously made my way up and came out onto a corridor that was sunken down where the ceiling had bulged downstairs. There were lots of holes in the ceiling. Wires and cables hung like drawn guts. Dirty water pooled all over the floor. People on this floor would have been badly injured at the very least.

I moved slowly down the corridor. Some of the walls had been knocked down and so there were higher piles of debris to navigate. I went in and out of individual bedrooms, nudging open the doors that weren't lying on the ground. Beds, blankets, and pillows were covered in ash. Chairs were in pieces, cabinets were overturned, clothes were strewn about. Sinks and toilets were smashed and wastewater was pooling everywhere. Glass crunched under my boots.

The first three bedrooms on my left had street-facing windows and the correct down-and-right line of sight to the entrance. But they were single rooms with single beds, and therefore far too small to have accommodated six people. It took fifteen minutes to get round the third floor. I found nothing there, either.

The final flight to the fourth floor was cordoned off with a bunch of yellow tape. It was a hard scramble up and there was no fire door at the top this time. Nor was there any ceiling. The night sky was clear. The upper floors had collapsed and there were giant heaps of brick everywhere. It looked a bit like the landfill back in Chicago. Everything was crumbled and stained black. No survivors from here up.

I consulted the fire plan to see what was what. The fourth floor had a single corridor that ran all the way around it, like a rectangle. I was in the northwest corner. Immediately to my left was what the plan called *Treatment Room Nine*. It was a longish room, but only the corners of its walls remained standing. Its floor was covered in rubble.

Six hospital beds had been crushed underneath.

There was nothing left of the street-facing wall. I walked up to the edge and looked down and right.

This is it, the male voice said. *Exactly where she was standing.*

Which means all the brown folders were in this room on Wednesday, the female voice said.

I stood in the middle of the room and tried to imagine the six people lying around me. I pictured the guy with the white lab coat, too. I began shifting around some of the debris, uncovering a couple of long, silver poles and a few small aluminum bags.

Then I heard a noise.

You guys hear that?

Came from the opposite corner, the male voice said.

I stepped back into the corridor. Listened. Everything was quiet. I clambered toward the other side of the building, snaking side to side to avoid the gaps in the floor, dodging broken pipes that were sticking out of the rubble. I turned the northeast corner slowly. Listened again. Still nothing. I continued to the southeast corner.

Halfway down the corridor I heard another noise.

I drew the Colt.

I moved forward slowly. I pressed myself against the southeast corner and peered around it. The noise was coming from the third room along the corridor's southernmost side. The room didn't have a door anymore, but it still had its most of its ceiling and good part of the wall, too. I couldn't see inside. I looked at the piles of debris leading up to it. There was no way to make a quiet approach. I took a breath and cocked the Colt and then jumped around the corner and powered though the rubble and burst into the room.

And saw a black guy dressed all in black.

FORTY

THE BLACK GUY had a gun, too.

It was pointing straight at me.

The room itself was a lot bigger than I'd originally thought. The next door along the corridor also opened into it, about twenty feet to my right. A collapsed drug cabinet was lying in front of it. In the middle of the room there was what looked like a dentist's chair—but a dentist's chair from hell. It had a full array of restraints built in. Leather straps for the wrists, arms, waist, legs, and even forehead. I was glad I flossed.

Above the chair, there was a hole in the center of the ceiling. A shaft of moonlight was beaming through it, spotlighting the seat. In front of the chair, on the far wall, was a big roll-down screen, like the kind you play movies on. It had a ragged gash across it and was soiled with soot. The black guy was standing right in front of it.

He was about thirty, athletically built, and his gun was perfectly trained on my center mass. It was some kind of Berretta. He was holding a flashlight directly below the barrel, with his arms extended, and his feet staggered for balance. So was I. We were mirror images of each other. A standoff.

The male voice said, *Pretty fast reaction*.

The female voice said, *Meh… it was adequate*.

The black guy said, "Drop it."

I said, "You first."

"Ain't gonna happen," he said.

"So we'll shoot each other then?"

"I'll shoot *you*."

"Yeah, but I'll *kill* you."

The black guy said nothing.

The male voice said, *Pwned*.

I said, "You're the guy from SAD?"

The black guy narrowed his eyes.

I smiled and lowered the Colt.

"What, you didn't think you guys were the only ones investigating, did you?"

The black guy kept his gun where it was.

"ID," he said.

"It's with my decoder ring."

The black guy said nothing. I watched him run through some kind of calculation and evaluation. Then he lowered his gun and said, "What the hell does Mossad want with this?"

The male voice said, *Really*?

Might as well go with it though, the female voice said.

Which is what I did. I said, "We want the same as you do."

The black guy said, "I doubt it."

"All right you got me. I'm here for myself."

"Why?"

"Vengeance."

"For what?" he asked.

"Friend of mine."

"Brooks?"

"You knew her?"

"She's *dead*?" he asked.

"No thanks to SAD."

"Damn. When?"

"Couple days."

"She's supposed to be secure."

I said nothing.

"Used to be my CO," he said.

"In 2011?"

"Hell of a thing."

"Hell of a girl."

"How'd you know her?"

"Joint ops a year later," I said.

"Those three weeks in July?"

"August."

He nodded. "I always wondered about that."

We went quiet for a moment.

The male voice said, *Good job we read her file*.

Would have been easier just to shoot him, the female voice said.

That's your answer to everything.

Hey, I'm just worried you-know-who's gonna make a mistake and let this guy get the drop on us.

Hmmm. You make a good point.

The black guy said, "Pythons are standard issue now?"

I shrugged. "It's been suggested I may be overcompensating for something."

We both put our guns at the back of our belts.

The black guy said, "Hard to believe Brooks ended up here."

"What happened to her?"

"Whatever they made her do last."

"You don't know?"

"I've been in Germany," he said.

"You don't sound too pleased about it."

"Six months of crap."

"But at least you get to have fresh bratwurst," I said.

"I don't eat meat."

"Yeah? What do you do with it?"

The black guy said nothing.

"So how'd you get roped into this?" I said.

"Orders."

"Hays?"

The black guy said nothing.

"Makes sense," I said. "If what they're saying is true, that is."

"What are they saying?"

"Enough that this *would* warrant total black ops," I said.

He shook his head and smirked. "Blacker than black. Fuckin *noir* ops he called it."

"Wait, so it's true then?"

The black guy smiled, "You're nowhere are you?"

"Least I've got company."

"We ain't in the same boat."

"No, just the same blown-up building," I said.

"You spent the day in the coffee shop."

"And you spent it watching me?"

He said nothing.

I said, "Who's the old woman?"

"Impressive. I thought I deleted that footage."

I glanced around the room.

"Find anything?"

His right arm made a subtle move to cover his jacket pocket. He said, "Look man, I don't know you, I don't trust you, and I sure as hell don't need your help. So do yourself a favor and stay out of my way." He made to walk past me but I caught his right elbow and stopped him beside me.

I said, "MK-ULTRA? *Really?*"

He shrugged off my grip.

"Stay out of my way."

FORTY-ONE

I HEARD THE BLACK guy clamber down the corridor and then everything went quiet again.

The male voice said, *Still got it.*

I looked down at my hand. I was holding a crumpled scrap of paper. The black guy had stuffed it into his pocket the moment I'd burst into the room, and I'd taken it back out while he was telling me to stay out of his way. I flattened the paper out. It was a label, plain white, rectangular, about two inches by one, with rounded corners. The black guy had torn it off something.

The male voice said, *Pro-zee-tuh—Well, it's some kind of drug.*

The female voice said, *I wonder what's going on in Germany.*

Didn't sound like much, I said.

Kinda depends on his competence, doesn't it?

I suppose, I said.

That bit about "noir ops" though…

I know, I could almost hear Hays saying it.

The male voice said, *Excuse me but I think we're all missing the point.*

What's that? I asked.

That I was right. I told you this was MK-ULTRA but noooooo…

And that particular rant went on for quite a bit.

I stared up through the hole in the ceiling. I could see the moon. It was full but clouded over. The air was slightly warmer now, too. Rain was coming. Beside the hole, and directly above the restraining chair, was a small suspension rod. A couple of torn wires were hanging off it. Directly below, a metal box was lying by the base of the chair. I picked it up.

The female voice said, *A projector?*

The lens was smashed and the internal components were all broken and loose inside. It sounded like a cereal box. I looked at the big screen hanging in front of the chair.

The male voice said, *Kardashians?*

Could be, I said. *Torture was part of the original program.*

You think the black guy's really that far ahead of us?

No. He didn't even know Hays was dead.

Think he'll be a problem?

Guess we'll find out.

At which point I heard a burst of gunfire.

It was something semiautomatic. A short spray of bullets. Six of them, and then a pause, and then a second gun, firing twice. An exchange to be sure, but a lopsided one. The second shooter disadvantaged by his mere single-fire handgun.

I drew the Colt and scrambled back across the fourth floor corridor and looked down from the edge of a room on the street facing side. I saw a triple-flash of hard white light shoot out of the entrance and light up the road.

The female voice said, *Move it, Isaac.*

I darted into the stairwell and crashed straight into some guy clambering up the final step. He was holding some kind of carbine that got pinned between our bellies as we smacked together. We both went over, falling hard onto the rubble and sliding down the staircase. We hit the bottom one after the other, him first, then me, and then my elbow into the center of his face. A plume of soot got kicked into the air.

I scrambled to my feet. I was coughing and couldn't see a thing. The soot was in my eyes and lungs.

The gunfire kept cracking below me.

I kept moving. I stumbled out into the third floor corridor, still coughing badly, but not entirely blind, because the voices could navigate for me. They got me round the debris and into one of the ensuite bedrooms, whereupon I fell to my hands and knees and padded around until I hit a puddle of wastewater. I didn't hesitate for a second. I splashed it all over my face, desperately trying to get my eyes to stop burning.

Once I could see again, I ran back to the stairwell. The guy I'd elbowed was out cold. No kind of law enforcement. Just some punk. I picked up my Colt from beside him and put it at the back of my belt, and then snatched up his carbine, which actually wasn't a carbine, but rather a Heckler & Koch MP7. The MP7 is a good weapon. Small and compact like a submachine gun, but as powerful as an assault rifle. The one I was holding was set to *burst fire*. I put three bullets into the guy's chest and then hurried down to the first floor.

The gunfire had stopped.

Now I heard police sirens in the distance.

I hustled across the first floor and found a second guy

lying by the elevators with the piles of rubble inside. Again I put three bullets in him before moving on.

I found the black guy slumped against the Athena statue near the main entrance. He was in a bad way. He'd taken a hit to the stomach and was bleeding out.

"How many?" I said.

"Two," he said, wheezing for breath.

I heard the police sirens closing in.

I knelt down by the black guy.

"How bad?" he asked with a slight smile on his face.

I looked down at his stomach. The blood was black. He wasn't going to make it. I glanced back toward the elevators.

"Who were they?" I said.

But the black guy was dead by the time I turned back to him.

The police sirens got closer still.

The female voice said, *Let's go, Isaac*.

I rummaged through the black guy's pockets, stuffing everything into my jacket. Then I ran back to the elevators and robbed that guy, too. I quickly wiped the MP7 and then dumped it and ran outside, missing the cops by a close margin. A few blocks south I hit Bond Street, which had a tube station. The first train to arrive was the Jubilee, heading west toward Stanmore.

FORTY-TWO

I RODE FIVE STOPS and got off at London Bridge. I found a sports bar a short distance later. It was fairly packed. Football fans made up the majority. Highlights of the big game were playing on a couple of big-screen TVs. It was a masculine place to be sure, with dark colors, chrome highlights, and assorted memorabilia. The floor was sticky and there were some very powerful smells mixing together, too. No soot, though. The liquor was lined up along the back wall and there were a bunch of tables around the room. A line of booths extended down each of the side walls. Downstairs there were more TVs, leather couches, foosball, and pool tables. Nobody noticed I was caked in soot and toilet water.

The female voice said, *London: Where nobody gives a shit.*

I made my way across the room to the toilets in back. I stood in front of a small mirror above one of the sinks, looking at my reflection and flashing back to the SAD facility.

The male voice said, *Forty-eight hours and we're back in a toilet. Great progress.*

Yeah, and with a busted thumb to boot, the female voice said.

I looked down at my right hand. The duct tape was filthy.

I ripped it off to reveal a still-swollen thumb. I tried massaging it out a bit. It didn't do much.

I washed my hands and then filled the sink with soapy water and dunked my head into it. I sloshed around, trying to get all the crap of my face. I repeated the procedure a couple of times and then went back out to the bar and got two bottles of water. I took a seat in one of the rear booths and drained the first bottle in one swallow.

Then my jacket started ringing.

I reached into my pocket and took out the cause. It was a cell phone, obviously, and also the only thing the guy by the elevators had been carrying. It was a cheap affair. No kind of touch screen or anything. Just a simple cuboid with a keypad. A typical burner phone.

I looked at the screen. The number was blocked.

I answered the call.

A woman said, "Is it done?"

She sounded old. And impatient.

"Well?" she said.

I brought out Hays's photo. "You're five-eight," I said. "Silver hair, small build."

Silence on the line.

"Mr. Blaze?"

"Close," I said. "But it's usually pronounced 'Oh, *shit*.'"

The woman chuckled. "That would require fear on my part."

"Or common sense."

"You really have no idea where you stand, do you?" she asked.

"I'm sitting down."

"We've been watching you for quite a while now, Mr. Blaze."

"You know, you sound just like you look," I said.

"Excuse me?"

"Old."

I heard her grumble. Then she said, "I must confess I am curious about one thing, Mr. Blaze."

"What's that, dear?"

"How much did he pay you?"

"He?"

"Come now, Mr. Blaze. As I said, we've been watching you for quite some time."

"Actually you said 'quite a while,' but don't worry, at your age, it's to be expected."

The woman took a breath.

"How much did that prick pay you?" she said.

"I really do have no idea who you're talking about."

"Hays."

"*Hays*?"

"There's no point denying it. We saw you at the SAD facility," she said.

"Then you also saw I was handcuffed to the table."

"Hays was a prick, he wasn't stupid."

"And you think he paid me?"

"Well he must have offered you something. Why else would you be investigating?"

I said nothing.

She sighed. "SAD has fallen a long way."

"I'll be sure to let them know, dear. I just need your credit card details, and… I'm sorry, what home did you say you were calling from?"

"You're a dead man, Mr. Blaze."

"I'll see you soon."

"No, you'll b—"

I hung up.

I immediately called Marcel. I asked him to trace the last call made to the phone I was calling from, but when he called back just minutes later, he told me that the calling phone had gone dark. It was nowhere to be found. Which meant Tanner was both smart enough and quick enough to have ditched her cell, already. She wasn't about to be traced. And neither was I. So I did the same thing. I took the battery out of the phone and snapped the SIM card.

The male voice said, *All right, so where do we start now?*

How about with what she told us.

Love to, he said. *Problem is, she didn't tell us much.*

She said enough.

You mean the Hays comment? he asked.

She called him a prick. She knew him.

No shit. Hello? She put a hit out on him.

No, I mean she <u>knew</u> him, I said.

What, like personally?

Yeah, I said. *I think we were right about that angle.*

OK, but how's she been tracking us?

Well, you've got to figure Isabel set up a live feedback at SAD. Confirm the kill and whatnot.

Agreed, the female voice said. *And the old woman must've left those two guys watching the Lyndale Institute in case anyone suspicious showed up to investigate. Make sure they got away free and clean.*

Meaning there were three sets of eyes on us the other night. And here I thought I was just being paranoid, I said.

Congratulations, you were just sloppy.

I said nothing.

The male voice said, *So is the old woman running this or is it other guy in the photo?*

Still too early to say, I said. *And let's not forget about the dark guy in the white coat. We don't even have a picture of him.*

The female voice said, *What did we get from the black guy?*

I reached into my jacket and put all the black guy's possessions onto the table. He hadn't been carrying much. Just three items.

The male voice said, *Hmmm.*

The first item was a roll of money, 720 British pounds, a cylinder about two inches in diameter.

The male voice said, *Well, we'll take it.*

I moved on to item number two. It was another cylinder, again about two inches in diameter, but plastic, though, and with a removable cap. Inside were fifteen small circular pills which the label on the outside identified as a kind of antidepressant.

Germany's not that bad, the female voice said.

Well he was a vegetarian, I said.

Item number three was not a cylinder.

It was a ticket.

The male voice said, *Would you look at that.*

At which point my booth was suddenly invaded by two girls. They were in their late twenties and wearing paint on their faces and pink fairy wings on their backs. Both were extremely leggy and in very short skirts. They had broken off from the group of twentysomething women on the other side of the bar. I figured the women had probably been moving from bar to bar, eventually settled in the sports bar for some fun with the football lads. Some of those women were a right state but the two girls in front of me were fairly goodlooking.

One was blonde, the other a redhead. But both were looking at drunk in the rearview mirror. Confidence high, inhibitions low. Even sitting down they were off balance. Their heads and shoulders kept swaying around. Their eyes were wide and glazed over. Their cheeks were flush and they were wearing giggly smiles.

I nodded at them, "Ladies."

They giggled.

The redhead said, "Why are you so wet?"

"Yeah why are you so… so wet?" the blonde repeated, breathlessly.

I said, "I just soaked my head in the sink."

Nothing happened for about a minute and then their heads tilted sideways in tandem. Expressions of puzzledness and sadness.

The redhead said, "Why did you do that?"

"Yeah, why did you do…" the blonde started but couldn't finish. She paused for breath, and then managed, "…do that."

Another pause followed.

The blonde's level of inebriation meant she forgot to include any rising intonation to the end of her sentence. It just came out like a statement. So for clarity she added an upward hand gesture like a waiter holding a tray.

I said, "I killed three guys and got dirty doing it."

The girls leaned in close to each other and exchanged a bunch of *oh, yeahs* along with much supplementary head nodding. Then they turned back to me and the redhead said, "Your hair is really black, you know. Like, *really* black."

"Yeah," the blonde said. "And why are you so wet?"

The female voice said, *Wow.*

I drained the last of my water and asked the girls about getting us a round of drinks. The idea was met with much approval so I got up and made my way to the bar. And then I just kept going.

FORTY-THREE

I GOT BACK TO Heathrow's Terminal Five at six the next morning. I had spent the night in a motel, which although very unusual for me, I really did need a shower. The minibar came in handy too.

I found the same guy behind the concierge desk. I gave him the black guy's ticket and he looked at it, and then at me, and then he nodded and went into the storage room.

He came back with a briefcase.

It was your classic 1960s corporate attaché. A sleek sliver rectangle with combination flick-out locks, and a solid aluminum exoskeleton.

The female voice said, *I swear if this thing has any bandages in it…* Which sentiments I conveyed to the guy behind the desk, who, in true airport-customer-service style, didn't care, and didn't try to hide it. I glanced around cautiously, then took the briefcase and walked away.

I stayed inside the terminal. The VIP lounge I'd come through on the flight in was off limits to me now, but there was a Costa coffee shop. It wasn't that busy. It would do. I bought a bottle of water and a small snack and sat down at a table. I put the briefcase on top and tested the locks. They were both closed. Each lock had big square sliding button next to which was a rotary input that required a three-digit code. One thousand possible combinations would take a while to get through, but old-style briefcases are pretty easy to break into. All you have to do is rotate each wheel until you find a number with a small dark mark next to it. If the number has a mark, it's the correct number for that wheel. Kinda stupid? Yes. But without those "secret" marks, manufacturers would be inundated with distress calls from businessmen with lousy memories.

There were three things inside the briefcase.

A laptop.

And two thick brown jiffy envelopes.

I unfolded the laptop. It was fairly thick by current standards, but seemed to have all the latest processing power inside it. There were plenty of silver stickers below the keyboard attesting to that fact. I hit a button on the hinge and powered it on and confirmed that it really was no ordinary laptop.

There was no standard start-up procedure. The screen was black and then a green underscore started flashing in the top left corner. Three seconds later, reams of data began scrolling down the screen, after which a message box popped up informing me that my connection was secure. Which was strange. The laptop definitely wasn't connected to the airport's Wi-Fi, and yet somehow it had acquired an Internet connection.

Must be some kind of direct satellite uplink, the male voice said.

Explains the bulky casing, I said.

The female voice said, *But what's it connected to?*

I hit the return key and found out.

The laptop was patched into what was basically a secure messaging server. Pretty much the exact same thing the guys in Iran had been using to communicate with the SAD facility in Chicago. The correspondence was between two parties. Both of whom had been using code names. Both of whom were now dead.

I read through the entire correspondence—every message between the black guy and Hays. Every message was time-stamped, dated, and supplemented with the origin of transmission.

The black guy had been called to action on Saturday at 3:24 p.m. Central Time, which was 10:24 p.m. Germany time, which was where the black guy had indeed been stationed prior to all this. He'd been in Berlin, mostly, and the majority of the correspondence detailed his activities during that time. The first big brown jiffy envelope was stuffed with pertinent files.

The male voice said, *Wait. This is why they were looking at Germany?*

Yeah, no wonder the black guy was getting nowhere, the female voice said. *SAD has no idea what they're dealing with.*

They really didn't. But in any case, Hays had ordered the black guy to drop everything and head straight for London. His target: the Lydale Institute. But while the black guy had moved on double-time, he had gotten to London in the early hours of Sunday morning—which of course was too late. The Institute had already been bombed.

He had, however, uploaded a message on Sunday evening containing a number of .jpg files. I opened them up. The picture of the old woman and the mystery guy was .jpg file number one. Then came a bunch of other surveillance shots that captured Sophia along with the five other brown folders Hays had been researching. Following that, the black guy— after seeing his former CO somehow mixed up in whatever it was he was looking at—had questioned Hays about Sophia's involvement and what her current situation was. Hays had simply replied with: *Brooks is secure. Find Tanner.*

The male voice said, *Tanner?*

Gotta be one of our mystery duo, the female voice said.

I scrolled to the bottom of the screen. The black guy's last message had been made on Monday, at 10 p.m., London time. It said: *Tanner trail cold. Lyndale still out of play. Continuing surveillance.*

But that wasn't the last message on the screen.

It was the second to last.

The last message was unread and had been posted just over thirty-six hours ago.

It was one word long.

Watch.

I clicked on it.

A video began to play.

"My name is Adrian Hays."

FORTY-FOUR

HAYS WAS SITTING in the big green leather chair, in his home study. His back was ramrod straight and his hands were clasped on top of the desk. He was wearing a dark cardigan, probably moleskin or cashmere. There were two brown folders on the desk, to his right. He was looking straight into the camera.

"The situation at hand was brought about by a chain of events set in motion seventy years ago."

He reclined in the chair, steepled his fingers, and looked up at the ceiling.

"In 1945, in the aftermath of World War II, the US government initiated Operation Paperclip, which brought over 1500 leading foreign scientists to American soil. September 18, 1947 was the official date of formation of the CIA. In 1950, and with the use of these scientists, the CIA embarked on Project Bluebird, which became Project Artichoke on August 20 1951."

I leaned back in my chair and folded my arms. In the bottom right corner of the screen there was a time stamp: 09–27–2015, 11:47:33.

Less than an hour after the black guy had sent the pictures.

Hays said, "At first, the scope of these projects was limited to actionable intelligence purposes, and predominantly to the development of advanced interrogation methods. But within six months, these underlying concepts began to shift. And what began as an intelligence program quickly evolved into something else. In particular, this shift was made toward finding an answer to a single question: Can a human being be controlled, and if so to what extent? On April 13 1953, this became the basis of Project MK-ULTRA."

Hays paused, then reached out and picked up the first brown folder. He held it up for a second and then dropped in the middle of his desk. It was labeled *MK-ULTRA* and *Top Secret.*

Hays said, "MK-ULTRA's activities went far beyond any legal or ethical limits. Experimentation involved the use of various physical and psychological treatments, including verbal and sexual abuse, sensory deprivation, prolonged isolation, and other forms of what can only be described as *torture.* Furthermore, the project's subjects included hundreds of unwitting subjects—both US and Canadian. This was accomplished by the CIA operating through front organizations such as hospitals, universities, pharmaceutical companies, and prisons."

Hays took a deep and contemplative breath. His eyes dropped down and he stared at the folder for a while. Then he looked back into the camera.

"In 1969, I was recruited by the CIA to their Special Activities Division and became affiliated with the MK-ULTRA project. The same year, a young and brilliant psychologist published a thesis on subconscious suggestion and mind control, and was also brought into the project. Her name was Christine Tanner."

Christine Tanner.

CT.

One mystery solved.

The male voice said, *Wait, so the old woman was one of them?*

I thought back to what she had said on the phone: "SAD has fallen a long way."

Hays continued, "It wasn't until 1973 that investigations into the CIA's activities caused the project to be officially halted. However, in order to mitigate the potential damage, the then-director of the CIA, Richard Helms, ordered the destruction of all MK-ULTRA files. So while over twenty thousand documents have now been released under the Freedom of Information Act, much of the project's information has never been recovered."

The male voice said, *Still think this isn't about MK-ULTRA?*

The female voice said, *Why don't you just shut the f—*

Hey! I said. *I'm trying to watch, here!*

Hays continued, "Naturally, the course of these investigations eventually turned to individuals, and, in turn, the prospect of federal consequences meant that many of these individuals fled the country and went to ground. Christine Tanner was one such individual."

See? I said.

Yeah, I see, the male voice said. *Guess you were right.*

It was actually quite an impressive feat. Because, as the tape clearly showed, there was absolutely no doubt that Hays had used the word: *individual.* And yet, at the same time, there was also absolutely no doubt that Hays had just called Tanner a *haggard bitch.*

A personal connection.

Hays went on, "As it turned out, my specific involvement

in the MK-ULTRA project never came to light. I remained clean of it and without reproach inside the agency. But a man can only run from his conscience for so long." He looked away from the camera. His face went stern. "What we did is unforgiveable." He paused and then looked back down the lens. "Which is why I have made it my life's work to put an end to the project once and for all."

Hays sat up to the desk again and addressed the second folder. It was thick and full of paper.

Hays said, "For the past twenty years, I have tracked down and eradicated any and all attempts to recreate the MK-ULTRA program."

Hays turned the folder round and showed it to the camera. He began flicking through it. The first thing in the folder was a picture of a woman lying dead in an alley. She had been dumped on top of a pile of garbage bags, half naked, and utterly emaciated. Next came a close-up shot of her arms and face. Thick black veins, insomnia streaked across her eyes. Similar photos followed.

Hays said, "In truth, most of these attempts were just that. *Attempts*. Run by amateurs with no real understanding of the science. And any more serious endeavors were limited by the same factors the original project encountered. But forty-eight hours ago, a new case was brought to my attention. And it would seem that the landscape has now changed."

Hays closed the folder. He squared the edges, placed it on top of the first folder, and centered them on his desk. He clasped his hands on top and then looked back at the camera.

He contemplated his next words very carefully.

"For the reasons mentioned herein, I confess to using SAD resources to suppress the truth. Enclosed with this video, however, are the facts of six cases, all of which are testament to both the efficacy and danger that this newest case represents."

"The recent explosion at the HBL laboratory was the first of the six. It is also what brought the situation to my attention. Upon interview, the culprit in question was both entirely unaware of their actions and bore physical, emotional, and psychological symptoms consistent with subjects from the original project. Without question, someone from the original team is involved. They have come the closest to not only replicating the MK-ULTRA program, but, based on their recent results, I fear they are on the verge of a breakthrough."

Hays paused. Breathed in. Out. He addressed the final item on his desk. "Forty-three years ago, Christine Tanner disappeared. And for forty-three years, she has remained disappeared."

He lifted up the item and showed it to be the photo I'd found in his safe. "This photo was taken three hours ago," he said. He reclined in his chair again and stared down at the photo in his hands. "I had hoped my part in the MK-ULTRA project would never come to light. But it would be naive to think that this recent development is no cause for alarm. Indeed this video is both my confession and my plea." He grunted and tossed the photo onto the folders. "The MK-ULTRA program was a blackest of marks against our country. It was an abuse of power and a betrayal of trust. One that I actively and willingly participated in." He took a thoughtful breath. "Perhaps, on some level, I believed that going after those who have attempted to perpetuate the MK-ULTRA program—that going after the worst criminals period—would somehow serve as penance for my crimes. Perhaps it has. But if you are watching this video, then it would seem that fate has decided otherwise."

The female voice said, *Man, this guy was really something else.*

Hays said, "I enclose also a document containing all the MK-ULTRA information at my disposal. My tarnished credibility aside, I cannot underscore the importance of this case enough. Christine Tanner and those she is working with must be stopped."

He stared at the screen.

"I regret my actions. I am sorry."

The video went to static.

FORTY-FIVE

BOUT FIVE SECONDS later, the video automatically closed down and a dialog box popped up on screen. It told me a .pdf file was attempting to download and asked me whether I wanted to allow that to happen, bearing in mind a potential security risk. I clicked *Allow* and the file opened up on screen.

It was a digital copy of the first folder on Hays video.

MK-ULTRA.

Top Secret.

I started going through it.

The female voice said, *Oh, wow*.

There was an old photograph paperclipped to the one of the pages near the beginning of the file. A brown snapshot of a research team in a laboratory. Ten people total, five behind five. They were all wearing lab coats. A young Christine Tanner was front and center, and an afro-sporting Adrian Hays was standing ramrod straight on the far right of the back row. The photograph was dated in the bottom right corner *08/12/72.*

The male voice said, *Huh. So Tanner was always ugly.*

Guess so, I said. *But having said that, Hays does look like a bit of a prick in this.*

A little further on in the file, I came across a document numbered *#190527*. Across the top of it someone had scribbled *TBD*.

The female voice said, *TBD?*

The male voice said, *To be redacted.*

I read through it carefully. It was a full write-up of two experiments, the first of which almost perfectly described a situation like Sophia's. It involved two subjects, both female, both of whom were placed into deep trances, during which time they were each given certain specific instructions. When awakened, each of the subjects was to proceed to a certain room and await a telephone call. Each subject was to engage in that call as they normally would, but, upon hearing their own specific code word, they were to immediately fall into a trance-like state and carry out their own individual mission.

Subject A was told to proceed to the women's bathroom where upon another operative, Subject B, would identify herself via the code word *New York*. Subject B was given a briefcase containing an incendiary device, and was told that after identifying herself, she was to instruct Subject A as to the incendiary device's correct use, specifically how to set the timer, for how long, and where it should be planted. Subject B was then to instruct Subject A that after planting the device, she was to take the briefcase, proceed back to the Operations Room, sit on the sofa, and immediately fall into a deep sleep. Subject B was likewise to do this upon completing the handoff.

Both subjects were made to believe this was a real operation.

And both subjects carried out their parts perfectly.

The comments in the report also highlighted the fact that, during the entire experiment, both subjects acted completely normally, their movements easy and natural. Nobody in the building suspected anything. There was a single minor point of concern in that, although both subjects were instructed to forget everything that had happened, some memory fragments remained. Despite this, however, the experiment was deemed a success.

The second experiment in the document was simpler in nature, with the goal being to steal the wallet from an unconscious man. It was likewise a success.

Amazing, I said,

And check out where it took place, the male voice said.

Damn, I said. *If this gets out, the CIA's going to have a massive problem.*

You thinking what I'm thinking? asked the male voice.

I think so.

The female voice said, *What do you mean if?*

Hhn?

Think about it, would you? said the female voice. *Hays clearly set this up as a failsafe, didn't he? Anything happens to him, and these files get sent out forty-eight hours later.*

Yeah, so what? said the male voice.

So you really think he only sent them to the black guy?

The male voice and I said nothing.

Then I said, *So much for what we were thinking.*

The male voice said, *But would Hays actually send this video to <u>everyone</u>? I mean, sending it out to the rest of SAD is one thing, even to the CIA as a whole, but to send it to other agencies and news channels? He'd bring down the entire agency.*

And? the female voice said. *Why wouldn't he? Not like he cares anymore. Might as well take as many people with him as he can.*

No, said the male voice. *Hays wasn't that guy. He was all about honor. And a play like that would be anything but. Not to mention it would undo all the good work he was doing as penance. Right, Isaac?*

I said nothing.

Isaac?

Yeah… I said. *That must be it. Got to be.*

Care to fill us in? the female voice said.

Why did Hays come after us? I asked.

What do you mean?

Well when we were back at SAD, we assumed that Hays had brought us in because he thought we might be involved with the incidents he was investigating. Except that can't be true, can it? Because we now know that Hays would have never suspected we were involved.

Hey that's right, the male voice said. *Because Hays knew this was all about MK-ULTRA the whole time.*

OK, I see your point, the female voice said. *So what's the answer? Why did he bring us in?*

I said, *The contract.*

You think Hays knew about the contract?

Actually, I think he was counting on it.

In what way?

I picked up the photo of Tanner, again.

Well, I said. *The whole reason Hays made this video was because he saw Tanner in this photo. And haggard bitch or not, she's former SAD and has managed to evade them for the past 43 years. And with Hays trying to do this black-book-style, he was playing a very risky game. One wrong move and it was game over. Tanner knew who he was and probably had a ton of files just like these with which to incriminate him. All she had to do was leak the info and Hays would be on trial. Which is exactly what she should have done.*

But she chose to put a hit out, instead, said the female voice.

Yup. And that bad blood gave Hays an opportunity.

I get it, said the female voice. *You think Hays wanted to use us to track Tanner.*

It was his last chance. The Lyndale Institute had been destroyed, the black guy was nowhere, and Sophia had just bombed HBL. If Hays wanted to stay in the clear, he needed to find Tanner and take her out.

Which is why he took over all of Chicago's surveillance cameras. To watch out for people like us. To watch his back and see who Tanner would send.

Exactly. And it probably would've worked too.

Except for the fact we weren't the one coming to kill him.

Yeah. And that hit him like a ton of bricks. I thought back to the interrogation room. *Remember that look he gave us when Isabel burst in? It was like he was thinking… But I thought… you're supposed to be the one?*

The female voice said, *Poor bastard.*

The male voice said, *All right, so where does that leave us now?*

Depends, I said. *Assuming you're right about Hays being Mr. Honorable, which I think you are, then SAD is probably all hot and bothered, right now. I figure we've got a 24-hour head start, at most.*

To find a woman that's managed to stay off grid for 43 years?

I didn't say it would be easy.

FORTY-SIX

THE MALE VOICE said, *Well, I doubt she's still in London.*

Agreed, the female voice said. *Blowing up the Lyndale Institute would suggest she's finished up, here.*

Unless it's some kind of double bluff. Like a last-place-you'd-expect kind of thing.

Doubtful.

Great, so she could be anywhere.

We're coming at this the wrong way, I said.

The wrong way? What's the right way? said the male voice.

With a different question.

Which is? asked the female voice.

Why now?

I don't follow, she asked.

OK, I said. *Tanner's been off grid for over <u>forty</u> years, right? "<u>Disappeared,</u>" to quote Hays.*

So why choose now to reappear? asked the female voice.

Exactly. She's former SAD. She could have stayed gone if she wanted to. But she didn't. So there must be a reason.

OK. Makes sense.

She'd also need help, I said.

Which is where the guy in the photo comes in, the female voice said.

Yeah, we need to find out who he is.

And how are we supposed to do that? the male voice said. *We don't know anything about him. Hell, we can't even see his face.*

But we do know what he must be offering her, I said. *Why-now reasons aside, in order to replicate the project, Tanner needs resources. She needs funding, she needs facilities, and she needs subjects.*

Lots of people can offer those, said the female voice.

True, but I'm willing to bet there must be at least a few specifics that she needs that almost nobody can offer. After all this is cutting-edge research we're talking about.

OK, like what specific things? asked the male voice.

I don't know. First we have to understand how this project works.

Then we should start with her thesis, the female voice said. *The one Hays said she got recruited because of.*

Which was easy enough to do since it was included in the information on Hays's PDF.

The thesis was entitled: "The Effect of Chemical Psychedelics on Neuroplasticity, Subconscious Suggestion, and Cognitive Conditioning."

I read the whole thing.

Tanner theorized that, provided a subject was placed in a susceptible enough state, exposure to a powerful enough suggestion could allow for the development of an alternate personality. This personality, if properly built, would be completely subservient and without inhibition—even to the extent of suicide.

She gave examples of possible suggestion mechanisms, but ultimately concluded that the state of susceptibility necessary could only be induced chemically. Mere hypnosis would never be adequate. During the original MK-ULTRA experiments, the

CIA had been using LSD for this purpose, but Tanner believed that there were better chemical alternatives.

The paper went on to describe the exact properties of such chemical substances, along with pharmacokinetics, dosage, toxicity, and detectability, but the technology for synthesis was simply not available at the time.

The male voice said, *Hays did say he thought she was on the verge of a breakthrough.*

The female voice said, *So maybe now someone's come up with a way to synthesize these drugs.*

Right, I said. *In which case that's the reason she waited until now. And it's also what our mystery man is providing.*

I minimized the pdf and closed down the secure communication network and opened up the browser. I input all of the information about the drugs and did a search for any relevant research projects and trials that had taken place over the past five years. What I found was that numerous grants had been awarded for development in this general area but only one team had made a truly significant contribution: Dr. Galabin Vanev from a small company called Dasintex, which was based in Sofia, Bulgaria. He had been experimenting with scopolamine and its derivatives, and, in combination with various other psychedelics, he was synthesizing new, more powerful hallucinogens, the properties of which matched Tanner's specifications almost exactly.

Vanev's team had been in the human trial stage of testing, and they had been showing promising results. Three months ago, however, the trial was suspended. And the reason for that was because Dasintex had been bought out, taken over, and finally absorbed into a much bigger machine—a giant conglomerate known as the Silverton Group.

The male voice said, *Son of a bitch.*

FORTY-SEVEN

I WAS STANDING ON a sidewalk 4,000 miles west of Heathrow's Terminal Five, looking up at the penthouse apartment of the Georgian Terrace Hotel on the opposite side of the street. I had spent the majority of the day going over the rest of the MK-ULTRA files as well as becoming an expert on all things Senator Kane. It turned out, after much digging and a call to Marcel, that if you traced the Lyndale Institute's financials far enough, you hit a shell corporation that, once cracked, revealed the Silverton Group to be its parent.

Which actually answered a question that had been bugging me since SAD: Why had the photo of Kane been on their computers in the first place? I mean, they weren't exactly the NSA. So the only conclusion was that Hays must have followed the Institute's financials like we had, and must have been looking into Kane when he got shot. Which, all things considered, the voices and I agreed wasn't exactly a great conclusion, since it meant a huge piece of the puzzle had been right in front of us the whole time.

The direct-to-Atlanta was an afternoon flight, and, after standing in line at the Fed-Ex desk, behind a very loud and very annoying Swiss banker, I had mailed the laptop and Germany documents to Marcel, and then deposited the briefcase containing the Colt I'd never fired at the luggage drop, and then bought a first-class ticket for said direct flight with the credit card of said annoying banker. The flight had departed from Heathrow at 5:30 p.m. GMT and arrived in Atlanta at 9:00 p.m. EST. A twenty-minute drive from Hartsfield-Jackson, plus a leisurely stop for dinner, meant it was now 11:00 p.m., EST.

Senator Kane was not a difficult man to find. The guy was a social-media addict. As a result, could easily be located at any given moment. Kane didn't like living outside of the city. He wanted to be right in the center of the action, all the time. To that end, the Georgian Terrace's penthouse had long since been his primary residence. He had once tweeted that it was "the perfect position," and, to be fair, he had good reason for thinking that. Just half a mile away was the Georgia Institute of Technology, his alma mater, and directly across the street was the Fox Theatre, where he had spent most of that time. Less than two miles southwest of the hotel were the Georgia World Congress Center and the Georgia Dome—perfect for the hardcore Atlanta Falcons fan that Kane was.

More importantly, however, the hotel was just one mile east of the Technology Enterprise Park, the epicentre of Atlanta's booming biotech industry, to which Kane himself had contributed massively. Silverton Group's current head-quarters was stationed in prime position in the park, adjacent to Coca-Cola's own world headquarters—Coca-Cola's standing twenty-nine stories high, Silverton's standing thirty-three. Quite simply, Atlanta was Kane's town.

The male voice said, *What do you think he's up to?*

The female voice said, *With what we know about him, I'm afraid to find out.*

I crossed the street and walked into the hotel.

The lobby was in the center of the building, at the bottom of a huge glass rotunda that ran all the way to the top and acted as a walk-around balcony in the center of each floor. From the outside the hotel looked like a huge Coca-Cola can with an I-Pad stuck to either side. I came in through the large sliding doors and assessed the lobby area. It was fresh and spacious and I could see all the way up to the roof. Everything was white and red, everything gleaming and spotless. The reception and concierge desk was to the left, behind which was a Taiwanese woman in a fitted jacket. There was a long mirror on the wall behind her. The name of the hotel was embossed above it. The woman was alert but fairly relaxed. Not much was going on at this time of night except for the occasional telephone call.

The male voice said, *Hello, hello…*

My eyes slid across the lobby.

Opposite the reception desk was a large sitting area. A guy in a black suit was sitting on a couch, his eyes scanning the lobby.

First thing I noticed: He was strapped.

Looks like some kind of 9mm, the female voice said. *Beretta, if I had to guess.*

The guy's eyes locked on to me. Assessing, concluding, then moving on. Not a threat. All clear. He didn't know me. But I knew him. I recognized him instantly from the research I'd done on Kane. As a billionaire Senator, Kane never went anywhere without protection. His security detail consisted of three people: two black suits—of which the guy in the lobby was one—and a monster. The suits, from the looks of them, were ex-servicemen who had made the popular choice of transitioning to private security. The monster was something else. He stood six foot three and had probably never worn a suit in his life. He was former Atlanta Falcons' defensive tackle, Markus Redding, who—much to the relief of every Quarterback in the NFL—had been banned from the game for life after violating the three-strikes rule for steroid abuse. Now he was Kane's personal bodyguard.

The female voice said, *OK, so one guy down here leaves the other two somewhere else.*

Got to figure the big guy's up there with Kane, the male voice said.

Yeah, I said, *And the other suit is probably patrolling.*
So how do we get up there?
Let's try the easy way.

I walked over to the reception desk. The Taiwanese woman gave me a courteous smile but was more than a little hesitant when I asked her to call up to Kane's Penthouse for me. It was late at night and disturbing a prized guest could cost her job. She did do it though. She waited for Kane to pick up and then handed me the phone.

"…Kane," a tired voice said.

"Guess who."

"MOTHERFU–"

Again I had to pull the phone away from my ear. The expletives came fast and loud and the receptionist didn't know where to put herself. I smiled and told her that Kane and I were old friends. She didn't seem to buy it. In the mirror

303

behind her, I saw the suit watching me very carefully. Like maybe he was starting to recognize me.

I waited for Kane to take a breath and then put the phone back to my ear and said, "Correct. Now listen carefully Kane, we need to talk. There's a—"

"No *you* listen, asshole," Kane shouted back. "You should have never made an enemy out of me. I'm going to *find* you, and *gut* you, and then I'm going to—"

"You do realize I'm downstairs, right?"

The line appeared to go dead.

I pictured Kane muffling the phone with a tight clutch, frantically waving his other hand as he tried to get the attention of his security detail. In the mirror behind the desk I saw the guy on the couch touch his ear piece.

He started to get up.

But then he didn't.

Instead Kane came back on the line and said, "Put Lin on."

I handed the phone over the reception desk. Lin held it to her ear, looking worried and then going stiff. Her eyes dropped straight down to the floor. She listened carefully. Her eyes lifted back up. First to me, then to the entrance, and then back down again. She said, "Yes, sir."

I glanced in the mirror again. The guy on the couch was still watching me. His hand had moved off his ear and was now hovering around his mouth. A group of people walked in through the main entrance and started chatting in the middle of the lobby, directly between the seating area and the reception desk. I saw the suit say something into his cuff.

Lin was still listening to the phone. I couldn't hear what Kane was saying, but he seemed to be repeating something over and over to which Lin kept nodding and replying, "Yes, sir."

After about three minutes she put the phone down. She glanced at the elevators and then shot a quick look over to the seating area. In the mirror I saw the suit nod at her.

"Everything OK?" I asked.

Lin said, "Senator Kane would like you to join him upstairs."

The male voice said, *Well, that was easy.*

Lin disappeared into a staff room behind the desk, coming out into the lobby a few moments later, holding a key.

"Please follow me," she said.

She led me straight through the lobby, passed the main hub of elevators, and down one of the corridors. The guy in the suit didn't follow.

I scanned her up and down as we walked. She had a slim figure wrapped up in a tight pencil skirt and the fitted blazer. Her hair was tied up in a fancy way and held in place with a long silver hair stick. She led me all the way to the back of the rotunda, to a separate and isolated elevator with the word *Private* painted above it. She hit the call button and offered me a nervous smile as we waited for the car. I glanced around. Nobody about.

The female voice said, *It's a good a plan as any.*

Guess we'll see, I said.

The car arrived and we both got in. There were only five buttons, each one corresponding to one of the penthouses. Lin inserted the key into a small slit adjacent to the button labeled *Penthouse 1*. She turned the key and pressed the button and then smiled at me again before moving to leave the elevator.

At which point I caught her hand and spun her into me and covered her mouth.

The doors closed.

FORTY-EIGHT

I T TOOK TWELVE seconds to reach Penthouse 1. Lin fought the entire time, just like Sophia had back in Chicago, except in this case it was an altogether useless endeavor, since, even if she had broken free, she'd have still be locked in a metal box with me.

I kept my eyes on the small LED screen above the button panel, counting off each of the lesser penthouses as we passed them. When we passed Penthouse 2, I took my hand off her mouth, yanked the hair stick out of her hair, and then pulled Lin down into a crouched position with me.

The elevator gears clunked to a stop.

The car stood still for a moment.

And then the doors opened and three bullets smashed into the back of the elevator, two feet above me, exactly where my chest had been seconds earlier.

The male voice said, *Son of a*—

Shards of mirror glass rained down onto me. I slid my hands down Lin's body, over her hips, and under her butt, and then exploded up out of my crouch and launched her straight through the doors and right into the second black suit who was standing directly in front of the elevator with his right arm outstretched and a silenced 9mm Berretta at its end. Their heads smacked together, knocking like coconuts, and knocking them both out. Which left me standing in the middle of the doorway, with the entire penthouse spread before me, still looking pretty, but then hearing three things in quick succession that left me looking less pretty, and more like a blur.

The first was the sound of Kane shouting from the far left corner of the penthouse.

The second was the subsequent slamming of a set of double doors as he barricaded himself inside a room.

And the third was the snapback of a gun.

My eyes locked on to Redding.

He was standing twenty feet in front of me, in the middle of the living room, wearing a shiny green Adidas tracksuit, and holding another silenced 9mm Berretta.

I felt my eyes stretch wide and an immediate impulse hit my legs, and then the male voice shouted, *Move it, Blaze*, which is exactly what I did.

But Redding was quick on the trigger.

I saw the muzzle flash in the corner of my right eye as I dove forward and left, toward the nearest shield. I was hanging in midair, fully outstretched. A massive target.

But lucky.

Because a split-second after the boom of the bullet, I saw a vase explode in the corner of my left eye. It was sitting on a table by the elevator and shattered into a million pieces. The two sounds came immediately after one another. *Bang, tink*. I pictured the bullet flying across the room, rippling through the air at the speed of sound, passing right behind my back, and missing me by no more than a few inches. And then the next thing I knew, I had crashed onto the floor and skidded straight into the back of a leather sofa, hitting it hard and in a fetal position.

Redding kept firing.

He fired two bum shots and then the third bullet hit the sofa, bursting through tight leather skin and out the back. The next bullet did the same thing, skimming my leg in the process. I was a sitting duck.

Redding said, "Come on out, little man."

"Toss the gun and I will," I said.

Redding fired another bullet into the sofa.

"Guess it's true, then," I called. "You *are* a pussy."

Redding stopped firing.

There was silence for a minute, and then I saw the gun fly through the air and skittle across the floor, toward the elevator.

I peeked over the back of the sofa.

Redding was just standing there.

"I ain't no pussy," he rumbled.

I looked back at the elevator. Both handguns were lying on the ground, much closer to me than him.

So just an idiot then, the female voice said.

Redding said, "You wanna fight me like a man, bring it on."

I turned back to him and took a breath. I also pushed the hair stick up my right jacket sleeve, pointed end first.

I stood up slowly and walked out from behind the couch with my hands held up innocently. To my far left, a set of double doors opened and Senator Kane poked his head through. I kept my vision focused on the big guy. Kane took a moment to assess the situation and then shouted, "What the hell are you doing?"

Redding said nothing. Just cracked a smile and waved Kane down with one of his giant paws.

We both just stood there. Squared up, staring each other down. The penthouse was all open plan. The kitchen, dining room, and living room without division, a 2500-square-foot luxury apartment with plenty of furniture—exactly none of which now stood between me and Redding. I considered the board. Kane to the left, out of play. Lin and the black suit likewise, in a tangled heap behind me, three feet in front of the elevator. Seven feet past them was me and the dead couch, with Redding twelve feet dead ahead.

I said, *Well, guys?*

The male voice said, *He's big.*

The female voice said, *Not necessarily strong, though.*
But near enough body-armored to be a problem.
Point.

Redding's shiny bright green tracksuit was an ultra-lightweight item. The jacket was half zipped and there was just a white undershirt behind it.

The male voice said, *Good mobility.*

The female voice said, *And this hooligan can fan-fight, too.*

Which was true. During my investigation into Kane earlier in the day, I had come across a YouTube video that had gone viral the year before, when five guys armed with baseball bats had tried to attack the Senator after a big football game. The Atlanta Falcons had visited the Baltimore Ravens, and, after seeing their home team lose, the five guys had decided it was Kane's fault, and that they would have their revenge in the parking lot immediately afterwards. The two black suits had reacted as they should have, making their priority to rush Kane to safety. While they did that, Redding had handled everything else. And according to the web, all five guys were still on respirators.

The male voice said, *Remember this guy's NFL stats? Four-point-nine second forty yard dash.*

Meaning he's six-four, 310 pounds, and about point-seven seconds away from us, the female voice said.

Any good news? I said.

Well, we're prettier, the male voice said.

Smarter too, I'd imagine.

And faster.

And a better fighter.

We're also going to cheat, the female voice said.

Redding cracked his neck from side to side.

He said, "You ready, motherfucker?"

"I'm ready," I said.

"Last words?"

"That tracksuit is ridiculous."

Redding snarled and descended into an athletic stance. I saw the face that must have been the last vision many quarterbacks had seen before they blacked out. I wasn't worried. This guy had quite literally thrown away any chance of winning.

Redding said, "I'm gonna break your face."

I smiled.

The male voice said, *Toro, you big ape.*

Redding juggernauted me.

A stupid move.

I dropped my hands and let the hair stick slide down to my fingertips. Attacking gorillas is relatively simple. Provided, of course, that you can hold your bottle. There are two rules: Use their momentum against them, and attack the base. I watched Redding explode off the mark. One step and he was already moving quickly. Which, combined with his mass, made his momentum great. Which made him hard to stop. But also made it hard for him to stop himself. So while Redding was coming straight at me, he was only coming straight. If I dodged to the side, that momentum wouldn't let him follow.

I watched his second step land and shifted my weight to my right foot.

Dodging to the side was all well and good, but it wasn't going to do anything to put Redding down. He'd recover quickly and come at me again. And while I could have probably dodged him for an entire few minutes, eventually he was going to catch up and land a blow. And if he did, I was going to die. So I needed to end the fight early. Ideally right then and there. And preferably with one blow. Which although would seem hard to do—what with his thick muscular cocoon and all—it wasn't actually that implausible. In fact, it wouldn't even be that hard. Because while muscles grow, joints don't. They are the weak points in any structure. They take all the load and all the stress. More load, more stress, more pain.

It only took Redding three steps to cover the distance. His right foot planted down hard about two feet in front of me, his entire weight falling onto it, his right hand stretching out and back.

I edged my left leg edged outward, dropping my center of gravity, preparing to move.

Redding drove powerfully off his right foot. His hip was popping, his shoulder was leading, and his right hand was coming around fast. It was swarming though the air and coming straight at my head. A kill stroke. Like a tiger mauling its prey. Redding put all his momentum into it. The predictable gorilla, doing exactly what I wanted. I pushed off my right foot and dodged under his arm. That was all it took. Just a quick bob to the outside and Redding was at the mercy of his own momentum. He was left twisting away from me, with his entire weight collapsing onto his left leg, and his entire backside now exposed.

My weight also shifted onto my left foot. But it didn't stay there long. My right hand was reaching across my body, winding up its power, and gripping the hair stick tightly. I exploded off my left foot, driving my entire body to the right, and throwing my right hand down toward the back of Redding's left knee. The hair stick speared powerfully through the air, scything a long arc, and carrying every ounce of my power with it. Redding's entire weight collapsed onto his left leg and the hair stick smacked straight into it.

The stick wasn't particularly sharp but it punctured his skin easily. I jammed it deep between his hamstrings and then yanked it to the side, ripping the muscle from the bone.

Redding went down.

His knee joint collapsed completely and his entire weight fell straight through it.

The only problem was: He fell right on top of me. All 310 pounds of him. He fell backward and flattened me. My chest hit the ground and all the air got knocked out of my lungs. Redding was convulsing around on top of me. The stick was embedded in a large nerve, and he was shrieking in pain. My ribs took a beating. I couldn't breathe at all, but then, mercifully, Redding finally stopped screaming. And moving. The pain had overloaded his system and he had simply shut down. He became a dead weight on top of me. I crawled out from beneath him.

I stood above Redding, with my hands on my knees, trying to get my breath back. My ribs were definitely bruised. The penthouse's foyer was a mess. The elevator car was standing open and full of broken mirror glass. Lin and the black suit were lying in a heap just in front, and there were pieces of ceramic vase all over the floor. The couch that Redding had killed was leaking stuffing, and the two bum shots he'd fired had landed in a decorative pillar. I walked over to the black suit and dragged him halfway into the elevator. I didn't want anyone else coming up.

I picked up both handguns. Put one at the back of my belt and kept the other in hand. Then I walked back to Redding. His hands were grasped around his thigh. The hair stick was jutting out between them.

Walk again? the male voice said.

Not well, I said.

The female voice cleared her throat.

I looked over at the far left corner of the penthouse.

Kane was white.

He was frozen in the doorway with nowhere to go.

I reached down and yanked the hair stick out of Redding's leg. The release of pressure caused a column of blood to spew out after it.

I paused for effect, and then took a step toward Kane.

The guy just about shit himself.

FORTY-NINE

I DIDN'T HAVE LONG. Between Redding's shrieking and the nine bullets that had been fired so far, the police were most definitely on their way. Which meant SAD wouldn't be too far behind. Which meant I had less than five minutes to get the info I needed from Kane. Which is why the first thing I did was break his nose.

"Motherfucker!" he shouted, throwing his hands over his face.

"Easy Kane, we're just getting started," I said.

We were in the room he had been cowering in previously. It must have been some kind of den in the original plans but Kane had turned it into an office. It looked exactly like the kind of place a Senator would use too. There was dark paneled wood all around, and a big old desk in front of the west wall, which itself, like the northern wall, was all glass, and looked out over the city. I could see the Georgia Dome way off in the distance. I could see the red and yellow lights of the cars on the freeway. The south wall of the office was basically a huge bookshelf, with lots of books, lots of pictures, and a big plasma TV in the middle. The news was on, and a certain

London based mental-health institute had made international headlines—again.

I threw Kane onto a sofa that faced the TV. He was wearing a plain blue shirt, sleeves rolled up, dark trousers, dark shoes, and a hefty gold watch. He leaned forward and spat out a mouthful of blood. Then he looked up at me – his blonde hair disheveled, his chin covered in red, his eyes wide and angry.

"We had a deal," he shouted.

"Yeah, I remember," I said.

"Then why is my Lear in the hands of some Chinese prick?"

"What?"

"You sold my jet, you bastard."

I smirked. *Isabel.*

Kane shouted, "You think this is funny?"

"I think you need to calm down."

"Who do you think you are?"

"The guy who'll shoot you if you don't calm down."

"You don't scare me."

"Then you're an idiot."

I walked over to his desk. It was cluttered with work. A laptop in the middle, various papers, memos, documents, and spreadsheets everywhere else. Nothing of any use though. I turned around and perched on the end of the desk.

Kane said, "What the hell do you want?"

I said, "Grand scheme? Meet a nice girl, settle down, have a couple of kids. But right now I'll settle for revenge."

"Revenge?"

I pointed at the TV.

Kane said, "What about it?"

I said, "I know you're involved."

"Then *you're* an idiot."

I shot the sofa, right between his legs.

Kane reeled back on the sofa. "NO! WAIT! *Don't SHOOT! Don't kill me! Please!* I'm involved. OK? I'm involved."

"Involved in what?"

"You know what."

"I want to hear you say it."

"MK-ULTRA. *OK? There, I've said it. DON'T KILL ME!*"

"And?"

"*And*? *And <u>what</u>? There's no <u>and</u>.*"

I shot him in the kneecap.

"No *and*?" I said. I pointed at TV again. "Take a look, Kane, there's the *and*."

Kane was clutching his knee, rolling around on the sofa and crying in pain.

"*OK, OK, yes*, people are *dead*," he said. "But if you think I'm the one pulling the strings you're wrong."

"*Ohhh,* so now you're just a puppet?"

"Just the money," he cried.

"Where's Christine Tanner?"

"*Who the hell is Christine Tanner?*"

I sighed and raised the Berretta again.

Kane coughed blood and spat it out. "No. *Stop. Please.*"

"Then stop lying."

"*I'm not, dammit! I don't know anybody called Christine Tanner.*"

I took a breath. I was getting impatient.

The male voice said, *Running out of time here, Isaac.*

The female voice said, *Shoot out his other kneecap.*

Kane said, "Listen. *Please.* I'm *just* the money."

"Yeah? You're funding the entire project?"

"Yes, yes. Labs, equipment, premises, people—"

317

"Dasintex?"

Kane gritted his teeth and looked up at the ceiling and shouted, "*Fucking Dasintex!*"

"…Yeah," I said. "I'm going to need a bit more than that."

Kane looked back at me, his eyes burning with rage.

"You're a dead man," he yelled.

"That's great. Now tell me about Dasintex."

Kane shook his head. "You don't understand."

"I don't care, either. Now tell me about Dasintex."

"What's there to tell? They told me to buy it, I bought it."

"Just like that?"

"I'm the money."

"OK, so you bought it, dismantled it, and then…?"

"And then I had to explain to the board why I bought a company with no prospects."

"Don't get cute with me, Kane. Besides, we both know that wasn't true was it?"

Kane said nothing.

I said, "You wanted Vanev."

"*They*," he said. "*They* wanted Vanev."

"And now I do. So where is he?"

Kane gritted his teeth again.

I tossed the hairpin onto the couch, next to him.

"Believe me," I said. "There are worse places I can stick that than your leg."

Kane started begging. "Please," he said. "Please. *Enough*."

"Where's Vanev?"

Kane cried out. Gave it up. "BexuTech. He's at BexuTech."

"BexuTech?"

"It's a company. A subsidiary of Silverton. Army research."

"You've got another MK-ULTRA lab there?"

"Yes."

"And how many other labs are there?"

"None."

"None?"

"Yes, none. I'm telling you the truth. There are no other labs. They destroyed Lyndale and now they've gone to BexuTech. I've just set it up for them."

"OK. What else do you know?"

"Only that testing is over."

"Meaning what?"

"Meaning now they're going after *real* targets."

"What's the endgame?"

"I don't know, I swear."

"Then what's the next target?"

"The conference. On Friday."

"What, at the Congress Center? Big business, Big problems?"

"Yes, yes, that one."

"You know all that and you don't know Christine Tanner?"

Kane didn't reply. He just kept crying in pain.

I charged over to him and threw him on the ground. I knelt down, putting one of my knees and most of my weight on his chest. Then I took the picture from Hays's safe out of my pocket and shoved it in Kane's face.

"Look at the photo, Kane. That's Tanner. Now who's she talking to?"

Kane's eyes were squinted tight. He could barely breathe. He was about to go into shock.

I said, "Answer the question. Who's the guy?"

Kane opened his eyes and focused on the photo.

He knew.

"Who is he, Kane?"

Kane shook his head. He started laughing.

"They're going to kill you," he said,

"Who is?"

"You have no idea how far this goes."

"So enlighten me, Senator."

Kane kept laughing. "How do you think I became senator in the first place?"

I thrust the Berretta into his stomach.

"Last chance," I said. "Who's running this?"

Kane stared up at me, still laughing, and getting more hysterical by the second. He lifted his head off the ground and stretched up to say something.

He said, "Fuck you."

I shot him in the stomach.

FIFTY

BEXUTECH WAS LOCATED 6.4 miles northeast of the Georgian Terrace Hotel. It took twenty minutes to get there by cab. It was now almost midnight. I had spent less than thirty minutes at the hotel. The only way to and from Kane's penthouse was the elevator, so after removing the body from between the doors, I had ridden down to the lobby, and stepped out to find the first black suit standing six feet in front of me, watching another receptionist shouting at the hotel's maintenance guy to fix the elevator. Black Suit immediately went for his gun and I shot him. I had walked out of the hotel just as the police had turned up.

The cab dropped me off at the side of a road, which ran north-south, a short distance east of the BexuTech compound. I went on foot from there and spent the next hour walking around and assessing the place.

I did not like what I saw.

The compound sat a mile north of Emory University. The Centers for Disease Control and Prevention had premises smack in the middle of the two. The Yerkes National Primate Research Labs and the VA Medical Center were a drive to the east. They were all situated in a huge and thick and dense woodland. According to the Google search I did with the second black suit's cell phone, the place where I was standing had originally been a ring of houses, a nice suburban family area called Castle Falls Drive, but then, about seven years ago, during the peak of the recession, Silverton had brokered a new contract with the army, bought the people out of their homes, and built BexuTech in their wake.

The compound itself was the size of nine football fields— three on a side, a perfect rectangle. In addition to the surrounding forest, the perimeter was enclosed by a fifteen-foot-high razor fence.

The main building stood in the exact center of the compound. It was a cube made almost entirely of blue mirror glass. Spotlights beamed up from the ground onto each of its sides. The whole thing sparkled in the darkness.

The cuboid took up most of the compound's space, but there was another building behind it in the northeast corner. It had steel siding and looked like a warehouse. But it must have been something else because it also had a big cylindrical chimney on top. The remaining area of the compound served as parking. It looked to be at about 10 percent capacity, with most of the vehicles parked near the warehouse.

The male voice said, *I wonder what's going on in there.*

Must be something important, I said. *Or at least it's where the action is tonight, anyway. The main building looks quiet.*

I stayed back in the forest and kept moving around the perimeter. The compound had copious amounts of lighting. The lights stood atop twenty-foot poles and beamed pure white cones onto the gravel, illuminating every inch of the parking lot. Hubs of rotating cameras were affixed below the lights and missed nothing inside the fence. The only way in was through a manually operated barrier on the eastern side. There was a security hut there and a guy inside it.

I said, *Ideas?*

The male voice said, *Not many.*

The female voice said, *What did you expect? Like Kane said, it's army research.*

Man, that guy was a psycho.

We still should have searched his office. He probably had a key card for this place. Or at the very least a parking pass.

Maybe, I said. *But then we'd have had to deal with the cops.*

Yeah… and?

And I've got a busted thumb and a set of bruised ribs here.

Poor baby.

You two are out of order.

The male voice said, *What did I do?*

The fact of the matter was that when BexuTech had secured the army contracts, it had been both entitled and forced to install some of the highest spec security available. There were going to be layers upon layers to their defense, each one more restricting than the last. But no security system is perfect. And after I swept the entire compound, it was clear to me that BexuTech's first layer had one major weakness.

I tracked back through the forest and took up position on eastern side of the compound, looking out from behind a tree. The entrance gate was just a retractable section of the fence, twenty feet wide, fifteen feet high. It was fully motorized and moved on a set of wheels. There was a bank of cameras monitoring it, and just, like the rest of the fence, the gate had warning signs all over it. The security hut was situated outside of the gate.

That was where the weakness lay.

And it was a mistake I'd seen countless times before.

Yes, BexuTech's security cameras were undeniably top of the line, and without question they surveyed every part of the compound. There were even camera turrets set up specifically to watch the surrounding forest, as well. But what good are a bunch of cameras if the only person watching is a complete and utter doughnut?

The male voice said, *Seriously? Netflix?*

The guy in the hut was about forty years old and on the heavy side. His job was to monitor the perimeter and check or issue permits via the hut's Plexiglass window. He had a phone, computer, and multiscreen feed of the parking lot cameras to help him do all of that. Not that he was paying attention though. Not with over ten thousand titles at his disposal.

I sighed. *All right, let's take this dope out.*

The female voice said, *What about your ribs?*

The compound sat a mile north of Emory University. Which, therefore, meant it was a mile north of approximately 15,000 students. And since students have, for one reason or another, been drawn to the woods for countless decades, it was not inconceivable that, every so often, one of them would get hopelessly lost and wander onto BexuTech's property, and become BexuTech's problem.

So the guy in the hut was probably well used to it.

And, since the first thing to do was to get the guy out of the hut without his raising the alarm, I figured that was my best approach.

I emerged from the forest and staggered straight up to the

gate. My hair was messed up and my clothes were pulled here and there. I swayed and stumbled and walked straight into the gate, bouncing off it and landing flat on my ass. I then began the challenge of getting back to my feet, making sure to shout about my appropriate euphoria once I was.

Then I unzipped my fly and began watering the security gate.

I heard the latch release on the security hut's door.

"Hey," the guy called. "Ya'll clear off now, you hear?"

I kept a firm focus on what I was doing.

"I SAID—" The guy hustled over. He marched straight up behind me and put a firm hand on my swaying shoulder.

Two minutes later, I was seated behind the Plexiglas window, with a clean face, a security jacket on my back, and security cap on my head.

FIFTY-ONE

THE SECURITY HUT was bigger than it looked from the outside. It had a long counter below the Plexiglas window, on which were a computer, landline phone, personal laptop, and half-eaten snacks and empty wrappers. The hut had good lighting, a comfortable chair, and a little fridge. It even had its own toilet.

The male voice said, *This guy had a pretty good shtick going.*

Too good, the female voice said. *I mean, just look at him. Total incompetence.*

Let's just hope the rest of the security is, too, I said.

The security guard was slumped in the corner. Bound and gagged and therefore still about as useful as he had been before. I had found a toolbox under the countertop and used a roll of duct tape to bind his arms and legs and then seal his mouth. It had been a quick knockout, but, apart from a couple of bruises and a splitting headache, he'd be fine. Jobless, perhaps, but fine. His jacket was baggy on me, but I figured that wouldn't matter too much. The cap was the main selling point.

The Plexiglas window was in the center of the hut's northern wall. It was made of two rectangular panels, one of which could be slid behind the other. To the right of the window was a set of shelves stacked with various files and equipment. To the left of the window were nine monitors, each one receiving multiple feeds from the security cameras, and changing between them every five seconds. Below the monitors was a big control box. It had lots of buttons, lots of switches, and lots of dials. Some controlled the cameras, some controlled the gate. One of them was a big red thing that sounded the alarm.

The computer had no Internet access. It was solely for vetting any would-be entrants. It was hooked up to some kind of ID scanner and contained a database of all the employees at BexuTech. Unsurprisingly, I did not find Christine Tanner or Dr. Galabin Vanev in there. I did, however, see that there were five levels of clearance to which one could be assigned—*five* being the highest, granting access to any part of the facility.

The security guard didn't have a gun. I had three 9mm Berrettas. But I didn't need three Berrettas. So I ejected the magazines and used the bullets from one to top up the other two. Since Redding's had been fired the most, I deemed it to be the most trustworthy and clipped in a full magazine. Again, I put it at the back of my belt, with the other full magazine going in my pocket as a spare. I stripped down the other two guns and threw their firing pins into the woods.

The male voice said, *I don't know, Isaac, we go in guns blazing and someone's bound to hit an alarm.*

Agreed, the female voice said. *The direct approach is out.*

Who said anything about guns blazing? I said.

The male voice said, *What you got in mind?*

Way I see it, we're going to need some help.

And how do you plan on getting that?

Remember that time in Kabul?

I remember it didn't work, said the male voice.

Yeah, but how many war zones do you think these guys have ever been to?

I started rummaging around the hut. The security guard had a radio on his belt, and, using a flathead screwdriver from the toolbox, I cracked it open and pulled out all of the wires and components. Then I opened the fridge and hoped that the combination of the security guard's girth, the wedding ring on his finger, the shocking obesity statistics of America, and the somewhat proud display of junk food wrappers on the counter, would mean I'd find what I was looking for.

I did.

And I *tsked* at the guy because of it.

The fridge was stacked full of Red Bull energy drinks. Understandable but of absolutely no use to me. It was the lovingly prepared and totally untouched cellophane-wrapped sandwiches in the door that were perfect.

There were four blocks of them. Each block contained two slices of bread with some kind of meager filling in between, cut in half in order to produce the illusion of two sandwiches. I began squeezing each block, squishing the bread into a kind of doughy consistency. I used the duct tape to stick all four blocks together, leaving me with one single doughy mass. Then I took the components from the radio and started pushing them in and around the block. Finally, I took the guy's cell phone and stuck it to the front.

Et voilà.

The female voice said, *You know, actually, it doesn't look that bad.*

Guess we'll see, the male voice said. *Here comes someone now.*

*

The north–south road I'd come in on ran straight through the woodland, splitting off due west for access to BexuTech. I saw a set of headlights make that turn in the distance. It was a small hatchback and it was carrying a rather tired-looking fellow in a lab coat. He pulled up to the hut, lowered his window, and stuck his hand out. I slid back the Plexiglas window and reached out to take his laminate ID card. I swiped it into the ID scanner and his profile popped up on the computer screen. He was a general technician, with Bexutech for the last couple of years, a Level Two clearance.

Not what I was looking for.

I handed back his card and worked the gate and he drove through.

The male voice said, *Well that was a bust.*

The female voice said, *Get used to it. This could take a while.*

It took well over two hours. Which actually wasn't that bad. It was past midnight, after all. The interesting thing was that Bexutech's main building remained quiet. It was the warehouse that was the main attraction. All five cars that pulled up to the gate went and parked right outside it. Just like the first guy, each person handed over their ID, waited patiently, and then got let through by the new and very good-looking security guard. But, just like the first guy, none of them had what I needed.

So I had to wait.

Mercifully, though, at a quarter past three, a rather expensive four-door sedan pulled up to the hut and phase two of my entry plan began.

FIFTY-TWO

THERE WERE TWO people inside the car. A man and a woman. They were both wearing lab coats. The guy was in the passenger seat and he passed his laminate to the woman who then passed it to me along with her own. I scanned each card into the computer system and checked out their profiles. Dr. Daniel Patel was the man in the passenger seat: fifty-three, an engineer, a longtime employee. Last entry was the night before, at around the same time. Dr. Paula Emerson was the driver. She was thirty-six and the head of metamaterial research at BexuTech. Her last entry matched Patel's. Clearly, they carpooled.

The male voice said, *She's the one.*

As head of metamaterials, Emerson had a Level Five security clearance. She had full access to the facility. Patel was part of the same team, but only had Level Three. But that didn't make him useless. In fact, he was actually going to do me a big favor.

I reached back out of the Plexiglas window to return the laminates. Emerson's hand went to receive them but I quickly retracted my arm at the last minute, having suddenly been alerted to something. Emerson's hand was left hanging in midair.

I snatched up the hut's phone to my ear. I listened very carefully and then began nodding and Yes-sir-ing. I put a stern look on my face and started shifting my eyes suspiciously between Emerson and Patel, both of whom stared back at me, utterly perplexed, and eventually a little worried. I kept it up for about a minute and then said a final "Yes, sir" before putting the phone down.

Emerson said, "Is everything OK?"

I didn't reply.

Instead I made a big show of scrutinizing their laminate IDs and then signaled for Emerson to hold position. I closed up the Plexiglas window, put the roll of duct tape in one pocket, my arts and crafts in the other pocket, and then I took the hut's phone off the cradle, grabbed a flashlight, switched the entrance gate to automatic, tipped my hat to the guard, and exited the hut. I made sure to lock the door and tossed the keys into the woodland. Then I walked around to the idling sedan, where Emerson was craning her head out of her window.

"Is everything OK?" she asked again.

Again I didn't reply.

I started walking around the car like the guys back at Wright-Patterson had. The car was a Mercedes—newish model, four doors, silver. I walked slowly, counterclockwise, shining the flashlight over every part of the vehicle, and making a big deal of looking into the back seats. I came around Patel's side, putting the beam straight in his face. He squinted away. Not a confrontational guy. I continued around the hood and came to the driver's door.

I leaned into the vehicle.

"Nothing to worry about, folks," I said. "But I'm going to need you to pop the trunk."

Emerson looked at Patel and then back at me.

I said, "Ma'am, the trunk."

She nodded and hit the button.

I gave them both a look and then went to the back of the vehicle. The trunk was completely empty.

The male voice said, *Nice accent.*

I said, *What, I'm not allowed to have some fun with this?*

The female voice said, *But why always with the gum chewing? Every time you go Southern it's smack, smack, smack?*

Helps me get into character, I said.

And that character is Colonel Sanders?

I closed the trunk and walked back to the driver's window. "All right, thanks, folks."

Emerson said, "Is there something we should know?"

I handed back their laminates.

"Afraid there's been some trouble at the Texas facility," I said.

"Trouble?" Emerson said.

"At Texas?" Patel said.

BexuTech had a sister facility down in Texas. It was smaller than the Atlanta facility, but just as valuable.

I nodded. "Seems a couple good-for-nothings were after some of our research."

Emerson said, "They got into the facility?"

"Mm-hmm. Forced a couple of lab techs to sneak them in using the trunk of their car."

"That's awful. When did it happen?"

"Couple of hours ago."

"Are the lab techs OK?"

"No doubt they're shaken, you can be sure. But they'll be fine."

"Did they get anything? The people I mean."

"Yes ma'am. Yes indeed. *Caught*. Caught is what they got."

She relaxed a breath and nodded back.

I said, "So what you're experiencing right now is heightened security measures. Fact is, we got sloppy. It could have just as easily been a bomb back there. We won't make that same mistake again."

"That's terrible," Emerson said. "I'm glad you guys are on top of it. Thank you."

"No thanks required, ma'am. Just doing our job. Besides you folks ain't got nothing to be scared about. Scariest thing in your trunk is that there set of golf clubs. Now I don't play much myself but from what I hear Callaway is a friend."

Emerson exhaled an uneasy laugh. Nodded again.

And then she snapped rigid and shot me a look.

"Wait, what golf clubs?" she said. "I don't have any golf clubs back there. I don't even play golf."

"Ma'am?"

Emerson just stared at me, wide-eyed, confused, and then she turned to Patel, who offered nothing, and then back to me, who gave her a smile, and then she shook her head and undid her seatbelt and popped the trunk again and got out of the vehicle. Patel got out too, and we all convened at the back of the car.

Both doctors stared into the trunk, pontificating at the empty space. Emerson in front to my left, Patel in front to my right. Both of them were confused, but Emerson got the message first. Specifically, she got it when she felt the cold steel of the Berretta's extended barrel on the back of her neck. Patel got it a few seconds later when he turned around and saw the situation.

I smiled at him.

"Lab coat," I said.

I kept my voice calm and even, speaking in a very matter-of-fact kind of way, though, for some reason, still with the accent. Emerson was frozen and holding her breath. Patel was stunned for a second but then complied quickly and silently, shucking off the white coat and handing to me.

Not a confrontational guy. No kind of hero.

I said, "Phone, keys, and wallet."

He dropped them in a neat pile on the ground.

I glanced around and back down the road. Everything was quiet, nobody coming. I took the duct tape out of my pocket and nudged Emerson into action.

"Mouth, hands, and feet."

She hesitated.

"Faster you do it, faster it's done," I said.

Patel nodded at her. Emerson got to it. She worked quickly and he didn't resist. She knew what she was doing, too. She tied Patel's hands behind his back and then he brought his feet together and she knelt down and did the same to his ankles and knees. Then she wrapped a full length of tape around his mouth and head. Once she was finished I nodded at the trunk and Patel folded himself into it. He was not a big man, not the size of a golf bag either, but after a little shuffling around he actually looked quite comfortable inside the spacious trunk.

Emerson said, "Don't worry, Daniel. It'll be fine. I promise."

At which point I pulled out what looked like an IED.

Both of their eyes widened at the same time.

Emerson said, "Oh my G-d!"

I put the bomb in the trunk with Patel and quickly closed the lid. They had seen what they wanted to see. Any more time to process and they might have seen through it.

Emerson was stiff as a board and still holding her breath. I brought the gun down a fraction, then nodded at Patel's belongings which she hurried to pick up.

I said, "You drive."

Emerson got back into the driver's seat and I got in behind her. We had to reverse a few feet and then reapproach the gate in order to activate the sensor. I had no doubt that people would wonder about the empty security hut, but so long as they had no trouble getting in, I figured they'd forget about it by the time they parked.

The Mercedes rolled into the compound.

FIFTY-THREE

THERE WERE ONLY twelve vehicles parked in front of the main building. One was a big black SUV, the rest a mix of middle- or upper-class sedans. I told Emerson to park among them, indicating a space between the SUV and an Audi. She slid the Mercedes in and then shut down the engine.

We sat in silence for the next few minutes.

The Mercedes was quite spacious. Emerson had gone for the dark interior. Black leather, silver highlights. The back seats were comfortable and I had plenty of leg room. Better than the catering van, but a far cry from the Jag. The SUV was to our left. An eight seater. Big, imposing, and blocking out a lot of light from the nearby floodlight. Emerson was staring at me in the rearview mirror.

There was something oddly calming about the head of metamaterials research. She had brown eyes and a ponytail of the same shade of brown. An altogether gentle appearance. She was wearing just a faint trace of perfume, or possibly none and it was just her shampoo, but, in any case, the scent lit up my senses quite pleasantly.

She said, "I need to ask you something."

I said, "You got me. I'm not Southern."

"Have you honestly thought this through?"

"Honestly? No. But that's what we're going to do now."

Emerson said nothing.

I leaned forward and handed her the picture from Hays's safe.

I said, "Do you know this woman?"

Emerson held the photo up to her face. Then she looked at me in the rearview mirror and gestured at the dome light. I nodded that it was OK and she flicked it on. She studied the picture carefully for about thirty seconds.

She said, "I don't know who this is."

"You're sure?"

"Yes."

"You've never seen her around here?"

"No."

"What about the name Christine Tanner? Does that ring a bell?"

"No."

"How about Dr. Galabin Vanev?"

"No."

"There's no way they could be here?"

"I've never seen or heard of either of them."

"But it is possible."

"No."

"Why not?"

Emerson paused.

She said, "How many people do you think are working here?"

I looked out at the giant cuboid.

I said, "Five hundred?"

Emerson shook her head. "You're not even close."

"More?"

"Less."

"Two-fifty?"

"Sixty."

"All right so two hundred and sixty people. Surely you don't know *all* of them."

She shook her head again. "No. Not two-sixty. *Sixty*."

"What, in this whole place?"

"Yes. And two weeks ago, there were only twenty of us."

I said nothing.

Emerson said, "This is why I asked you if you had really thought this through."

"I don't understand."

"BexuTech was founded seven years ago," she said. "Silverton acquired a selection of army contracts and this place was built specifically for those purposes. State-of-the-art facilities, some of the brightest minds in the country. And, yes, back then, about three hundred people worked here."

"So what happened?"

"Simple. We lost the contracts."

"All of them?"

She sighed. "The real problem was the timing. Since we acquired all the contracts at the same time, they all came under review at the same time. Five weeks ago the Army put the contracts back out to tender. We lost six out of seven, and therefore just over 85 percent of our funding."

"So all those people got laid off?"

"Unfortunately. Yes."

"But not you."

"Materials was the contract we managed to keep. I'm head of materials."

"Lucky you."

Emerson said nothing.

I said, "You're telling me this place is basically shut down?"

"Yes," she said. "Apart from a small group in the bio department, plus what you can see over there, my team is currently the only active user of the facility. BexuTech is 85 percent shut down."

"And nobody else can use it? What about the university? Surely they can make use of these state-of-the-art facilities?"

"Well that's the set up most other research facilities have in place. But the conditions of Silverton's original deal make that extremely difficult. The main reason Silverton was granted all seven contracts in the first place was because they agreed to construct a purpose-built facility, and put it under US Army jurisdiction. Everyone on site at BexuTech must possess an Army-accredited security clearance. The kind of thing that takes about a year to sort out, and includes background checks, financial histories, and polygraph tests."

"Everyone?"

"Everyone."

I took back the photograph.

Emerson switched off the dome light.

I said, "So what is going on in that other building?"

"It's a separate department."

"Why is it separate?"

"It's a precaution. Because of what they're working with."

"And that would be?"

"Extreme combustibles."

"Sounds like a blast."

Emerson said nothing.

I said, "They're really making bombs in there?"

"Not bombs. Combustibles."

"How about some specifics?"

"That's classified."

I gave her a look.

She said, "Do you know what a *catalyst* is?"

"Something that lowers the activation energy of a reaction."

Emerson gave me a look.

I said, "Application?"

"Enhanced fuel delivery systems."

"Jet fuel?"

She nodded. "For fighter jets."

The male voice said, *Just the money, eh?*

I said, "Let me guess, one of the contracts you lost has just come up for tender again?"

"Yes," Emerson said. "And if we can reacquire it, it will mean millions in funding. Most of the people in there now were part of the original team. This is their chance to get their jobs back. They've been working round the clock."

"And I'm going to take another stab in the dark and say HBL were the ones who won it five weeks ago?"

"What are you implying?"

"Enough."

Emerson said, "What exactly are you hoping to achieve, here?"

I said, "Talk to me about security."

"There's a lot."

"In a facility that's 85 percent empty?"

Emerson said nothing.

I pointed at the glass cuboid. "Start with the ground floor. What's the layout?"

"There's a security desk."

"A guy there 24/7?"

"Two guys."

"You know them?"

"Doug and Joe."

"How old are they?"

"How old are they? I don't know. Late twenties, maybe. Young guys. Ex-military, I think."

I smiled. "Same battalion as the guy in the hut?"

Emerson said nothing.

I said, "OK so that's Doug and Joe. Anybody else?"

"There are more guards."

"But they're in the other building?"

"Why are you doing this?"

"You have access to the entire facility, correct?"

"It's 85 percent empty."

"And 15 percent full."

"Look," she said. "This *isn't* going to work. I don't know what you're hoping to find, but even if we had no guards, even if we had no one here at all, you still wouldn't have the time to look."

"Explain."

"I told you the original contracts came with certain conditions. Security was one of the major ones. We've got a military spec system in place. Facial recognition. Getting past the gate is one thing, but the actual building is something else. It's basically a 'smart' building. It scans everyone who enters and it will go into lockdown at the first sign of threat. And if it does, there's no way out. *You will be caught.*"

"What constitutes a threat?"

"You."

"Me?"

"Anyone with any kind of criminal history."

I nodded. "OK, me."

Emerson said, "Certain decibel readings will also set off the lockdown."

'In other words, a gunshot."

She nodded. "And police response was tested at five minutes."

I looked out at the giant cuboid. Then at the other building. Then back at the security hut.

The female voice said, *Guess we were lucky.*

The male voice said, *Yeah, if this place hadn't been deserted for the past few weeks we probably would've had to deal with someone far more competent than that doughnut.*

Still, it does explain how Tanner could set up a lab here.

I met Emerson's gaze in the rearview mirror. "I noticed that the security hut didn't have Internet," I said. "I take it that's the same situation throughout?"

"Of course," she said. "It's a security measure. Mandatory in this day and age. Internet access means exposure. We can't afford to get hacked."

"What about government Intranet? Your facial recognition system needs a database."

"Yes but it's a closed-loop system. A direct link to the database and nothing more."

"E-mail?"

"Only internal."

"So how do you communicate with the outside world? Snail mail?"

"Or fax."

"That's all you have?"

"That and telephone."

"What about when you want to hand over something to the Army?"

"We do it once a month," she said. "Someone comes here. Official US Army courier. We release the information to them directly. A hard copy. It's another bunch of protocols and a whole other procedure."

The male voice said, *So much for Marcel's help.*

The female voice said, *Which means we'll have to do this old-fashioned way.*

Emerson watched me think.

I said, "So all I have to do is beat the facial recognition and I'm free?"

"How can you beat facial recognition?"

"Easily. But answer my question first."

She sighed. "No. Even *if* you beat the facial rec, you still wouldn't be free to move around."

"Why not?"

"You're thinking that because I've got a Level Five clearance you'll be able to use me to get around, right?"

"Maybe."

She shook her head. "Except you won't. The building also tracks how many people are in each sector. You need a key card to access a sector, and the building will match faces to key cards."

I looked down at Patel's laminate ID card. There was a passport-size photo in the top right corner.

The male voice said, *Not even close.*

I asked Emerson, "How does someone get a key card?"

"They are issued by the front desk."

"Doug and Joe?"

"In this case."

"Then we have our way in."

"No, I told you, everyone needs a security clearance just to be on site. You can't be issued a key card without proper documentation."

I waved away her comment. "Details," I said. "You'll figure it out."

Emerson said nothing.

"Doesn't need to be complicated," I said, "And feel free to think outside the box. Personal physician, attorney, outside consultant, anything can work. Just spin them a simple story and we'll be good to go."

"And what if they don't buy it?"

"Come now, Doctor, we both know that those two guys spend about 90 percent of their time thinking about one thing. And we also know that if you're around they're not going to be doing any thinking, at all. At least not with their heads anyway."

I saw her blush in the mirror. She didn't deny it though. Women, lab coats, and very little else make for powerful fantasies. And Dr. Paula Emerson definitely knew that.

She said, "But… "

"But what?"

Emerson turned in her seat and looked back at me.

"But this will make me an accomplice," she said.

"I think that ship sailed when you taped your friend's knees together."

Emerson faced forward again. She contemplated for a few moments and then said, "Even if I did vouch for you, you'd still only be issued with a limited access pass. And you'd still have to pass facial recognition."

"But as long as I'm with you my pass will work anywhere, right? That's usually how these things work."

She said nothing.

"Excellent. Now, you got any makeup?"

"What?"

"Relax. You look fine. I mean for me."

"What? Why?"

"Well if you're running facial recognition, I want to look my best."

Emerson just stared at me in the rearview mirror.

"Makeup," I said.

She hesitated for a moment and then reached across dash and opened the glove box. There were a bunch of things inside. She retrieved a small compact and a tube of lipstick and placed them on the armrest between the front two seats.

I said, "You got any blush?"

She gave me another look.

"Seriously," I said.

She went back to the glove box and came back with a rectangular blush palette. There were nine colors to choose from, all deep and warm. I loaded the accompanying brush with a deep purple and then pulled down the over-head mirror and got to work. I applied a thick layer of the blush all over the bridge of my nose and under my eyes. I made use of a dark red, too.

Emerson continued to watch me in the rearview mirror, totally bewildered.

I said, "Duct tape."

She handed the roll back to me.

"And whatever that rectangular box is."

She took it out of the glove box and gave it to me. It was a pack of throat lozenges. I removed the contents and unfolded the box. It was rectangular in shape, completely blank on the inner side. I tore the box into a smaller shape, keeping only one of the long narrow sides plus an equal section from the adjoining "face" and "back" sides. I placed the long edge down the center of my nose and folded the flaps down over the sides. Then I used duct tape to fix it into position. One strip down the length of my nose, another across my fore-head, and a final one from cheekbone to cheekbone. By the time I'd finished, it looked like I'd broken my nose real bad.

"OK," I said. "This'll take care of facial recognition, and you can take care of Doug and Joe. We'll play it by ear after that."

Emerson said, "What about Daniel?"

"Don't worry about Daniel."

FIFTY-FOUR

EMERSON AND I got out of the car. She said my best way in would probably be as an outside consultant and told me to put on Patel's lab coat. The guard's jacket had been too big and Patel's lab coat was too small. I rolled up the sleeves to try and hide that fact, and then told Emerson to lead the way.

We scuttled around the SUV, past some flower beds, and over to the cuboid. It was chilly, and the breeze blew through Emerson's ponytail and unbuttoned lab coat. She was wearing black trousers, a dark red top, a plain wristwatch, and heels. Her laminate ID hung around her neck.

The main entrance consisted of a pair of double glass doors that opened automatically for us. The lobby sat in the exact center of the eastern face of the cuboid. It was large and very corporate looking. Neutral colors, highly polished, minimalist. The floor was made of shiny square tiles. There were two crude sitting areas on either side of the room, hard sofas around glass coffee-tables. There were a couple of water coolers and some fake plants too.

There were also fifteen security cameras scattered across the ceiling.

I could almost feel the facial recognition start running me.

The reception-security desk was straight ahead. It sat squarely on the back wall, where the BexuTech logo was embossed in chunky letters, just like at the Georgian Terrace Hotel. There was a big metal box on either side of the desk. They looked like body scanners at airports.

Emerson brought a hand to mouth.

I said, "What?"

"I forgot about the degaussing boxes," she said.

"What about them?"

"They bombard you with a super powerful magnetic field. Any electrical device is wiped clean, if not destroyed."

"Yeah, I get it. No technology in, no technology out. So what?"

"So you see? This isn't going to work."

"You're still assuming I'm here to steal something."

"Aren't you?"

"I've got no interest in your tech. Or your research."

"Fine. But you *do* want to bring in your cell phone."

She had a point. Since I couldn't fire my gun without the lockdown going off, the only real leverage I had against her was the bomb in her Mercedes. A bomb supposedly triggered by my cell phone.

I said, "Then I won't go through the box."

"Everyone goes through the box," she said. "On the way in and on the way out. No exceptions."

"*No* exceptions?"

"None."

"I bet Daniel could think of a few."

*

We walked over to the security desk. As promised, two young men were sat behind it. But contrary to the doctor's advertisement, they were exceedingly average in every way. Competent, perhaps, but certainly no military backgrounds. Again, had BexuTech been in better shape, they would have been replaced with an upgrade. They were wearing white shirts, black ties, and name tags. Doug was sitting on the right, Joe on the left. They were chewing the fat and passing the time. Both guys perked up upon seeing the doctor.

Doug said, "Evening, Dr. Emerson."

Emerson said, "Evening, guys."

She was ever calm, her voice even and controlled.

Then Joe said, "Where's Dr. Patel?"

"He got tied up," I said.

Eyes shifted over to me.

Doug pulled a face, stretching his mouth sideways and sucking in some air. He said, "What happened?"

"Bingo at the local senior center," I said.

He gave me a blank look.

Emerson said, "Dr. Patel is going to be away for the next few weeks. My colleague… Dr. Vaughn, here, is assisting in Daniel's absence. He's going to need a pass."

The male voice said, *Vaughn?*

The female voice said, *Yeah not great. But we can make it work.*

Joe waved me over to his side of the desk.

"Full name?"

"Victor Atriums Vaughn."

"Spelled?"

I spelled it.

"Date of birth?"

I made myself thirty.

"Occupation?"

"Retired."

"Retired?"

"Used to be in advanced polymer-based silicon-spectroscopy. Now Google is."

Another blank look.

"How I have time to consult and get into fistfights with female octogenarians."

"Err… I'll just put consultant, then."

He typed in the information and then looked up and said, "Security clearance documentation?"

At which point Emerson butted in, saying, "You should already have it, Joe."

We all looked at her.

Joe said, "I should?"

"Didn't Jason send it to you this morning?"

Joe started clicking away at his computer. Came up with nothing. He searched through a paper tray on the desk.

"I've got nothing here," he said. "You, Doug?"

Doug checked his computer, too. He looked at the empty fax machine sitting next to him. He shook his head.

Emerson exhaled like she was tired, frustrated, and more than a little pissed off. She looked at me and started shaking her head. She said, "I'm sorry about this, Dr. Vaughn."

I said nothing.

Emerson turned back to Doug and Joe again.

"You know Jason *really* is getting on my nerves," she said. "It's been one thing after another. There was that whole thing at the beginning of the week and now this. Daniel wasn't supposed to leave until Monday. That's what we agreed. But then Jason decides he needs him in Texas three days early and of course that's that. So at eight o'clock this morning I had to drive Daniel straight to the airport, straight from work, and then I had to wait there to pick up Dr. Vaughn, here, four hours later. Except naturally Dr. Vaughn's flight got delayed, meaning we've only just come from the airport, now. So, basically, I'm running off zero sleep, with a project delivery deadline in two days, a project that Jason himself was supposed to have done, but instead passed off to me, and now you're telling me that the only help I've got to do that can't, because Jason hasn't bothered to send the necessary particulars?"

She took a breath. She had worked herself right up.

Doug and Joe and I said nothing.

The male voice said, *Where did that come from?*

Doug and Joe looked to me.

I shook my head and shrugged.

They looked at each other. Then back at Emerson. Then back at each other.

Doug said, "You know... I'm sure... "

Joe nodded quickly. "Yeah, Jason will send it all over in the morning. We can give you a guest pass until then."

Emerson exhaled and massaged her forehead. "I'm sorry guys. It's not your fault. It's just been a hell of week. You two are brilliant. I really mean it. Thank you."

They both made *aw shucks* faces and then Joe got to work. He took my picture via the webcam atop his computer and did some fast and furious clicking with his mouse. To my right, Emerson started up a deep conversation with Doug. She was leaning forward on the desk, her arms crossed loosely, and her breasts resting on her forearms and swelling up. She was looking right at Doug, seemingly pouring out her troubles to him. Doug was nodding but looking slightly lower.

Joe rattled open a drawer and took out a laminate card. He waved a handheld scanner over it and something beeped and after a few more mouse clicks he handed it over to me saying, "OK, you're all set Dr. Vaughn."

I looked at what I'd been issued with. It was just piece of paper sandwiched between two sheets of plastic, flimsy, almost square, with a BexuTech logo on one side, a barcode on the other, and a metal clip affixed to one edge so I could hang it on my jacket. Below the logo was the letter *G*.

I said, "No picture?"

Joe said, "Not for a guest pass. But you'll get your full ID tomorrow when the paperwork comes through. For now though you'll be linked with Dr. Emerson. She'll have to be with you at all times."

"That's fine."

"Great. Now I just need your cell phone and any other electricals before you go through degaussing. You can pick them up on your way out."

"Actually, Joe, he can't," Doug said.

Joe and I turned to him.

Doug said, "I understand you have a medical condition, Dr. Vaughn?"

I looked at Emerson. "...Yes."

"And you wear a pacemaker for that?"

I smiled. "That's correct. I've got a slight arrhythmia."

"Then you can't go through degaussing. It'll fry your device."

"So what does that mean?"

"Well technically it means we can't let you into the building."

I looked at Emerson again. She seemed to be holding her breath.

Doug said, "Now Dr. Emerson, here, has vouched for you, but we're still going to need to take some precautions. You understand."

"What kind of precautions?"

"Well you're shoes and such can go through degaussing, no problem there, but we'll have to pat you down."

I said nothing.

Emerson eyes widened. She was looking straight through my stomach to the back of my belt. She turned and snapped at him, "Oh come on, Doug, is all that really necessary? He's with me."

Doug was taken aback. He turned to Joe, who said nothing and kept his head down, and then he looked up at me, who could offer nothing but a broken nose, and then he looked back at Emerson and decided he didn't want to be like Jason and said, "Um… all right, go ahead."

Emerson didn't wait around. She immediately started walking, going straight through the box to the right of the desk. I followed quickly.

I said, "Who's Jason?"

"He's our CEO."

"You two weren't married were you?"

"What? No. Why?"

"You can't tell me that was all an act."

She said nothing.

I said, "Well, in any case, nicely done."

"Just tell me what you want."

"You said there were people in the Bio Department?"

"They're from the Army."

"What are they working on?"

"I don't know."

"Take me there."

FIFTY-FIVE

MERSON TOLD ME the quickest way to the Bio labs was via the elevator a few feet away from us. But I didn't want to go the quickest way. I wanted to go the least quick. Or the least-intuitive anyway. Basically, I didn't want a repeat of what happened at Kane's penthouse. So I told Emerson to show me something in a side entrance.

Emerson led me down a short corridor, which had a couple of corporate-style boardrooms on either side. We turned off south and immediately came to a thick set of double doors. They were made of steel and looked just about impenetrable. No windows, no handles. Just a cold blue tint and the number *1.3* imprinted in their center. Above the doors were two cameras, and on the adjacent right wall there was a rectangular glass panel. *It tracks how many people are in each sector, and matches faces to ID cards.* I held my ID pass to the panel and a second later a red light blinked on and a sharp buzzer went off, like on a game show when a contestant gets a question wrong.

I looked at Emerson.

She said, "I have to scan, first."

She held up her laminate to the glass, and this time, a

green light blinked on, followed by a much more placid tone of beep. I then scanned mine again and only after that did the steel doors unlock.

Emerson pushed through and the corridor continued straight ahead, turning right at the bottom, about halfway to the southern face of the cuboid. The left hand wall was made entirely of glass and looked into a gigantic laboratory, with a fifty-foot ceiling, and which occupied the entire southwest corner of the cuboid. It was filled with massive machines and grand work benches. There were huge sculptures all over the place. Half-built conceptual design ideas that although looked impressive clearly hadn't made an impression: The whole lab, and indeed the whole sector, was dark and totally shut down. Without the lights on, I could see straight through the southern wall, out of the cube, over the forest, past the university, and into the far distance.

The right wall had a short staircase up to a second level, but was otherwise lined with doors, each one with a small window showing a either a dark empty lab or a dark empty office beyond. There was nobody around.

I said, "What department was this?"

"Robotics and Engineering," she said.

"The mandate?"

"Next gen smart missiles. Conceptually brilliant but practically a bust."

"What was the problem?"

"Even the army has a budget."

"Are all your labs this big?"

"Hardly. R and E just had the biggest toys to accommodate. But they were also the best-funded. Highest number of people, too."

"How many?"

"Sixty-four."

"And the other departments?"

"Between forty and fifty."

"Except yours which only has twenty. "

"We manage."

"Where exactly is your lab?"

She hesitated.

"Relax," I said. "I told you I've got no interest in your work."

"Materials is *1.9*," she said. "The northwest corner."

"That why you went through the degaussing box on the right?"

"I thought it'd be suspicious if I went through the left."

I nodded. "Good thinking."

We rounded the southeast corner, the giant robotics lab coming around on our left with us, until we hit another set of steel doors. We swiped our IDs and then pushed through into sector *1.4*.

It was a T-shaped corridor, with the crossbar continuing ahead, and the stem extending from the middle of the right wall to the center of the cuboid. The left hand wall remained see-through, and showed a large room filled with computers. Down the stem of the T there was a set of sealed double glass doors that looked into a huge room filled with vending machine shaped equipment. They were arranged in regimented rows, each unit encased in titanium, painted black but speckled with tiny red and green lights. Coming down from the ceiling high above them were large aluminum cylinders, all part of an intricate cooling and fire-prevention system. A server farm. Terabytes of processing power stacked in a temperature controlled room.

Again the entire sector was dark and shut down.

"What department was this?" I said.

Emerson said, "Information Sciences. Cyberdefense systems and such."

We went through the next set of double doors and came out in a small vestibule. There were toilets, fire stairs, an elevator, and a couple of vending machines. There were also two sets of double doors. One set went east, toward the middle of the cuboid, sector *1.6*, and the other continued ahead, toward the south-west corner of the cuboid, sector *1.7*. But Emerson pointed to the fire stairs instead.

"The Bio department is down there," she said.

"The basement?"

"Sunlight and chemicals don't mix."

"And you think a team from the Army is down there?"

"Probably not *now* but during the day."

"How do you know they're from the Army?"

"Because it's always the Army. I told you, any outside party needs to get clearance before they can use the facility. So far they've all just gone somewhere else."

"How long have they been here?"

"Since Monday."

"How many people?"

"I didn't see them arrive. Jason handles all of that."

I thought about the big black SUV in the parking lot.

The male voice said, *How bad could it be?*

I pulled out the Berretta.

FIFTY-SIX

WE CAME DOWN the fire stairs slowly. No sense coming in the side entrance if you're going to alert everyone with a clunking elevator. I pushed open the fire door at the bottom of the stairs and peeked ahead. I saw a long corridor that went right at the bottom. It was painted metallic blue and had no glass walls. The ceiling was low and there were doors on either side, some of which required an ID scan, all of which had dark windows. I focused on trying to hear round the corner.

The female voice said, *Looks quiet enough.*

The male voice said, *It always looks quiet enough.*

So we'll keep <u>this one</u> *in front of us*, said the female voice.

You don't like her?

Meh…

I turned to Emerson. "All clear," I said.

"All clear from whom?"

I stepped out of the stairwell and eased the door closed after Emerson. Then I ducked into the first room on the right. It didn't require an ID scan and looked like a kitchen. It was a small rectangular space with built in counter tops on either side. A couple of computers, a couple of microscopes. Nothing in use. Empty.

Emerson said, "Who do you think is down here?"

I said, "What are these guys supposed to be working on?"

"I told you I don't know."

"Well what was the Bio contract you had before?"

"Performance supplements."

"Like steroids?"

"Not exactly. But essentially yes. For the brain, anyway. Neural boosts. Ways to make soldiers sharper, keep them awake for longer, that sort of thing."

"What happened?"

"Same thing that always happens with this kind of research. The costs outweighed the benefits."

"Costs as in side effects?"

"I don't know the ins and outs."

"But you did carry out the tests down here?"

She shot me a look. "*Not at all*," she said. "Are you crazy? We only do research here. Sure we work with the chemicals and synthesize potential serums, but we'd never actually *test* them here. We're far from equipped. Live trials are only ever done at approved army medical centers. Under the supervision of doctors, nurses, and a whole slew of other professionals. We're talking about soldiers lives. Human beings for goodness sake. We'd never do something so stupid. Never."

I said nothing.

"And that quip you made before, the one about HBL and how we might have had something to do with the explosion at their labs? You must know that's totally ludicrous."

"Is that a fact?"

"Yes it is. I mean, how could you even think that?"

I tried a door on the opposite side of the corridor. It had an ID scanner next to it.

But it opened freely.

Which seemed to quiet Emerson down a bit.

It was another small lab. Black rubberized flooring, gray walls, a suspended ceiling. But there were signs of use. There was a big box on one of the counter tops. It had a Silverton Group logo on its side. It was open.

I checked out the contents.

The male voice said, *Microchips?*

The female voice said, *Not like any I've ever seen.*

Emerson said, *DNA Microarray Chips.*

I looked at her. Shrugged.

"They help tailor drugs to individuals," she said. "It's the main problem when testing any new chemical compound. Deliverance and dosage protocols are one thing, but *how* a drug interacts with a system is far more important. It all hinges on the pharmacogenomics. You have to factor in individual gene expression in order to optimize and stabilize the pharmaceutical effect."

The male voice said, *Sounds pretty familiar.*

It did. Emerson could have quoting directly from Tanner's thesis paper.

I walked out of the lab and we carried on down the corridor. About halfway to the end we passed a window showing a room with number of green and red lights glowing inside it. Not as many as I'd seen in the Information Sciences Department but nonetheless another sever room. Again the door opened freely despite the ID panel.

We approached the turn at the bottom of the corridor. I hugged the wall and looked round the corner. The corridor continued toward the center of the cuboid. It was four doors long, and there was a set of heavy doors at the end. They weren't sector doors but they were just as solid. There was an access panel next to them. Cameras above. It was some kind of special lab. Each door had a square porthole with a mesh grating over them. I couldn't see through it, but I didn't need to in order to see that the lights were on inside.

As were the lights in two of the rooms leading up to it.

I turned back to Emerson and held a finger to my lips.

We crept up to the second door on the left and looked in through the window.

Emerson said, "What in the world?"

She hurried to open the door, rushing inside only to stop dead as if shocked to find what she'd just seen through the window.

Which was not a lab.

Or an office.

It was a room with six beds inside.

Five of which had a body lying on top of them.

They were all unconscious and they were all wearing hospital gowns. They were all young. No one over twenty-five. Three men, two women. The men on the right, the women on the left. *One mile north of the University. One mile from over ten thousand potential subjects.*

The beds were not proper hospital beds. They were crude low-height military cots. No headers, no footers, no pillows, no blankets. Just a strip of canvass on folding legs. The only accessory was a clipboard, which hung off the end and was presumably some kind of medical chart.

To our right, in the corner of the room, there was a video camera attached to a tripod.

I saw Emerson working hard to process what she was seeing. I could see her mind flooding with questions. Everything from who these people were, to what was being done to them. I also saw that one question was beating out all the rest.

Why were they all strapped down?

All five people were anchored to their cots via six thick leather belts. One across their chest and upper arms, one across their waist, one across both thighs, one across both shins, and two smaller ones for each wrist. Only their heads had freedom to move.

To the left of each bed was a vital-sign monitor. They showed sinus waves and heartbeat blips and numbers over numbers. All of them were beeping at a similar speed.

Emerson turned to say something but immediately got interrupted by a loud moan. It came from the guy in the middle cot on the right. He was about twenty years old, white, with blonde hair, and about four days of worth of stubble. He had been perfectly still like the others, but was now twitching and shuffling around under his restraints. His head started tossing from side to side. His heart rate shot up and his monitor started beeping loudly.

Emerson rushed to grab the clipboard from the foot of his bed. She wasn't a medical doctor but she snatched through the pages, frantically trying to make sense of what was happening.

I didn't need a chart.

To the right of each bed was a tall stainless steel pole. Each pole had two silver bags at the top. Each bag had an IV line running down from it, one ending up in the person's right arm, the other in the person's left.

All ten arms had thick black veins standing out in bold relief.

Emerson said, "What the hell is going on?"

I walked out of the room and diagonally across the

corridor to the other door with a light on. I looked in through the window glass. I pushed it open.

The male voice said, *Damn.*

Emerson came marching in after me.

"Hey, what the hell is—"

Her hands shot up to her face and cut the words right off. It was an instant reaction—partly because of what she saw, partly because of what she smelled, and partly to stop the whole array of things besides words that wanted to come gushing out of her.

In the middle of the room, there was what looked like a dentist's chair—but a dentist's chair from hell. It had a full array of restraints built in. Leather straps for the wrists, arms, waist, legs, and even forehead.

The girl from the empty bed was strapped into it.

She wasn't moving, but her eyes were wide open. Clamped open. Four thin metal rods came out of the headrest, reaching around to her eyelids and pulling them apart via the little hooks at their ends. Her eyes were completely bloodshot and staring straight ahead.

At the projector screen.

It was the only source of light in the room. But what it showed was pure darkness. It was one of the worst things I've ever seen. It was deranged. Horrible. It was a series of the most depraved sexual scenes conceivable. Rape and necrophilia, followed by cannibalism. The majority was child-based. Short clips had been randomly stitched together to make a twenty second film. It was utterly disturbing. And it was on a continuous loop.

There was no sound to the film. Just a constant stream of white noise coming from the four speakers in the corner.

The effects of all this were clear to see. The girl's cheeks were streaked with tears and there was a pool of urine on the floor beneath her.

In the far corner, another video camera was set up.

Emerson had zombied toward the projector screen. Her hands were still clamped over her mouth. She had gone completely pale. She turned to look at me, but before I could say anything, two guys stepped into the room behind me, both of whom were wearing black shirts, black trousers, and black boots—the exact same attire as the guys back in London—which obviously made them Tanner's henchmen. They both had their weapons drawn and were looking at me and looking at Emerson and reaching an altogether *not good* conclusion, but, fortunately, a little too slowly, because I had already received orders from the voices, who had long since worked out the most effective response, meaning that I had already shot them—and they were already dead.

FIFTY-SEVEN

T HE ALARM DID not go off. No lockdown, no nothing.

I turned back to the room. Emerson was crouched down by the dentist's chair. Her eyes were wide and kept flashing between the dead guys and me. Her hands had muffled any scream.

I shot the projector on the ceiling.

Emerson fell on her ass and into the puddle of urine.

I pointed at the girl. "Get her out of that."

I turned away and scrambled over the bodies, checking the corridor quickly before I stepped out. I ran straight to the end and burst through the double doors, Berretta first.

Tanner.

Vanev.

Five other people.

They all froze.

The lab was a big rectangular space, about thirty meters by fifteen. It was clinically clean with a sharp antiseptic smell that burned my nostrils. Everything was either titanium white or metallic gray. Four huge lab benches with reagent shelving were arranged two-by-two in front of me. Centrifuges, microscopes, test tubes, beakers, and other assorted chemistry equipment cluttered the work stations. Fume cupboards ringed around the outskirts and were punctuated by tall refrigeration units that were stacked with hundreds of vials and chemicals and containers, all of which were plastered with bright warning labels. Computers and plasma screens were peppered about, one of which was a fifty-incher on a freestanding wheelable mount, about seven-and-half meters in front of me, in the middle of the intersection, showing a picture of the girl in the chair, along with copious supplementary notations. Tanner, Vanev, and some other guy were standing together in front of it.

I aimed the Berretta straight at them.

They stared at me. Shocked, flustered, processing. Then they each did something different.

Tanner was on the left. She was the only one who recognized me. She grimaced. "Shit."

The other guy was on the right. He was the only one not wearing a lab coat. He was like a dear in the headlights. His eyes just kept getting wider.

Vanev was in the middle. He looked about as opposite to Tanner as possible. She was a pale white ghost; he had thick black hair, olive skin, a heavy beard, and a big purple wart on the end of his nose.

Which is where the bullet hit him.

The plasma screen blew up behind the three of them and the contents of Vanev's head splattered all over it. Tanner and the coatless guy ducked their respective ways, neither one escaping getting wet. The other four people dropped to the ground simultaneously.

The coatless guy threw out his hands. "*Whoa, whoa, whoa!*"

Tanner was looking at a set of doors in the far left corner. She had taken a step toward them but then stopped. She knew it was too far. She took a breath and straightened up. She wiped the side of her face. She looked down at Vanev. She turned back to me. She gritted her teeth.

She said, "Kane."

I nodded.

"I told them he was weak," she said.

"Well I did shoot him, first."

"You think you've won?"

"Haven't I?"

"You have no idea who you're messing with. You're a dead man, Mr. Blaze."

"That's what Kane said. Then I–"

I shot her in the face.

The female voice said, *You couldn't have done that straight off the bat?*

He tried, the male voice said.

Wait, that first one was a miss?

I got overexcited, I said.

I moved the Berretta to the right. The coatless guy came into focus. He still had his hands out. *Because they were going to stop a bullet.*

I said, "The rest of you get out here."

Nobody moved.

"*Now.*"

The other four people crawled on hands and knees to the center of the room. They all whimpered at the sight of the bodies. I pointed at the near right lab bench and they sat together, in a line, with their backs leaning against the side of the bench, their legs out straight, and their hands resting on top. One of them was a dark woman who looked like she might have been part of Vanev's original team. She had plenty of fear in her eyes.

The coatless guy stayed frozen where he was.

I said, "So who are you?"

Which question was answered when Emerson rushed in behind me.

I glanced back at her.

The male voice said, *Now that's an angry woman.*

It was. Emerson's jaw was set tight. Her eyes were ablaze. She scanned the room. Me, the bloody monitor, the two bodies, the coatless guy, the people the ground.

Then back to the coatless guy.

She said, "Jason?"

The coatless guy said, "Paula? I… What are—"

"What have you done?" she said. "What the *hell* have you done?"

Jason started but nothing much came out. His eyes were still glued to the Berretta.

Emerson said, "Answer me, Jason."

Yeah, Jason. Answer her, the male voice said.

Jason said nothing.

Emerson came and stood next to me.

I said, "So… I'm pretty much just going to shoot him now."

Jason said, "No, wait, you don't understand. They *made* me do it."

"They make you blow up the HBL lab, too?"

"That was Kane's idea."

Emerson said, "Senator Kane's involved?"

"He *was*," I said.

She looked at me.

Jason said, "Please, you don't have to kill me."

"Yeah? Why not?"

He stumbled and stuttered and stared at the Berretta.

He came up with nothing.

I said, "All right, tell you what. I'll give you all the same chance I gave Kane."

I lowered the Berretta and fished Hays's photo out of my pocket.

"Take a good look," I said. "First person to tell me who this guy is gets to live."

I walked toward Jason, showing the photo to each of the people on the floor on the way.

The dark woman said, "This man was in London. I saw him."

"What's his name?"

She shook her head. "I don't know."

She sank back down.

The other three had nothing to contribute.

I showed the picture to Jason. He stared at it. He thought hard.

He said, "He must be one of the people running this."

I pistol whipped him.

He fell to the ground, clutching the side of his head.

"Better?" I said. "Or is there still some stupid left?"

"What do you want me to say?" he said.

"Give me a name."

"How? I've never seen the guy before."

"You said *they* made you do it."

"I meant Kane and Tanner. I have no idea who's further up. None of us do."

I pointed the Berretta at him.

"Then I've got no use for you."

He reeled away, flashing a desperate look to Emerson.

Emerson said, "Wait. Please."

I waited.

"Don't kill them," she said. "They should go to jail. That's what they deserve. That's what's right."

The male voice said, *Right*?

The female voice said, *Yeah, very compelling.*

I looked down at Jason. He looked back. Wide-eyed, holding his breath. He swallowed hard. The other four were all staring at the floor, shaking.

I sighed and relaxed the Berretta.

"Well," I said, "I guess it's your lucky day."

Jason breathed out.

"You'd have a *terrible* time in jail."

I raised the Berretta and shot Jason in the head.

Then I swept it right and fired four more times.

Bang.

Bang, bang, bang, bang.

The noise crashed off the walls and all around us.

Then there was silence.

Then Tanner's body started ringing.

FIFTY-EIGHT

I T WAS A cell phone. Not the one she'd called me with before, but a secondary unit, presumably to be used only for contact with a third party. I retrieved it from her pocket and looked at the screen. It showed a green square with the silhouette of a person's head and shoulders inside. No name, no number.

I answered the call.

The caller said, "Update."

The voices started profiling.

Male.

Forty.

European?

Something.

Swede?

More like Dane.

But upper-class.

Definitely.

In charge?

Well it wasn't a question.

Then we've got our guy.

Looks like it.

I hung up the phone and again immediately called Marcel for a trace. He told me to hang tight.

I went through the rest of Tanner's pockets.

I found a USB stick.

Vanev and the others had nothing on them.

I turned to Emerson. She was standing still, just staring at the seven bodies on the ground.

The male voice said, *I think we broke her*.

The female voice said, *See what's on the USB*.

I called to Emerson, "You still want to know what this is about?"

She didn't respond.

"Hey, Emerson."

She looked at me.

I nodded to a computer. Emerson walked over and sat down at it. I stood beside her and worked the mouse. The computer was linked up to the monitor that was now covered in two sets of blood. On screen was the picture of the girl in the chair and the supplementary notes. It was a copy of her complete medical profile. I closed it down and went back to the parent folder. It was entitled *104* and contained two other files. The first was called *.log* and had a bunch of information to do with dosages, subsequent responses, and hourly medical updates. The second was a video file.

I double-clicked it.

A big window opened on the screen.

It showed a close-up still of the girl in the chair. The camera was zoomed in so that her face filled the frame. Her terrified expression was frozen in front of us—her eyelids held back, her bloodshot eyes bulging and looking to the right.

I hit the play button.

Her eyes shot to the left. Then back to the right. They

darted around in every direction except straight ahead. Anywhere but the film. The volume was loud, and her screams filled the lab. She was begging them to stop.

The video was seventy-three minutes long.

I closed it after four seconds.

Emerson's hands were covering her mouth again.

I clicked out of folder *104* and went to its parent. It was entitled *Project 1* and contained subject folders *101* through *106*, a project summary report, a file labeled *Objectives*, and five video files. The summary report stated that the project had commenced ten hours ago, at 18:03 on Friday October 2, 2015. Subjects were responding well and no problems had been encountered thus far. The *Objectives* file was still being typed up, but, as far as I could tell, it contained no references to the upcoming conference at the World Congress Center.

I double clicked the first video file.

It began with the six students lying strapped to the military cots, vigorously struggling to get free. There was no audio, but it was clear that they were all shouting and crying and pleading to be let go. Tanner's two henchmen were standing over them, guns in hand, expressionless faces.

There was a time-code running in the bottom right corner.

10/02/2015—18:03:44

The dark woman appeared onscreen. She was carrying a tray with six syringes on it. Steady, composed, another day at the office. She handed the tray to one of the henchmen, and then took the first syringe over to the guy we'd seen having a nightmare. He watched her approach. Tensing, straining, begging. It made zero difference. The dark woman held up the syringe, did the air-squirt thing. And then she sat on the guy's right arm and sunk it into a vein. The guy's head was craned up as he watched it happen. He went berserk.

As did the other subjects.

They were next.

The dark woman pulled the syringe out and put it back on the tray. Then she turned back to the guy and waited. The guy kept screaming and fighting at full force for about thirty seconds. And then he just went still. Instantly. Like he'd suddenly died.

At which point Jason popped up on screen.

He appeared from the left side of the screen and ran up to the guy's bed. He was waving his arms about and seemed to have a go at the dark woman. The other five students watched on in horror. Their desperation magnified a thousand fold. But the dark woman remained calm. She simply hooked the guy up to both IV lines, attached his vital monitor, and then proceeded to the next subject.

Five minutes later all six subjects were lying perfectly still.

I hit the fast-forward button.

Nothing happened for thirty minutes. The subjects remained flat on their cots. Then, at 18:32:24, they began moving again. Slowly at first, just restless limbs and random twitches. But before the hour was up, they were jerking around beneath the restraints. It looked like they were seizing. Like Sophia in the motel room. These seizures kept getting worse until suddenly, in almost total unison, all six subjects arched their bellies up to the ceiling, holding this position for several seconds before collapsing back down into total stillness.

Thirty minutes later the cycle repeated itself.

The other video files were just a continuation of the first. Each one about two hours long.

Emerson said, "But why? What's the point of all this?

What were they doing to them? What were they trying to accomplish? And who are these people, anyway?"

I answered by sticking the USB into the computer.

A folder window appeared on screen. It was entitled *MK-ULTRA* and contained everything Tanner had about the project. Which was a lot. There were hundreds of files. Files from the original project. Tanner's personal notes from 1972. She talked about the problems they were having. Brian damage, coma, death. She talked about ideal subjects. An age range of twenty to forty was deemed mandatory. Outliers simply couldn't handle the process. It was also preferable for the subjects to have an underlying mental illness. Nothing too crippling. Any kind of advanced stage disease would be unsuitable. But a mind with just a few cracks was considered optimal. It made the subject more susceptible to the program.

Tanner went on to talk about where the program was strong and where it needed improvement. It turned out the depraved film we'd seen was the same one they'd used in the original project. Tanner had created it. It did not need improvement.

Tanner's thesis paper was there, too. As were a selection of project test reports. Hays' stuff was interesting but you wouldn't have been able to recreate the MK-ULTRA program with it. Tanner's stuff, on the other hand, was pretty much a blueprint.

Emerson read along with me. Silently, gravely, her eyes constantly shifting to the bodies on the ground.

I clicked open another file. It was entitled *Procedure* and outlined the entire MK-ULTRA protocol.

The protocol was in fact quite simple. It was built on two pillars, the first of which was the cause of all the "complications" the MK-ULTRA program had ever encountered, and was where Vanev's breakthrough had made all the difference.

The drugs.

For the duration of the program the subjects were continuously administered an ultrahallucinogenic cocktail of psychedelics, dissociatives, and deliriants. Originally this was a blend of the most powerful hallucinogens, including LSD, mescaline, PCP, psilocybin, peyote, and DMT. But Vanev had come up with a new drug called DVH2. Its properties were hybrid and in reality nothing too groundbreaking. It was essentially just LSD on steroids. But with the help of the microarray technology, the way it interacted with the brain was more efficient than anything before. Which made it that much more powerful. To make matters worse, barbiturates and stimulants were also used. They were simultaneously pumped in to the subjects, each arm taking a different liquid. The barbiturates would depress the nervous system, causing a sedative effect, and the stimulants would amp everything back up. The result was a brain-breaking continuum of sleep paralysis and night terrors, the sole purpose of which was to break the subject's mind and allow the protocol's second pillar to work.

The second pillar was essentially the "programming" part—the part where Tanner took over. With Vanev's drugs putting the subjects into a "susceptible-enough state," Tanner could begin cultivating an alternate personality—one that was entirely subservient. She accomplished this by periodically exposing the subject to her damned film for up to ninety minutes at a time, though, of course, with all the drugs in their system, this would have felt more like ninety hours. At various intervals the film would shut off and the white

376

noise would stop and Tanner would talk to the subject over the speakers.

Each subject averaged three programming sessions per day, for between five and ten days total.

Emerson said, "This is unbelievable. They were actually trying to make this work?"

"They've already got it to work," I said. "Here, take a look."

I opened a folder marked *Trials*. It contained everything that had gone on at the Lyndale Institute. Every subject that had been tested on had a file. And there were a lot of files. I went through all of them. The older files showed mostly failed attempts. Bad science, dead subjects. But as the files became more recent, they began to show progress. And then came a breakthrough. A group of subjects who'd survived the program.

The brown folders.

I found Sophia's file. She was subject *209*. Her *.log* file said she had resisted. It said she had taken much longer to break than anyone else. Unsurprising, given her training. But that only worked against her. Her dosages had to be made higher as a result. Longer exposure to Tanner's film was likewise necessary. Her file also mentioned that she had been interrogated. The last thing in her file was a section that detailed her objectives and her results. She was the program's first success. The first subject to survive the protocol. But at no point in her file had Sophia ever been referred to by name.

My hand crushed into a fist.

Then Tanner's phone started ringing again.

Marcel had traced the phone.

FIFTY-NINE

I PULLED THE USB out of the computer. With the Lyndale Institute destroyed, and Tanner, Hays, and Vanev dead, I was holding perhaps the last remains of the MK-ULTRA program.

The male voice said, *Got to figure the Dane has a copy, though.*

And we'll still need to wipe these computers, the female voice said.

Emerson said, "We need to call an ambulance. They all need medical attention."

I nodded. "First help me with the hard drives."

"The hard drives?"

"Everything in here is about to become evidence. I'd rather it all got destroyed, wouldn't you?"

She paused a moment. Glanced back at the computer. To what she'd just read the government did the last time they had this technology. She turned back to me and nodded.

We walked back to the server room and ripped out every single hard drive. We took them back to the giant lab and put them in a pile on one of the benches. Then I went back to the room with the military cots. Emerson had carried the girl in the chair back to her cot and unhooked all the IV lines. All six subjects were now lying inert on their cots.

I went into the room directly opposite. It was cluttered with the desks, chairs, and other office equipment that they had removed from the other two rooms. There was a toolbox on one of the desks. It had a big drill sticking out of it. They had used it to set up the projector in the other room. I took the toolbox back to the lab.

As any computer-savvy person will tell you, nowadays a simple software wipe is basically useless. Data is never *really* destroyed. Now some will argue that even hard drive shredding isn't enough, but with paranoia at a level where the government using atomic reconstruction is a real possibility, those guys really are lunatics. And while I do hear voices, I'm not *that* far gone.

A hard drive consists of a stack of miniature disks encased in a metal box. The disks are called *platters*, and are generally 2.5 or 3.5 inches in diameter, and made from either glass or metal. The platters are what computer data is actually recorded onto. And therefore what need to be destroyed.

Emerson held each drive in place while I drilled a hole straight through. It took about fifteen minutes to get through all of the drives.

"You're going to have a busy few days," I said. "Obviously there'll be an investigation. CIA will take you in. They'll ask you questions, they'll keep you for a while. Do yourself a favor and tell them everything."

Emerson said, "We have to call an ambulance right now."

I nodded. "Give me ten minutes and then make the call."

"What about Daniel?"

"Ten minutes," I said again. Then I walked out and left Emerson alone in the big bio lab in the basement of the giant glass cuboid at 5:28 on Saturday morning.

SIXTY

I WAS SITTING IN the big lounge. The one to the left of the big staircase. It was empty like before. Just a faint hanging of cigar smoke, and the somewhat muted sounds of the things going on in the upstairs rooms.

It had taken most of Saturday to get back to Chicago. I'd first swung by Armand's place to pick up Hays's card, then "borrowed" an appropriate car from a nearby parking lot and driven over. It was now a little past nine in the evening.

The male voice said, *Man, we've should've been on to this guy from the start.*

How'd you figure?

Come on. That look he gave us? Dead giveaway.

Yeah. In hindsight, maybe. Besides, they were all giving us looks.

Whatever. We still should've known. Anyway, point is, the guards upstairs are gonna come running. Either of you get a count? I had seven.

One more than me, I said.

The female voice said, *Hey, isn't that our guy?*

I looked across to the big staircase. Coming off the bottom step was a guy in a charcoal suit. Forty-five years old, a full head of gray hair, one hand in his pocket, the other on his cell phone. It was the same guy who'd given me the odd look the first time I'd gone to the club. The *other* asshole. He paused at the bottom of the stairs, typing something into his phone—which he was still grinning at—then made a left and headed into the dining room.

I got up and followed him.

He went and sat at a two-seater in the middle of the dining room. As before, there were only a handful of other patrons around. He took out his membership card and Nicolas was standing beside him before it hit the table. I hung back and watched him order a scotch without lifting his eyes from his phone. I waited for Nicolas to go into the kitchen, then walked up to his table and took a seat opposite him.

He glanced up from his phone.

His eyes widened a fraction.

He said, "Mr. Blaze."

I said, "Hello."

His momentary panic subsided quickly. The grin came back.

"I suppose I should have expected this," he said.

"Depends what you think *this* is."

"You know, we *do* have security. I could call for help."

"You could…" I said, and then cracked the hammer of my gun into position under the table.

His eyes dropped down. Then came back up.

He didn't call for help.

"How did you find me?"

"Traced your call."

"But we were using burners."

I nodded. "You were."

"They're supposed to be untraceable."

"Why? Because you paid cash?"

"No names, no details," he said.

"Right," I said. "No names, no details. You buy a burner, your personal information is entirely blank."

"So?"

"So that has nothing to do with the *phone's* information. That's still up for grabs. Model number, place of purchase, current location—you make a call, you give it all up."

"But I thought it took time to trace a call? You hung up after two seconds."

"Sure," I said. "And if this were a movie, the guy playing me would have kept the guy playing you on the phone for at least three minutes. But in reality, there's no need for all that. It's much easier. You make a call, I get your number. And, providing I know a guy—which clearly I do—your location follows pretty quickly."

He grunted. "Good to know."

He dropped his phone onto the table. Slightly disgusted, almost disappointed with it.

Nicolas came back out of the kitchen and presented one glass of scotch. The way he reacted to my presence, you'd never of thought we'd met. With Hays's card still in my pocket, I didn't exist. He simply placed the scotch within easy reach of my dining partner's left hand and followed it with a "*Your order, sir?*" kind of look. He got a shake of a head in response, so Nicolas swiveled around and attended to another patron, tout suite.

"So who are you?" I said.

"You don't know?"

"Like you said, personal information is blank."

He picked up his drink. Took a sip.

"Good scotch," he said.

"It better be," I said.

He took a second sip before placing the glass back on the table. Then he took a breath and reclined in his chair and crossed his legs.

"I'm an investor of sorts," he said. "I see an opportunity, I try to take advantage."

"Investor, eh? All right, *Mr. Investor*, so walk me through this one."

He shrugged. "Honestly, it was no different than any other. I simply happened to come across a research paper a few years ago."

"*Happened* to come across?"

"It's the first key to successful investment. The more information you have, the more opportunities you can see, and the more informed your decisions are. Which is why I employ a number of people to sift through and send me all sorts of interesting material."

"So you read Tanner's work and thought: gold mine?"

He waved a hand. "Actually I thought it was a joke," he said. "Science fiction, nothing more. I dismissed it completely."

"So what changed?"

"I got more information. About a year later I learned that certain parties were taking such research projects very seriously. Tests were being done, money was changing hands. A lot of money."

"So you decided to give things another look."

"Yes I did. But I dismissed yet again. I mean, sure, *if* Tanner's work was viable, the potential value was obvious. Mind control? The military and intelligence applications alone would be huge. And then there are the much sicker fantasies it could enable."

"Except it wasn't viable."

"Exactly. It was still all just theoretical. Despite all the interest, no one was actually getting any results. And they hadn't been for years. The technology simply wasn't there yet."

"Until Vanev came along."

He nodded. "Vanev changed everything. I'd been keeping a close eye on his and other similar projects. And when he had his breakthrough, I moved quickly."

"Or at least you got Kane to. What did you have on him anyway?"

He chuckled. "More than enough, believe me."

"He said you made him senator."

"I may have put him in touch with some people."

"Another investment?"

"The man *is* worth a few billion."

I gestured at his three-thousand dollar suit, the Rolex on his wrist, and the gold pen sticking out of his breast pocket. "Not that you're doing too badly yourself."

He brushed a hand over a five-hundred dollar sleeve. "Yes, well, that's the second key to successful investment. Never use your own money."

"How'd you find Tanner?"

"Actually I didn't. She found me. Turned out she'd been tracking Vanev's progress too."

"How'd she find you?"

"I honestly have no idea. But suffice to say I welcomed her proposal."

"Proposal?"

"She gets to finish her life's work, I get to profit from it."

"A partnership."

"Indeed."

"Equal?"

"Had to be. After all, Tanner was the only one who knew

how to run the program. Research papers are one thing, but actually recreating the MK-ULTRA program required more. And to do it successfully? You'd need both access to documents from the original trials—most of which were destroyed in 1973—as well as an expert in the relevant field. And who better than someone from the original project?"

I shrugged. "Even so," I said. "I'd have taken her files and got rid of the old bag. Hired someone less ugly."

He shook his head. "Inefficient. Tanner would get it to market quicker."

A glint in his eye.

"Better to get rid of her afterwards."

I smiled. "That's exactly what she thought too."

"Pardon me?"

"You were planning to double-cross her; she was planning to double-cross you."

"Is that a fact?"

I nodded. "How'd you think I knew who you were?"

"You said you traced my phone."

"Yeah, but that only gave me your rough location. Remember, personal information is blank. You could have been anyone in this place."

"So how then?"

"Couple of things." I took out the picture from Hays's safe. "This was the first."

He picked up the photo and studied it for a moment.

"The Lyndale Institute," he said. "Another of Kane's contributions. I was there for a demonstration. Tanner had had a breakthrough. First success was some girl."

"Sophia."

"I'm sorry?"

"That was her name. Sophia Brooks."

He nodded. "Yes, that's right. In fact one of Hays's people as I recall?"

"Speaking of Hays, how *did* you figure out he was on to you anyway?"

"Yes, well, I suppose I got lucky there." He pointed to the table I'd sat at the first time I was in the club. "That was Hays's table," he said. "He always ate there. Every time he came to club. Same table, same time. And always alone. So you can imagine my surprise when the first time I see him with company it's with Ms. Brooks, who's supposed to be dead."

"Hey, I'm still surprised you let a test occur in your hometown. HBL was massive risk on your part."

He nodded. "Not the most prudent of decisions, I agree. But then, the potential benefit to Kane was enormous. And of course if Kane were to benefit…"

"Hmm," I said. "So you knew who Hays really was the whole time?"

"Oh, not in the least. Tanner was the one who revealed that particular nugget. I thought he was banker." He leaned forward. "You know Hays was part of the original project too. Him and Tanner."

I said nothing.

He leaned back. "In any case," he continued, "once Hays got involved, we had to move quickly."

"So you blew London and put the hit out on him."

"Correct."

He put the photo back on the table.

"It's a nice picture of the back of my head," he said. "But I'm afraid I still don't see how it identifies me."

"It doesn't. But it did tell me there was at least one other person involved."

I put the photo back in my pocket.

"What gave you away was a file I found at BexuTech. Kane said your next target was the big conference next week?"

He nodded. "It would have set certain events in motion."

"Yeah, well, apparently Tanner had other ideas. One of which being to send one of the subjects after you."

He smirked. "Interesting."

I raised my eyebrows. "I gotta say, you're taking this all pretty well."

He shrugged. "Well that's the third key to successful investment. Win some, lose some, move on."

He picked up his glass and drained the last of his scotch.

"Which brings us to the here and now," he said. "And to what I think *this* is."

"Which is what?"

"An opportunity."

"Is that so?"

He smiled. "Let's be honest, Mr. Blaze, you could have killed me ten times over by now."

"Yeah, I am moving a bit slow today. But hey, a man deserves a last drink."

"Look, why don't we make this simple? Clearly, I'd rather have you as an asset than a liability, and obviously that's not going to come cheap. Now, I take it that Tanner and the rest of them are—shall we say—in the red?"

I smiled. "Nicely put. And yeah."

"OK. And tell me, do you still have her files?"

I shrugged. "There may be a memory stick floating around somewhere. Why?"

"Because something like that could be worth a lot of money."

"Yeah? How much?"

He smiled again. Relaxed a little more and seem to gain

387

supreme confidence. Like he was now in his element and knew exactly what to do. He proceeded to take the gold pen out of his breast pocket and scribbled something on the menu standing in the middle of the table. He put the pen away and swiveled the menu around for me to see.

The male voice made a long whistling sound.

"That's a big number," I said.

"As I said, Tanner was never going to be part of this forever. Your killing her now merely saves me from having to hire someone next week. So I guess you can consider this payment for services rendered."

"What abou—"

"And you could add another two zeros to that for the memory stick."

The male voice said, _Two zeros?_

Yeah, not bad, the female voice said. _Definitely more than we were thinking, anyway._

He watched me think.

I said, "How come you don't have a bodyguard?"

"Better privacy," he said. "Besides, the circles I roll in, there are usually more than enough of them around at any one time."

"I want the money up front."

He said nothing. Now I watched him think. Watched his eyes move down and up again.

"OK," he said. "We have a deal."

"Mazel tov."

I threw him a cell phone.

He looked down at the PayPal transaction page on screen. He gave me a look.

I said, "_Two_ zeros remember."

He grumbled a little but started typing all the same.

When he was finished he turned the phone around and said, "There. Done. See?"

I looked at the screen. It attested to a successful transaction. The amount as promised was in the account.

I said, "What does that bit at the bottom say?"

He turned the phone back around and read the confirmation message I'd programmed in an hour before.

"Thank you! Your donation to the Sophia Brooks Mental Health Fund is greatly appreciated. Please look up."

He looked up.

I shot him in the face.

The female voice said, *All right, well that was fun. So what now?*

Well, we're probably going to have to deal with them, first, the male voice said, referring to the five bodyguards hustling off the staircase ahead of me, weapons drawn.

Yeah, the female voice said. *But then what?*

Germany sounds like fun.

So does Shanghai.

Isaac?

Yeah, I said, getting up from my chair… *Could be.*

ABOUT THE AUTHOR

So you're probably expecting to see an author bio, round about now. Born here, got rejected there, did the self publishing thing, etc.

Well, think again.

Because the way I—or *we*, if you've been reading—see it, is that after 390 pages of nosying into my life, this is where I get my own back. But before I get to *you*, let's talk about the guy who's responsible for that 390 pages.

Axel Cruise.

British born, Jewish made, and admittedly a rather handsome devil too—though, of course, nothing for me to worry about. Childhood-wise, little Axel came up watching Deadpool, Seinfeld, and all things Tarantino—which probably explains a lot. He's a sly one to be sure, and also a pretty good writer, if you believe all the hype. Which I guess you must, if you made it all the way here.

In any case, I don't like him.

What's that? You think I'm ungrateful?

Yeah, how about you go back and read that first sentence again.

Mm-hmm. That's what I thought.

Not such a nice, after all.

OK. Now, on to you. Well, you've got taste, I'll give you that. Like I said, Axel can put words to paper—even if they are someone else's. (Who's ungrateful now? I mean, I didn't see a "Thank You, Isaac" anywhere, did you?) The other thing I can tell you is that you'll buy the next book in this series. Why? Simple. If you don't, you'll never know if you won the secret competition or not.

—Isaac Blaze, 2017

Printed in Great Britain
by Amazon